TAKEDOWN

LEONARD RUHL

Published by **B**ig **C**orner **P**ublishing

Copyright 2023 by Leonard Ruhl

Cover art by Clarissa Schmidtberger
Author photo by Samson Ledesma

AUTHOR'S NOTE

Anyone familiar with South-Central Kansas will realize that I have taken several liberties in naming the roads and cities and in describing the geographical and topographical details of the countryside surrounding them. While the cities and the areas exist, I've altered them according to the demands of the story and my whims, therefore they should be regarded as totally fictitious.

ACKNOWLEDGMENTS

Many thanks to best-selling author Rob Leininger for his advice, countless edits, and tireless support. Thanks to the folks at Big Corner Creative, especially DeeAnna Stout, Ian Roseberry and Clarissa Schmidtberger. Special thanks to retired undersheriff and lifetime law enforcement officer Mike Yoder for his help keeping the firearm and ammunition passages accurate. Thanks to Police Chief Tracy Heath and Jessie Cornwell. Thanks to Evan Watson for insight into professional visitation in various county jails. Special thanks to Shelly Steadman, Ph.D for guidance regarding the DNA passages. Thanks to Amy Mott, C.R.N.A. for guidance regarding the benzo (roofie) passages. Any mistakes in the text are mine, not those who I've leaned on for help. Special thanks to Marilyn Targos, whose help with finicky programs kept me from smashing hardware to bits.

Also by Leonard Ruhl
Verdict Denied
> A fast-paced and exciting work of crime fiction.
> —*Kirkus Reviews*

www.leonardruhl.com

This book is for

Amy, Will and Caroline.

Peace if possible, truth at all costs.

> – Martin Luther

What is truth? said Pilate; and would
not stay for an answer.

> – Francis Bacon

1

THE EVENING SKY had gone to purple and rose and cottonwoods were swaying when Geronimo stepped onto an old friend's porch in Missouri. Grassland sloped from the cabin to where I sat with my two preteenagers in a bass boat idling on the lake as the sun sank in the west. As I motored toward the slip, I clipped a 9mm Glock 19 inside my waistband. It wasn't likely that Geronimo had shown up to kill me, but trouble followed him like noxious fumes behind a speeding diesel.

"Who's that?" Leo said from the back of the boat.

Lindy studied my face from the front seat, waiting for the answer. She was ten, two years younger than Leo.

"An old friend," I said, misstating reality by a wide margin. Last I knew, Geronimo was a hitman in a drug cartel, forty years old, face brown and seamed like old leather, a "friend" only due to circumstances now two years in the past. Our relationship, such as it was, was complicated.

Lindy narrowed her eyes at me. "A friend? Then why do you need that gun?"

"Hope for the best, prepare for the worst."

She blew air between her lips, not buying it.

I smiled. "You're just like your mother."

Their mother, my first wife, died five years ago. I pulled out my phone and called my second wife, Keri, who was in town according to her text a few minutes ago.

She answered the phone with, "Catch any—"

"Geronimo found us."

"What—how?"

"No clue." The dock was twenty feet away.

The four of us had spent the last two years in the Sawtooth Mountains of Idaho hoping to avoid blowback from our part in the dismantling of a Mexican drug cartel operating in the south of Kansas. We got to Idaho just before the pandemic hit. At the time, I told the kids to look on the bright side—at least we weren't missing anything. But that wasn't true. They missed their friends and the world they knew, which, judging from the news I'd read, would never be quite the same. We home-schooled them and lived off the land, sparing no effort to stay off the grid. Cash transactions, burner phones—all of it. But here we were in Missouri, first leg of an attempt to return to our lives in Kansas. And here was Geronimo, like a bad dream. The boat bumped gently against the dock.

"What the hell does he want?" Keri said.

"Only one way to find out. Gotta go, babe."

"Be careful, Benny—"

"I'll call when he's gone. I'm sending the kids out on the lake while we talk." I ended the call, grabbed my little cooler, and got one foot on the dock. "Leo."

"Yeah, Dad."

I nodded at the driver's seat. "Take it out to the middle of the lake. Don't come back 'til I call."

His eyes were wide. "What if you don't call?" He stacked two cushions on the seat and sat behind the wheel.

Lindy rolled her eyes. "Then we'll call Keri." I couldn't tell if she was annoyed by Leo's question or having to utter her stepmother's name. She was still adjusting to having a "new" mother.

I kept my eyes on Leo. "I'll call. Just keep it afloat, okay?"

Twenty-seven months ago we'd all survived a kidnapping attempt from a cartel operating in Kansas. Things happened that should never happen to kids their age. That, and the survival and firearms training I'd given them in the last two years left each of them harder and more aware than the average kid.

Half-melted ice in water rattled in the cooler as I walked up the slope. Geronimo watched me from an Adirondack chair by the front door. I couldn't read his expression but a pistol was lying on the arm of the chair.

I set the cooler at my feet. "Beer?"

He nodded.

I dug into the cooler and tossed him a dripping can of Modelo.

I took a chair next to his. "How'd you find us?"

He shook the question off.

Great. "Okay, then, why are you here?"

He popped the top and took a pull, looked out at the boat circling slowly in the lake. "Calling in a favor, Your Honor."

Your Honor. Shit. A title I gave up two years ago when I had to disappear. Now, at thirty-eight, I was probably among the youngest former judges anywhere.

"Thought we were even," I said.

Twenty-six months ago I'd been forced to form an uneasy alliance with Geronimo—sworn enemy of the Mendez-Rodriguez Cartel, a rival in crime. MRC had taken my sister during an attempt to kidnap the rest of us. The price for her return was for me to deliver a judgment of acquittal in a capital murder trial to free a drug lord's grandson. Geronimo helped me save my sister, and I helped him find and kill most of MRC's major players, including the drug kingpin who'd killed Geronimo's father back in 1989—a dish of revenge served ice cold.

"Yeah, we're square," he said. "That's why I'm calling it a favor."

"You said you were calling *in* a favor. That's different."

He closed one eye. "Picky. You're still an attorney, right?"

"Yeah, but I haven't—"

"I need you to represent somebody."

I stared at him. "I'm not that kind of an attorney. I was a judge and before that I was a prosecutor. I've never done criminal defense work. I don't even practice law right now."

His eyes narrowed. "What do you do for money?"

Truth was I was running low. I hadn't been able to sell my farmhouse back in Kansas and the mortgage was a month overdue. Perhaps my rawboned look told him everything he needed to know about how we were doing, but I wasn't about to confirm that for him. He pulled five bundles of cash bound with paper bands from his jacket pocket and made a five-inch stack next to the gun.

I glanced at it. I didn't want to get in bed with Geronimo again, but I didn't want to work at Walmart, either. I thought about the best way to start this negotiation, because that's what it was. Finally I said, "I don't need money."

"Said no one ever."

"What if I say no? I get to walk away from whatever this is, or do you use that gun?"

"It's not like that." He forced a smile which came off like a wolf baring its teeth. "That's fifty thou. Off the books so it's tax free," he added.

I didn't look at the money. "Whatever it is, I'm not taking the case."

"You haven't heard what it is yet."

"Doesn't matter what it is."

He thumbed the bills in a packet of hundreds. "A young woman named Mia Delarosa is in a Wichita jail for murdering her neighbor. Allegedly," he amended. "An ex-cop named Jimmy Ray. Someone almost took his head off with an axe. I need you to represent her."

"Christ, Geronimo. An axe murderer?"

He picked up the pistol and held it in his lap. "Is that a no? Haven't been told that in a while."

"Don't worry, I won't tell anybody."

He forced another smile. "I have me one of those nicknames now I guess. They call me El Tiburón."

"The shark."

He tilted his head. "You spend some time in Mexico during your hiatus?"

"No. Just happen to know that one."

"I got credit for some of your work. You oughta be called Little Shark."

I'd killed four cartel members during the kidnapping attempt, then, later, the kingpin's youngest son while trying to find my sister. I liked hearing that people in Geronimo's world thought all of that was his doing, but the blood on my hands was part of the reason we'd been living in a remote cabin in the Sawtooth Range. "I have no idea what you're talking about."

"'Course you don't, Tiburón Pequeño. What'll it take to get you on this case?"

I closed my eyes and gave it some thought. "Start-up costs would be a lot," I said after a minute. "And I'm not looking to start a new career as a defense attorney so the number would be high. What's this woman to you, anyway?"

He set the gun on the arm of the chair. "Doesn't matter."

"Does to me. I want to know what I'd be getting into."

He smiled. "A suit and tie, *pendejo*. Isn't that what lawyers wear to court?"

"If I take the case, and I'm not saying I am, I'd be representing her interests, not yours, not anyone else's."

He gave me a *What the fuck* look, then gazed at the lake again, the boat all but invisible in the dark, its motor a soft murmur across the water. "All this talk and I never heard a number," he said.

"Fifty grand isn't even close. I'd need to rent office space. I'd need computers, a good laptop, malpractice insurance, other stuff I can't even think of at the moment. And I would have to hire an investigator."

"I'll get you an investigator."

"I've got a guy." Which was a lie, but if I did this, the last thing I wanted was some guy in Geronimo's pocket.

"Does he work for free? Because my guy does."

"I get my own investigator. That's not negotiable."

Geronimo laughed.

"Then find someone else," I said.

Geronimo leaned forward. "Okay, so use your own guy. Hypothetically, how much money would you need?"

"Hypothetically? Two hundred thousand to get started— office, legal secretary, investigator, equipment. Then I'd need living expenses, food, gas, insurance, taxes, all of that. And I've got kids. They're expensive."

"Christ, just give me a number."

I thought about it. "Office, secretary, PI, eight grand a month. Living expenses, another eight, but let's call it ten."

"I'm hearing eighteen a month. I'm generous, so let's call it twenty. So I come up with six months' living and legal—three hundred twenty thousand up front and twenty G's a month after half a year until this is over." He looked at me. "Done?"

I squinted like I was considering the offer against my better judgment, but in my head the deal was already done. Money talks. "Okay, fine. If this woman agrees to let me represent her."

"She will."

"And if this is another cartel deal—"

"It's not."

And just like that, I was a criminal defense attorney.

*   *   *

Geronimo stood, slammed the rest of his beer, and stepped off the porch, leaving the money on the arm of the chair. "I'll get you the rest tomorrow."

He walked off toward his pickup parked in the driveway. He was three inches shorter than me, still taller than average at six feet, though his build—blocky, wide, powerful—gave the illusion of a shorter man. He was about my age, but you'd never know it looking at him. His craggy face was that of a guy who'd lived a hard and savage life, collected on too many unforgiveable loans.

"Geronimo," I said to his back.

He stopped, slumped his shoulders, then turned. I wanted to ask him why he was doing this, but decided against it when I realized his patience had worn thin.

So I made a joke.

"Open container laws in this state are a bitch. Toss me the empty and I'll get rid of the evidence."

His eyes lit up. "I get rid of my own evidence."

Dark humor? Veiled threat? I held up the money. "Who is this Mia Delarosa? Why you doin' this?"

Geronimo made a face. "The ex-cop she killed was a chomo."

Child molester.

"Ugly, but last I checked, that's not a defense for murder."

"Should be," he said. "Hell, she deserves an award." He caught himself. "If she did it."

2

MANNY HERNANDEZ'S LAW office was located in downtown Wichita, Kansas, directly across the street to the east from the Epic Center, a skyscraper shaped like a box cutter with the blade out. It was the tallest building in the state, not far from the federal and county courthouses and the jail where Mia Delarosa was being held.

Manny was an uncle of my childhood best friend, Tony Cornejo, who'd mediated our arrangement. I was to pay fifteen hundred a month for a room vacated by Manny's recently deceased partner. I'd need to get my own equipment, staff, and phones. This wasn't going to be a partnership. Tony had told me Manny was retiring at the end of the year and leery of entanglements, so I was going to be a tenant on a month-to-month basis, which suited us both. Neither of us planned to be in this building long. I'd have a key to the front and back doors and access to the hallways, bathrooms, and my office. That was it. Our agreement wasn't in writing yet, but I wasn't too concerned. By all accounts, Manny Hernandez was a man of his word.

When I stepped into the place, a receptionist looked up from behind a formidable desk. It was seven in the evening and I knew Manny had stayed late to accommodate me, but I was surprised to see staff still in the building and even more surprised to see her answering a phone while giving me a curt nod, not a hint of Midwestern hospitality. "Hernandez Law, state your business," she said into a hands-free mike.

I walked to the counter as she transferred the call and looked at me again, this time with arched eyebrows. The name plate on her desk read: RASHONDA PHELPS. Up close I could see powder buildup in the little cracks of her face.

"Benjamin Joel," I said.

She sized me up, then said, "Mr. Hernandez will be with you in a moment. Please have a seat over there."

I'd been on the road for over five hours and didn't feel like sitting, so I stopped in the center of the room to check out a life-size bronze statue of a young woman in a toga holding a mirror to her face. Egad! She held a snake in her other hand, which, by her facial expression, didn't seem to bother her at all.

"Prudence," said a man's voice.

I turned. Manny Hernandez was lost in his clothes, thirty pounds lighter than the last time I'd seen him five years ago, and he wasn't overweight then. His tie was loose and the top button of his shirt was undone. The tie, fussy red paisley, hung around his shrunken neck like a noose yet to be tightened. He was short of breath and tiny beads of sweat glistened on his brow despite the air-conditioning.

He nodded at the statue. "My partner's idea. Blame him. It's Greek, I think. Supposed to be the personification of the virtue, prudence. Cost him twenty thousand dollars."

"Prudence—how ironic."

He frowned briefly, then a smile flared. "Given the amount of money ol' Tom made in this profession, I guess I wouldn't label the purchase 'imprudent.'"

"In his commercials, your partner wore a cowboy hat, rode a bull, and shot computer-generated money out of a computer-generated gun into the air like it was confetti, as I recall."

"He said the bull represented the insurance company he was suing—taming for the benefit of his client. Judging by the money he raked in, about eighty grand a month, I'd say his marketing campaign was a success. The bull was a metaphor the masses seemed to relate to, unconsciously, no doubt. Or maybe it was the money being shot into the air."

"I need office space, Mr. Hernandez." I gestured toward the statue. "Prudence dictates that I shut up or change the subject until I get our agreement in writing."

Manny laughed. "Tom represented injured people and took on insurance companies. My nephew tells me you're representing an axe murderer who took a cop's head clean off."

"Allegedly. And the guy was an *ex*-cop whose head was still more or less attached, from what I've read."

"I think you missed my point. How's what you're doing for money any better than what Tom did?"

"Maybe it's not. But I'm not about to slap a red clown nose on my face while I do it, that's all."

Manny smiled. "That's as good a place as any to draw a line in the sand." He turned and pointed down the hallway. "Come on, I'll show you Tom's old office."

As we left, Rashonda's eyes tracked us out of the room.

The dead partner's office smelled of new carpet and fresh paint. The desk and office chairs I'd had delivered were arranged in the middle of the room like props in a low-budget play. The IT people I'd hired were supposed to have had the phone and the electronics with all the relevant software set up by the close of business today, but for some reason that hadn't happened. I thanked Manny for keeping the doors open and told him I hoped to get the computer geeks in tomorrow. He turned to leave, then paused and asked if everything looked okay.

"Looks fine," I said. "Just need the keys to the place."

As Manny dug in his pocket, my cell trilled. It was Russ Osborne, the private investigator I intended to hire. I knew Russ through Tony who'd used him to track bail skips for his bonding company. I'd talked with Russ for the first time on the phone about the case on the way back from Missouri and found him to be blunt and humorless, but he sounded competent. When I told Tony what I thought of his PI, he laughed and said "Ozzie" must've been having one of his good days.

"Where you at?" Russ said.

"My new office." Manny gave me two keys and left. "What's up?"

"I need you to come five or six miles out in the county to meet someone with me. I'm watching her place now, waiting for her to get home. Write this down."

He gave me directions that eventually led to a trail through a cornfield where I could meet him. Said he knew the farmer and had permission to use it. I plucked a new pen from a wire basket on my new desk and wrote the directions on my palm. When I finished, I said, "I'm supposed to meet with Mia at the jail in thirty minutes. What's goin' on?"

"Maybe nothin'. Maybe something important. I might need you with me to help figure out the difference. I don't know anything about this case of yours yet."

"I don't either, other than she's charged with murdering an ex-cop. What've you got?"

"An escort with X-rated photos of this client of yours."

"Escort?"

"Paid companionship."

"Got it."

"Her name is Annie Black. She's facing possession charges and missed court last Thursday. I tracked her down for Tony. Found her sleeping in the front seat of her Mustang this morning behind the strip club where she works. When I got her in cuffs, she asked me to put something in the trunk for her so it wouldn't get stolen. 'No problem,' I told her. I got her key fob out of her pocket and she pointed out an envelope in the back seat. I asked her what it was. She told me it was none of my business. I told her that since she asked me to hide it, it was my business. I dropped it back in the car and shut the door. Then she told me to go ahead and take a look if it was that big a deal to me, so I did. The envelope was full of porn pics. Maybe twenty of 'em. Group scene stuff."

"Of my client?"

"She's in every one of them. With the same guys at the same location. Guys are all wearing masks of recent ex-presidents."

"That's bizarre. How many guys?"

"Three. Reagan, Bush Two, and Bill Collins."

"When did you see these pictures?"

"This morning around eight."

"Why'd you wait so long to call me about this?"

"It was only after I started doing background on your case this afternoon that I realized the girl in the photos was your client. When I saw Delarosa's mugshot from the jail, it hit me. At least I think it's her."

"You think?"

"Looks like her. I'd bet money on it."

"Do you have the photos?"

"No. All I did was look. Figured it wasn't my business."

I laughed. "Despite telling the escort it was your business."

"It's your business now."

"Maybe."

"Then shut up and listen. We might be able to get the photos back. Tony put up another bond for Annie on the condition she talks to us. She told Tony she'd be home in the next half hour or so. Be easier if you come down the trail behind me like I said and get in the car with me. And bring a check. I don't work on credit."

"You'll get your money," I said.

Rashonda was on her feet with a purse over her shoulder and keys in hand. She feigned a smile when I nodded at her on my way out the front door with the phone to my ear. The heat pressed around me as I stepped onto the sidewalk. Buses and cars passed, sunlight flashing off chrome and glass. Rashonda came out behind me and walked away without a word.

"This Annie better be worth it," I said to Russ. "I'll cancel my meeting with Mia and be there soon as I can."

3

I FOUND RUSS where he said he'd be. In a dusty Malibu parked on a trail that bisected a cornfield. A head-high wall of cornstalks rose up on either side. I parked behind him and climbed into his front passenger seat. He sported a goatee and a ponytail and had a muscular, ropy neck. The sleeves of his khaki snap shirt were rolled up his forearms.

"This woman home yet?" I asked.

He nodded. "Annie pulled in five minutes ago."

"Why didn't we meet at her place?" I said.

He squinted through a windshield murky with dust and sun glare. "Wanted to get a few things straight with you before I take this on. Maybe we start with the money."

A sheen of sweat had formed on his face in the August heat. An expanse of pasture was spread out in front of us across a dirt road. A quarter mile away I could make out a mobile home. Binoculars rested on the console between us.

I dropped an envelope on his lap.

He opened it. Peered inside. "Ten thousand in cash?"

I'd tripped Russ's personal alarm by paying in cash. I'd have set off the IRS's alarm by depositing Geronimo's cash into the bank. Easy choice.

He got cigarettes from his shirt pocket and shook one out. "What're we gettin' into?"

"I do the legal work. You do the investigating."

Russ lit the cigarette and blew a stream of smoke through the window. "It don't look like you're carryin'."

"If you think a gun is needed to interview this woman, I'll wait in the car while you do it."

"Ain't worried about Annie. I'm worried about you."

"What about me?"

He gazed across the road, smoke coiling around his head. His flat affect gave the impression he was nursing some physical discomfort, maybe a hangover. His accusation or misgiving about me, whatever it was, hung in the air long enough for me to once again wonder what Tony saw in this guy—this guy who now had a lot of my money on his lap. I reached for it and his head turned, his gaze meeting mine. I couldn't read what it meant.

"You got something to say," I said, "say it."

"Already did. Someone drops that much cash on me, I start thinkin' about hazard pay. It's a natural progression."

"No offense, but you look like someone who'd appreciate tax-free money."

"I'm not lookin' to wade into something I'd have to hide from for the rest of my life." He drew on the cigarette, blew out smoke. "You've been off the grid for two years and show up with ten grand in cash? Makes me wonder where it came from, that's all."

"A shoe box. You can't go off-grid charging up a credit card, so yeah, we used cash. And that ten grand isn't the last of it, either."

He glared at me.

"Tony didn't tell you why I went into hiding two years ago?" I said.

"He said you didn't feel safe with all the murder and mayhem going on. Somethin' like that. I didn't push him, but I knew it wasn't the whole truth."

"The body count started rising of folks associated with a trial I was running, so I got out. Took my family and ran. If you find that peculiar, then we aren't the same. Or maybe you don't have a family."

Russ blew smoke out the window. "That's all there was to it, huh?"

I didn't say anything. From Tony I knew Russ had fought in Afghanistan and was a former ATF agent who'd worked undercover operations. I assumed he still had connections to law enforcement which meant there was a good chance he knew that my brother-in-law, Rotten Rodney Crudup, was trying to cause me problems with any cop who'd listen. Rotten Rodney is an idiot and an asshole and I beat his ass one time for laying hands on my sister, but what he was telling the cops this time was the truth. When my sister went missing for thirteen days two summers ago, she hadn't been hiding from her abusive husband like she told investigators. She'd been kidnapped by the Mendez-Rodriguez Cartel.

Russ squinted at me. "I'm not your preacher and I'm not investigating you, but before we do business, I need to know one thing."

I waited for it.

He held up the envelope. "This have anything to do with that trial two years ago? You taking off with your family?"

I shook my head. "No."

My answer fell somewhere between more-or-less true and a white lie. The cash came from a cartel hitman who helped me save my sister, but other than that, I had no reason to believe my representing Mia Delarosa on this murder charge now was connected to what happened two summers ago.

Russ looked at me. "While you were gone, your brother-in-law told the sheriff and the KBI your sister's disappearance back then was connected to that trial."

"Pops told me Rodney's been doing that. KBI showed up on Pops' doorstep last year, asking where I was." Pops was my grandfather. He'd raised me and my sister since we were in grade school.

"If some folks kidnapped your sister back then, maybe it's the same people who killed that detective in the middle of the trial. That's why the KBI still cares."

"No shit."

"No shit? If there's nothing to your brother-in-law's story, why don't you talk to the KBI and lay it to rest?"

"Maybe I did."

"You didn't say squat. Don't jerk me around."

"I thought you weren't investigating me?"

Russ gave me a flat look. "We're both doing the same thing here."

"What's that?" I said.

"Telling each other bits and pieces of the truth and lying by omission. I have an old friend who knows a lot about your situation. Label that an investigation and call me a liar if you want, I don't give a shit."

"This case with Mia has nothing at all to do with that cartel trial. If you can't accept that, I'll move on. Simple as that."

Russ picked up the envelope. "Where'd this come from?"

"You don't want to know."

"That may be the closest thing to the truth you've said so far." He handed me the money. "Shove it under the seat for me over there, would ya?"

"So we're good?"

Something in the sun-soaked distance caught his attention. He dropped his cigarette out the window and put the binoculars to his eyes. "Get me another ten grand in cash tomorrow and we're good as we're gonna get."

Fair enough. Tony said Russ was the best PI in Wichita and I figured the final bill would be closer to twenty grand anyway, so I agreed.

His eyes were still glued to the binoculars.

"Damn," he said.

"What?"

"Guy named Rick Butler just showed up at Annie's. I know his Lexus. He owns the escort service Annie and Mia work for."

"How do you know this guy?"

He lowered the binos. "Every cop around knows him. Strip club owner who's been in the sex trade long enough to have the goods on enough high-level people in the right positions that he's never been in any serious trouble. He's kind of a genius that way, though I hear he's been slipping lately. Used to be, if he couldn't get dirt on a cop or councilman or prosecutor, he'd pay someone to get it. Top dollar, too. Time has taken its toll on him though. Now, among other things, he's a has-been drug dealer who dabbles in his own product."

He put the binos to his eyes again. "What the fuck is he doing? He's just sitting in the Lexus."

"And we're just sitting here. That because you don't want him to know we're talking to her?"

"Nothing gets by you, does it?"

He kept watch with the binos. I stared into the distance long enough to know whatever was going down was too far away for me to see it. Storm clouds swept along the southern horizon with long, dark tendrils of rain dropping to earth in the distance. Cattle moved from a muddy pond bottom into an enormous stand of cottonwoods in a creek that cut through a pasture. I answered a text from Keri about dinner. Before I looked up from my phone, Russ laughed.

"Fat sumbitch can barely get out from behind the wheel."

I looked down at my phone. Answered another one of Keri's texts. Then another. *Tacos sound good.*

Russ dropped the binos abruptly and started the engine, slammed the car into gear and tore out.

"What's going on?"

"He forced his way inside. Looked like they were fighting."

We raced southward, dust rising in our wake. When we were clear of some trees, the mobile home was visible again through tall weeds and sun-dried grass, backlit by a low sun. Russ reached over and opened the glove box and handed me a Glock 17 in a holster. I made sure it was loaded and had a round in the chamber before shoving it inside my jeans at the small of my back.

Russ glanced at me. "You're not callin' 911?"

"No. They'd tell us to hang back, wait for deputies. Wouldn't get here in time to do this woman any good."

Russ nodded. "My kind of lawyer."

We turned into the sun, both of us reaching for the visors at the same time. We roared up a long, rutted driveway that ended at a double-wide trailer. Russ slid the car to a stop behind a Lexus SUV near the front door. A newer-model blue Mustang was parked beneath a tree.

We pulled our pistols and leaped out. Before we reached the door, a blonde in shorts and an oversized T-shirt pushed it open. Held it open and looked down at us. Her cheeks were flushed, like maybe she was angry.

She glanced at the guns. Her eyes narrowed but otherwise her expression didn't change. Her hair was bundled in a big pile on her head, showing off an elegant neck. She looked to be in her mid-forties and wore a middle-aged thickness well.

"Everything okay here, Annie?" Russ said.

"Why wouldn't it be?" She focused on me. "You the attorney?"

"Everything alright?" Russ said again. He tried to see past her into the kitchen.

"What'd I just say? But right now isn't a good time. How 'bout you come back later?"

Russ shook his head. "We're here now."

"I know why you're here. How long'll this take, anyway?"

She stepped outside barefooted onto a stack of cinderblocks fashioned into steps. Russ got by her and yanked the door open, bounded into the room with his gun drawn. Seconds later he yelled at someone to drop their gun.

No gunfire, so I gave Annie a look and went in behind Russ. Rick Butler was on his ass on the floor, back against a wall, rubbing his neck with both hands. Tears rolled down his red face, which looked the redder in contrast to his thick, white hair. A pistol was on the floor within his reach. I kicked it away, then picked it up. It was a cheap little Bersa .22 with a scratched nickel finish.

"What the hell's wrong with him?" I said to Russ.

Butler's eyes blazed with fury. "Bitch," he said, the word sounding raw and liquid in his throat.

Annie watched from the top step, propping the door open with her rump. Russ glanced at her, then at Butler. "Lady fucked you up a bit, didn't she?"

Butler glanced at Russ, then his eyes settled on me. His pupils were pinholes. He was on something. Probably opioids.

I knew the look. He squinted, sort of tilted his head, gave me a confused look, then smiled a little. "Paco? I thought you was dead."

Russ looked at me. I shook my head. "No idea."

"You got shot," Butler said. "They carried you off into the woods."

Weird.

"I'm not Paco," I said.

"Sure, you are." He blinked several times. Licked beads of sweat off his upper lip. "I mean, you, you, gotta be. 'Cept, 'cept I saw you dead. Curtis shot you."

"Curtis?"

"Dean Curtis."

Russ and I exchanged a look. Dean Curtis? Curtis was a local billionaire socialite the media dubbed the *Darth Vader of Dark Money* two election cycles ago. Investigative reporters had pegged him as the likely source of tens of millions of dollars of so-called dark money funneled through nonprofits that anonymously funded everything from mayoral candidates in New York to campaigns for the presidency. Which meant Butler was somewhere off in dreamland.

Russ made a face. "You on the pipe now, Rick?"

I crouched in front of him. "I'm not this Paco guy," I said again. "Whoever he is."

Butler's gaze sharpened somewhat and he searched my face. "You . . . then you're like his son. Or something."

I laughed, holstered Russ's gun, and stepped down into the yard, still holding Rick's crappy little pistol.

Annie came out into the yard with me and the door banged shut on a spring.

"You hit him in the throat?" I asked.

She nodded.

"He have this gun on you at the time?"

"He pulled it. That's as far as he got."

I popped the magazine, ejected the chambered round and put all of that in a pocket, dropped the pistol on the Malibu's front seat. "Why'd he push his way into your house?"

She looked away. "Don't know what you're talking about."

"Guy's dangerous. He's going to kill you someday."

"No he won't. Farmer don't kill the milk cow." She stared at me. "You two got no right rollin' up in here like this, both of you with guns."

"Call 911 on us. I won't stop you."

She raised her eyebrows. "Yeah, right. Get sheriff's deputies out here. I wouldn't make that call on a bet." She nodded toward the house. "How long've you known your investigator?"

"Just met him, why? You know him?"

She shrugged. "Kinda. He say anything about me?"

"Said you worked for Butler. Told me you had photos of my client I oughta know about. Why?"

She shook her head. "Just curious. So if you're here about Mia, ask your questions. Let's get this over with."

"How do you know her?"

She shrugged. "We both work for Rick."

"As what?" I searched for the word. "Escorts?"

She gave me a flat look. "What if we are?"

"Not my business. What were you doing with those photos of her?"

"What do you mean, what was I doin' with 'em?"

"Russ said you were awfully protective of them this morning."

"I didn't want 'em stolen. Didn't want 'em out there for anyone to see. Common courtesy amongst us girls, that's all."

"Where'd the photos come from?"

She shook her head. "Dunno."

"No idea, huh?"

"Nope."

"Who were the men with Mia?"

"How would I know? They wore masks."

"Where are the photos now?"

"I burned 'em."

"They're not still in your car?"

Her face got hard. "What'd I just say? I burned 'em."

I glanced at her car. "Mind if I have a look?"

"Knock yourself out. It's unlocked."

As I walked to the Mustang she trailed after me. "Porn's free y'know. Find anything you want online."

Her car smelled new and was clean inside. I found nothing of interest regarding Mia Delarosa. The only thing of note was a hundred dollar bill crumpled on the floor in the back seat. I handed it to her on my way to the trunk.

Nothing in the trunk. I shut it and asked what her case was about.

She shrugged. "Possession."

"Knew that. Possession of what?"

A light sprinkle fell and the air cooled as wind blew in from the south. She hooked a lock of hair that had come loose behind her ear and faced the breeze. "Meth."

"Bullshit charge or what?"

She closed her eyes against spits of rain. She opened them and faced me. "I don't use drugs. Don't possess them either."

I tried to look sympathetic. Not sure it took.

She frowned at me. "My lawyer gave me that look."

"What look?"

"The one that says she thinks I'm lying."

"About what?"

"I told her the same thing I told the cop that searched my purse. I've never done meth in my life."

"I bet your attorney hears that a lot."

Annie blurted out a laugh. "That's what she said. Your next question's gonna be, 'So, where'd the drugs come from?'"

"Where did they come from?"

She sighed softly. "What's with you lawyers?"

"Drugs had to've come from somewhere. What's the explanation? Maybe I can help."

She smiled. A glimpse of the girl she'd once been. Her teeth were straight and white and despite a long night and a rough day her eyes were clear. She wore a touch of makeup that suited her. She didn't look like a drug user to me and I'd seen hundreds of them in court. Even lived with a couple when I was a kid—my mother and her live-in boyfriend.

"I don't do drugs," she said. "Never have. That's my explanation. Figure it out from there."

"For what it's worth," I said. "I believe you."

Her expression softened.

"Come on. You must have some idea how the meth got in your purse. Let's hear it."

"I know exactly how it got there, but I think telling you would be a mistake. Haven't even told my lawyer."

"Why you keeping this from your lawyer?"

She shrugged. "That day I met with her . . . if she gave me that smug little smirk again I was afraid I'd . . ." She trailed off and shook her head. "I'm tired of it, y'know?"

"Tired of what?"

"Everything." The lock of hair was out again, dancing across her face in the breeze. "Not being believed. Even by my own attorney. I know you guys have heard it all, and who set me up on this charge is just another ridiculous story—"

"I'm a connoisseur of ridiculous stories."

She sighed. Looked off into the distance. "Clint Brown planted the drugs on me. Whole thing was a setup."

When she looked at me again, I pointed a finger at my face. "Not smirking."

"You don't even know who Clint Brown is, do you?"

"No . . . guess not. The name sounds familiar though."

"He's the undersheriff in this county."

"Okay, that rings a bell. Why would the undersheriff plant meth on you?"

"Because I made him pay for a date."

"A date? Is that what you call it?"

She nodded. "What else should I call it? Anyway, Clint's not the kind of guy I'd be interested in if money wasn't involved. That didn't sit well with him."

"You're sure he planted meth on you?"

"He came right out and told me he did. Said he was teaching me a lesson."

"He framed you because you wouldn't have sex with him unless he paid for it?"

She pursed her lips. "I told him to set up a date through Ricky—Butler—like everyone else." Her eyes turned glassy. "What he wanted last night was some action to make the possession charge go away. He called it bartering. Showed me his key to the evidence locker and said he could hide the drugs from my case in the wrong bin. When the trial rolled around and the cops couldn't find the drugs, the prosecutor would have to dismiss the case. That's how he was going to pay."

"He raped you."

Her face lost color and she looked away. "I told him I'd just as soon take the conviction. Told him I wouldn't have sex with him for all the money in the world. He put a gun to my head. When he finished, he pinned me down . . . stuffed that hundred dollar bill you found into my mouth."

* * *

She said she hadn't reported the rape and that she'd taken a shower and washed her panties. She assumed this meant there wouldn't be any DNA evidence to collect. I told her that wasn't necessarily true. She said it didn't matter because even if a prosecutor could prove Brown had intercourse with her, people would assume she wanted it because she was a "whore who got her money in the end." She paused and added, "Or in the mouth, as the case may be." I ignored her attempt to lighten the mood and told her I was sorry for what happened, that I wanted to help her do something about it. She told me I was obligated say that, denied my offer, but nevertheless thanked me for the kind thought.

I peeked into the Lexus on my way to check on Butler and Russ and saw a used hypodermic needle and a tourniquet on the console. That's probably what Butler was doing in the Lexus.

I stepped onto the cinderblocks and pulled open the door, but didn't go inside because Russ was standing in the way with his back to me looking down at the gelatinous form of

Ricky Butler. Russ looked back at me and Annie, who was practically in my hip pocket. His hands were on his hips and he was breathing heavily. So was Butler.

"What's going on?" I said.

"Trying to get this fat fucker outta here," Russ said. "It's like fighting with a goddamn sumo wrestler." He wiped sweat off his brow. "It's hot as shit in here."

He stepped outside with us. We stood by the doorway staring in at Butler. He was flat on his back, his eyes were half open. We were close enough that I could smell his funk.

I said to Russ, "Did you find the photos of Mia in there?"

"Told you I burned them," Annie said. "I think it's time for both of you to leave."

Butler sat up slowly, grunting with effort as he did. It was a process. When he got himself stabilized, he looked at me. "Whass your name?"

"What's it to you, fat ass?" Russ said.

Butler's doped-up eyes held mine. "Paco's your dad, ain't he?"

I rolled my eyes.

Russ laughed. "Here we go with this Paco shit again. He's so smacked out."

Butler squinted at me, trying to focus. "You're from Worthington, aren't you?"

That startled the hell out of me. I was from Worthington, a nearby town of ten thousand people, thirty miles south of Wichita.

"Don't answer," Russ said. "He's just fucking with you."

I kept my eyes on Butler. Worthington. Where'd he come up with that?

Butler wet his lips. "Your mother was there when Curtis shot Paco, but she slipped away."

I took a step toward him. "What the fuck are you talking about?"

Russ shook his head. "Give it up, Ben. Waste of time."

"They had to kill her, you know," Butler said.

"Who had to kill who?" I said.

Butler's heavy eyelids opened wider. "Your mother. To keep her quiet. Back in, in, think it was in '93."

I felt my whole body stiffen. My mother OD'd on heroin in '93. I was eleven when I found her body.

Russ gripped my arm. I shook it off.

Butler swallowed hard, then coughed. "She died of a heroin overdose, but that ain't the whole story."

My neck turned hot. "Yeah? What's the whole story?"

"Let's get out of here," Russ said. "He's full of shit."

"Wait a moment. I want to know how and where he came up with any of this." I nudged Butler's foot.

"Cops killed your mother," he said. "Made it look like an overdose."

"Where're you getting all this?" I said.

"You gotta be Paco Correa's kid. I knew Paco. You look juss like him. You ever know him?"

My stomach knotted. "What's my name?"

He thought for a while, mouth working silently. "Gotta be Joel," he said at last. "Your mom's last name was Joel. I heard her son became a lawyer. Then a judge. Don't know if I ever knew your first name, but you must be Judge Joel."

He smiled at me with an air of superiority. Maybe there was a simple explanation for this. He'd gotten information about me from God-only-knows-where, knew who I was when he first saw me, and was mixing it with lies and guesses and half-truths to mess with me. But, maybe not. Men like Butler sometimes had access to the kind of information that very few people did.

Russ tugged on my arm. "Come on. Let's get outta here. He's just fucking with you."

I held back. "Who are these cops you're talking about?"

Butler shook his head. "You don't want to know. I tell you that, I'll get us both killed."

I wasn't sure what to do. Russ might be right. Butler might be fucking with me. Time to cut this off. "Let's stuff his ass in the Lexus and take him for a ride."

* * *

Butler didn't like being stuffed into the back of his Lexus like old laundry. Judging by the berating we took from Annie, she didn't care for what we were doing either. Can't say I liked it either, but I didn't want to leave Butler with Annie and I wasn't about to call for deputies who might answer to Annie's rapist.

Russ zip tied Butler's hands behind his back and drove him three miles down a dirt road and parked on a bridge. I followed in the Malibu. Watched Russ toss Butler's key fob into the creek, open the hatch, and cut the zip tie. Butler tried to hit him. Russ deflected the blow and punched him twice in the face, dragged him out of the Lexus by his hair, and beat his head against the back bumper for as long as it took me to pile out of the Malibu and pull Russ off him.

Butler moaned and rolled around in the gravel. A couple goose eggs bulged on his forehead.

Russ came back from the front of the Lexus carrying a laptop with a decal of the rock and roll group AC/DC stuck to it.

"What are you doing with that?" I said.

"There's gotta be some interesting shit on it."

"Names of Johns?"

"Probably more than that, but yeah. Some of those too."

"Leave it," I said.

"Why?"

"What are you gonna do with it? Extort people?"

"No. But he might."

"Throw it in the creek if you want, but we're not taking it."

Russ made a face and walked past me to the Malibu. I looked down at Butler. He was playing possum on the ground, one eye cracked open. He saw Russ toss the laptop over the railing. I didn't hear a splash.

I stepped to the railing and looked down. The creek was narrow and shallow. I figured Russ had thrown the laptop into the thicket on the bank, but I couldn't see it.

Fine, I thought. It'll be dark after Russ drops me off and gets back here. These two idiots can hunt for that thing and fight over it all night for all I care.

4

WE WERE PARKED on the trail between the cornfields again in the Malibu. I was in the driver's seat, and we were nose to nose with my black Ford F350 in the gray light. In the miles leading back here, I'd told Russ how, as an eleven-year-old, I'd found my mother dead in a Worthington trailer park and that I didn't know who my father was.

When I opened the door to leave, Russ asked me if I wanted him to look into what Ricky Butler had said.

I shut the door. "Yes. If you can."

"What year did your mother die?"

"Ninety-three."

He nodded. "Time frame fits. That's disconcerting."

"How much to get you started?"

He waved his hand dismissively. "What did Annie say about those photos of Mia?"

"Nothing significant. She's lying about what she knows. I'm sure of that, but I don't know how those photos could make any difference in Mia's case. So it probably doesn't matter."

"You're probably right." He shrugged.

I told him about Annie's allegation of rape and how that tied in with her possession charge. As I did, his eyes grew distant. Looked like he took it personal.

"You believe her about the rape?" he asked.

"Yes."

He tilted his head. "A one-word answer from a lawyer?"

I shrugged.

"Yet, you think she lied about the photos. Explain that."

"She was straightforward with me about when she was lying."

"I believe it'd take three years of law school to learn some stupid shit like that. Is that lawyer logic?"

I shook my head. "Observation, mostly. The study of nonverbal cues. A skill you should've honed as a cop. There was defiance in Annie's demeanor when she lied about the photos. Like a juror saying whatever is necessary to get off jury duty. Looking at you like, *you and I both know I'm lying and there's not a damn thing you can do about it.* It's like that."

I studied his face. He'd wore that pissed off look since I told him about Annie being raped—looked more like a father who'd just been told his daughter was raped than a hardened investigator. I wanted to know why, so I stirred the pot to see what bubbled to the surface. "You believe Brown raped Annie, just like she said, don't you?"

Russ's mouth fell open. "Never said that."

"Didn't have to. I'm just reading the cues here."

He faced me. *Read this, motherfucker.*

I smiled. "Could be I'm reading them wrong."

He looked away. Flush creeped across his cheeks. This was a big deal to Russ. I watched him until his shoulders relaxed, then turned up the heat. "You're upset because you like this woman."

He blew out a breath and rubbed the back of his head. "I've known Annie since we were in high school together—Valley Center."

Valley Center was a small town just north of Wichita—one of Worthington's rivals in high school sports.

"I take it you believe her?" I said.

"You read me right."

"How well do you know her?"

Russ looked at me like he was deciding whether I was worthy of hearing such a thing, then looked away like I hadn't passed muster.

I reached for the door to leave when he said, "She was my first. I got her pregnant when we were sixteen."

"What the hell? That should've been the first thing you told me about Annie . . . wait—you took her to jail this morning."

He buzzed his window down and lit a cigarette.

"And a few minutes ago you're beating the shit out of that asshole who's taking advantage of her. What the hell's going on?"

He stared through the mist-coated windshield.

"You said she was your first. Love, or just sex?"

"Both."

"She have the baby?"

He shook his head. "Miscarriage. At least that's what Annie's father, Pastor Arlen Black, told his congregation from the pulpit one fine Sunday morning."

"Seems highly inappropriate."

"By the time he found out she was pregnant, she was five months along. Can't keep a secret like that for long in a small town, so I guess he felt like he needed to face the problem head on—get it out in the open and preach about it. Use it as a teaching moment."

"An all-have-fallen-short-of-the-glory-of-God kind of message?"

"More like if you sleep with dogs you get fleas. His version was that she'd made some poor choices by running with the wrong crowd. Privately, he maintained that Annie was raped."

"By you?"

"By me. That's what he put out there in his chickenshit way. Never to the cops. Never from the pulpit. But behind closed doors to anyone who'd listen."

"What did Annie say about that?"

"She told her friends the truth, but she was a kid. She couldn't stop her father from spreading lies any more than I could. Two weeks after finding out she was pregnant, Annie's parents sent her to live with her uncle in Texas. I never saw her again. Until recently. I heard from a friend of hers a few years after high school that there'd been no miscarriage."

He flicked an ash out the window. "And no birth."

"Abortion?"

He nodded.

"Is that what Annie wanted?"

"I dunno."

He seemed to mull that over.

Finally, he said, "When I was in grade school, it was always a big event when the teachers brought in Pastor Black to show us his collection of large snakes. Every kid in the class either loved the snakes or loved hating them, y'know—the darkness they evoke in the mind from just watching them move. Turns out he used the snakes to lure young girls into his home so he could molest them. One woman came forward with her allegations about what he'd done to her when she was a child and that started the ball rolling. When all was said and done, fifteen women came forward, all with similar stories. He was arrested in '02 when I was overseas. Before I was stateside, he'd been sent to prison and murdered—gutted with a shiv by his cellmate."

"So you've never talked to Annie about any of this."

"No. I never looked her up. She never looked me up. About a year ago, we saw each other at the grocery store. She turned her shopping cart around and pretended not to see me. I let her go."

"What about Clint Brown?"

"What about him?"

"You just letting that go?"

Russ smoked. "Not my circus, not my monkey."

"Staying in your own lane, huh?"

"As far as you know."

I suspected Russ's arrangement with Annie's bondsman, my best friend, was a way for Russ to get close to Annie. I could call Tony and ask when he started using Russ as his skip tracer. Find out who approached who about doing business together. Maybe then I'd know if Russ had set up his current involvement with Annie. Maybe I'd do that, but I wasn't sure it mattered. He still cared for his first love. There were worse things in the world.

I told Russ I'd be in touch, then left him there between cornfields, but I figured he might pay Ricky Butler another visit before the night was through.

5

THE TECHNOLOGY GUY arrived at my office at nine the next morning to set up phones and computers. I watched him work and drank coffee, trying to shake off the funk from a restless night and the dream I had of pedaling across Worthington on a mission to tell Pops about how I'd found his daughter dead in her trailer home. In the dream, I passed the same houses, crossed the same streets, darted down the same alleys with the same barking dogs, only to repeat the trek, over and over, never arriving, never delivering the news, as if telling Pops about Mom was the ultimate horror to be avoided. Three cups of coffee and two hours later, the fog from the night was gone, and the IT guy had the Joel Law Office up and running.

I called Pops and told him that Keri and I were cooking him dinner tonight. A long overdue reunion. Then I called the Sedgwick County Detention Center to reschedule my initial meeting with Mia, but the jail was in lockdown for reasons the guy manning the phones either didn't know, or wouldn't tell me. He told me to call back in four hours.

Since I didn't have the discovery packet from the DA's office on Mia's case, I was fresh out of office work. I considered calling my old law school buddy, Blaine Swartzmiller, the elected DA, to get the discovery fast-tracked to me, but then had better idea. I called Russ and told him I had the rest of his money. He gave me an address and told me to "swing it by." People tend to make themselves available for money. I was hoping the payday would inspire him to look into the whole Paco Correa thing for me before we had anything more to do on Mia's case.

I ditched the suit and tie for hiking boots and jeans and drove north on Broadway Street until I reached a boxy concrete place called Crossroads Bar & Grill that sat adjacent to a railyard on the outskirts of the city. An enormous grain elevator glowed white under a clear blue sky further up the road.

Russ was behind the bar wiping it down when I stepped into the place, which had just opened. He glanced at me, said something through the serving hatch to someone in the kitchen, then pointed me to a round-top table in the corner and followed. He sat across from me with a towel thrown over his shoulder.

I looked around. Two booths by the front window. Three more round-tops. A lotto kiosk in the corner by the restrooms. "I assumed I was getting directions to your office. Maybe your residence."

"The PI business isn't all that lucrative if you want to know the truth, and this is my residence. Got a manager's room with a bed in back."

I pushed an envelope across the table. "Maybe this'll help."

"You meet with Delarosa yet?"

"Jail's in lockdown for some reason. I'll try again this afternoon."

He peeked in the envelope. Gave me a sideways look. "I won't have time to start on the Paco thing today if that's what you're thinking."

Arrogant and rude or savvy and straightforward. Russ Osborne as human inkblot. My assessment reflected more on me than him so I went with savvy and straightforward. I'd like to think of myself as a charitable man capable of cutting the arrogant prick some slack.

The morning's first customer came through the door, glancing at the big-screen TV above the bar that the waitress had just turned on.

"I guess you'll have your hands full in here today."

"Got the rest of the day off. You eaten yet?"

"No."

"Grilled ham and cheese is today's special. By special, I mean on me. Hungry?"

"Sure. Thanks."

He stood. "What are you drinking?"

"Ice water."

He left and came back with sandwiches, steak fries, and drinks. He crushed lime slices over his Coke, dropped them in, then gulped down half the glass while I made a puddle of mustard next to my fries. The sandwiches weren't complicated—grilled in butter to a toasty crispness with melted pepper jack warming thin cuts of black forest ham and flat slices of cool dill pickle.

"What's on your agenda today?" I said.

"Clint Brown." He pulled up something on his phone and showed it to me. "Check out this spread of his."

I did. Stopped breathing for a moment. Felt a flutter in my gut. Big Georgian-style home featuring six white columns and a white-railed balcony that ran the length of the front, accented with an antique brick exterior. A bank of dormer windows overlooked the balcony from a steeply pitched roof. Behind the house in the distance sat a huge, circular barn built around a silo. Impressive, yes, but that didn't explain what raised my hackles. This estate was the focal point of what might be my earliest memory, one that periodically came to mind in idle moments—some vestige from the past that stayed with me, free of all context except that I knew I was very young and with my mother when I saw the place from the passenger seat of her El Camino. Why this image lingered in my mind through the years had always been a mystery to me. Now I wondered if it had something to do with the deaths of my parents.

"By the look on your face," Russ said, "I'm guessing you're wondering how a man who makes eighty grand a year can afford this place."

Good guess, but I didn't tell him he was wrong and that I was certain I'd seen the house sometime in the past. I shrugged, trying to pull myself back to the present. "Inherited it, maybe?"

"Yes and no. Brown's been with the sheriff's office his whole career. Same as his daddy. The story is that his old man got lucky on some stock pretty late in life. After his parents died, Brown invested that money with a solid money manager and hit it even bigger than his daddy did. Bought this place with some of the proceeds in the early nineties."

"You've been investigating Annie's rapist. Good for you."

Russ blew out air in mock amusement. "Yeah, good for me. I'm meeting him at this place in an hour."

"Meeting? You gonna rip him a new one about raping Annie?"

"Mm, not exactly."

"How'd you manage to get a meeting with him?"

He shrugged. "Called him."

"And said what?"

"Told him I wanted to give him a heads-up about something I came across involving Rick Butler and one of his girls. Some bullshit involving him he might want to get ahead of before it got any bigger. Common courtesy—one cop to another. Not the kind of thing that should be talked about over the phone."

"He knew who you were?"

"Said he did. We were both cops. We've seen each other around."

"Like at the policeman's ball or something?"

Russ rolled his eyes.

"What?" I said. "Police don't have balls?"

"Ask your wife. She knows better. Can I finish my fuckin' story now?"

"Let me take a moment to say how honored I am to have been here to witness your first attempt at levity."

He gave me a blank look, no laugh, so I said, "Guess I was wrong. Keep talking."

"Brown suggested a meeting at his place this afternoon."

"So you said."

"I didn't tell you it was his idea. He wanted to have the meeting before his wife and daughter got home. You're fucking up the flow of the conversation."

"This is none of my business, but if you confront Brown about what Annie told us, aren't you putting a target on her back?"

"Not the way I'm gonna play it."

I thought about what he meant. Went with the first thing that came to mind. "You're going to tell Brown that Rick Butler's raising hell about him raping one of his girls."

"That obvious, huh?"

"Thought maybe you went back and beat the shit out of Butler last night."

"He was gone when I got back to the bridge."

"And you didn't find him in or around the creek looking for the laptop?"

He shook his head. "Didn't find the laptop either. He must've found it. I knew exactly where it landed."

"So now you sic one asshole on the other. Sit back and watch them fuck each other up. That play's been around a long time."

"For good reason. It works."

I nodded. "Mind if I tag along?"

"What the hell for?"

"Brown's place—what you just showed me on the phone. I'm pretty sure I've been there before. Saw it from the road in my mother's car. I couldn't have been more than five or six."

Russ guzzled the rest of his Coke. "So what?"

"Where's this place at?"

"Thought you'd been there before?"

"I just said I was five or six at the time. I've seen the house, but I don't know where it is."

Russ nodded slowly. "Brown being a lifelong cop, you think there might be a connection between him and what Butler said yesterday?"

"I don't know. Maybe. Butler said a cop killed my mother. Brown is a cop. I saw his house when I was very young."

"One chance in a hundred, if that."

"Uh-huh. Still a chance. So where is this place?"

"West of here. Northwest part of Sumner County. There's a lake a few miles west of there. Maybe your mom drove you by his place on the way to the lake. No connection there."

"Anything's possible. I'm just not ruling it out."

"Okay, fine, but he's not expecting anyone but me. What's gonna be our excuse for you being there?"

"We'll tell him I'm Mia's new attorney. Annie and Mia both work for Butler, so—"

"So what?"

I shrugged. "We'll say we're investigating Butler."

He squinted. "Doesn't make any sense."

"Doesn't have to. Just get me in the door, I'll make it work."

Russ gave me a long look. Finally, he said, "I still don't like it."

I reached across the table. Picked up the envelope full of cash and dropped it on the table for effect. "Customer's always right, right?"

Russ held his glass near his mouth, jiggling loose Coke-colored ice. "Whatever you say, boss."

6

RUSS DROVE US west out of Wichita on U.S. Route 54, then south into Sumner County. Several turns later, we were on a dirt road that every other mile or so took us past farmhouses and barns, a good half of which had long ago been abandoned. The most decayed structures had caved in roofs and slumped to one side. The roads were well maintained and cut through gentle rolling land that appeared to stretch beyond the rim of the world. The wind blew hard, chasing clouds across the sky. We crossed an intersection where a street sign was perforated with buckshot.

"Feel like you've been down this road before?" Russ asked.

I shook my head.

He pointed at a huge house in the distance. "That's Brown's place right there."

It disappeared from view as we rode down a gentle slope.

"Are you gonna be alright in there with this guy?" I said.

"What do you mean?"

"Guy rapes your high school sweetheart and you ask 'what do I mean'?"

"A lot of years have passed since Annie and I were together. I'm over it."

"I don't think so."

His look told me he didn't want to talk about it.

"I'm thinking you might lose your shit in there and take this guy's head off," I said.

"Told you I'm over it."

"Whatever you say."

Brown's estate was behind a ten-foot mortared field-stone fence I'd never seen before. We turned into a gravel driveway and parked in front of a wood gate between two stone columns. A security camera perched on one of the columns swiveled on its mount and aimed at us.

After a moment, the gate swung open, revealing a red-brick driveway lined with trees on either side. The treetops had grown together over the road, giving the illusion of a tunnel.

We drove through. Eighty yards later we came out from under the canopy and saw Brown's home. To the left of it a round barn surrounded a silo in the middle distance. Russ rounded a fountain centered in the circular drive and parked the Malibu by the front door. He killed the engine and looked at me. "Still think you've been here before?"

I nodded. "The fence out front wasn't here back then. Neither was the fountain. And the trees were smaller, but this is the place. I've been here before. Out front on the public road at least."

"If there's anything to what Rick Butler said about Paco, seeing your face might scramble Brown's circuits."

I opened the door and put one boot on the bricks and looked back at Russ. "I figured you would've caught on sooner than that."

"If he sees a resemblance to Paco, let's hope he doesn't have a good poker face."

"Let's hope he won't even know he's playing poker."

*   *   *

Undersheriff Brown opened the front door looking anxious, his bushy mustache standing watch over thin lips. His eyes darted between us and he said his own name and shook Russ's hand with the enthusiasm of a politician. His paunch, narrow shoulders, and disproportionately short legs made me think of a penguin. Take the man out of his button-up Oxford and put him in a tuxedo and the whole world would see it.

He cocked his head as he shook my hand. "Have we met? You look familiar."

Familiarity, but no obvious scrambled circuits. Innocent enough, maybe. But if he'd killed my mother he probably knew her name. Likely knew she had a son. Some killers are like that. He hears my name he might remember why my face looked so damned familiar.

"Ben," I said, releasing his hand.

"Ben . . ." Brown waited for me to tell him my last name.

"Benjamin Joel." I watched his eyes to see if the name Joel would make them flicker, make them reveal something he wanted to keep hidden. My mother was Paula Joel.

A hint of something flitted across his face. Recognition? It was gone in an instant, but a look of animal caution remained in his eyes. For a moment we locked eyes. I didn't smile, didn't say anything. I let my gaze work on him. I might be staring into the eyes of my mother's killer as he stared into the eyes of the son whose parents he'd killed. Or maybe he was just a nervous rapist.

"Ben used to be a judge," Russ said. "Face has been on TV a few times over the years. Maybe that's where you saw him."

"On TV. Yeah, right." Brown stepped back, rubbing his palms on his jeans. He reminded me of a boxer trying not to look hurt to the referee. Russ and I went past him into the foyer without being invited.

A staircase was centered in the marbled foyer which echoed with the ticking of a grandfather clock. What looked like recent photos of Brown sat on an entryway table—Brown the family man, the cop, the hunter, then I saw one that caused my whole body to tense. It was of a much younger Brown with an also-younger yet easily identified Dean Curtis, the local billionaire Rick Butler said had killed some guy named Paco he thought might be my father. Brown and Curtis were in what looked like an art gallery, posing for the photo in front of a painting that probably went for half a million dollars and looked like something my daughter drew on the living room wall when she was four. The picture of Brown and Curtis seemed out of place out here in the foyer, but maybe the display was intentional, as if Brown wanted his guests to know who they were dealing with—a connected cop with serious juice. But then again, maybe not. There might be a deeper connection between the two men I didn't know about—something to do with my mother and this guy named Paco. I shook that off and told myself there could be fifty ways these two might know each other, none of them having anything to do with me. Something innocent. Good, even. Perhaps the two men were family.

I tried to look impressed and waved at the photo, gently probing for information. "Old friend of yours?"

Brown brushed by me without a word. I looked at Russ. He'd also seen the photo, and with Brown's back to us he gave it another look. As did I. In the photo, Brown was grinning and his cheeks were flushed, probably from the wine he was holding, but maybe from the photo-op with a famous person. He looked tipsy, if not drunk. Curtis's face—thin, angular, with the deep-set eyes of a monkey—was also smiling. Sort of—there was something stealthy in his expression, something sly that I didn't like. Snap judgement I know, but I'd learned to trust my primal instincts.

We followed Brown down the hall into a room with a fireplace. In front of the fireplace, matching cornflower-blue couches faced each other on an expansive burgundy and gold area rug. Between the couches was a leather-topped coffee table. Some sort of ottoman hybrid. Brown gestured to one of the couches. Russ and I sat as Brown took a seat across from us.

Brown looked at me. "Former judge, huh? You lose an election?"

"I resigned," I said, thinking about how to again inject the subject of Dean Curtis into the conversation. But I quickly decided against doing that, at least for the moment. Brown obviously wasn't in the mood to talk about Curtis, and I figured we'd find out the connection soon enough on our own anyway.

Brown gave Russ a sidelong look. "You didn't say you were bringing anyone with you."

"You didn't ask," Russ said.

Brown cleared his throat. "Why's he here then?"

"Mia Delarosa," I said. "I'm her attorney. Russ here is my investigator."

Brown's mustache made an upside down U. "Mia Delarosa. That's the woman charged with murdering Jimmy Ray, right?"

I leaned forward. "Yes. You knew Jimmy Ray?"

Brown shrugged. "He was retired PD. I've seen him around over the years."

I gave Russ a half-concealed grin. He shook his head. *Don't say it.*

I looked at Brown. "Like at the policeman's ball?"

Couldn't help myself.

Brown leaned back. For an instant he looked at me like I was an idiot, then his face took on a wary expression as he reevaluated my response.

"You also knew Rick Butler," I said.

"Yeah, so what? Where're you going with this shit?"

I gave him a hard look. "He claims you raped one of his girls. Woman by the name of Annie Black. My client, Mia, worked for Butler too."

"Scumbag like Butler lies about me and you think it has something to do with Jimmy Ray's murder? That's the stupidest thing I've heard in years."

"Butler exploited my client. I need to know everything I can about the guy. I like to say, 'you don't know what you don't know.' So I ask questions. I'm thorough. I like to look into the corners, see all the angles, even ones that might not yield anything useful. It's one of the ways I guard against confirmation bias. And I'm a bit of a control freak, which is why I'm here."

I gave Brown a predatory smile. "I want to make sure certain questions get asked. I want to hear the answers myself. Secondhand doesn't work for me."

Brown examined a fingernail. "Yeah, well since you've been a judge, you've had plenty of practice thinking you were the smartest sonofabitch on the planet."

Russ stifled a laugh, or pretended to.

Brown glared at me but wasn't able to hold it for long. "I don't know anything about Butler that Russ here doesn't know. Maybe you let him do his job and you stick to the courtroom." He turned to Russ. "Is that what you came here to tell me—this dumbass pimp says I raped one of his whores?"

"There's more to it than that," Russ said. He told Brown how he'd found Annie Black asleep in her Mustang in the parking lot of Butler's strip club, leaving out any mention of the photos. Then came the lie: "Butler showed up. Began ranting about you raping Annie."

"I've never raped anybody in my life, but why would he tell *you* something like that?"

"We've known each other for years, but he must've thought I was still with ATF because he asked me what I was gonna do about the rape. I told him I was a PI hired by Annie's bondsman to take her back to jail, that's all." Russ's eyes narrowed and his voice got harder. "That's when he threatened to come after you. That's what I came here to tell you. Give you a heads-up. Maybe you do me a favor sometime if I need it."

Brown's cheeks flushed and his jaw was clenched. He was scared and angry. Looked like he wanted to kick us out, but if we had more information he wanted that too. "Why are you really here?"

Russ looked hurt. "Jesus Christ, I didn't say we believe you raped anybody. Now that I'm a PI I've been cut off from access to the kind of information I used to get as a cop. You know how this works. You didn't think I'd come right out and say it, did you?"

Brown nodded. "Quid pro quo. I'm listening. You came all the way out here to tell me what Butler said, so get on with it."

Russ frowned. "He said he was coming after you for raping Annie. He didn't say how. By then, Annie was awake. She heard Butler tell me all of this and told him to shut the fuck up, told me Rick was high and didn't know what he was talking about."

"If Butler had just showed up," Brown said, "how the hell did he know anyone raped her?"

Russ shrugged. "Said he had it on video."

Brown laughed. "Every cop in this county knows Butler doesn't have surveillance in that parking lot. Crimes are committed back there every other night."

Russ had been nodding while Brown spoke. "I told Butler the same thing you just said—that there's no way he's stupid enough make a record of the drug deals he's got going down back there. He laughed, told me he'd set up surveillance and the police were too stupid to figure it out. He had trail cams hidden behind the cedar fence back there, cameras with a live feed you can watch from a phone. The cameras are hidden in trees and aimed through missing slats in the fence. He even had one hidden in a tree at just the right height to see into vehicles. One of the recordings showed you raping Annie. It's backed up to the cloud, but he wasn't sure what to do with it because Annie told him what he caught on video was consensual and with a customer from the bar, not Undersheriff Brown. Butler thinks she's scared of you because of who you are."

Brown's face was pale. He opened his mouth but nothing came out. He looked like a fish. His eyes looked hunted. I knew what was going on in his slow-moving brain. Were there really cameras? Had he really been caught?

Finally, Brown said, "Butler said he was coming after me?"

Russ nodded. "He said he knew how to handle things like this."

Russ pretended to force a smile, then turned to me. "Okay, then. You done here, Ben? If so, I got things to do."

We all got up and Brown walked us to the door. He thanked Russ for the heads-up and lied to me about how nice it was to meet me.

As we left Brown's estate in the Malibu, I said, "Did you see his face when he heard my last name?"

Russ lit a cigarette and nodded, pointing the Malibu toward Wichita. "Yeah, that might've connected some dots for him."

"And—are you freakin' kidding me—he's got an old photo of himself with Curtis right there in his damn foyer."

He glanced at me. "It's possible Paco Correa isn't just a figment of Butler's imagination. Brown flinched. That and the fact he seems to know Curtis personally means there might be something to what Butler said about how your mother died."

Murdered. I thought about that. There'd been an autopsy, and the cause of death had never been in question. Accidental overdose. I thought about how that could be. Maybe someone held her down while another person pumped her full of heroin. After we'd traveled a few miles I forced myself to think about something else.

I looked at Russ. "What you said about Butler having trail cams behind his strip club. Brown might check that out for himself."

Russ smiled. "I put some up back there to keep him on edge if he does. Even put one up in a tree close to where Annie's car was parked. He'll find it if he looks hard enough."

"You know Brown's going to hammer the shit out of Butler, don't you?"

"That's the plan."

"Could be a mistake. Brown seems like a leave-no-witnesses-behind kind of guy to me. There's a good chance he goes after Annie too."

"When I decided to dump this on Brown, I thought Butler was most likely just fucking with you yesterday. I didn't know Brown knew Curtis personally, and I certainly didn't figure either of them for murderers. That still feels like one hell of a stretch to me."

"Brown knew this meeting was about him raping Annie the second you called and told him you wanted to give him a heads-up about one of Butler's girls. And you're on the list of skip tracers who can bring bond jumpers to his jail, so he probably figured you'd brought her in a few hours after the rape. Once you set up the meeting, we had to stay the course and try to make him think Butler was his real problem."

Russ nodded. "I know, but knowing what I know now, I wish I'd never done any of this. I'll tell her what I did. Put her up somewhere safe, if she'll let me."

Water under the bridge. It was time to clock in for the person we were being paid to defend—Mia Delarosa. "How good a look did you get at the guys in those photos with Mia? See anyone shaped like a penguin?"

Russ laughed. "Brown is shaped like a penguin, isn't he? The men looked middle-aged. Not in great shape. So yeah, Brown could've been one of them."

We rode in silence for half a mile.

I pulled out my cell and called the jail. The lockdown was over. I told the jailer I'd be there in an hour to meet with Mia.

When we reached the outskirts of Wichita, I got a call from Ernie Watson, Mia's public defender. I'd left him my number yesterday. He advised that Mia told him I was going to be her new attorney and that she seemed real happy about it. But not as happy as he was. She'd been a difficult client. Additionally, the case had been assigned to an ADA named Claire Riddle, a prosecutor he apparently didn't get along with.

But most of his complaints were about Mia. He said she wasn't being straight with him about her case, but admitted there wasn't anything unusual about that with criminal defendants. He was concerned that an inmate named Ellen "Bigknife" Wilson had turned Mia into a "Bible thumper" and that, against his advice, she'd been discussing her case with Bigknife. According to Ernie, Mia had it in her head that if Bigknife was good enough to bring Jesus into her life, she was good enough to confide in about everything.

Ernie pledged to help in whatever way I needed. I took him up on his offer and asked if he could send me copies of whatever discovery materials he had so I could familiarize myself with the case as soon as possible. He agreed and told me he'd have it to my office before five today.

Suddenly he told me a judge was on the other line and that he had to run, then laughed obnoxiously.

"One more thing," Ernie said. "Mia told me that God sent you to her. So I'm like, 'I take it the good Lord doesn't think much of my legal skills,' and Mia replies with a straight face, 'No offense, but it is what it is, Big Ern.'"

Ernie's laughter roared through the phone again. He wished me luck, then abruptly ended the call.

7

I MADE MY way into the bowels of the professional visitation wing of the Sedgwick County Jail, past a metal detector and a guard suspicious of new faces and lawyers in jeans, through a labyrinth of sterile halls, up one floor on an elevator, and finally, beyond a pair of steel doors, each of which unlocked with a metallic clack as I approached, then locked with rude efficiency behind me. I found myself alone in a room with a chubby young guard sitting at a circular desk.

The young face of a Hispanic woman in an orange jumpsuit peered through the safety glass of a door adjacent to us.

A metallic clack sounded in the door. She pushed through it and stepped in. No cuffs, no leg chains, no escort.

"Mia?" I said.

Consistent with what her public defender had told me, she looked happy to see me. We introduced ourselves and shook hands. The guard pointed down a long hallway and told us to go to room seventeen.

We walked side by side to the sound of her orange flip-flops flopping against her heels. About halfway down the hall, we found our room. Only a few of the rooms were occupied, including the one next to ours.

Our conference room was seven by seven feet. A legless table was fixed to a wall and hovered between two plastic lawn chairs. The walls separating the rooms consisted of soundproof safety glass waist-high to the ceiling. It was the kind of glass with what looked like chicken wire trapped inside. I followed Mia into the room, put the representation agreement I'd drafted on the table, and looked through the line of glassed-in rooms on either side of us. Nothing about visual privacy with your attorney in the Constitution, so these are the rooms we get. At least the design gave the illusion of space, a comfort mostly undone by the woman in an orange jumpsuit next to us pacing her small cage like a tiger.

We sat. Mia folded her hands on the table and looked up at me with dark brown eyes. I knew she was twenty, but she looked sixteen to me.

"I've been hired to represent you, but you have the option to decline my services and stay with the public defender if you want."

She smiled. "Why would I do that?"

"I wouldn't know."

"Do you know what they call the public defender's office in here?"

"The public pretender?"

She nodded. "You heard that one before, huh?"

"Don't take advice from inmates. And don't talk about your case—"

"If we were that smart, we wouldn't be in here, right?"

"Let me finish. Assume anyone in here pumping you for information about your case is looking to trade that information to the DA for a break on their own case. You're accused of killing a former cop. Everyone knows the DA wants to nail you to the wall."

"Watson said the same thing."

"And he was right."

I needed to ask her what she'd told Ellen "Bigknife" Wilson about her case, but first things first. I wanted her to sign the representation agreement.

"I take it that you're fine with me as your new attorney?"

"Yes, of course. I was told you've never lost a case."

She smiled, giving me grateful and optimistic. The optimism bothered me because she had too much of it. It seemed like a good time for the subtle art of managing expectations.

"Someone told you I've never lost a case?"

"That's not true?"

"It's true. But it's also misleading."

"How so?"

"I was a prosecutor. First for the state, then the feds. And I didn't do it all that long before I became a judge."

"Still, you've never lost a case."

"I know how to pick a winner. That's what prosecuting criminal cases is all about. I'd look for cases with a stacked deck. Facts I could prove in court. Guilty sonsofbitches I could damn well prove were guilty sonsofbitches."

"Cases you couldn't lose."

"If you don't know what you're doing, you can lose any case. Like I said, I looked for a stacked deck. After that, it was just a matter of sharpening my knives."

"Sharpening your knives?"

"Prepping the case tirelessly. No surprises. I worked to make a guilty verdict as inevitable as the sun coming up in the morning."

Her smile lit up the room, like the sun had just come up.

"Mia?"

"What?"

"Did I miss something?" I looked behind me, thinking maybe someone was making funny faces through the glass. Nope—the inmate next door wasn't pacing anymore. She was lost in conversation with a suit.

I turned back to Mia. "Why are you smiling?"

"You're intense. I can see why God sent you to me."

It was all I could do to keep from rolling my eyes.

"You know who sent me and it damn sure wasn't God."

She laughed. "It damn sure was." She pursed her lips, then gave me a cute smile. "You know what I mean."

"You need to open your eyes and see where you are."

She leaned toward me and put both her hands on top of mine.

I looked down at our stack of hands on the table next to the representation agreement.

"The Lord will see me through this. When this is over, I will walk out of here. I have faith."

"'Faith,' she says." I mumbled this so she could hear, then slid my hands out from under hers and leaned back in my chair.

She said, "I take it you're not a Christian."

"I'm a believer."

"But only on the good days?"

"This is a good day. When I walk out of here in about twenty minutes, I'm going to a butcher shop and buying the five best steaks in the building and taking them home to my family. I'll probably drink some beer while pretending I'm the king of the universe. I'll hug my lovely children and kiss my beautiful wife. Odds are, I get laid. Now that's a good day."

I immediately regretted my words.

She looked at me like I'd punted her rabbit. "You don't believe the Lord will save me?"

"Faith won't save you from what a government wants to do to you. You know how St. Peter died, right?"

She shook her head. "No."

"Crucified upside down after multiple trials in Rome. Most of the apostles were tortured and martyred. Killed."

"What kind of Christian are you?"

"A realistic one. The Good Book counsels us to be wise as serpents. People forget that part."

"You don't believe God will protect me?"

"Like he did the apostles?"

She leaned forward. "I know you think it's cliché, but I found God in here."

"You found Ellen Bigknife Wilson, not God."

"God put us in here together so I could know Him and be saved."

"That's an odd story, don't you think?"

"You don't want to hear my story."

"The story of how Jimmy Ray's son found his father with an axe in his neck so you could find Jesus?"

She leaned back and crossed her arms. "You can leave. I'll stick with the public pretender."

Me and my big mouth. All I did was tell her the truth but often it's the one thing people don't want to hear. This wouldn't make Geronimo happy. Not to mention my wife and my creditors. I had to fix this.

She averted her eyes. Finally, I stood with the unsigned representation agreement in my hand.

Nothing.

When I opened the door she said, "Mr. Joel."

I looked back.

"Why should I trust you?" she said.

I sat down. "Interview me and make a judgment. Go with your gut. I'll make a promise to you. I won't lie. Not even to make you feel good."

Mia combed her hair behind her ears with her fingers. "Do you even know how to defend people?"

"I know what I'm doing," I said. "But don't get the idea that I'm some sort of magician. I read the online news stories about your preliminary hearing. An axe in Jimmy Ray's neck, his blood on you, and your confession to having killed him. I don't want to talk about all that until I get a chance to look over the evidence for myself, but I want you to know that getting a not guilty verdict from a jury isn't going to be easy. I can't promise you anything but my best efforts. Many times, the only thing an attorney can do is damage control."

"Plea bargain?"

"Sometimes that's your best bet."

"The pretender told me that too."

"Please call him Mr. Watson. Show some respect."

She nodded. Slumped a little.

I said, "I talked to Mr. Watson before I came in today. What have you told Ellen Bigknife Wilson?"

She answered after a long pause, moving her hand in a dismissive gesture. "It's okay."

"What's okay? I don't know what that means."

"It means she won't run to the prosecutor. What's that paper on the table?"

"Okay, fine, we can talk about Bigknife later."

I handed her the agreement. She flipped through the pages while I explained it to her. She interrupted me by asking for a pen. I gave her one.

She signed the back page, pushed the agreement across the table with a bit of a snarl, and watched me check the signature.

"I'm curious about something," I said. "Who told you I've never lost a case?"

"My sister."

"Carmen?"

She drew her head back a little.

"Read online you lived with her at the time of the murder. I need to talk to her."

"Good luck with that."

"What do you mean?"

"It's not your decision."

I shrugged. "Whose is it?"

"Geronimo's."

"How do you know him?"

She stared at me for a moment. "How do *you* know him?"

"He hired me to defend you."

"He didn't say how he knows me, did he?"

"No."

"Then he doesn't want you to know. Which means I'm not gonna tell you either."

"Look," I said, "it's my job to defend you. I don't take orders from anybody."

She laughed. "Mr. Watson's got nothin' on you. I should call you the pretender."

She smirked at what she must've thought was the empty bravado of her attorney. Since it was a bad idea to explain my past with Geronimo and why I didn't fear him to the extent others in his orbit did, there wasn't much I could say to gain her trust. I'd have to earn it.

"I'm not trying to be rude," she said. "I'm just telling you: Geronimo's not gonna allow you to talk to Carmen. And in case you were wondering, I have no idea how you can find her either."

"How old is she?"

"Twenty-eight."

"What's she to Geronimo?"

"Why don't you ask him yourself?"

"Because I'm asking you. Anything you tell me stays between us. Strictly confidential."

She shook her head. Pressed her lips together.

I shrugged. "What're you protecting your sister from?"

"Nothing. It's just that Geronimo makes his own rules. You don't get to change them."

Quibbling with Mia wasn't getting us anywhere so I changed the topic before she clammed up completely.

"Why does Annie Black have pornographic pictures of you with a group of naked men in masks?"

"What?"

I raised my eyebrows.

She slumped a little and said, "I have no idea how she got those. How do you know her?"

"Never mind that. Who are the men in the photos?"

She shrugged. "Dunno. Like you said. They had masks on. What's this have to do with the murder case?"

"Not sure. Maybe nothing, but it's important that I find out all I can about it, so help me out. What do you know about these men?"

"They're sick and full of darkness."

"That's a given. How many were there?"

"Three. Four if you count the guy running the video and taking pictures. But he didn't join in. They tried to get him to, but he wouldn't. He was younger. They called him, Youngblood."

"You think that was a nickname or his last name?"

"I think the older men called him Youngblood because he was so much younger than them. I wasn't supposed to know who any of these people were. Youngblood wore shorts. Had really amazing legs. Like a dancer's."

"How old was he, if you had to guess?"

She shrugged. "Late twenties, early thirties."

"I take it he was wearing a mask too."

"Yeah. A mask of President Trump."

"You have no idea who these guys were?"

"No."

I sensed a lie. "Describe the masks."

"Recent presidents. Bush, Slick Willie, and one I'm not sure his name. You've seen the photos."

"No, I haven't. I apologize if I gave you that impression. Annie says she burned them. They're gone."

"Oh."

"Where'd she get them?"

Mia shrugged. "Stole them from one of the men, probably."

"Or maybe the photographer?"

"Maybe."

"Could she have gotten them from Rick Butler?"

Her eyes widened. "Rick wasn't one of the men in the masks if that's what you're asking. Unfortunately, I know what he looks like nude and it's not good."

"Okay, but he set up the date with the men, right?"

She shrugged, then nodded. "Yeah."

"So maybe he arranged for the photographer too."

She shook her head. "They brought their own photographer. These were VIPs. They had their pick of Butler's girls and called all the shots. Pickup, location. All of it."

"What makes you say these guys were VIPs?"

"That's what Ricky called them. Told me they asked for me."

"Was one of the men in the masks Clint Brown?"

Mia's eyes narrowed and darted around the room. "A few minutes ago you told me I needed to be wise as a serpent. Maybe you oughta take your own advice."

Clint Brown, the undersheriff, might have something to do with running this jail, but I doubted he was stupid enough to bug the interview rooms. The risk of getting caught was too high, the reward too low. Nevertheless, she had a good point. Better safe than sorry. I nodded and asked Mia to help me check the entire room for listening devices, surveillance of any kind.

"The room's clean," I said, finally satisfied.

"Can you get me out of here," she whispered. "I'm scared they're going to kill me."

"Who?"

She bugged her eyes.

"What's your bond set at?"

"Two million dollars. Big Ern tried to get it lowered, but the judge wouldn't do it."

I nodded. "I take it Brown was one of the men in masks."

"No."

We sat down. I leaned forward, put my hands on hers and talked in a whisper. "Explain to me how you know he wasn't one of the men."

She gave the room a nervous look. Whispered, "I don't know the guy. I mean, other than knowing he's an undersheriff or something. What would be the odds that he was one of them?"

"This is the only place we can talk. If you can't talk to me about the case in here, I can't defend you. I don't mean that to sound like a threat. It's just the truth."

Tears welled up in her eyes. "I don't know who any of the guys were."

I patted her hands and told her that was enough for the first day. I picked up the agreement and looked it over, thinking maybe she'd written me a note about who wore the masks while I was checking for listening devices beneath the table. She hadn't. We stood, and I pocketed the agreement as we walked down the corridor toward the guard manning the doors.

When we entered the room a metallic clack sounded in the door leading to lockup. The guard watched us without speaking. Our good-byes would have to be short. She motioned for me to lean down so she could tell me something. When I did, she whispered into my ear.

"The undersheriff was the one in the President Collins mask."

8

I WALKED BACK to my office in the punishing heat of the late afternoon sun to find Keri leaned way back in the executive's chair she'd picked out for me. She wore a grey skirt and her legs were crossed and her bare feet were propped on the desk next to an open envelope. She had on a wireless headset that made me think of a helicopter pilot. My laptop was open on her thighs and she was pattering on the keyboard.

"How'd it go with Mia?" Her eyes stayed glued to the screen as she traced her finger along the touchpad.

"She's onboard." I plopped down in the chair in front of the desk and told her it was time to formally notify the court that I was Mia's attorney.

Keri lifted an index finger vaguely in my direction as she pressed a button on the laptop. "Done. You're officially a defense attorney. Welcome to the dark side."

I laughed.

She sized me up. "Well?"

"Well what?"

"Did the undersheriff recognize you?"

"Oh, that. He said I looked familiar. When I told him my last name fear flickered across his face like a hologram. Makes me think there's something to what Rick Butler said."

She made a quick frown. "You okay?"

"I'm fine."

She nodded skeptically until her face brightened like she'd forgotten to tell me something. "Hey, if you know—any idea what's up the receptionist's butt?"

"Rashonda?—I'm pretty sure it's a corn cob, why?"

"Because it's about to be my foot, that's why?"

"What'd she do?"

"Well, for starters, she's rude. And she gets in my face about the inconvenience of having to do her job."

"We're renting office space from Manny, that's it. Rashonda's not our employ—"

"I know that, but we have to talk sometimes and there's no excuse for her being a royal B every time we do."

"I'll talk to Manny about it." I pointed at the envelope on the desk. "That come from the public defender's office?"

"Yeah, that's the latest thing that set her off."

"Shit."

"Someone dropped it off an hour ago and poor Rashonda had to walk all the way back here to give it to me."

While she gave me an unabridged account of her conflict with Rashonda, I noticed Keri's toenails were now cobalt blue and it looked like she'd gotten that pedicure she'd been looking forward to. It occurred to me that her skirt was new. So was the blouse she was wearing. She'd spent a good portion of her day enjoying the perks of civilization. I nodded, to let her know I was listening and agreed with everything she said, then reached across the table and picked up the envelope. It was empty.

She pointed at the thumb drive in the laptop's USB port. "It's right here."

In the last two days Keri had become the de facto manager of my office, an administrative assistant, and my paralegal. Even when she wasn't in the office, calls were forwarded to her cell phone. While answering phones and setting up a law practice were new to Keri, the paralegal duties weren't. She'd been working as a trained paralegal when we met. Any information I'd learned from Mia could be shared with Keri or Russ in pursuit of a zealous defense and still be squarely within the protection of attorney-client privilege. I'd laid this out for Mia in the representation agreement that she'd signed, but hadn't read.

Keri lifted her feet off the desk, sat up, and passed me the laptop.

I sat forward and put it on the desk and oriented myself to the long list of computer files on the screen. "Have you looked through any of this yet?"

"Some of it, not all."

Keri came to the front of the desk and sat in the chair next to me.

"What's the story in a nutshell?" I said.

"Jimmy Ray was found dead in his home on St. Patrick's Day by his adult son, Brian, age twenty-four." Keri clicked through the files with the touch pad. "The son got in the house through the back door like he usually did, went through the mudroom and found his father dead at the kitchen table looking like this."

A digital photo appeared on the screen.

Jimmy Ray was faced away, sitting in a chair with an axe buried in his neck on the right side at a forty-five degree angle, the handle pointing back at the doorway where Brian would have been standing. Jimmy Ray's head was canted grotesquely to the left, hanging by a strap of neck muscle and skin. He was slumped against the backrest as far left as the arm of the chair would allow, his legs spread wide, feet resting flat on the floor, the left one in a pool of blood. His left arm dangled outside the arm of the chair in a way that made it look like he was angling for something on the floor.

The chair was pushed back from the table like he'd just sat down. Or maybe he'd been preparing to stand when the axe fell. A fountain of blood had sprayed in all directions, the victim, chair, floor, walls.

Keri said, "Brian told police that he noticed red smudges on the floor of the mudroom on his way in, but it didn't occur to him they were shoeprints until after he saw his father. He called 911 while following the tracks that led through the screen door and across the concrete patio where the trail disappeared into the grass. Despite being admonished by the

911 operator to immediately go to the street in front of the house for his own safety, Brian went where the bloody path pointed, straight across some freshly mowed fescue to a chain-link fence between his father's backyard and that of his neighbor's. He told the 911 operator he could see a woman, Mia Delarosa, going into her house covered in blood. That's when the operator lost contact with him.

"When the cops arrived a few minutes later, they found Brian and Mia in Mia's bathroom. Brian had her pinned to the bathroom floor in her bra and shorts. Her shirt was in the sink and the shower was running onto the curtain and rod which had been knocked into the tub."

"You watch the video of the confession yet?"

Keri shook her head and clicked to a file that read: DELAROSA INTERVIEW. "This should be interesting."

"No doubt. Let's see how big a hole she dug for herself."

9

KERI HIT THE play icon on the screen.

Mia appeared alone at a table in an interview room. Her shirt was clean and way too big for her. The time stamp on the video read: MARCH 17, 10:37 p.m.

Detective Riggins came through a door and sat across from her. He was sweaty and his tie was loose. He read the *Miranda* warnings from a card the way a teenager recites the Pledge of Allegiance—in a monotonous drone. This was by design, an old detective's trick. The idea was to blend the momentous occasion of waiving one's constitutional rights into the humdrum of the day. Not a big deal. Mia waived her rights at the end of the routine without a word—just a nod of her head and her signature on a card that Riggins' promptly put in his wallet. She would answer questions without an attorney. Mia Delarosa versus a detective built like tree stump with a flat top.

Riggins started with basic biographical questions, the most important of which was about her current living situation. Mia said she'd moved into her sister's house on North Waco Avenue three years earlier.

"Do you know the man who held you down in your bathroom?"

Mia nodded. "My neighbor's son, Brian."

"So, you know him by name."

"Oh yeah."

"How long you known him?"

"My whole life basically. We were neighbors growing up."

"I'm confused. Thought you said you moved into your sister's house on Waco three years ago."

"Our families were neighbors growing up in Delano, not where we are now."

Delano was a neighborhood in Wichita west of the downtown area.

"When you moved in with your sister, was Jimmy Ray, Brian's father, already living there behind her?"

"No. He moved in last spring."

"Just a coincidence?" asked Riggins. His expression didn't change. His voice conversational. No big deal. Nothing to see here.

"What do you think?"

"I don't know what to think. That's why I'm asking you."

"No way it was a coincidence."

"So he must've been following you."

Mia nodded.

Riggins put his elbows on the table. Interlocked his fingers as if in prayer. "Who put the axe in his neck?"

"Me."

Riggins grunted. "Why?"

Tears filled Mia's eyes. "He raped me. When I was a child. More times than I can count."

Riggins pushed a box of tissues toward her. "Can't say how sorry I am to hear that." He waited for her to dry her eyes. "How old were you when it started?"

"Seven."

Mia explained that her father was out of town a lot, and her mother worked second shift, so Jimmy's wife sometimes watched her and her sister Carmen at the Ray house. Many times it was just Mia because Carmen was older and played a lot of team sports. Couple times a month Jimmy's wife would go to the store and Jimmy would be alone with Mia. He'd hustle her up to his bedroom and have his way, then show her his gun and tell her to keep her mouth shut. Told her if she told anyone, he'd kill her and whoever she told.

"What about your sister, Carmen?" Riggins said. "Jimmy ever do anything to her?"

"I asked. She says he didn't."

"You believe her?"

Mia shrugged. "Sort of. But I'm not sure."

"Did you tell anybody what Jimmy did to you?"

Riggins waited. Mia gazed at nothing in particular, like she was perplexed by the question.

Finally, Riggins said, "Can I get you a drink of water?"

She shook her head. "I told my sister. That's it."

Riggins made a note on his pad. "Who helped you kill Jimmy Ray?"

"Nobody. Just me."

"Really."

It wasn't a question but Mia nodded like it was.

"You just came through the screen door with the axe and whacked Jimmy Ray before he could turn around in his chair. Something like that?"

"Pretty much."

Riggins pursed his lips. "Then you ran out the back through the screen door, across the yard, over the fence, and into your house. Is that how it went?"

Mia shrugged. "Pretty much."

"Not much time passed after you killed Jimmy before Brian was there, right?"

"Yeah. I was surprised."

"Before Brian got there, you weren't jumping back and forth over the fence, were you?"

She squinted at him. Sat back in her chair.

"You understand the question?" Riggins asked.

"What happened is all kind of a blur to tell you the truth."

"Who are you protecting?"

She hesitated. "What makes you think I'm protecting someone?"

Riggins threw out his arms. "For starters there are two sets of footprints around Jimmy Ray, and two clusters of blood smears on the fence. They're twelve feet apart."

Mia looked away from him, wouldn't make eye contact.

Riggins said, "We found a brick by the fence beneath the place where either you or your accomplice climbed over. The brick—it was smeared with blood. What was the brick for?"

Riggins waited for an answer. Didn't get one. "What are you, a hundred and thirty pounds?"

"One twenty-eight."

Riggins whistled. "That's one helluva blow with an axe for a gal your size."

"It was sharp, what can I say?"

"Sharp?" Riggins smiled. "I don't care how sharp it was. A blow like that would've taken more strength than I think you got."

"I'm stronger than I look."

"Maybe. But those bloodstains on the back of your shirt tell me a different story than the one you're telling."

"You have a lot of people confessing to crimes they didn't commit or something?"

"It happens. I've seen plenty of folks take the blame to protect their friends and family. Where was your sister this evening?"

Mia shrugged. "Dunno."

"Not with you?"

"Nope."

"Where can I find her?"

"No idea. She moved out last week. Don't know where she went, or when she'll be back."

"You have a boyfriend?"

She hesitated, then shook her head.

"Someone else was in the kitchen with you when Jimmy Ray was murdered. How about you tell me who it was. Tell me what really happened."

"Already did."

"I don't think so. Where'd you get the axe?"

"I remember holding it. Swinging it. Who cares where I got it?"

Riggins drummed his fingers on the table while he watched Mia. "Someone or something was real close to Jimmy Ray when that blade sank into his neck. That person or thing was on his right, down low, around his thighs. If it was a person, they were either incredibly short, or kneeling. Probably on their knees. Bent over. So close they could touch him down there—the crotch area. His jeans were unsnapped and his zipper was down." Riggins leaned closer. "Then, to put it as mildly as I can, there was this bloody interruption to something that was going on that brought you and me here together like this."

Mia folded her arms across her chest.

"Know how I know you didn't swing that axe?" Riggins said.

Mia didn't move. Her face was blank.

"Jimmy Ray's blood is on the back of your shirt—the one we found in your bathroom sink—it shows us you were bent over on your knees right beside Jimmy Ray when the axe fell. Inches away."

Mia stared straight ahead.

"That means you couldn't have swung the axe. Guess what else it means?"

She took another tissue from the box, slumped back again and cried into the tissue.

When she regained her composure, Riggins said in a soothing tone, "I need you to tell me the truth. Maybe you didn't know what was coming. Didn't see it and suddenly there it was. If that's the case, you're not responsible. You just happened to be there when Jimmy was murdered. Maybe you go home tonight if things check out."

She shook her head. Sniffled. "I did this alone."

There was a knock at the door of the interview room.

Detective Riggins stood and left. Came back five minutes later. "Talked to my partner, who's been talking to Brian. Brian thinks you killed his father for having an affair with your mother when you both lived in Delano. When you were kids. Says the affair broke up your family. His too. Anything to that?"

"This is getting twisted."

"What's getting twisted?"

"Maybe I need a lawyer."

"Tell me about your parents."

"They split up when I was thirteen. My mother's with a guy in Arizona now and my dad's back in Mexico."

"Did your mother have an affair with Jimmy Ray like Brian says?"

"Yes."

"Did she know he was molesting you?"

She hugged herself. Even on video, I could see that Mia was blanching.

"You told her, didn't you?" Riggins said.

"Yeah, I told her. She didn't believe me. Thought I was making it up to get her to stop seeing him."

"When did you find out they were having an affair?"

"When I caught them fucking."

Riggins shoulders slumped a little. "How old were you when that happened?"

"Nine."

"When did your father find out about the affair?"

"Four years later when he caught them at it."

Riggins frowned. "Brian says you told him you were going to kill his dad someday. You ever say that to him?"

"As a kid, I said that to him several times. Then we moved away. I didn't kill Jimmy because of the affair."

"Why does Brian think you did?"

"Because that's what I told him when he asked why I wanted to kill his father."

"You never told him his father molested you?"

"No. My own mother didn't believe me, why would Brian?"

Riggins sighed. Went silent. Finally, he said, "I'll ask you one more time, who helped you kill Jimmy Ray?"

"I'm through talking. I want a lawyer."

"I got a feeling this goes better for you if you tell me who swung the axe."

She stared back at him, but didn't seem to see a thing.

Riggins took in the look. Waited. Finally shook his head. "Have it your way." He stood and left the room.

*   *   *

Keri toggled through the files on the laptop. "The lab confirms that Jimmy's DNA is on the shirt found in Mia's bathroom sink and the blood spatter expert confirms Riggins' theory that whoever was wearing that shirt was bent over Jimmy's lap when he was killed."

Keri brought up the blood spatter expert's report and I began reading. There were two "void patterns", or bloodless spots, surrounding Jimmy Ray that weren't caused by furniture. The first one was to be expected. It was right where the person swinging the axe would have been standing when blood sprayed from the wound in Jimmy's neck. The second bloodless spot was consistent with a person on their knees bent over Jimmy's lap during the murder. In the expert's opinion, the back of the shirt found in Mia's bathroom sink has a bloodstain pattern on it—that if placed into the bloodless spot on and around the victim's lap area—more or less completes the pattern of blood spatter surrounding Jimmy Ray. Kind of like a missing puzzle piece, but three-dimensional and dynamic. Mia and Jimmy would've probably been moving some and the spray uneven and pulsing and landing on surfaces with much different properties. It was far from an exact science, but that didn't stop the expert from concluding that the shirt was the object that was present in the area directly over the victim's lap at the precise moment of the murder, and its removal from the scene explained this bloodless spot in the pattern.

Keri said, "Correct me if I'm wrong, but you got something to work with here. If she didn't swing the axe, they have to prove she was in on a plan to kill Jimmy. That she did something to help the killer do this. We might actually win this case."

The phone rang. Keri took the call, speaking into the microphone on her headset.

I clicked on the file containing the state's complaint and saw that the state was prosecuting Mia for aiding and abetting an unknown accomplice in the premeditated murder of Jimmy Ray, which, if proved by the state made her as guilty of murder as if she'd swung the axe herself. The penalty was the same too—life in prison. I toggled through the files and reviewed the DNA report. The lab had tested samples from stains on the bottom of Jimmy Ray's screen door, the chain-link fence separating the two properties, and a brick found in the grass beside the fence. They'd compared the DNA in the samples to samples taken from Jimmy Ray and Mia. I perused the file containing the photos of the stains at the scene of the crime and put it all together. Jimmy Ray's blood was smeared on the bottom of the screen door and the brick. Mia's blood was on the top rail of the chain-link fence where she'd cut her hands on its barbed selvages. She'd dropped the brick so she could use both hands to get over the fence during her getaway. The state's theory of the case became obvious to me. I clicked on the file containing the preliminary hearing transcript and skipped to Claire Riddle's closing argument to see if I was correct.

Claire Riddle: . . . the evidence conclusively proves that the defendant fled out an already open screen door behind the person who wielded the axe. I submit that the defendant did so without any fear for her own safety because—if the murder came as a shock to the defendant—wouldn't she run screaming out the front door in the opposite direction for her life? Instead, the defendant follows the killer into the backyard and over a fence, but not before taking the time to remove the brick holding the screen door open, and in the process, leaving blood from the victim smeared at the base of the door. Incredibly, and this is important Your Honor, this is the only blood investigators could find on that door. As bloody as the defendant and her accomplice must have been, I submit the only rational explanation is that the screen door had been propped open with the brick.

Which brings me to the million-dollar question. Why was the screen door to the mudroom propped open? What's the best explanation for this? Recall the testimony of the victim's son, Brian Ray. He'd never known his father to leave open that screen door, let alone prop it open. That particular screen door, like many screen doors, was loud and creaky. I submit that it had been propped open by the defendant so the person with the axe could enter through the mudroom undetected while the defendant diverted Jimmy Ray's attention. This is solid evidence of a plan. Of premeditation.

Unfortunately for the defendant, this brick with the victim's blood smeared on it was found at the foot of the chain-link fence separating the backyards. I submit to you that the forensic evidence and the injuries to the palms of Ms. Delarosa's hands paint a vivid image of what happened during her failed getaway. Ms. Delarosa dropped the brick to

free up her hands so she could lift herself over the chain-link,
cutting her hands on those sharp barbs in the process.

It was the argument I was expecting. Factually, the state's case made sense but a jury sympathetic to a child rape victim might be inclined to bend over backwards to find her not guilty. I kept reading the transcript and found a preview of how the prosecutor planned to handle the sympathy a jury was likely to feel for Mia.   The state wasn't conceding Mia's stated motive for the murder. Instead, Ms. Riddle argued Brian's theory—that Jimmy Ray was murdered by Mia and her accomplice because Jimmy had broken up Mia's family. She argued that Mia's allegations of child molestation against Jimmy Ray were part of her plan to ruin his reputation and gain sympathy for what she'd done.

I was still reading Brian's testimony when Keri got off the phone. "Have you had a chance to read the prelim transcript?" I said.

"No. Why?"

"The prosecutor doesn't argue that Mia might've been the one wielding the axe, despite her confession to the contrary. Instead, she argues that Mia aided the killer. Created a diversion to get her accomplice in the house undetected."

"Seems to me Detective Riggins suggested our best defense in that interview we just watched—maybe Mia didn't know what was coming. You could argue she had no idea what was about to happen and do it with a straight face, right?"

"Sure, but let's analyze our argument to see how strong it is. Put yourself in Mia's position. For whatever reason you're about to give Jimbo a hummer?"

"Gross, but okay."

"Someone basically takes his head off with an axe and you had nothing to do with it. You're in total shock, and you have his blood all over you. Now what?"

Keri thought about it. "Are you suggesting that if she were innocent, she wouldn't have followed the killer out the back door? That she would have feared for her own life and went out the front door or called 911. Is that what you're getting at?"

"What—you don't you think that's a good argument for the state?"

"Not really. Who's to say Mia didn't stay in the room in a state of shock for ten seconds, or twenty, or a full minute, before going out the back door. By then, the killer was long gone, so she would have no reason to go in the opposite direction."

"Good," I said. "Now assume the jury doesn't buy this argument and thinks an innocent person would've run the opposite direction on instinct."

"We could argue that while the murder was a surprise to Mia, she didn't actually fear for her life because she must've known the person who did this. Why else would she be willing to lie and take all the blame? We could even suggest that she knows why this person murdered Jimmy Ray—retribution for molesting her as a child. Whoever swung the axe must be close to Mia. She may be guilty of lying to the police, but that's it. Something like that would be what I'd argue."

"Realistically speaking, for that to work, the jury's probably going to want to hear from Mia. Which means she'd have to take the stand and testify. Problem is—"

"The prosecutor will ask Mia to name the actual killer."

"Bingo."

"And when she won't give it to them, it'll look bad."

I shrugged. "Jury might conclude she's loyal as hell. Maybe they'll like that under the circumstances, but I doubt it."

"She needs to tell us the whole story, so we know where we stand."

"That'd be nice, but I wouldn't hold my breath. She refused to answer some of my questions today. She's going to be a difficult client."

"However this plays out, maybe sympathy for Mia keeps us in the game here. Maybe the only thing we need to do is give the jury something to hang their hat on."

"If what the prosecutor argued at the prelim is any indication, the state's not conceding that Jimmy Ray was a child rapist. If the jury buys Brian's theory that Jimmy was murdered for breaking up Mia's family, then comes to the conclusion that Mia is making up the rape allegations, they'll hate her. And she'll spend the rest of her life in prison."

"I don't believe Mia would do this over Jimmy's affair with her mother, even if she believes that's why her family broke-up. Can't see how a jury would believe that either."

I shrugged. "Maybe Mia's father killed Jimmy and she's covering for him."

Keri's eyebrows went up. "Chickenshit thing for a dad to do—leaving his daughter at the scene like that. Then leaving her to rot in jail." She laughed. "Other than that it makes sense, especially if he thought Jimmy Ray had an affair with his wife and molested his little girl."

"Point is, the state is muddying the water the jury has to drink. The jury will know Mia's the one person with the answers. If she doesn't take the stand and tell them what happened and why, they'll resent her for that, even though they'll be told by the judge not to. The state's strategy is to keep the negative feelings a jury will have for Jimmy Ray to manageable levels, while dampening the sympathy factor that favors Mia. Makes it easier for the state to keep the jurors' eyes on the ball and convict."

"Do you think Mia is lying about her motive?"

"No," I said. "But we need to keep our eyes open."

"Mia also needs to tell you who swung the axe. Any person willing to kill for her would probably take her off the hook and say she wasn't in on the murder."

"And if that person says the two of them planned the murder and that it went down in a way that is consistent with the physical evidence in this case, Mia will be worse off than she is now."

"It might be worth the risk."

"Maybe. I'll talk to Mia about it. If nothing else, we might be able to get a favorable plea offer from the state if we give them the name of the actual killer. But—"

"If Mia wanted to go that route she would've already done so."

"Exactly. I'll talk to her, but there's a good chance she won't tell me, and we'll have to figure it out ourselves."

"If we know who the killer is, we'll be better able to predict what that person will say about Mia's involvement when and if they're ever arrested."

I cocked my head, working through the probabilities. "The thing is, if the killer wanted to help her out, why hasn't he or she already done so?"

Keri nodded. "I still like it. Maybe Mia's would-be savior just needs a shove in the right direction. Maybe the person just can't stomach the idea of spending the rest of their life in prison. But if the killer knew they were going down anyway, why not take Mia off the hook?"

"I like it too. So let's try to figure it out, with or without Mia's help."

Keri clicked through the files on the laptop and found a photo of the axe handle suspended in midair, the business end of the thing still lodged in Jimmy Ray.

She ran a finger along the length of the image of the axe's shaft. "See all these shiny red, wet-looking droplets."

"Blood spatter."

"Right, but see how there's no wet stuff here near the grip end?"

I nodded. "Where the killer's hands would've been during the eruption of blood."

She pointed at a dark red stain where the killer's hands likely gripped the handle. "Yeah, but look at that? What's that?"

"I dunno, dried-up blood maybe. Looks like that one's been there a while."

Keri bugged her eyes. "I agree. The lab didn't test that stain because the cops didn't ask them to. They didn't take a sample of it or anything. I checked the evidence custody receipt."

"I'm not surprised."

"The source of that stain may be our killer."

"It might also be a chicken. Testing it isn't gonna tell us who killed Jimmy Ray."

"Jesus—they should at least test it, and if it contains human DNA, they should run it through their DNA databases for a hit."

"I'm not disagreeing with you, but right now I'm glad they didn't until we know if it helps us or hurts us."

I stood. Stretched my legs. Thought about how our involvement in this case started.

Keri walked around the desk and pulled her purse from a drawer. She was talking as she did, but I was lost in thought.

Finally, Keri raised her voice. "Hey, Benny. What's the matter?"

"It's probably nothing."

"Spit it out."

"After Geronimo hired me at the lake, I told him he shouldn't get into his truck with an open can of beer. You know—open container laws and all that. He wouldn't leave the can, even though I'd just seen him finish off his beer. He took it with him—an empty can."

Keri made a sound in her throat. "You think he was being paranoid about handing over something that probably had his DNA on it."

She plunked her purse on the desk. I knew her pistol was what weighed it down.

"He's exactly what Detective Riggins is looking for," Keri said. "A strong guy who can create a lot of torque. Someone with the stomach for murder. And we know he's somehow involved because he hired you. Shit, if he's the killer, it pretty much means he's paying you to keep Mia quiet."

"Despite all the signs, I don't like Geronimo for this murder. I can't see him leaving Mia there alone, all covered in blood for the police to find. The risk she might give him up in a situation like that is too great and completely unnecessary. Geronimo's a professional killer. He would've never panicked like that. It's a loose end he wouldn't have allowed."

"Yeah, and Brian Ray—"

"Wouldn't be alive right now if Geronimo was the hatchet man."

Keri nodded and looked at the time on her phone. "Speaking of right now, we need to get to Sig's before it closes."

Sig's was the butcher shop where we sometimes bought our meat.

I walked around the desk and hugged her from behind, watching her look up the business hours for Sig's on her phone. It closed in an hour.

I took the phone from her hand and set it on the desk. "We've got time to check something off your bucket list."

We had quite a bit of free time in the mountains. Sometimes we shared fantasies. One of hers was sex on an office desk.

She turned around. Kissed me. "Rashonda's still out there. Just heard her talking to someone in the hallway."

"It's almost five. She'll probably be leaving any minute."

"She stays late sometimes. There might be other people here."

"We'll have to be quiet."

"You know I'm not good at that."

"Think of it like a game. Make too much noise, you lose."

"You need this don't you?"

I nodded. "It's been a rough couple of days."

"Then lock the door."

* * *

We didn't find Rashonda in the building when we were done. We found Geronimo. On the couch in the reception area with the statue of Prudence. He was reading a *Sports Illustrated*. He wore thick rimmed glasses and what looked like an auto mechanic's shirt with a patch on the breast that read: ALEX. His version of a disguise.

He grinned. "Nice and cool in here. Yet, you're both sweaty."

I looked at the front door, then back to Geronimo. "How'd you get in here?"

"Place was locked up so I knocked on the glass. Black lady let me in after I told her I was looking to hire you for my divorce lawyer. She tried to buzz you on the intercom but you didn't answer. Then she went down the hallway all pissed off and shit. Came back more pissed. Said you'd be with me whenever you were done doing whatever it was you were doing."

He was beaming at me.

"We were moving furniture," I said.

He laughed. "Oh I'm sure the furniture was moving."

"Glad we could brighten your day," I said.

"You did."

Keri faked a smile.

"It's family night," I said, "so we really do need to get out of here."

"Ooo, family night," he cooed. "Is this how it usually starts?"

"Maybe you should mind your own business," Keri said.

He stood with the magazine he'd rolled into a tube. "Relax. I'm just here to see how things are going with Mia."

"I met with her and everything is on schedule. Keri and I have already gone over some of the evidence. I'd like to talk to Mia's sister. Can you get me in touch with her?"

He looked surprised by my injection of this into the conversation. "What for?"

"Nothing I can discuss with you. I just need an address or a phone number. Maybe you could have her meet me here."

"I'll see what I can do. No promises."

I took that to mean he wouldn't be setting up my meeting with Carmen Delarosa any time soon. When Geronimo approached me at the lake, I'd wondered if Mia was his girlfriend. Now, I wondered if Mia's sister was the person he most wanted to keep out of prison.

He stepped past us, pushed open the front door part way, and looked back. "If there's anything else you need to help Mia, let me know."

"There is," I said. "Do you know Rick Butler?"

"Yeah, Mia's pimp."

"He's got a laptop computer. I'd like to know what's on it before it disappears."

"What makes you think it's going to disappear?"

"Because the undersheriff in this county is going to go after Rick Butler. I think his laptop might shed light on how these two are connected."

His eyes narrowed. "What's that got to do with Mia's case?"

"I'll know for sure once you get me the laptop. Maybe nothing, but I don't think so. You'll know it if you find it. It has an AC/DC sticker on it."

Geronimo popped his thigh with the magazine. "I'll take care of it."

He pushed through the door. Keri and I watched it shut.

She said, "Did he just steal Manny's *Sports Illustrated*?"

"Yes. Yes he did."

"Do you think his DNA would've been on it?"

"Maybe."

"Think that's why he took it?"

We looked at each other and then out the window at Geronimo crossing the street.

10

WHEN WE TURNED onto the dirt road that led to our home, we were driving toward a shelf cloud that had blotted out the evening sun save for one corner of the horizon that glowed like incandescent coals in a fire. Keri drove her Honda Civic. I followed in my pickup. We lived way out in the country west of Worthington in a low-lying area where the roads washed out during heavy rains and the dried ruts made for a bumpy ride.

Pops was sitting in a lawn chair beneath the large overhead door of our pole barn watching the kids hit balls in our outdoor batting cage. Cicadas buzzed in the trees and the air smelled of rain and woodsmoke from the grill and the grease of countless meals. Behind Pops, five potatoes in char-marked aluminum foil sat on a card table with a stack of paper plates and silverware. I went to the grill with steaks still wrapped in butcher paper.

"Hold off on that for a few minutes," Pops hollered out. "Hell, I've waited this long."

I set the steaks on the grill's shelf as Keri set up two lawn chairs next to Pops, then left to make a salad in the kitchen.

I plopped down next to Pops. He slipped his hand into the cooler by his side and handed me a Busch Light. I popped the top, gulped down half the beer, and breathed in the smell of the coming rain, gazing past the batting cage, through a gap in the shelterbelt, and across a tilled field disappearing into the gathering dark. The kids were now arguing about whether it was too dark to keep playing. Near as I could tell, Lindy wanted one more turn at bat, with softballs this time, and Leo was hungry.

"Welcome home," Pops said.

He got up and turned on the outdoor floodlights, buying the kids more time in the cage. He moved well for a seventy-five-year-old and carried a 1911 pistol in a holster on his jeans, the same model he carried as a marine in Vietnam. What hair he had left was shaved close, silver and white.

He sat again. Drank.

"I was starting to think I might not ever come back," I said.

"How does it feel?"

"Strange."

"Strange how?"

"Having to deal with people again I guess."

Pops set his empty on the concrete and fished out another beer from the cooler. "You're at that age when you see a certain pattern you didn't see before. A certain downward trajectory to society."

"I see the world for what it is."

"And what would that be?"

"A giant dumpster fire making laps around the sun."

"Where would you rather be?"

"Right where I am, I guess."

"Then stop your bitchin'. You weren't put here to be comfortable."

"You mean enjoying a beer with you isn't the purpose of life?"

"Enjoying a beer with me is more like a gift."

"Really?"

"Don't take it for granted."

"I don't."

"Tell me about this client of yours."

"Mia Delarosa. She's that woman in Wichita charged with murdering an ex-cop."

"Woman?"

"Yeah, a woman. That surprise you?"

"Not really." He took a drink. "Well, I take that back. It kind of does."

"Women commit about ten percent of the murders in this country."

"Women aren't usually prone to kill unless a man's bent 'em into something that was never meant to be."

"I might be wrong, but that's probably considered a sexist comment these days, Pops."

"I don't give a shit about that. How old is your client?"

"Twenty."

"If she did it, why?"

"Either because he raped her as a child or because he broke up her family by having an affair with her mother." I shrugged. "Maybe both."

Pops grunted. "I rest my case."

We watched Lindy lay down some bunts.

"So, how'd she do it?" he asked. "Shoot him or something?"

"No. Somebody sank an axe into the guy's neck, you haven't heard anything about this?"

"I don't watch or read news anymore."

"I guess not."

He shook his head. "This is supposed to be some kind of revenge killing, right?"

"Both motives appear to involve revenge, that's right. Why?"

"Ah, never mind." He took a drink. "I don't know this woman."

"Something not making sense to you?"

"Her supposed motives. Don't buy either one, but like I said, I don't know this woman. Do you buy it?"

"Yeah, according to my client's statement to the detective she killed Jimmy Ray because he raped her as a child. To me, that's a plausible motive. I get it."

He gave me a doubtful look. "Revenge?"

"Yeah. It's a classic motive. Why does that seem so farfetched to you in this case?"

"I've seen what fear does to men in battle. Good men. I know what it did to me. I turned it into anger, and when things came completely unhinged, vengeance. But in my experience, women don't lash out that way." He shook his head. "Revenge killing? That seems off. That's not what women typically do."

"What do they do?"

"Don't give me that, Benny."

"What?"

"I heard your tone. No such thing as a typical anything anymore, right? That what you're thinkin'?"

"What won't a typical woman do?"

"A good woman will do whatever she can to protect herself and her family. She'll sacrifice everything. Whatever she ends up doing, whatever steps she takes, it's got nothin' to do with vengeance. It has to do with the future. Going forward."

"You might be on to something. I think she's protecting someone."

"Who?"

"Her accomplice. Someone she cares for somehow."

He nodded and drank from his beer. "Don't listen to me. I'm a tired old man who never understood women, typical or otherwise."

Heat lightning flashed in the distance and I stepped to the grill and sent the kids to the house to wash up for dinner. Pops followed me, and was watching as I plopped the steaks on the grill away from the direct heat like he'd taught me. Once the inside of the steak was good and warm, I'd put them directly over the fire to finish them off. Light rain soaked our heads and hissed and steamed on the grill's iron shell.

"Can I ask you something about Mom?"

Pops nodded.

"She ever tell you who my father was?"

"Where the hell'd that come from?"

I told Pops about what Ricky Butler had said about a woman murdered in a Worthington trailer park and how he thought I was a dead ringer for a guy named Paco Correa who was killed by some dirty cops. I told him about the undersheriff and my memories of his Georgian-style estate and the recognition I'd seen in his eyes when we met.

"You think your mother might have been murdered and that some guy named Paco might be your father?"

"I don't know what to think. I didn't go looking for this."

"Your mother died of a heroin overdose and never told me who your father was. Maybe you leave it at that."

"Maybe I don't. Did Mom have any old photos I can go through? Who knows? Maybe this Paco guy's in one of them."

"She didn't have any old photos. Other than pictures of you and Ashley."

"You sure about that?"

He nodded.

The wind picked up and black clouds moved over the top of us. Pops looked to the sky and closed his eyes against the rain. "There's no future in the past."

"Yeah, well, the past showed up a couple days ago with a gun and fifty grand in cash."

"Tell me you're speaking figuratively."

"Wish I was."

I told him how I became Mia Delarosa's attorney. Pops knew what happened with Geronimo two years ago.

He wasn't happy about any of it.

11

Friday, August 13

RUSS CALLED AT five minutes after eight the next morning. I took the call as Rashonda stepped into my office to have a word with me. I pressed the cell phone against my chest and told her to shut the door behind her on the way out. Kind of brusque of me, I know. The slammed door sounded like a gunshot.

"The hell was that?" Russ said loudly over the sounds of the road on his end.

"A pissed off receptionist."

"What'd you do?"

"Office drama. What's up?"

"Someone followed Ricky Butler home from his strip club last night. Beat the shit out of him, took his keys, tossed his Lexus and his house."

I ran the odds in my head. Even money said it was Clint Brown's doing, or Geronimo's. I'd know soon enough. "What were they looking for?"

"They wanted to know where the laptop was that you wouldn't let me take."

"How do you know that?" I said, thinking it was probably Geronimo's men. Then again, I hadn't received any news from Geronimo about this, so I still didn't know what to believe.

"Butler called Annie at four in the morning. Said they kept asking him where the laptop was. He wouldn't tell them. Told them if he dies, his records—including everything on the laptop—gets sent to the press. Some sort of dead man's switch. Must have something pretty good on that computer for that to work."

Brown's men, I thought. The threat of releasing records to the public wouldn't have slowed Geronimo down a bit.

"Butler threatened to kill you and me by the way," Russ said. "I just got off the phone with Annie."

I loosened my tie. "Why's he want to kill us?"

"He thinks we sicced Brown and his goons on him."

Which we did, I thought. Butler's IQ must've gone up a few points since I saw him at Annie's place. "What gave him that impression?"

Russ groaned. "What the hell you think? Annie says she's never seen Butler this mad."

I smiled. "Understandable, if he thinks he's getting his face kicked in for saying things he never said."

"He doesn't think it. He knows. These guys knocked his teeth down his throat, told him about our meeting with Brown. Told him to keep Brown's name out of his mouth."

"Bet he was hard to understand with missing teeth."

Russ laughed. "Annie said he had to repeat things over and over. Said he sounded like her grandmother when she had a stroke."

"Do you believe Butler—that he didn't give up the laptop to Brown's men?"

"I don't know what to believe. Records go missing, that's bad for business, real bad if you run an escort service. He's not gonna want anyone to know their secrets might've fallen into Brown's hands, if they actually did. We should've taken the laptop when we had the chance."

He was right. Too late now. The threat of whatever was on that laptop might've been the only thing that had kept Butler alive. Perhaps it could do the same for Annie and Mia. It was more important to protect them than to play by the rules. I needed to remember that going forward.

"You know what that sonofabitch Butler tried to get Annie to do last night after he got beat up?" Russ said.

"What?"

"Told her she needed to call Brown and tell him I'm playing him for a fool. That he never told me Brown raped Annie. That there never was any surveillance behind Butler's strip club."

"She didn't do it, did she?"

"She says she didn't."

"Where is she now?"

"Riding around in her Mustang, too scared to go home. Too scared to go to court this morning like she's supposed to. I'm on my way to meet with her now. Gonna put her up in a hotel under an alias."

"What're you going to do with her Mustang?"

"Put it in storage somewhere."

"Good. Swing by the office later and pick up the discovery materials Keri texted you about."

When the call ended, I warned Keri and Pops of Ricky Butler's threat. After that, I called Geronimo. He didn't answer.

Something occurred to me. Earlier this morning I'd looked over the files and saw something about a Mustang in Mia's neighborhood on the night of the murders. What Russ said about Annie's Mustang moments ago clicked and I powered up my laptop, opened a file on the thumb drive that read: NEIGHBORHOOD CANVASS. Detectives Antonio Trillo and Olivia Naldoza were put in charge of interviewing the neighbors. Trillo worked Mia's street while Naldoza interviewed the neighbors on Jimmy Ray's street.

I started with Detective Naldoza's report. On the night of the murder, she knocked on the door of every house on North Fairview Avenue within four blocks of Jimmy Ray's residence. The only person to report witnessing any activity at Jimmy's house in the hours leading up to the murder was Rosa Cortez, the elderly neighbor one door south of Jimmy Ray. Ms. Cortez told Naldoza that she saw her neighbor to the north (she said she thought his name was Jimmy something) in the backyard with a young child about half an hour before the cops descended upon the area. She volunteered that the only way for her to see into Jimmy's backyard was to be on her deck, which put her just high enough to see over the bushes. She was smoking a cigarette, waiting for her dog to do his business. She made a point to tell Naldoza that she wasn't snooping, but heard the little girl's voice and wasn't sure where it was coming from and when she laid eyes on the girl everything seemed okay. As far as she knew, she'd never seen the child before, and guessed the girl to be Jimmy's grandchild or some other relation. She thought maybe the girl was five years old, but couldn't describe her other than that.

Detective Trillo's interviews with residents up and down North Waco Avenue produced one interesting tidbit. Mia's neighbor directly across the street, an auto mechanic by the name of David Velasquez, told Trillo that he'd noticed a newer-model blue Mustang he'd never seen before sitting on the curb in front of his house when he got home from work that evening. He never saw anyone in or around the car and could only say that it was sitting there around six thirty when he got home, and was gone by the time the cops were swarming the neighborhood just over an hour later. Other than that, he didn't see a thing.

I clicked out of the neighborhood-canvass file, and searched the icons for interviews with Annie Black. There were none, nor were there any reports regarding any investigation into who might have been the owner of the Mustang.

I called Russ.

"What's up?"

"Do you have Annie with you yet?"

"Yeah, why?"

"Call me as soon as you've got her safe in a hotel and the Mustang hidden."

"Okay, what's this about?"

"You'll see."

* * *

Russ put Annie up in the Ambassador, a former bank building turned high-rise hotel on South Broadway in downtown

Wichita. It was a quarter mile south of my office, so when Russ called just after lunch, I strapped on my shoulder holster and threw on a suit coat to hide my Glock and walked to the hotel. The sun was directly overhead, so the tall buildings provided no shade. No relief from the heat. By the time I reached the hotel, I'd ducked into two buildings and backtracked three times, never seeing any sign that anyone was following me.

From the outside, the Ambassador looked like what it was—a classy hotel. Its western entrance sat across the street from another high-rise building, a weathered-brick structure with a legion of blown-out windows, most of them boarded up. The few that weren't had pigeons on their sills. Several homeless people were spread out along the sidewalk, squatting, sleeping, or leaning against the building. One grizzled old man was smoking a cigarette. From across the street, I couldn't tell if he was watching me, or just staring into oblivion. The hotel lobby was a whole other world— chandeliers, marble, conversational groupings of wingback chairs and velvet sofas. Not overly ornamental, but sleek and modern, decorated in a way that gave the place a patina of old- world quaintness, like something a rube from Kansas might imagine seeing in France maybe, except for the sixty-inch flat- screen TV on one of the walls.

I rode the elevator to the fourteenth floor and went to Annie's room. Russ answered the door and let me in.

"Nice place," I said.

"Don't worry, it's on me. It's my fault she's here."

Russ shut the door behind me as I glanced around. Spacious room with muted colors—creams, lavenders, and shades of gray on a patterned charcoal-colored carpet. The brightest things in the room were the purplish throw pillows on stylish chairs and a love seat. They matched the folded- down comforter on a king-sized bed with enough pillows on it to keep the starting lineup of the Kansas City Royals comfortable. The curtains on the huge window were pushed to the sides and offered a view of downtown Wichita. I could see Riverfront Stadium and the Epic Center, the building across the street from my office.

"Where's Annie?"

"Shower."

I handed Russ the thumb drive containing the discovery I had in Mia's case so far. He slipped it into his pocket.

We walked past the mini-bar and the closet to a small table sitting in front of the window. Maybe this was how the hotel had the room set up, but I doubted it. It looked more like a modification made by long-lost lovers anticipating a romantic room-service lunch because the table seemed a little too close to the bed, given the available space in the room. As we sat across the table from each other, he asked me what was up. A pack of Marlboros and a .40 caliber Glock were sitting on the window sill next to Russ and I could hear the shower running beyond the bathroom door behind him.

"I need to ask Annie if she was with Mia at her home on the day of the murder."

"What makes you think she was?" Russ said, sounding defensive.

"The cops canvassed the neighborhood. A blue Mustang was parked across the street from Mia's house an hour before the murder."

"What year Mustang?"

"Newer model was all the report said."

Russ made a face like he was sucking on a lemon.

I said, "You got a problem with me asking her questions about that?"

"No." He frowned "Why would I?"

"Oh, I dunno. Do you happen to know how many times Annie's been arrested?"

"Yeah, we talked some this morning. Just the one time when Brown set her up on the possession charge. Why?"

"Because, when you look at the photos of the murder weapon, you'll see what looks like a dried stain on the grip of that axe handle. No one's tested it yet to see if there's any human DNA there but I might be in a position to call for that one day."

His eyes narrowed. "When you have a better idea about what the person swinging the axe has to say about Mia's involvement in the murder."

"That's right. If I think that person will say Mia wasn't in on the murder, I'll be asking the court to order the state to run whatever DNA profile they find through the state's DNA database. Maybe that old stain is the dried blood of the real killer—what the state now calls Mia's unnamed accomplice."

Russ faced the city, his eyes squinting against the glare. "The KBI's way behind on entering DNA profiles of arrestees into its system. It can take months. Years even."

"But you see what I'm getting at?"

He shot me a look. "Annie's DNA profile will eventually be in the state's database. I get it."

The shower shut off.

I leaned forward and lowered my voice. "If it ends up being Annie's DNA on that axe handle, and the state can put together a case on her, say, through my client's testimony—"

"You're afraid I'll hide her," Russ whispered.

"Yeah. Would you do that?"

Russ leaned forward, stabbed a finger into the table, and spoke in a fervent hiss. "If Mia told you Annie killed Jimmy Ray, just tell me—"

"You're not answering my question."

He leaned back in his chair. Cupped his mouth with his palm and stroked his goatee. "Would I help Annie be a fugitive from murder?" He reached for the cigarettes, then drew his hand back. Old habit. Smoking was as forbidden as firearms in this place. I glanced at the Glock beside the Marlboros.

Russ said, "I should probably be offended."

"But you're not."

He shook his head and we stared at each other for a long moment. "No. It's a fair question."

"Then answer it," I whispered. "If it looks like she murdered Jimmy Ray, would you hide her?"

The bathroom door opened. Annie emerged from a puff of steam in a white terry-cloth bathrobe with a towel wrapped around her head. She spotted me and by way of greeting said, "Russ said you wanted to talk with me again."

"I can leave and come back after you're dressed."

She brushed by Russ and sat on the bed a few feet away. I caught the scent of shampoo as she faced us. She crossed her legs and removed the towel from her head, letting her wet mane fall to one side. She worked to rub it dry with the towel. Her robe parted below the waist and I got an eyeful of long, well-muscled legs before I could look away.

"Ask your question," she said.

Her tone was blunt. I took it to mean, *I want you out of here.* When her green eyes shifted to Russ, they seemed to suggest something like, *if you lose the lawyer, I'll lose the robe.* But when she looked at me again, I sensed something more provocative in her eyes. It gave me the unsettling vibe that I could stay, watch, maybe more. I tried to tell myself I was imagining this, but I knew what I saw. A look like that was always intentional, but it didn't necessarily mean she wanted anything to do with me sexually. Perhaps it was meant to throw me off. Maybe she'd killed Jimmy and figured Mia had told me the whole story. Maybe she'd managed to turn Russ into one more lonely sap caught in a honey trap.

He picked up the pistol and stood. I had a fleeting vision—him pointing it at me. Firing rounds into my chest. I gave him a questioning look.

Russ noticed. Grinned knowingly and held up his pistol. "Better put this away before room service gets here. Wouldn't want to give anyone the wrong impression."

As he walked away, he said, "You eaten yet?"

"Yeah." I needed a drink of water. My throat suddenly felt dry. I realized I didn't know Russ as well as I would've liked. "Grabbed a sandwich already."

He went to the closet.

I stood. Picked up a bottle of water off the nightstand. "Mind if I drink this?"

Annie shrugged.

I chugged most of the water.

Russ locked his gun in the hotel's safe. Annie stood and re-tightened her robe and sat back down.

When Russ and I returned to our seats at the table, I smiled at Annie. An attempt to reassure her that I meant her no harm. I wasn't sure it would turn out that way, and neither was Annie. She didn't return my smile.

"How well do you know Mia?" I asked her. "And don't tell me you only know her because you both worked for Ricky Butler. You two were close enough that you, for whatever reason, had intimate photos of her in your car."

"Like I told you before," she said. "I was looking out for her."

"That's your story and you're sticking to it."

She shrugged. "Do you have a daughter?"

I looked at her for a moment, then nodded.

"Would you want pictures like that of her out there for anyone to see?"

"No. I wouldn't."

"That's all there was to it," she said. "Just looking out for a young girl."

I'd started to drink the last of my water, but stopped. "Was there a video made of the activity captured on the photos?"

"The 'activity,'" Annie said, laughing her way through the words. "You mean the gangbang?"

I nodded.

"Ask Mia."

"I'm asking you."

"I wasn't there, so I don't know."

"Where'd you get the photos?" Russ asked.

Annie turned to him and shrugged. "Not sure I want to tell you that."

"Why not?" I said.

Annie's gaze took in the room. "This is a nice place, but I have to hide out here because of what you two bozos told Brown."

Russ held up a hand. "My mistake, not Ben's. Like I told you earlier, I was trying to put the heat on Butler. All I can do now is say I'm sorry and try to make it up to you."

"How could you ever do that?" she said.

Russ and I shared a look. I could see he didn't have an answer for her.

I swirled the last ounce of water around in the plastic bottle, absently staring at it. "We can't make it up to you, but we can help each other."

She drew her head back. "How?"

"Brown is dirty," I said. "Maybe you help us bring him down."

"You represent Mia," she said. "No one hired you to bring down a dirty cop."

"No one had to. What happened at your place with Butler, things that've happened since, I think Brown may've had something to do with the death of my mother."

Annie's chest rose as she drew in a slow breath. "And a guy named Paco something."

"Maybe. What do you know about him?"

"Nothing. Don't even know if Paco was an actual man, or a figment of Ricky's fried wires. I heard what you both heard. That's all I know."

Russ said, "Butler never said anything about a possible link between Brown and Paco Correa? The thing involving the woman in Worthington?"

She shook her head. "Hey, I still don't know if this Paco guy exists. And like Ricky's gonna confide in me if he does."

"Brown is in the photos you had in the back of your car, isn't he?" I said, switching gears to keep her off balance—maybe loosen those tight lips.

She crossed her arms. Gave me a blank look.

"You're way too smart to destroy those photos like you say you did," I said.

She pursed her lips.

"If it helps. I already know Brown is in those photos," I said. "Just need you to confirm it."

"Which one was he?" Russ asked. "Which president?"

She averted her eyes. "I'm assuming Mia already told you that."

Russ leaned in close to her. "We need corroboration. And we need those photos. Where are they?"

If she'd lied to me two days ago about destroying the photos, she didn't repeat it now. But it was clear she wasn't about to answer Russ's question either. She closed her eyes and shook her head. She couldn't believe the mess she was in. She could stay here with us and take a brow beating, or she could take her chances with Butler and Brown.

"Did you get the photos from a guy they called Youngblood?" I said, hoping to spark a reaction.

I did, but it was Russ who shot me a look. He recognized it as new information. I'd tell him what Mia told me later. Maybe.

"Never heard of him," Annie said. "What do the photos have to do with the murder?"

"Can't see why anyone would give them to you. Maybe you stole them?" I said.

"Answer me, goddamnit. What's this have to do with the murder?"

"Pulling on a thread to see how things are connected in your world."

"World I'm in is a snake pit. You have no idea."

"I think I do. Looks like one giant mating ball from where I sit. Can't tell where one snake ends and the other begins. So I ask questions."

"And I'm not answering that one."

"Okay," I said, "Let's try this one. Did you have any contact with Mia on the day of the murder?"

She shrugged. "Don't remember."

"You don't remember?" I said. "How's that possible?"

"I've slept since then."

I glanced at Russ. He'd gone pale. I took that he was concerned for Annie.

"Come on," I said to Annie. "Cut the bullshit."

"What makes you think I talked to her that day?"

"I've got information that suggests you were at Mia's house on the day of Jimmy Ray's murder."

"You think I killed him? Is that why your eyes lit up when Russ picked up his gun a few minutes ago? Thought maybe for one second I'd confessed a murder to him. And being such a nice piece of ass in high school, you thought Russ just might put you down to protect me."

"Something like that flashed through my mind, yeah. You're a beautiful woman."

"I'm a sure thing. If Russ wants a piece of this all he has to do is pay me like anyone else. Same goes for you."

"Annie!" Russ said. "Stop it. Ben is just trying to help Mia. We're trying to figure out what was going on at her house prior to the murder. Maybe you know something that can help her."

She fixed her eyes on me. "From what I hear, Mia had a front row seat for the whole show. Why don't you ask her what happened?"

"I'm asking you. Were you at Mia's house at any time on the day of the murder?"

"What makes you think that?"

"Because. Your blue Mustang was parked there that evening." I didn't know this for sure, but I said it like it was a fact.

She looked at Russ, then dropped her eyes to the floor. "If that's true, I wonder why the cops haven't been by my place to ask me about it."

"You know why," I said.

Confusion clouded her face, which was what I wanted. Confused people make mistakes.

"Because you're lying," she finally said. "Because there was no blue Mustang parked across the street from Mia's house that night."

I smiled. "You seem to remember more than you think."

"What are you talking about?"

"I never told you the Mustang was parked across the street from Mia's house," I said.

Annie's face tightened.

I gulped down the last of the water. "Yet, that's exactly where it was parked. Given that people park up and down both sides of North Waco Avenue, and there's a driveway in front of Mia's house you could've parked in, that's a strange thing for you to have said. That you weren't parked across the street from Mia's house." I shrugged. "Makes me think you were, and that you're lying now."

"That don't mean anything. I'm done talkin' to you."

"Who was the little girl in Jimmy Ray's backyard thirty minutes before the murder?"

Her breath caught. "I'm done with this." She stood and pointed at the bathroom. "I'm going in there to get dressed. If you're still here when I get out, I'm leaving."

I said, "Why won't you—"

But she stepped into the bathroom and shut the door.

I was still looking at the door when she cracked it open a second later and peered through a six-inch opening. "I'll tell you the same thing I told Russ this morning. It'd be a mistake to underestimate Rick Butler. His junk don't work no more, but he still got that pride that makes him want to fuck up people that cross him. Now more than ever. I think that chip on his shoulder doubled in size when his dick went limp. He was gonna be dead in a year until you two came along and gave him something to live for." She nodded at me. "You can carry that pistol around with you all you want, but when Ricky finds you, you won't be expecting it. You'll be outmanned and outgunned. You can't stay vigilant forever, and he won't ever forget."

She shut the door again.

"How old is the little girl?" Russ asked.

"Jimmy Ray's neighbor thinks she was about five."

"Cops haven't figured out who she is, huh?"

I shook my head. "Not from what I've read anyway."

There was a knock at the door. A man's voice in the hallway said he was room service.

I smiled. "That could be Ricky at the door now. Or Brown. You sure that safe is the best place for your pistol?"

Russ glanced lazily in the general direction of the bathroom. "As long as I'm in here with her it is."

"Sure, Russ. You're afraid of her now."

"I'm not?"

I laughed. "No, I don't buy that. But maybe you should be."

I followed him to the door. He peeked through the spyhole and told the guy on the other side he'd be right with him. He put his hand on the door knob, then turned to me. "You can trust me."

"Would you hide Annie from the cops?"

He took his hand off the knob. Pondered his answer. "Aren't I already doing that?"

"Would you do it to keep her from being arrested for Jimmy Ray's murder?"

He shook his head. "No."

"Not sure I believe that."

Russ shrugged. "Believe what you want. Did Mia tell you Annie was the killer?"

"No. She won't talk about that. Not yet anyway."

"She's either afraid of the killer, or she has someone in her life worth protecting."

I nodded. "You need to remember who you're being paid to protect."

He shrugged. "You paid me in cash. Makes me think you got paid in cash. And no way does Mia have enough money to get you out of early retirement."

"What's your point?"

"Makes me wonder: Who exactly am I being paid to protect?"

12

Friday, August 13

RICKY BUTLER PARKED his SUV on a country road and opened the door against a hot wind, his eyes almost shut against the afternoon sun. He gripped the steering wheel and swiveled his heft so that his feet dangled over the running board, then squirmed ever closer to the edge of the leather seat until gravity triggered a short skid to where his sneakers hit the gravel. He groped for, then wrestled with the ground-facing belt on his pants, the snap, the zipper, the part of him he would never again see without the benefit of a mirror—the dance of a morbidly obese man taking a leak. When he was finally free to cut loose, he was sweating. Now came the waiting.

He caught a whiff of burnt garbage and glanced north, then south toward Wichita, the direction from which he'd come. From this relatively high ground, Ricky felt like he could see the road behind him for twenty miles, which wasn't true. But he could see a long way, and was sure no one had followed him. There were no vehicles in sight, and he had always said that seeing is believing. He blinked several times in an effort to lubricate his eyes, then looked down to shield them from the wind. His belly prevented him from seeing the little puddle he figured to be making in the rocks by his feet and he'd lost so much feeling down there that he could no longer tell for sure if he was done urinating, or if he'd even begun. He jiggled himself to kick-start the process or keep things moving and waited some more. Blinked his eyes and waited.

The smell of burnt garbage came to him again.

He looked west across the plain, squinting against the prevailing wind, then south down the road again. Nothing burning anywhere he could see and still no vehicles. Just pasture and cattle and wide-open spaces and a contrail blooming from a jet in a cloudless sky. His eyes were among the few things he had that still functioned properly.

Twelve hours earlier, his list of ailments was shorter. Before men claiming to be with Undersheriff Brown had kicked teeth down his throat and set off an alarm inside his head. The ringing in his ears was still loud enough that he couldn't hear the hum of his Lexus or wind blowing through his thick, bone-white hair. He traced the stitches sewn into his swollen lips with his tongue, then used it to explore the holes in his gums where three of his favorite teeth used to be—both upper incisors and a canine, giving him a Halloween grimace. He wondered what Lucky would think when she saw him and this caused him to look up the road at her single-story clapboard house, half hidden in tall weeds. She wasn't outside anywhere he could see and the curtains were closed so he knew she wasn't watching him, which was good. He was an old fat man with multiple health issues. He wasn't looking for new ways to remind her of that.

When he parked next to Lucky's pickup in front of a ramshackle shed in the backyard, he wondered what she had in store for him. He wondered if she'd even understood that he was on his way to her house for their weekly rendezvous. It'd been a frustrating phone conversation. He couldn't hear her and she couldn't understand what he was barking into the receiver through swollen, anesthetized lips and missing teeth. Maybe she was angry enough to put a gun to his head and make him go down on her. That's how she'd kicked off the festivities last time. He'd been watching last Friday's video all week, reliving his dark fantasy. He shut off the engine and looked at himself in the rearview mirror and it dawned on him that whatever they did, it wouldn't be a reenactment of last week. Not with a lip full of stitches that would irritate her when they touched her down there. Lucky specialized in delivering pain, not receiving it. She looked the part too, which was half the fun. She had broad shoulders, large hands, and an Adam's apple the size of a racket ball. She even had a fully functioning penis that could dole out agony in spades. He regarded it as her defining characteristic.

He used his key to get into her back door, which put him in the kitchen. The stairs to the basement were to his immediate left and from where he stood he could see all the way through the small living space to the front door. The three doors along the left wall of the living area were closed. The place was full of rental furniture and electronics and had always smelled like what it was, an old, refurbished farmhouse—some amalgam of mildew, sweat, and his grandad's trailer-home when he was a kid. Today, the only odor that came to Ricky was burnt garbage and it occurred to him that the wires in his head were delivering signals that bore no relation to reality—a product of the severe beating, he guessed.

A half-empty bottle of well-brand vodka sat next to a note on the kitchen counter and he could feel the wood floor vibrating under his feet, pulsing to a beat. Sound was getting through and he could tell it was music—like a song heard underwater. Muted as it was to his ears, he still pegged it as grunge rock from the early nineties, when Lucky was born and her name was Chad.

He stepped to the counter and read the note. She was waiting for him in the basement. He pulled ten hundreds out of his pocket and dropped them next to the vodka. In this house, he was a customer. Five hundred for the sex, five hundred for the video.

The noise of the world increased and clarified with each step into the living room like for a swimmer coming up from the depths. He didn't want to hear this tired, over-hyped clatter on the recording later. If he could hear at all, he wanted to hear the insults and his own moans and the crack of the whip. When he stood before the stereo system, the vibration coming up from the floor thumped into the bottom of his feet through his sneakers and he saw that the volume was pegged to the max. He recognized the song and was able to make out a familiar refrain about a mosquito and a libido—a singsong flow of meaningless lyrics that satirized a meaningless life. He wasn't usually into all the melodramatic woe-is-me shit from that era, but standing here in this living room the way he was, he could relate. His whole life was about chasing highs. Drugs and orgasms. And the orgasms were getting hard to come by, he liked to joke, even if it wasn't funny. He wondered how many he'd had and how many were left in the tank, which caused him to think about what he was and what he'd become, the kind of self-reflection that slipped in without warning and illuminated a truth he didn't want to see. He'd sold women so men didn't have to jerk off into a sock and now he was paying big money to be the sock. Right now, it's all he could think about. Mosquitos and libidos indeed.

When he killed the power to the stereo he found himself alone with the incessant ringing inside his head again. He worked his jaw up and down like people do on planes until something clunked open inside his skull behind one of his ears and he thought he could hear the house creaking against the wind. The ringing continued, but at a lower volume. He covered it up by humming the song about mosquitos and libidos as he descended into the basement, a very quiet voice in his head telling him this wasn't what he'd envisioned for his life back in high school . . . Not even close.

* * *

At the bottom of the stairs Ricky surveyed the small, square chamber, tinted green by a string of party bulbs hanging from the basement rafters. To his left was a bong shaped like a skull on a table with whips and chains and ball gags. To his right, a platinum blonde with a heavily made-up face and two days of stubble stepped out from behind the furnace in a black mini-skirt and combat boots and told him to get on his knees.

Butler smiled, figuring this was Lucky's lover. Same age, same build, except the blonde had muscular legs like a professional dancer. Butler had offered to pay Lucky double for a threesome some time ago and hadn't thought she liked the idea, but it was an old story. Money talks. He craned his neck to the left in a failed effort to see around the furnace.

"Where's Lucky?" Butler said.

"Never mind that. Get on your knees."

Deep voice. Muffled. But enough of it got through that he understood her. Her?

Butler grabbed a beach towel that was slung over the stair railing and folded it into a fluffy pad. "What are your pronouns?"

"My what?"

"Your . . . pronouns."

"Oh. I'm an asexual asshole, born with an honest-to-God dick, dressed like a woman, if that helps."

Butler laughed.

"Get on your knees."

"Lucky told me I should ask about pronouns in a situation like this."

"What kind of situation do you think you're in?"

Butler shrugged.

The blonde said, "You've lived a life consumed by fripperies."

"Fripperies?—"

"Trivial shit." The blonde pointed to a spot in front of the table. "On your knees. I'm not going to say it again."

A bit over the top, Butler thought, but so were his fantasies. This is what he paid for, so he rolled with it. Took several steps forward, threw down the towel, and struggled to place his knees on it. When he was comfortable, he looked up and saw feet, toes up, sticking out from behind the furnace. A kaleidoscope of butterflies inked into the calves were migrating toward thighs still obscured from his view. Butler's face reddened under his white hair and he yelled for a timeout and when that didn't bring Lucky to her feet he began hollering her name.

The blonde looked down at Lucky's body before turning back to Butler, whose eyes were wet and useless and still staring at the legs. Butler wheezed and seemed to utter something to himself.

"What are you saying?" said the blonde.

"I'll take you to my laptop. You can have it."

"That's not why I'm here."

"I never told anyone Brown raped one of my girls."

"Brown didn't send me."

Butler opened his mouth. Not to talk. He was struggling to comprehend.

The blonde said, "The one who sent me believes Brown raped your girl. Just like you been tellin' people."

"I never said that."

"It doesn't matter now."

Butler swayed, then crumpled to his hands and knees, lightheaded and nauseous. When the urge to puke passed, he raised his eyes enough to see the combat boots before him and his last lover's legs in the periphery to the right. Lucky's legs twitched and moved like she was restless, or having a nightmare. Then she coughed.

The blonde looked over his shoulder and saw her legs moving. He took a hypodermic needle off the top of the furnace and Butler understood.

"Dean Curtis sent you," Butler said.

The man in the blond wig wore clear plastic gloves. Butler had missed that detail until now. Butler watched him straddle, then bend over Lucky. He couldn't see their upper bodies past the furnace. He watched until Lucky's legs stopped moving.

The man raised up, set the hypo on the furnace, and looked at Butler.

"You don't have to choke me out," Butler said. "Just give me the needle."

The man's chin came up, like a question.

"I won't fight you," Butler said.

"Wouldn't be much of a fight."

"Wouldn't have to be. Bruise me up and you got a murder investigation on your hands."

"This'll look like two sodomites overdosing on smack no matter what you do." The man stepped behind Butler. Got down on one knee and said, "You know how I'm going to kill you?"

Butler nodded. "Same way Brown and Curtis—"

The man pounced on Butler's back and shot his right arm around Butler's neck and they rolled and knocked over the table, sending the skull-shaped bong and the sex toys clattering across the concrete. They ended up the way they started, with the man's arm wrapped around Butler's throat, except the man was on bottom and Butler was condemned to a bug-eyed view of the rafters. The wig was cockeyed on the man's head and his eyes were rolled back. When he clamped his legs around Butler's girth, his mini-skirt rode up past his waist. He cupped the back of Butler's head with his left hand and tightened the vice, pressing the carotid arteries on either side of Butler's neck with his right bicep and forearm. Butler tried to wedge his fingers between his neck and the arm, then launched into a string of slurred, seemingly nonsensical ramblings about someone named Joel and a woman murdered in Worthington as the green lights above him faded and his eyes saw no more.

* * *

Geronimo was ten feet from the front bumper of Butler's Lexus, crouched inside the shed, looking out. Behind him, shafts of light poured through gaps in the raw, weathered slats, striping the dusty museum of forgotten farm things behind him. He wore jeans and an untucked western shirt with the arms cut off. Holding gloves and a ski mask, he eyed the back of Lucky's house through a two-foot gap in the shed's weary double doors, still huffing from having run through the pasture behind the premises.

A short-haired man in garish makeup he'd never seen before exited the back door of the house in a mini-skirt and combat boots and headed up the driveway toward the road with a blond wig dangling by his thigh like a dead rabbit. The man had a phone to his ear and the clear glove on the hand that held it glinted in the sun. When a pickup appeared on the road from the south, the man lowered his phone.

Geronimo pulled out his phone and whispered for it to call Pablo. When Pablo answered, Geronimo spoke in Spanish and asked him if he was seeing this.

"*Sí,*" Pablo said.

He asked Pablo if he was in position to see the tag on the truck. He was not.

The truck decelerated to a slow roll as the man with the wig kept pace and opened the passenger-side door and jumped in. The door slammed shut and the truck tore off up the road.

Geronimo spoke in Spanish. "I'm going in. Be ready."

"*Sí.*"

He put the phone away and slipped on his mask and gloves, then shuffled sideways through the gap between the doors. He strode to the passenger side of the Lexus and dropped to his belly. He reached underneath the SUV and wrenched a GPS tracker free from the undercarriage, bounced to his feet, and dropped the tracker in his pocket while pulling his pistol from its holster on his way to the back door.

The door was unlocked. He slipped into the kitchen and saw what he guessed was a man in a turquoise wig, pale and unmoving, slouched on the couch in the living room. He peered down the basement stairs and listened, then moved to the living room where he saw a used syringe and a tourniquet on the coffee table in front of the man, who looked to have died wearing black-laced panties and a black corset with silver zippers and buckles. Geronimo cleared the three rooms behind closed doors like a cop and approached the man for a closer look. He was dead. Frothy blood had oozed and partly dried under his nose and around his mouth.

Geronimo found Ricky Butler naked and dead on the basement floor next to a table with an assortment of sex toys and drug paraphernalia on it. A ball gag was crammed in his mouth. His right cheek was planted on the cement and his glassy eyes were half open. Geronimo squatted down and looked into them but they didn't look back. He found a track mark on Butler's arm, then stood and looked at the table. Another tourniquet and another used syringe were within a few feet of another dead body.

"Bullshit," he whispered.

He quickly found the key fob for the Lexus in pants rumpled on the floor then bounded up the stairs.

Outside, he searched Butler's SUV for the laptop. Didn't find it.

When he was clear of the scene and back on the highway with Pablo, he called Ben and told him what he'd found.

13

ON MONDAY MORNING a KBI agent named Caroline Gordon sat across the desk from me in my office, leaning a soft-shell leather briefcase with a shoulder strap against the chair at her feet. She wore a black, sleeveless tactical women's top that showed off her sinewy arms and hung below the waist of her jeans, covering her pistol. Her blond hair was parted down the middle and woven into a pair of French braids. Her red-rimmed eyes suggested exhaustion unfazed by the four-dollar coffee in her hands.

Two years ago, she was ambushed and shot in the leg trying to locate a missing detective who was involved in the capital murder case that caused me to resign as a judge. Four days after being shot, she showed up on my front porch and confronted me about the whereabouts of my children and a report from my brother-in-law that my sister was missing. Caroline suspected someone had gotten to me about the capital case by threatening my family—I suppressed her spot-on suspicion by letting her talk on the phone with my kids, whom I'd sent to Idaho with Pops after a failed kidnapping by the Mendez-Rodriguez Cartel. I blamed my sister's absence on my brother-in-law, a man with a well-documented history of domestic violence, by suggesting that she was probably hiding from him. A day later when my sister was saved from the kidnappers and the defense attorneys missed court and the case was heading for an inevitable mistrial, Caroline came to my chambers and all but told me she thought I'd been compromised and had settled the score my own way, which, of course, I had. Then she hinted she was going to let it be.

But she didn't.

I didn't hold that against her. The defense attorneys were found dead in a hole on a grazing pasture north of El Dorado. Coyotes had feasted on their bodies. The detective Caroline had been looking for was found dead, folded into the basement freezer of a house in Wichita. The murders were high profile, sensational, not the kind of crimes that could be quietly placed on a back burner.

I loosened my tie as I looked at Caroline. "I've been expecting you."

Her eyes narrowed. "That right?"

"Whispers in the wind."

Her lips twitched. "Did your father give you my number?"

"Pops is my grandfather, and I already had your number."

She nodded. "Why didn't you call?"

"Didn't think it would do you any good."

"Me? What about you?"

I didn't answer.

She glanced around the office. "You're a defense attorney now. I gotta say, I didn't see that coming."

"Keri and the kids were tired of the seclusion."

"But you liked it."

I nodded. "Yeah, I liked the quiet. But I'd had my fill of home schooling the kids, so, in the end, we all wanted the same thing. All of us were pretty excited about regular school this morning—first time back and all that."

"Good for you."

I shrugged. "It was time."

"Can't hide forever."

She stared at me without expression for a long moment.

I waved my hand in front of her face. "Did you forget why you're here?"

She leaned back and crossed her legs. "I don't wanna make you feel like you need to plead the Fifth or put you in a bad situation with ... with whoever. But, I'm investigating several murders. You know the cases. Anything you can do to help me with them?"

She gave me what she probably thought was a reassuring smile. I didn't fall for it. I'd killed five men two summers ago, four during the kidnapping attempt and one after I'd broken into a house trying to find my sister. Four rock-solid self-defense killings, and one that an over-officious prosecutor might reasonably think was murder. Legend had it that an avenging *sicario* named Geronimo had pulled the trigger on all five men. A good story. I wanted to keep it alive without saying anything that might get Geronimo locked up.

I shrugged. "Can't think of anything. You looking for anything specific?"

"Specific? No."

I shrugged. "You're a cop, so I figured Detective Mallory's murder would be at the top of your list."

She nodded. "He was a decent man that didn't deserve what happened to him."

"And the rest of them did?"

"The rest of them were criminals." She shrugged. "Or defense attorneys. But I'll take whatever information you have about any of these cases."

I could only imagine what happened to the defense attorneys, but I was there when Detective Mallory was executed. The cartel brought him to me in the bed of a John Deer Gator, hog-tied and red faced, screaming against the duct tape over his mouth. They dumped him on the ground and one of them put nine rounds in his head and chest. The triggerman—a cartel lieutenant named Miguel Mendez-Mendoza—set me up, leaving himself the option of framing me for the detective's murder when the trial was over in case I ever got it in my head to tell the cops what actually happened. Five days later, I watched as Geronimo put a bullet through Miguel's brain on the gravel road in front of the Slate Valley Baptist Church.

"Wish I could help you," I said.

She stared at me for five seconds. "Okay, how 'bout this? It's just you and me talking here. Off the record. If you had one guess, who would you say killed Detective Mallory?"

I smiled. "You want me to guess? Just jump out there with a name."

"Yep."

"Osama bin Laden."

"Very funny. Mallory had three children."

"Bin Laden had a litter of kids, so what? One guess is as good as another. That was the point of the joke."

"You're the one missing the point."

"Don't think so."

"How 'bout an opinion then. Who killed Mallory?"

"Since I have no idea who killed Mallory, it wouldn't really be an opinion, would it?"

She gave me a look—amused, but annoyed. "Let's not call it an opinion then. Let's call it a . . . random drawing . . . of a name . . . out of a hat."

"A random drawing of a name out of a hat?"

She nodded. "Yeah."

"What's the difference between that and a guess?"

"A guess can be educated. With a guess, the guesser could be using instinct or maybe even inside information, kind of like a professional gambler."

"Okay, fine," I said. "Let's do the random-drawing thing."

"Really?"

I nodded. "Sure, why not?"

"Good."

I waited with an expectant look on my face until her eyebrows finally went up. "What's the matter?"

"Where's the hat with names in it?"

"You have to pretend."

I smiled. "That would be a guess masquerading as a random drawing. But I can do that." I mimed taking a name out of a hat and reading the card. "Osama bin Laden."

Her face looked like I'd spit in her coffee. "How 'bout this then. Give me the name of Detective Mallory's murderer, or I make you the target of my investigation."

"Oh, okay. A threat. That might work."

She shrugged. "Would something like that make whatever you tell me inadmissible in court?"

"Depends."

"On what?"

"On whether or not you lie in court about how you got me to give you a name."

She uncrossed her legs, and set her coffee on the desk, then pulled her pistol out of its holster and leaned back, crossed her legs again and held the gun flat against her thigh.

"What's this?" I said.

She shrugged. "What's it look like?"

I shrugged back. "Another threat you could lie about."

"I'm a lot of things, but I'm not a liar."

"If I don't give you a name, you'll shoot me?"

"Oh yeah."

"Guess I have no choice then."

"Nope."

I nodded at her cup. "Do you need any more coffee?"

"No. Just a name. And not Osama."

"No problem. How 'bout . . . Miguel Mendez-Mendoza."

"He's dead."

"I read that somewhere. Shot dead in the head on a road in front of a little country church, right?"

"Point blank. That's the name you want to give me?"

"No. That's the name you forced me to give you. I'll tell you he killed Kennedy too if you want."

"No, that's alright. But you can tell me who killed Miguel?"

She gave me a fake smile.

"You gonna shoot me if I don't keep pulling imaginary names out of imaginary hats?"

"Yes."

"I'm recording all of this."

"Doubt it."

I was getting tired of the banter. No way was I giving up Geronimo. By any objective measure he was a horrible human being, but he'd been the key to saving my sister's life, and it didn't matter to me that he had his own selfish reasons for helping me do it. He and I were in it up to our ears together. Besides, he would kill me and my family if I snitched him out.

So there's that.

Caroline holstered her gun. "Actually, this has been fun, always is with you, Ben, but I'm here about another matter."

* * *

She reached into her briefcase and pulled out a laptop embossed with the logo of the KBI and opened it on my desk. "I want you to watch a video, then answer a few questions."

"What's this about?"

She punched some buttons and spun the laptop around. "Just watch."

I was looking at a shot of a concrete floor bathed in eerie, green light. The display on the screen logged the date and time. It read: 2021. 08. 13 15:43:36 and counting. I put it together fast—*three days ago was Friday the thirteenth and 3:43 in the afternoon was maybe half an hour before Geronimo called about finding Ricky Butler and another man dead in a Harvey county farmhouse.* Why was she showing me this? First thought that hit me—Geronimo. Had he been caught on camera? My stomach tightened.

Caroline watched me for a reaction. When I didn't give her one, she took her coffee off my desk and leaned back in her chair.

A man's voice from the video said, "*Get on your knees.*" A second voice—slurring—asked about someone named Lucky.

Caroline's eyes peered over the top of the screen at me as we listened to two men having a bizarre conversation.

"*On your knees. I'm not going to say it again,*" said the first voice.

Butler lumbered into the frame. A knot formed in my throat, thinking I was about to watch him die.

He dropped a towel on the concrete and awkwardly went to his knees. His lips were swollen and lined with stiches. He looked to his right with a look of terror on his face, yelling for a timeout and repeating the name, Lucky. He wheezed and offered to give the man his laptop, but the man wasn't interested.

"*I never told anyone Brown raped one of my girls,*" Butler said.

"*Brown didn't send me.*"

Confusion clouded Butler's face. I didn't get it either. If Brown hadn't sent this guy, who did? Caroline gazed down at her cup, clutched in both hands.

The man, still off camera, said, "*The one who sent me believes Brown raped your girl. Just like you been tellin' people.*"

The tone and the phrasing—the one who sent me—struck me as god-talk—religious rhetoric.

"*I never said that,*" Butler said.

"*It doesn't matter now.*"

Butler dropped to his hands and knees. His head was down. He looked like he was about to puke.

A man with a stubbly beard in a blond wig, mini-skirt, and combat boots stepped into the frame.

I shot Caroline a look. "What the hell?"

She smiled.

Someone in the basement coughed and the man in the wig looked over his shoulder.

"Pause the video," Caroline said.

I did.

"That person coughing or gagging off-screen is Lucky Andrews. She was born Chad Andrews before changing her name and identifying as a woman. This all happens in a Harvey County farmhouse—Lucky's residence. She met the dude in the wig at a bar called The Closet last Friday. Surveillance camera shows them leaving together at two o'clock—an hour and a half before what you're watching happened. We don't have any idea who the guy in the wig is, but the fat man was his target all along. Know why I'm showing you this video?"

"No," I lied, still thinking a cameo appearance by Geronimo was probably coming up.

"You'll see." She waved her hand. "Keep watching."

I hit the play button.

The man in the mini-skirt stepped out of frame.

Butler watched him, then said, "*Dean Curtis sent you.*"

I leaned forward and looked over the top of the screen at Caroline with wide eyes.

She was nodding—*yep, that Dean Curtis*. The billionaire that Butler said killed Paco Correa. The guy in the photo with Brown in Brown's foyer. Dean Curtis's name was on everything from fine arts centers in Chicago to basketball arenas in Kansas. Working a case with him as a suspect would put her out there on a very slender limb. No wonder Caroline looked so damned tired.

Butler said, "*You don't have to choke me out. Just give me the needle. I won't fight you.*"

"*Wouldn't be much of a fight.*"

"*Wouldn't have to be. Bruise me up and you got a murder investigation on your hands.*"

"*This'll look like two sodomites overdosing on smack no matter what you do.*"

The man in the mini-skirt stepped behind Butler and got on one knee. "*You know how I'm going to kill you?*"

"*Same way Brown and Curtis—*"

The man jumped on Butler's back and slipped his arm around Butler's neck. They rolled around on the floor and my view of their world disappeared into a whirling blur of scuffling and the sound of things crashing and skittering across concrete. When the camera stopped spinning, it was on the floor aimed at the stairs and I couldn't see either man, but I could hear Butler. He sounded like a man speaking in tongues, then I heard my name followed by a mangled phrase that put goose bumps all over me—something about a woman murdered in Worthington.

A few seconds later, all I could hear was heavy breathing.

Caroline said, "The fat guy said your name. How'd he know you?"

"Ricky Butler—met him five days ago when I went to interview a woman about a matter involving a client of mine."

"He owned Strictly Confidential Escorts—basically your client's pimp, right? Mia Delarosa's?"

"Yeah. You've done your homework."

She set her coffee on my desk again. "You won't see it on the video, but we think the man in the mini-skirt pumped a lethal dose of Fentanyl into Butler while he was passed out. Keep watching, and you'll hear him straining to pick Lucky up, and the combat boots will flash by and go up the stairs. Lucky's boyfriend found her dead on the couch. There was a needle and a tourniquet on the coffee table in front of her."

"Are the autopsies done?"

"Yeah. Of course the toxicology report will take several days, but the coroner is almost certain the cause of death will be opioid overdose."

"You said Fentanyl. I take it you field-tested the hypos?"

"Yeah." She lifted her chin and touched two fingers on her throat just above her larynx. "In our discussions about the cause of death in these two cases, the coroner explained that the small, fragile, horseshoe-shaped bone in the neck that guards the windpipe is called the hyoid. It often breaks during what my instructors at the academy called an air choke—what most people associate with strangulation or the cutting off of the air supply. Air chokes are a big no-no for cops, but many departments train their officers, in certain situations, to apply choke holds that will not damage the windpipe or the bone that protects it."

"The so-called blood choke."

Caroline nodded. "That's right. How'd you know?"

"Had a little training myself."

I watched the combat boots move across the screen and disappear up the stairs, then looked at Caroline. "Let me guess, the hyoid bone was intact in both of these victims."

"Correct. And there was no petechial hemorrhage in the eyes of either victim, which the coroner would've expected to see if their air supply had been cut off in any significant way. Air chokes involve the application of much greater force to the neck than a blood choke. The man in the mini-skirt knew what he was doing. He cut off circulation to their brains without causing any damage to their airways. That's how Butler was able to talk right up until he passed out."

"Is there video of this guy killing Lucky?"

"Yeah, the camera was hidden in a plastic skull that looked like a marijuana bong. It was on the table that got kicked over. It's motion activated and records through Wi-Fi to a system locked in a closet upstairs. The recording shows Lucky being put in a sleeper hold and injected about twenty minutes before Butler arrived. The killer dosed her again right before killing Butler. The coroner watched the video of both murders with us and explained that the killer simply cut the blood flow to cause a temporary hypoxic condition in the brain. Which leads to temporary unconsciousness, giving the killer time to administer a lethal dose of Fentanyl without a fight."

"Without the video, what would this case look like to the Harvey County investigators?"

"Accidental deaths, or some kind of suicide pact." She shrugged. "Or, maybe an accidental death followed by a suicide."

"Two more tragic deaths chalked up to addiction," I said, leaning way back in my chair, feeling the tug of stress-induced exhaustion. "Basically the same way it would've looked to the Worthington Police Department twenty-eight years ago when my mother was found dead in her trailer."

She gave me a frown of measured sadness. "I called the Worthington chief of police and told him what Butler said before he was killed. The chief told me how you found your mother dead when you were eleven."

I nodded. Twenty-eight years ago Chief Tom Bell was a detective in Worthington, probably in his thirties. He interviewed me after I found my mother. "What did he have to say about all this?"

"He was pretty blown away. Feels bad for the memories this'll bring up for you."

"He's a good man."

The combat boots were back on the screen. I heard sounds that made me think the killer was stripping off Butler's clothes.

Caroline said, "Butler knew about the hidden camera. According to Lucky's boyfriend, Butler not only paid her for sex, he paid her double for a recording of it. I know what he says on the video sounds more than a little nuts, but maybe . . . with his last conscious breath, panicked as he was, garbled as the message came out . . . maybe he was trying to tell us who killed your mother."

"Seems like it."

"Maybe Butler took a liking to you."

I looked up at her, then refocused on the video. "I doubt it. A few days ago he threatened to kill me and my investigator. Butler wanted to fuck with Brown and Dean Curtis, and since he knew he was about to die, this was his only option."

"Who's your investigator?"

"Russ Osborne."

"Oh."

"You know him?"

"Yeah. Used to be an ATF agent. People called him Oz."

"I'm curious," I said, looking up at her again. "Do you know why he's not with ATF anymore?"

Caroline shrugged. "Dunno. Maybe you should've asked him that before you hired him."

I shot her a look.

She smiled at me. "Tell me about Butler's threat."

I did, including what led to it—Annie's rape allegation against Brown and the beating Butler took from what he believed were Brown's men. I told her about Russ's and my meeting with Undersheriff Brown at his house and the photo of Brown with Dean Curtis in the foyer. I told her how Russ had attempted to protect Annie from payback by telling Brown that Butler had been the source of information about the alleged rape of Annie. I told her what Butler said to Annie about the attack—that men ransacked his house looking for a laptop and left him with orders to keep Brown's name out of his mouth.

By the time I finished, Caroline had a grimace on her face. "Do you know why these men wanted his laptop?"

I shrugged. Decided against making an educated guess. "I'd be speculating. Did you find a laptop?"

"No. We executed several search warrants trying to find it. Butler's house. All four of his vehicles. His strip club. No laptop. But it looked like somebody had torn through those places already so maybe somebody beat us to it." She tilted her chin upward. "I'll need to speak with Annie Black. Do you know where I can find her or how to get in contact with her?"

"Yeah, but let me set that up, okay? Annie's in hiding right now. She's pretty spooked."

Caroline's eyebrows went up. "There's a warrant out for her arrest, you know? Possession charge. She missed court again last Friday."

"Okay, but if you arrest her, you'll be putting her in a jail run by Brown."

"I won't arrest her." She shrugged. "Maybe."

"Maybe? She won't find that very reassuring. How bad do you want to talk to her?"

"Bad enough to arrest you for aiding a fugitive if you don't tell me how to find her."

"Talk to your boss. See if he's willing to let the warrant slide under the circumstances."

She nodded. "Okay, but whatever we decide to do about the warrant, I need the information you have about where she is by noon tomorrow."

"Sure," I said, about to change the subject and ask her if she knew how Brown and Curtis knew each other when a bumping sound from the laptop caught my attention. The green-hued view of basement stairs whirled and when the frame was steady again I was looking at the image of Ricky Butler prone on the concrete, naked, with a ball gag stuffed in his mouth. A clear watery substance bubbled out of his nose.

Caroline stood, flipped the laptop around, and looked at the screen. "The coroner told us the fluid on his lip, which is also in his lungs, is a telltale sign of opioid overdose."

She paused the video. I still didn't know if Geronimo had been caught on camera. If he had, I figured we were just getting started.

She sat down. "Tell me about your meeting with Ricky Butler five days ago."

Her question had nothing to do with Geronimo which surprised me a little, but I took it in stride. I told her that Butler was high when Russ and I confronted him in Annie's trailer, and that he told me I looked like a man named Paco Correa.

"Who's Paco Correa?"

"You tell me."

She shrugged with an amused, why-would-I-know-that expression on her face.

"I don't really know who he is either," I said, "but the things I'm learning make me think he might be my father. If he exists."

She frowned. "You have no idea who your father is?"

"Not counting Paco Correa, I don't."

"So you think there might be something to this?"

"My mother was white, and I have one of those faces that could pass for white or Mexican, so it's possible Butler was on to something."

She shook her head. "Your grandfather doesn't have any idea who your father might be?"

"He said he doesn't."

"Do you doubt him on that?"

"Hell, I don't know what to think anymore. Butler knew I was from Worthington. Even knew I was a judge. Knew my mother's name and that she'd died of a heroin overdose in '93, but said that wasn't the whole story. Said my mother was there when Paco was shot by Dean Curtis."

Caroline's jaw dropped a little. "Dean Curtis?"

"Yeah I know," I said.

"Did Butler say where this supposedly happened?"

"No, but wherever it was, he said my mother had gotten away. Said some cops killed her later and made it look like an overdose."

"Did you ask him who the cops were?"

"Yeah. He said if he told me that it would get us both killed."

Caroline's eyes grew distant. "Jesus."

"Turns out he had a tighter grip on reality than I thought," I said. "Any idea how Curtis and Brown knew each other?"

She puffed her cheeks out. "Yeah, that one's pretty easy. Brown hired on with the sheriff in '84. Curtis was on the sheriff's volunteer reserves from '91 to '94."

"What? Wasn't Curtis a billionaire by then?"

Caroline nodded. "A self-made man with no help from daddy, supposedly. I don't buy the self-made stuff myself, but whatever the case, in '93 he stood to inherit billions more when his father died."

I thought about that. "Why the hell would a guy that rich, with that background, join the reserves?"

"Who knows? NFL players serve turkey dinners to the homeless for the United Way and Dean Curtis volunteers for the reserves. How should I know? People do things. He did leave the reserves right after his dad died in '94."

"The Sedgwick County Sheriff's Office is pretty big," I said. "Any indication Brown and Curtis actually knew each other?"

Caroline nodded. "Oh, yeah. Brown was a deputy on third shift in the early nineties, and his partner in '92 and most of '93 was none other than Dean Curtis."

I sank back in my chair. "Partners. Shit. Partners in what?"

Caroline expelled a raft of air. "Besides what's in the public record, God only knows."

Her phone trilled. She pulled it out and looked at the screen. "I need to take this." She went out into the hallway.

I realized I didn't want any part of believing my parents were murdered. I'd grown comfortable with the old narrative, however false and however bad. I was the bastard child of a junky mother, orphaned by her addiction. Maybe Pops was right to let sleeping dogs lie. Could be too late for that. If Butler was right about his assassin, Dean Curtis had already let slip the dogs of war. Now that the KBI was on the scent, Curtis's and Brown's problems—whatever they were—would likely get worse. The conflict would widen, perhaps making me a target. I wondered if they knew about the video.

Caroline came back into the room and plopped down in her chair.

I said, "Have you approached Brown or Curtis with any of this?"

She shook her head. "Not yet. I'll let you know when that changes so you can brace yourself."

"No offense, but how long can a bunch of Harvey County cops keep a secret from a bunch of Sedgwick County cops? Brown and Curtis might already know about the video. How 'bout I go on high alert now?"

"That's what I'd do. In fact, that's one reason I'm here."

"Then thank you."

Caroline stole a glance at the clock on the wall. "Do you have any of your mother's old photos lying around I can have a look at? Maybe we get lucky and you have a picture of Paco in your attic you don't know about."

"If she had any old photos, I don't have them."

"What about your grandfather? Would he have them, if she had any?"

I shook my head. "I asked. He doesn't have any."

She sighed. "Anything else you can tell me about your past that might help?"

I told her about Brown's Georgian-style estate and my memories of having been there with my mother as a small child. I told her about the look of recognition in Brown's eyes when we met, and the look of fear that followed when he heard my name.

She said, "Seems like these guys had something to do with killing both of your parents."

"It's starting to look that way."

Caroline took that in, then stood with her briefcase and pushed the laptop closed. "To be continued."

She slid the laptop into her briefcase and threw its strap over her shoulder.

I stood to walk her out.

"I'll let myself out," she said, moving to the door quickly. "Gotta roll, I'm already late."

I came around the desk but she was already out the door. *To be continued?* Whatever she meant by that, for me it meant that I still didn't know if Geronimo had been caught on camera.

14

I MADE SURE Agent Gordon left the premises, then shut the door to my office and called Geronimo on my burner. He didn't answer. I left a one word voicemail: *Lebowski*. It was code we'd worked out and meant the cops were turning up the heat, which always required a change in burner phones and a discrete in-person meeting somewhere if possible. *Somewhere*—that was Geronimo's idea. He'd find me on his terms.

I called Pops and explained to him the bizarre and disturbing new information surrounding the death of his daughter. His response was operational, like the marine he'd always be, like there was nothing new under the sun. His house on B Street in Worthington backed up to the Catholic Academy's playground where the kids were in school. He said he would sit in the threshold of his open garage door and watch over recess in a couple of hours, just in case. He'd be packing his 1911 pistol and I knew there'd be other weapons stowed close by ready to go, including his M40 rifle, same model he used to notch approximately 283 kills as a sniper in Vietnam, 78 confirmed. When school let out, he'd walk down the alley and meet the kids at the front door. There was no hint of emotion in his voice and I couldn't decide if I thought him impervious to pressure or an echo of the man he must have been before the war. His daughter was dead and nothing could change that. The only thing he had was the present. Marines are practical people.

I was about to end the call when he surprised me with a change in tone.

"Benny."

"What?"

"You need to see me right away. There's something I need to show you."

Show me? My stomach dropped. Felt like bad news. An old secret crawling out of the gutter. I wanted to ask him what it was he wanted to show me, but didn't want to talk about it on the phone. Not until we put new burners in service anyway.

"I'm supposed to have a conference with Mia at the jail in an hour."

"Just get your ass down here now, okay."

"Okay. Be there as soon as I can."

"You eaten lunch?"

"No."

"Okay, good. Park in the alley. I'll roll a grill back there and throw some burgers on."

I called the jail and canceled my conference with Mia, then called Keri and told her what was going on. She would meet me at Pops' house in forty-five minutes. I changed into hiking boots and jeans. Opened a desk drawer. Pulled out my holstered Glock and shoved it inside my jeans at the small of my back.

*   *   *

I was fueling up at the turnpike service station when a man in his early twenties parked his Ford Explorer on the other side of the pump, got out, and said something to me. I didn't understand it because of his thick accent and the sound of traffic on the highways surrounding us. The wind lashed his long hair across his face as he pointed at a squeegee.

I waved my hand for him to take it.

He nodded and pulled the squeegee from its holder. Water spattered on the concrete and wet his running shoes, but his eyes were still on me.

"Geronimo," he said, louder this time. "Follow me."

We took the first exit off the turnpike. I followed him over dirt roads and paths to a spot behind a pumpjack bobbing up and down in the middle of an untilled field thinking there was no way this guy could've followed me to the gas station unless it was a multi-vehicle operation, which I doubted. I'd been paying close attention to my surroundings and never saw the Explorer until the man parked at the pump.

I pulled up next to him by the pumpjack and rolled down my window. He told me with a mixture of hand gestures and broken English to get in the Explorer with him.

"How'd you find me?"

He shook his head like he didn't understand but I saw a light of understanding in his eyes.

I buzzed the window up and shut off the engine. Got out and checked my truck's undercarriage and found a GPS tracker. I pulled it off and showed it to the man. He smiled and held up his cell phone. It had a map on it pinpointing our location.

I threw the tracker in the field and climbed into the Explorer, wondering how long Geronimo had been tracking me.

However Geronimo got that tracker under the truck, it might've explained how he found us on that lake in Missouri six days ago. Which got me to thinking about my departure from Kansas two years ago. I'd crawled around under my truck looking for trackers with a flashlight before leaving. I was thorough. Beyond thorough. Spent two hours checking and rechecking every inch of the truck. No way I could've missed a tracker back then when I'd just found one under the truck in less than ten seconds.

A sense of violation welled up in me as I considered the logistics of how this could've happened. Maybe, on our way to Idaho two years ago we'd been followed the old-fashioned way to a rest stop or a convenience store. A few seconds alone with my truck was all anyone would need. But trackers have batteries and batteries go dead. Someone would've had to replace them, or more likely, swap out the tracker for one with fresh batteries periodically, which meant Geronimo or someone sent by him would've had to have been under my truck in Idaho every month or so.

The driver took us down backroads to where Geronimo was waiting for me in a Suburban under enormous cottonwoods that lined the banks of the Arkansas River. He was parked on a weedy path next to concrete pilings that used to support a small house or maybe a hunting cabin. His windows were down and he was smoking a cigar. When I climbed into the passenger seat beside him and looked out the windshield, I could see mud-brown river water between a break in the foliage.

I told him about Agent Gordon's visit, including the video she showed me of a man in a mini-skirt and combat boots rendering Ricky Butler unconscious with a choke hold. I explained how Butler had been shot up with a lethal dose of Fentanyl. I didn't tell him that Dean Curtis's name had come up, and I left out the part about Ricky Butler uttering my name and making veiled references about my mother's death.

"I assume the guy I found dead upstairs—the dude dressed like a bitch—died the same way," Geronimo said.

"Yeah. How 'bout showing a little respect for the deceased? She was a human being."

Geronimo's eyes narrowed. "She?"

"Her name was Lucky Andrews. I'm told she identified as a woman."

"Uh, okay. If Lucky's a woman then my Mexican ass is a United States citizen—"

"Alright—"

"With a ten-inch dick."

"Look, Geronimo—"

"You think that shit would fly, man?"

I shook my head. "If that's what you want, you be you. You're Uncle Sam with a big flopper as far as I'm concerned. Just know it won't change anything. Your lady friends will still know the truth."

He grinned. "That's my fuckin' point, man."

"I don't have time for this right now. I'm concerned about you being caught on video."

"What?"

Something moving in the brush caught my eye and when I looked at it squarely I saw it was a St. Bernard padding toward the Suburban. Geronimo got out and opened the door to the middle row of seats for her. She jumped in heavily and stuck her wet nose and jowls across the center console onto my ear to say hello. I petted her, "Hey, Suzy girl, how you doin'?"

Over thirty years ago behind a bar in Laredo, an ambitious young trafficker named Jorge Mendez-Rodriguez unloaded three rounds of buckshot into a drug mule before taking off in the guy's pickup which had a pregnant St. Bernard named Suzy in the cab and five kilos of cocaine in the fuel tank. The drug mule bleeding out in the gravel was Geronimo's father, and Suzy was Geronimo's boyhood pet that Jorge kept as a living trophy that renewed itself with each new generation in Suzy's bloodline. When Geronimo finally killed Jorge two years ago, the revenge wasn't complete until he had the latest in a long line of dogs Jorge had named Suzy back where it belonged.

Geronimo climbed in and slammed the door. "So, what? Did you see me on that fucking video or what?"

"No, but the agent shut it off right after the man in the blond wig left. She told me the camera was motion activated and hidden in the bong on the table in the basement."

"There was a camera in the skull?"

"Yeah."

"Shit." He smoked—a slow meditation. "Then I'm on the video." He looked at me. "But my face was covered with a ski mask so I think I'm good."

Relief poured through me. "Good."

"This Agent Gordon, she the one that got herself shot looking for Detective Mallory?"

"Yeah, why?"

He picked a piece of tobacco off his tongue and wiped it on his jeans. "She's the smart one—the only one you think might be on to you, right?"

"She's the only one who's made it clear she suspects I know more than I'm telling. But by now, after two years of investigation, there's bound to be other suspicious cops"

"Yeah, okay I get that, but here's my point. She came to your office this morning and showed you this video, but didn't show you the part with me in it?"

"Yeah."

"She didn't break your balls about all that shit we went through two years ago?"

"That's right," I said, which wasn't really a lie because neither of my balls got broken.

He smoked. "That's good, I guess. Does she know I was Mallory's CI?"

"I dunno. Probably. She's good."

"That's weird, isn't it?"

I shrugged. "What's weird? That she's good?"

"No. That she didn't sweat you about her suspicions. Why the fuck wouldn't she? You better not be fucking with me."

"I'm not fucking with you."

"She's investigating Detective Mallory's murder, right?"

"Yeah. She did ask about that, but I told her I didn't know anything."

"But you were there when Miguel shot him to death."

"What's your point?"

He shrugged. "You didn't want to help her out with that, huh? A cop's murder?"

"I did want to, but I can't do that now can I?"

"And she accepted it?—that you didn't know shit about it?"

"Look, there's no way to just dip my toe in the water on this, so I lied. If I don't give her an inch, what can she do? This isn't Mexico. She can't just put a gun to my fuckin' head until she gets the truth."

He flicked ash off his cigar out the window. "You're not banging her are you?"

"What? No. Where'd that come from?"

"Not to sound like a fag, but you look like a guy the ladies get wet over." He shrugged. "Don't see it myself, but good for you. If this agent isn't jamming you up over the murder of a cop when she thinks you know what's up, I gotta think I'm missing something, and when I'm missing something I try to figure out who's payin' off who. But you're not the type to offer bribes and she don't strike me as the type to take 'em, so I'm thinking maybe you're breaking her off on the side, know what I mean?"

"I'm not, and you're way the hell off base."

"No offense, it's actually a compliment."

"No it's not, and here's what you're missing. Ricky Butler was Mia's pimp, remember? I represent Mia in a murder case and Agent Gordon has to go through her attorney, which is me, to talk to her."

He nodded and smoked. "She wants to talk to Mia, huh?"

She probably did, but it hadn't come up, perhaps because of time constraints. Caroline had ended the interview abruptly, saying she was already late for something. Geronimo and I locked eyes as I considered whether or not to tell him about Paco Correa and my mother's death and the billionaire named Dean Curtis.

"There is something else," I said. "But it's got nothing to do with you, or anything else from two years ago."

He eyed me through the cigar smoke drifting between us. I told him the whole story, from finding my mother dead in '93 to Ricky Butler's dying declarations, such as they were.

He opened the center console, pulled out an ashtray, and mashed the cigar into it. "Did the lady cop know who the guy was that killed Butler?"

"If she did, she didn't tell me. Why?"

"Maybe I can find him for you."

"You know who he is?"

"I didn't say that, but I might be able to find out. Professional murder-for-hire guys are a rare breed. Hard to find if you don't know where to look. But that's the easy part for someone like me. I know where to look."

I nodded. "Thank you."

He looked at me for long moment—long enough that it got a little weird. Long enough that I noticed things I hadn't noticed before, like Geronimo's bloodshot eyes and how loud the St. Bernard was panting behind us.

Finally he said, "I'll never forget what you did for me."

I nodded. "You trust me?"

"If I trusted anybody, it would be you. But no, I don't trust you. Why do you ask?"

"Because you need to trust me enough to let me talk to Carmen," I said. "Sooner, rather than later."

"What're you looking for?"

"I think you know. Mia didn't drop the axe on that ex-cop. Someone else did."

"I take it Mia still hasn't said who."

A hunch, but I didn't want to confirm it. "You're protecting Carmen, right?" I said.

He shifted in his seat and rubbed both sides of his neck with his hands. "Maybe. I'm not sure."

"Carmen's your girlfriend, isn't she?"

He sucked on his teeth. Stared through the windshield before finally nodding. "She won't tell me who did it, but I think she knows."

"The investigator working the case, Detective Riggins, thinks it was a man, or at least someone with some pretty good strength, more than Mia could do."

"Until Carmen tells me she didn't do it, you're not talking to her."

"Mia's petite. I figure there's a pretty good chance her sister is too."

"Carmen is almost as tall as you, brother." He looked me over. "And she's thicker than you. Big-boned girl, y'know what I mean? Put together well. She's fuckin' beautiful, man." He gazed out the windshield again. "She and Mia have different fathers. That came out when Carmen was in her teens. That's what caused their parents to divorce. That, and the fact that their mother was banging a neighbor."

"Jimmy Ray?"

"Shit, Ben, I didn't get a name."

"Jimmy Ray is the ex-cop that was murdered."

"I'm bad with names. I know him as that asshole-ex-cop-chomo-motherfucker."

"He was Mia and Carmen's neighbor growing up in the Delano district. The state's theory is that Mia killed him for having an affair with Mia and Carmen's mom and breaking up their family."

Geronimo shook his head. "That's some tangled-up shit right there. My understanding was that the guy was killed for raping Mia as a child."

"Carmen didn't say anything to you about an affair between her mom and this ex-cop that was murdered?"

"No, man, she didn't mention that her mom was bangin' the guy. I'd have remembered some messed up shit like that."

I decided Geronimo was telling me the truth so I moved on. "You said Carmen's a physically strong woman. Fits the profile Detective Riggins has in mind for the killer."

He nodded. "Yeah. She played softball at Wichita State. Led the Missouri Valley in homers one year." He squeezed his eyes shut. "See my problem here?"

"I can't defend Mia if everyone keeps me in the dark."

"Here's the thing. I don't think Mia told you who swung the axe. And Carmen won't talk to me about it either. Makes me think she might've done it. And there's something else . . . let's just say she has her own reasons to want to cut that fuckin' asshole cop's head off herself."

"Do me a favor will ya?"

His eyes found mine.

"Let me know if Carmen gives you the name of anyone else who might have a motive to kill this guy."

He nodded.

We exchanged cell phone numbers for our latest burner phones. I got out of the Suburban and faced him through the open window. "Hey, I found that tracker you put under my truck."

"It's convenient. For both of us."

"Bullshit," I said. "I took it off."

"Suit yourself."

"Did you track us two years ago when we left the state?"

"No."

"How'd you find us in Missouri then?"

He made a face like he'd caught a whiff of something rank. "Trade secret."

"Fuck you."

His face lost all expression. "Watch your tone."

I smiled but kept ice in my eyes. "Track me like that again and I'm off Mia's case."

Geronimo stared at me for a long moment. Finally, he said, "No tracker. We gotta trust each other even if we don't."

I nodded and walked to passenger side of the Explorer and climbed in next to the driver.

15

I PARKED UNDER the cottonwood tree on the east side of the alley behind my grandfather's detached garage. Keri and Pops were sitting in lawn chairs upwind from a grill and facing a playground flanked by baseball backstops on either end. Beyond the furthest backstop, the double doors of the school swung open and small children, probably kindergarteners, spilled into the sunlight.

When I stepped out of my truck, the smell of smoke from the grill was in the breeze. Pops got up and walked into the garage past his white Silverado. Keri stood and waited for me. We exchanged glances and joined Pops at his coffee-colored fiberboard workbench with its mounted vises and grinders and an intricate pattern of multi-colored stains I'd known for almost thirty years. The old beer fridge hummed as he sorted through keys on a ring. I ran my fingers over the bumpy pattern on top of the workbench, over a raised line of red paint I'd left behind decades ago, then picked at it until a piece of it flaked off.

Pops pulled the chain on an overhead light, opened a drawer with a key, pulled out a shoe box and dropped it on the workbench. "These were your mother's."

I looked at him. Pops' eyes were fixed on the box. Keri's were too—alive with anticipation and maybe a little fear.

"Go ahead," he said. "Take a look."

Pops glanced at me, then looked away. "You'll see."

I opened the box. It was full of three-by-five photos, some of them water damaged with curled edges. I splayed them out on the workbench. Most of them were childhood photos of me and Ashley in a time and place of which I had no memory. Our mother was in several of them: holding me or Ash as infants or toddlers; drinking beer with three other women in a low-rent motel room; standing on the shoreline of a lake somewhere in cut-off jeans. In all the photos, she wore the same pained expression that she tried to cover with a smile.

I picked up the photo of a man who looked more Mexican than me. Suddenly I knew what had sent Rick Butler and Undersheriff Brown reeling—a breathtaking moment when a long-hidden truth snapped through me like a jolt of electricity. I cleared my throat, staring into what felt like my own eyes. Keri's hand ran up the inside of my arm and gripped me tight.

The expression on the man's face was my own, like his cheekbones and the way he held his shoulders as he looked into the camera while sitting sunburnt at a Formica table in a wood-paneled kitchen somewhere with what looked like a glass of whiskey in front of him. I checked for writing on the back but there was none.

"Why didn't you tell me?"

"Assuming he's your father, he would've had more legal right to you than me. I couldn't risk it, so my plan was to keep this from you. That was always the plan, Ben. I'm sorry."

I nodded. "Do you know who Ashley's father is?"

"No, but I doubt it's that guy. She doesn't resemble him at all, but you never know."

"You ever meet this guy?" I said.

Pops shook his head.

"Do you know what became of him after Mom died?"

Pops drew in a deep breath. "I found those photos going through her things the day before her funeral. Saw the resemblance to you. So I visited a private investigator I knew in Wichita named Jake Brackeen and gave him a copy of the photo you're holding. Asked him if he could find the guy for me. I wanted to know if he was around. I wanted to know what to expect. I wanted to be prepared for the possibility he might show up one day and take you and your sister from me." Pops shook his head. "Jake didn't find the guy before the funeral and the guy didn't show for that, of course, but I decided I needed to find the guy anyway, so I could keep tabs on him from afar. In case he ever thought he wanted to dabble in fatherhood. After a week of poking around, Jake gave me my money back and said someone put a gun to his head and told him to leave it alone. He suggested I do the same."

"Did your PI find out anything useful at all?"

Pops grunted. "Useful? Don't know 'bout that. But he did tell me the guy's name."

Keri said, "Paco Correa?"

Pops nodded.

I looked at the photo, then back at Pops.

"Jake told me the good news was that he didn't think I had anything to worry about. Paco had gone missing. The fact that someone went that far to keep a PI from looking into it made Jake think Paco Correa might've been murdered."

"Anything else?" I asked.

He shook his head. "That's all I know. When a problem like that walks out of your life, you don't go chasing after it."

"Let it be?" I said.

"What's there to be gained?"

"Nothing, back then."

"Now, Ben." He glanced at Keri, then back at me. "What's in it for you now?"

"The truth," I said.

"At what cost?" said Pops.

He looked me in the eye, then Keri. He opened the fridge and pulled a plate of raw hamburgers out from between a battalion of Busch Lights and faked a smile. "Let's eat."

16

WHEN I STEPPED into the kitchen after getting home from work that evening, the kids were walking plates of spaghetti into the dining room and bickering about something. The timer on the oven was beeping. Leo yelled something about garlic bread. Keri bolted into the kitchen, handed me an unopened bottle of wine, and pulled the bread out of the oven. I stepped into the dining room. There was a big bowl of salad and four wine glasses on the table, two of them bubbling with sparkling water.

Keri handed me a corkscrew on her way past me with the bread, now steaming in a wicker basket.

"We celebrating something?" I said.

Keri set the bread on the table. "They wanted to make you dinner."

The kids were oblivious to our words because they were screaming at each other about whether or not we needed salad bowls.

When I realized Keri was watching me watch them fight, I returned her gaze.

Her eyebrows went up. "The wine was my idea."

Lindy was pro-salad bowl but Leo thought it would save a lot of trouble if we just put the damn salad on our damn plates.

"Stop cursing at your sister," I said.

"Why do we need bowls?" Leo said, his glare still on Lindy. "Just more dishes to clean."

"The heat from the spaghetti makes the lettuce gross." Lindy wasn't looking at her brother when she said this. Her appeal was to the adults in the room.

I nodded. "Put four salad bowls on the table and let's get on with our lives already."

Leo marched into the kitchen with a parting shot. "Fine, but she's doing the dishes."

Which caused Lindy to lag behind for one more point of order. "I did 'em last night, Dad."

I twisted the screw into the cork. "Ah, give it a rest, would ya?"

Lindy turned for the kitchen, utilizing patented body language she'd inherited from her mother, one part exasperation and one part *screw you.*

"Hey," I said sharply.

She flinched and looked back at me without the attitude she'd unwittingly flushed into the ether.

Leo stepped lightly into the doorway with a stack of bowls.

I smiled at the silence and nodded at the spread. "Thanks for dinner, guys."

* * *

After the kids were asleep, Keri and I set the security system to alarm mode and went to bed. We made love and fell asleep naked and spent in each other's arms.

I woke to what sounded like raindrops the size of pinballs pelting the roof. Keri was draped on me and my arm was asleep. I slipped out from under her. She moaned and found a pillow on her side of the bed. We lay on our backs and stared at the ceiling fan.

The rain hit harder.

"This thing with your mom," Keri said. "And Paco. I agree with Pops. I don't think we should push it."

"My mother may've been murdered. I'm supposed to let that go?"

"You could let Agent Gordon handle it. That's all I'm saying."

"She is handling it. Couldn't stop her if I wanted to."

"You know what I mean. Don't push it."

"You mean keep information from her. I thought about that and decided against it."

She touched my arm. "That's not what I'm saying. I meant, don't *you* get involved. You, Ben. Let her handle it."

"I'll give Agent Gordon the photo of Paco tomorrow, and when I do, like it or not, we'll be involved. More so than we already are. We'll be cooperating. Eventually, that will become apparent, and from the perspective of whoever may've killed my mom, we'll be pushing it."

"Then maybe you don't give Gordon the photo."

I shook my head.

"I'm sorry," she said, "but I don't think provoking these animals further is worth the risk."

"The KBI's involved, so it's too late. We're already at risk."

Keri sat up on an elbow. I could see her staring at me in the grey light. I waited for her to acknowledge that we were already at risk, but she never did.

I said, "If Dean Curtis doesn't know the cops are on to him about his hitman, he will soon. We're about to have one hell of a nervous billionaire on our hands, not to mention a nervous cop."

"You really think these guys will come after us no matter what we do from this point on?"

"They might. We have to be prepared for it."

"I think if we don't push the investigation, maybe the KBI won't either, and whoever has something to hide leaves us the hell alone. I think that's our best bet. I don't want to lose you."

"I don't want to lose you either, but I'm not comfortable banking on the mercy and humanity of degenerates. And the KBI is going to do what they're going to do. They're not going to back off just because we've gone silent about it."

"You make it sound so cut and dried and I don't think it is."

She got out of bed, put on her panties, then went into the restroom and turned on the light. Came back out and stood in the doorway. "If we're in that much danger already, then maybe we should go back to Idaho."

"We can't go back to Idaho."

"Why not?"

I told her about the tracker and the strong possibility that Geronimo had known our location for the last two years.

"Then we go somewhere else," she said.

"What about Mia? What about the two hundred grand Geronimo paid us?"

She shrugged. "We give the money back. We still have most of it. We're good for the rest."

"Is that what you want to do—go broke and back into hiding?" I said.

She shook her head. "God no. I'm just saying, if it's already that dangerous, and backing off won't save us, maybe we have no choice but to run. But you don't really believe we're already past the point of no return, do you? You're just using that as an excuse to do what you want and go after these guys."

She turned off the light and climbed into bed, propped herself up on her elbow again, looking at me. "If we're in that deep already, I say we pack our bags and leave. Now."

"We can think about it."

She shook her head. "Why wait?"

We stared at each other.

Finally she said, "You know this better than anybody. Sometimes the bad guys win."

"And sometimes they don't, but that doesn't just happen. Somebody has to stand up."

"Your mother has been dead for twenty-eight years. I don't want to offend you, but this has to be said. You're risking your life and the lives of everyone you love for two ghosts."

I thought about that. "Just polishing the rails of the Titanic, right?"

She nodded. "That's exactly right. So you push this thing, or God forbid, go after your mother's killers personally. Give me the best case scenario."

"What do you want me to say? That they end up in prison?"

"Would that satisfy you?"

My neck and ears felt as hot as my desire to kill whoever had killed my mother. If they had. I still didn't know.

She touched my cheek and traced a line to my chin. "You may never find out what happened back then, and even if you do, you can't change it and you can't change the world. Tell Caroline Gordon you don't want to open old wounds or something like that. Put the photo of Paco in a safe deposit box. Whatever you have to say or do to get her to drop it. But, if you really think it's too late, really feel that we're in danger, I think we should leave Kansas in the morning."

* * *

Two hours later Russ called and woke us up. Annie Black wasn't in her room at the Ambassador and he was calling from her trailer. She wasn't there either.

17

Tuesday, August 17

IT WAS RAINING when Annie Black walked under cover of darkness down the street from the Ambassador and met her Uber driver in a McDonald's parking lot. He took her south on Broadway over the John Macke Bridge past liquor stores and pawn shops, used-car lots, check-cashing joints and motels that rented rooms by the hour. She gazed through drizzle that was reflecting light from streetlamps along the strip, thinking about Russell Osborne and her last good kiss, back when she was sixteen, and how they had almost kissed again tonight. She'd felt her lips part when he leaned into her and caressed her cheek and said goodbye on his way out of her room, giving him a tender invite and a wordless yes, but one of them faltered. Maybe it had been mutual. She didn't know. The moment was intense, her memory of it already shrouded in fog. She knew Russ had a job to do and she had secrets she would just as soon die with. Maybe he did too. Maybe that's what stopped him—if he was the one that put on the brakes. Maybe he couldn't get too close because he had things he didn't want to tell her about himself. She hoped that was it. She wanted him vulnerable so she could accept him as he was and show him that none of it mattered. It would make it easier to tell him about her life, then there would be no secrets between them and they could finally see the truth of how the world conspired to keep them from a life together that should have been theirs.

The Uber driver tried to make small talk at first, but quit when he saw that Annie was preoccupied. She sat watching the world roll by outside her window, noticing the old building that used to be a waffle place and now housed her bondsman, then the hazy silhouette of a man urinating in the abandoned lot of a boarded-up porn store. She feared—being a pastor's daughter who'd been molested by her father—what the world would show her next.

* * *

Annie looked up at the gable of her five-year-old daughter's room, eyes pinched tight against the rain, a knapsack with a change of clothes and toiletries on her back. Except for light shining through a first-floor window, the old frame house was as dark as the sky and the miles of plains beneath it. She rubbed her eyes clear and looked behind her as the Uber driver turned left out of the gravel onto the blacktop. When the taillights disappeared into the night, she turned and climbed the steps to the front porch and dug in a planter full of dirt that sat next to the door for the key before remembering that she'd been given her own.

She pushed into the living room and jiggled her key out of the lock, shut the door behind her, then checked it twice to make sure she'd relocked it. The place was warm and smelled of cigars and cooking grease with a hint of something she'd always assumed was the stale odor of her uncle infused into the upholstered furniture, now stronger in the humidity. She pulled her coat tighter around herself and dripped water on the carpet on her way to the fireplace where her mother's brother had tacked a note to the mantle that told her to help herself to anything in the fridge. He'd had to leave for the hospital in a hurry because his daughter was in labor and there were complications. He didn't want to leave Annie's daughter, Amelia, alone for even twenty minutes but since it was late and Amelia was sleeping he figured it was better than taking her with him.

Annie went upstairs and down a hall to Amelia's room. She changed into dry underclothes, climbed into bed, and wrapped an arm around Amelia's tummy. On the edge of consciousness sometime in the night she heard a door open somewhere and figured her uncle was returning from the hospital. She sat up, listened. Decided she'd only heard sounds of the old farmhouse in the storm. Then she fell asleep.

* * *

Something nudged her shoulder. She opened an eye and shot bolt upright at the sight of a man standing over her and her daughter. Annie's throat constricted—felt like she was breathing through a straw. She saw by the glow of a lava lamp that the hair on the man's head was as short as the stubble on his face. His T-shirt cleaved wetly to his lithe torso. He put a gloved index finger to his lips.

"This doesn't involve her," Annie whispered.

"Then get up," he whispered back.

Annie got out of bed. The man had on combat boots that made her think this could be the guy that killed Ricky Butler. Russ had told her the whole story: how the killer had been dressed, how he'd met with a person named Lucky at a bar to get to Butler so that he could kill him and make it look like an accidental drug overdose.

Amelia mumbled, rolled over and faced away from them. They watched the child and when it was clear she was still asleep, the man grabbed Annie's elbow and pushed her ahead of him toward the door. At the bottom of the stairs he hooked an arm around her neck and shut down her carotid arteries.

She could breathe but was starting to black out. This was how Butler had been killed. With the last of her consciousness she realized her only hope was to give this guy information he might want.

"Cops know . . . you work for Curtis," she croaked.

He dropped her in a heap. She floundered, then got to her hands and knees, head hanging, feeling the blackness recede.

The man sat on his heels in front of her, elbows resting on his knees. She was breathing hard. And shaking. When her dizziness passed, she raised her eyes to his.

"What did you say?" the man said.

She'd gained a few seconds. She dropped her head again and breathed deeply.

The man cut his eyes to the top of the staircase, then grabbed her hair and pulled her head back up. "What. Did. You. Say?"

"The cops know you killed Butler."

She watched an artery throb in his neck.

"How do you know that?"

"You killed Butler on video, which the cops have. Now the KBI is going after Dean Curtis because you told Butler that Curtis sent you. But the KBI needs to find you to nail Curtis, which means—when Curtis finds out how bad you fucked up—he'll send someone to kill you whether you kill me or not."

Amelia appeared at the top of the stairs.

The man let go of Annie's hair and looked up at the little girl. "Goddamn you, woman," the man whispered.

Annie sat back on her haunches, tears filling her eyes. The man stood, his eyes on Amelia.

"Who are you?" Amelia asked.

"The tooth fairy," the man said.

"I haven't lost any teeth yet."

He nodded. "Right, your mom told me that."

The child wrinkled her forehead. "I thought you would look different."

"I get that a lot."

The man looked down at Annie. "I'm not supposed to let people see me. I'm already in a lot of trouble for that."

"I won't tell anyone," Amelia said.

Then man shook his head. "It doesn't matter anymore."

He walked out the front door into the storm.

18

THE STORM HAD passed when I parked my truck by the mailbox on the shoulder of the road in front of what Russ told me was Annie's uncle's house. I turned on the hazard lights in the gloom as the screen on my phone lit up. It was Russ. Forty-five minutes earlier he'd awakened me with a call to tell me that Annie had been attacked and her life threatened. She was okay, but scared. She didn't know the man's name, but we knew from what she told Russ that it was the same man who'd killed Ricky Butler. Since 911 would've dispatched deputies supervised by Undersheriff Brown to the crime scene, Annie didn't know what else to do but call Russ.

The house sat fifty yards off the road. A curtain moved in the front window. "Is that you out there?" Russ said. His Malibu was parked in the driveway near a side door.

"It's me," I said. "I'll wait out here until Agent Gordon arrives and gives me the okay to go in."

"The guy wore gloves, I told you that. There won't be any prints. There's nothing here to process."

"That'll be Caroline's call, not ours. I'll wait."

"Annie's not real happy with me for getting you involved. Please tell me that Caroline's supervisor agreed not to arrest her on the warrant."

"He did."

"And he's agreeing to leave the sheriff's department out of this investigation entirely?"

"For now, yes. I just got off the phone with Caroline. She even talked her boss into letting her take this call without backup from other bureau agents. Cut down the odds that word gets back to Brown. She should be here any minute."

"That's not gonna satisfy Annie."

I didn't mean to sigh, but I did, loud enough for Russ to hear.

"She doesn't trust anybody right now," Russ said. "She barely trusts me."

"I get it. Sit tight, I've already dealt the play."

I drank coffee and listened to the radio and waited. Not a car on the road. The casino several miles away lit up the southern horizon like a false dawn. I cracked the windows and cool air filled the cab with the smell of fresh rain. About the time headlights appeared from the north, I heard an engine crank up somewhere and before I could think too much of it something flashed in front of Russ's Malibu. I shut off the radio and buzzed the window all the way down. Whatever I'd seen was gone and I heard the unmistakable sound of an ATV engine screaming away into the night behind the house as a light came on over the side door. I snatched up my phone to call Russ but he beat me to the punch.

The screen door on the side of the house flew open and Russ shot out with a phone to his ear, stepping into the gap between the house and a shed. "She took off!"

"Get out of the way, Russ. I'm comin' through."

I put the truck in four-wheel drive and tore out down the gravel drive, past the Malibu, past Russ, into the back yard where I left deep ruts on my way to a trail in the woodland wide enough for a train, mumbling a string of curses. I clicked on the brights and followed Annie's tracks into a clearing where I stomped on the accelerator. The horses under the hood sang. I left a rooster tail of mud in my wake, making up enough ground to catch a glimpse of Annie on a four-wheeler as she disappeared through a narrow opening in the wildwood. I took my foot off the gas. No way through these trees in my truck and no quick way around them.

I dug a phone out of the center console that I'd dedicated to communicating with Caroline Gordon and called her.

She answered with, "Do you see her?"

"Not anymore. I take it you're at the house with Russ."

"Yeah, he told me what happened. Which way is she headed."

"West, last I saw. She's done trusting cops, and I'm about there myself. We don't need to involve any more agents, do we?"

"Not if we can find her," Caroline said. "I'll go west and try to get in front of her, but she might turn south or north. Pick a direction. The man that lives here is on his way back from the hospital I'm told. Russ will stay here with the kid."

She ended the call.

When I got back to the house Caroline was gone. Ten minutes later she called and told me her Crown Vic was stuck on a muddy backroad, buried to the axles.

"If you're going to work cases in rural Kansas, the KBI needs to issue you something with four-wheel drive," I said.

"Tell me something I don't fucking know or shut up."

I smiled, ended the call.

I picked her up and we cruised, windows down, listening for the whine of an ATV while Caroline scanned the countryside with a hunting spotlight she found in my back seat.

Just after six the sun came up and she put the spotlight away. I gave her the shoe box full of pictures of my mother and the one of Paco Correa. We continued searching for Annie, stopping only to grab McDonald's breakfast burritos and coffee. Three hours later we found a mud-caked four-wheeler in a shelterbelt near an overpass. It fit the description of the one taken by Annie. The engine was cold. The search for Annie wasn't over, but Caroline decided it was time to change tactics. I called Russ and told him Annie Black was in the wind.

* * *

Caroline called her boss to explain the situation while we made our way back to the house to talk to Amelia, Annie's little girl. I couldn't remember the name of Caroline's supervisor, something I blamed on exhaustion. Started with a "T" I thought. Whatever his name was, I could hear his voice seething with anger through the receiver for keeping him out of the loop, reminding Caroline that she was under explicit orders to keep him current on any new developments. He told her that once Annie made a run for it, it should have been his call whether or not to get other agents involved, or even the sheriff's office. The more he talked, the more convinced he sounded that Annie would have been found with a little extra manpower. The last thing I heard him say was that he was writing her up for insubordination.

When the call ended, I was busy picking a route through the sloppy backroads. I let her have a moment. Several. I waited for her to say something. She stared out her mud-spattered window at waterlogged fields glistening in the morning sun. Finally, I broke the silence. "You need more coffee? Another breakfast burrito? There's a Dunkin' Donuts on the turnpike."

"No thanks." Her voice was subdued.

More silence. I broke it again. "Look, I'm sorry—"

"It's okay. I made my decision. Now I live with it."

Ted—that was her boss's name. Ted Novacek.

"Is Ted involving other cops at this point? He didn't really say, from what I overheard."

Caroline shook her head. "Naw."

"How can you be so sure?"

"Ted's still an alright guy, but he's not the same man he used to be. He's learned the middle-manager game." She put a piece of gum in her mouth. "He has things right where he wants 'em. If the case blows up in the press and makes the KBI look bad, he'll sacrifice me to satisfy the brass above him. But if he calls the sheriff's office or some other agents in as reinforcements at this point and things go awry, then it's on him. His baby. His responsibility. And he can't have that."

"So he's mastered the subtle art of being a chickenshit. That's disappointing. I always liked Ted."

"You say that like he turned into a chickenshit the way people turn into zombies on TV—like maybe he got bit by another chickenshit or something."

"Maybe that's what's really going on. Metaphorically speaking."

She smiled faintly. "The chickenshit apocalypse?"

I shrugged. "They do seem to be multiplying."

"At least I can still get Ted to do the right thing most of the time. Might be for the wrong reason, but I can work with that."

"Life skills they don't teach you in school."

Caroline's smile dimmed. "Yeah."

*   *   *

Caroline tapped on the screen door with the back of her hand. We could see a burly old man in overalls with a beard the color of yellowed ivory sitting at a kitchen table.

"Come in," he called.

Caroline opened the door and we stepped in. The place smelled of old grease and cigarettes. Cigars maybe. Stale. Nobody was smoking at the moment. Russ was sitting across the table from the man and between them were dusty stacks of mail and a cast-iron paperweight in the shape of a revolver.

"Pull up a chair," the man said. "And help yourself to some coffee. Just made a pot." He pointed to the coffee maker on the counter next to some upside-down dishes on a towel.

We told the man we'd already had our fill of sitting and coffee. Caroline showed him her badge.

The man waved his hand dismissively. "Russ here already told me who you are." His eyes landed on me. "And you must be the lawyer that put those ruts in my yard."

He said "lawyer" the way folks that hate lawyers say lawyer—like an accusation. I told the man I was sorry and would repair the ruts or pay him for the damage. He told me a couple hundred dollars ought to settle the matter. I pulled out my wallet and handed him two hundred dollar bills.

Russ said, "Agent Gordon. Ben. This is Mr. Eugene O'Dell."

"Gene," the man said, setting the money next to his cup of coffee.

"He's Annie's uncle. He's also the legal guardian of her five-year-old girl, Amelia."

Caroline and I nodded our greeting.

Gene squinted at Caroline. "Amelia's asleep upstairs. Russ tells me you want to have a word with her."

"If you don't mind," Caroline said.

"I don't know what good it'll do," Gene said, picking up his cup.

"What makes you say that?" Caroline asked.

Gene took a drink. Swallowed. "On account she's five."

"Gene's right, she can't help us much," Russ said. "She saw a man at the bottom of the stairs standing over her mother. He said he was the tooth fairy. She didn't buy it, but pretended to. She didn't say this, but I think the kid somehow knew it was a good idea to play along."

"Can she describe him?" Caroline asked.

Russ shrugged. "Not well. She said his clothes looked wet. I got a couple other tidbits out of her. She said his hair was prickly and he had skin the color of mine. So . . . white guy with a buzz cut."

Gene put his cup down. "Lemme ask you somethin', miss. Is Annie in some kind of legal trouble?"

Caroline shook her head. "Not that I know of."

A lie, but necessary. There was a warrant for Annie's arrest, which the KBI said they wouldn't execute. The truth was complicated, and telling it to Gene was counterproductive to finding Annie.

"Not that you know of?" Gene shot me a look. Real deadpan.

"Your niece was attacked," Caroline said. "I'm . . . we're trying to protect her."

"Okay," Gene said.

"Okay, what?" Caroline said.

"Okay, so that's how you're gonna play it."

"I'm not trying to play you."

"Sure you are, you—" Gene had raised his voice. He seemed to check himself, but I could still see the fire in his eyes. "You mean to tell me you don't find the fact that she run from you suspicious?"

"Not particularly, no," Caroline said.

Gene made a face—amazed disbelief this time.

Caroline said, "I take it Russ hasn't told you what's going on."

"I didn't get into the sensitive details with him," Russ said. "Figured that's your call."

Caroline pulled back a chair from the table, sat, and gave Gene an earnest expression. "There might be some people out there with strong ties to the sheriff's office who want Annie dead. Some of them may even be cops."

"Which is why she called me," Russ said, "not 911."

Gene grunted. "I don't suppose any of you can tell me who these people are and why they want to kill her?"

"That's what I'm trying to figure out," Caroline said. "I need to speak with Amelia. Me, personally. Russ doesn't work for the KBI."

Gene considered that, then looked at me, his bearded jaw jutting out. "You're Annie's lawyer, what do you think I should do? Should I let them talk to her girl?"

"I'm not Annie's lawyer," I said.

"I never told you that," Russ said to Gene.

"You let me think it."

"How do I know what you're thinking?"

"What the hell's the lawyer for then?"

"I got Ben involved because I work for him as a private investigator and he's working a case that involves Annie. He got Agent Gordon involved because he trusts her. Annie ran because she doesn't know who to trust."

"That makes two of us," Gene said. He honed in on Caroline again. "What happens if I send you off without speaking to the girl?"

I cut in. "Then Agent Gordon will have a tough decision to make. She can just drop it. Or, run to the DA for a subpoena and hope no one in that office is connected to the people that want Annie dead."

Gene looked down at his hands. They were thick, dry and gnarled, wrapped around his porcelain cup. "My God. Annie's had a hard time of it her whole life. She never had a chance."

"I know," Russ said.

Gene looked up at him. "I remember you."

Caroline shot a questioning look at Russ, then me.

Gene continued. "You was a regular part of the family there for a while. I used to tease Annie about you before she got pregnant and her daddy sent her off to Texas."

Russ glanced around the room. Noticed Caroline glaring at him, then looked back at Gene.

"How'd you come out in life?" Gene asked him. "You have a family of your own now?"

"I had a wife and son," Russ said.

Gene grimaced. "Had?"

Russ nodded.

"Well," Gene said, "Sorry I brought it up then."

Russ leaned back and crossed his legs. "Son died of bone cancer. Once he was gone my wife and I turned on each other. Got divorced. Both our faults."

Five seconds passed. Finally, Gene said, "How'd you and Annie hook up again?"

"What do you mean?" Russ asked.

"I figure one of you must've looked the other up recently, then nature took its course." He smiled. "She called you tonight, so you must still be important to her. Maybe the angels started singing again."

Russ smiled. "I found her. Then took her to jail."

Gene frowned. Looked a question at Russ.

"I also work for a bail bondsman," Russ said. "She jumped bond. I brought her in six days ago. Talked the guy I work for into bonding her back out. That's how Russ-and-Annie two-point-oh got started."

"That don't seem right," Gene said. "That she meant so little to you that you could take her to jail like that."

Russ sucked on his teeth. Looked away from Gene.

I let my eyes wander to Caroline. She looked pissed off. I knew what she was thinking. Russ was on contract with Tony Cornejo to bring Annie in on another outstanding warrant. Cornejo stood to lose ten grand if Annie wasn't in custody within thirty days. Maybe Annie hadn't gotten away from Russ after all. Maybe he was still sweet on her and let her go when he learned the KBI was on the way. Maybe he just couldn't risk the KBI going back on its word and putting her in a jail run by a guy who'd raped her—a guy with a motive to silence her.

I thought all that and more. I wondered if the blue Mustang across the street from Mia's house on the day of Jimmy Ray's murder was Annie's. I wondered if the unidentified little girl who was in the back yard with Jimmy Ray was Amelia. And I wondered if Caroline had the police reports from Jimmy Ray's murder. If she did, we could be thinking the same thing. Annie Black might've murdered Jimmy Ray, and Russ might've just looked the other way while she made her getaway.

"Of all the people in the world, you had to be the one to take her to jail," Gene said.

"You can't make me feel any worse than I already do," Russ said. "I know what she's been through."

"You might think you do," Gene said. "But you don't. You don't know the half of it."

"You're probably right. I've barely talked to her since high school."

"You were just a kid. You don't know half the shit she went through back then either."

"Funny, I don't remember meeting you. Don't remember Annie ever talking about you either."

"One of the many things she never talked to you about." Gene stared into his cup. "I lived in Texas when you were in high school, so no, we've never met. I saw pictures of you two at the prom. Heard all about you from my sister."

Russ looked puzzled. "You're the uncle Annie was sent to live with in Texas?"

"No. That'd be her Uncle Mac. Father's side. Pastor Black's brother. He died in '05." Gene coughed into his fist. Fixed his eyes back on Russ.

"What don't I know about Annie that you think is so important?" Russ said.

Gene tapped a scaly finger on his mug. "When it hit me who you was a few minutes ago, I reckoned she may've told you."

The two men stared at each other in silence.

Finally, Gene shook his head. "This conversation would have gone much differently if she had."

Russ studied Gene for a moment.

"What doesn't Russ know about Annie?" Caroline said. "I'd like to know."

"If Annie wants you to know, miss, I'll let her tell you herself."

"Alright fine," Caroline said. "Do you know where I can find her? Any guesses?"

Gene shrugged. "If she doesn't want to be found, no idea." He pushed back from the table and stood. "Sit tight. I'll go wake Amelia. Won't do you any good but I guess you'll have to see that for yourself."

* * *

Russ and I stayed in the kitchen with Gene while Caroline interviewed Amelia in the living room. In the awkward silence, I wondered if Annie had hidden the pornographic photos of Mia somewhere in this house.

I sat next to Gene and asked him if Annie came to see her daughter often and he told me she did. I asked him if he knew who Amelia's father was and he said he didn't. Russ was slouched in his chair, watching us with a glazed look of exhaustion on his face. I asked Gene if Annie kept any of her belongings here and he bluntly told me he wasn't going to allow me to search for anything.

That amused Russ.

"What's so funny?" I said.

Russ stood and walked to the door. "Let's talk outside."

I followed him to the trunk of his Malibu. He opened it, reached in, and pulled out a Manilla envelope and handed it to me. "Annie gave me the porn photos of Mia before she left," he said. "There you go."

"Where'd she get them?"

"Said she stole them from Ricky Butler. Got them out of his safe at the club the night she was raped by Brown."

"Mia told me Ricky Butler wasn't in the photos."

"He's not."

"Then how'd Butler get his hands on them?"

"Annie has no idea, but she recognized Mia, of course, and she even recognized Brown, in that stupid President Collins mask. Brown was a regular customer of Annie's. She knows his body, right down to the birthmark shaped like Israel on his ass."

"Why'd Butler have the photos—blackmail?"

Russ shrugged. "Maybe, but they're of limited use for that purpose because the men wore masks, but that was Annie's guess too—blackmail. Butler's usual M.O.—collect info on anyone and everyone, then use it to thrive and survive. Law of the jungle."

"What was she going to do with the photos?"

Russ kicked at the gravel. "She was hoping to use them to get out of her possession charge with them somehow. Leverage Brown into pulling some strings for her. She hadn't worked out the details, but she thought she might threaten to show the photos to Brown's wife. Even with the Slick Willie mask on, his wife would recognize the birthmark on his ass. When Brown raped Annie, those pictures were in that envelope right there on the backseat of her Mustang."

Caroline came through the screen door, pointed up the driveway toward the blacktop and walked past us. We followed. Halfway to the road she turned and squared up on us. Asked me if I knew about Russ's relationship with Annie. I told her I did.

She glared at us.

Russ put a cigarette in his mouth.

Caroline motioned to Russ. "Tell me about you and Annie. Sounded pretty heavy."

Russ lit his cigarette and told Caroline that he'd gotten Annie pregnant in high school and that Annie's father had sent her to Texas for an abortion. He told Caroline about the lie Annie's father told his congregation about Annie's supposed miscarriage.

"Annie getting away like this looks bad for you," Caroline said.

Russ shrugged. "She got spooked. Thinks maybe the KBI is dirty, or would go back on their word and take her to jail for jumping bail, so she ran off."

Caroline smirked. "Or, maybe she thought I'd bust her for murdering Jimmy Ray?"

Russ gave me a questioning look.

Caroline noticed. "Don't look at him, I know about the blue Mustang at Mia's house and the unidentified little girl in Jimmy Ray's backyard on the evening of the murder from my source at the PD. I have all their reports."

We stared back at her like two kids in the principal's office. She seemed to be waiting for one of us to talk. Finally, she said, "I know Annie owns a blue 2020 Mustang."

"Has Detective Riggins put any of this together yet?" I asked.

"I don't know," Caroline said, her eyes still focused on Russ. "How long have you known Annie had a five-year-old girl?"

"Just found out tonight," Russ said.

"Was she the little girl with Jimmy Ray in his back yard on the evening of the murder?"

Russ nodded. "Yeah. I didn't get that from the little girl. I got it from Annie. All Amelia could tell me was that Mia was one of her babysitters and that she hasn't been to Mia's house in a while. And she doesn't remember any of Mia's neighbors, so I think that's good. I don't think Jimmy Ray touched her."

Caroline looked off in the distance. "I think we all know Annie is the prime suspect in Jimmy Ray's murder at this point, so no bullshit, Russ. Did you ask Annie if she killed Jimmy Ray?"

"Yeah, I asked. She said she didn't do it."

"Does she know who did?" I asked.

"If she does, she wouldn't say."

"Was that her Mustang that was parked in front of Mia's house on the evening of the murder?" I asked.

Russ nodded. "Yeah, but someone else was driving it that night. She won't say who." He shrugged. "Maybe she's lying and it was her, I don't know."

"Someone else picked up Amelia from Mia's house on the evening of the murder? Is that what Annie's saying?" I said.

"That's what she says. I asked Amelia to tell me all the people she could remember who have ever picked her up from Mia's house and all she'd say was her mommy. If someone else picked her up back in March, she has no memory of it."

"This looks real bad for you, Russ," Caroline said again.

"I'm aware of that."

"Did you tell Annie she ought to run tonight?" Caroline asked.

"Of course not."

"Maybe you told her where to run to. Maybe you're going to meet up with her later. Protect her. Sleep with her. Fall in love all over again."

"Fuck you," Russ said. "She went out the bathroom window after I told her you were coming. She doesn't know who to trust right now, that's all."

"You don't know that," Caroline said. "Maybe she's running because she's guilty of murder. According to her Uncle Gene, there's a lot about Annie you don't know."

Russ took a drag. Let smoke trickle out of his mouth. "I'll give you that one. I figure the old man knows what he's talking about."

* * *

On the ride home I called Caroline to speak with her alone.

"Did your source at the PD give you copies of the crime scene photos too?" I asked.

Silence. Finally, she said, "Yes, why?"

"Because there's a dried stain on the grip end of the axe handle. Looked like an older bloodstain to me. If the reports I have are accurate, no one's taken a sample of that stain and run it through CODIS."

Combined DNA Index System.

"You're thinking Annie's DNA profile is in the database because she was arrested?"

"No, not yet. I understand the KBI is way behind on entering the profiles into the system, but eventually it'll be there."

"Maybe by sometime next year."

"Way too late to help my client."

"Not my case, not my problem. Why'd you call?"

"To ask a favor."

"I'm listening."

"Can you think of any way to get a sample of the dried bloodstain on that axe?"

"Yeah, counselor, you hire a DNA expert and file a motion with the court. Think evidence and chain of custody."

"Do you trust Detective Riggins—or anyone else on the PD—not to manipulate the evidence if I get a court order?"

"Yeah, probably. I'm pretty sure Riggins is clean at least."

"Pretty sure?" I said. "Is that why you got the reports in this case from your source on the PD as opposed to just calling up the lead detective and asking for them?"

Silence. Then, "Detective Riggins never picked up the evidence from the lab. The axe is still there."

"How do you know that? Your source?"

"No. I know the DNA analyst assigned to the case. Cass Witham. We talk. Everyone calls her Mama Cass."

"You trust her?" I asked.

"Oh yeah."

"Well, there you go."

"There I go, what?"

Ask Cass to take a sample of the stain."

"And do what with it? Compare it to what?"

"To the samples you get out of Annie's trailer. I'll show you where she lives."

"I know where she lives. You want me to get a search warrant to swab Annie's trailer for her DNA?"

"Yeah, why not?"

"Because I don't work for you."

"You're a cop, solving a murder."

"It's not my case."

"It should be. Jimmy Ray was ex-PD. No way he doesn't still have friends on the force."

"He doesn't . . . because he's dead."

"You know what I mean. The PD should've handed this off to the KBI on day one. Ask Ted for permission to pursue this."

"I don't—"

"Do you know a judge who can keep his mouth shut about this if you approach him for a warrant to swab Annie's trailer for DNA?"

"Of course."

"There you go. That wasn't so hard, was it?"

Caroline laughed. "I'll run your idea by Ted. No promises."

"I'll owe you one. A big one."

"That and six bucks'll get me a latte at Starbucks. I got a better idea."

"What is it?"

"I need you to show something to Mia for me. Ask a few questions. Report back."

"You don't want to raise an alarm with Undersheriff Brown by visiting Mia in the jail."

"Yep," Caroline said. "You got it. And I don't want a latte. I want tacos. Grab some and meet me at your office in an hour. I'm going to download the video of Butler's murder onto your phone, and you're going to show it to Mia for me. I want to know if she recognizes the killer."

"Got it, I just need to know one thing."

"What?"

"Corn or flour?"

19

IT WAS MIDAFTERNOON when I sat across from Mia in the jail visitation room. Her jumpsuit was red this time, not orange, which meant she'd gotten herself into trouble with the jail staff.

"You look good in red. What happened?"

"Fight."

"You win?"

"No one did."

"No one ever does."

She rolled her eyes. "Guards broke it up."

No marks on her, other than some small abrasions on her knuckles. It was clear she didn't want to talk about the fight, which was fine with me. Put enough unstable folks in the same area together for months on end, shit happens. I was worried about her but decided to drop it for now. We had a lot of ground to cover and I was anxious to get started.

"I know Annie has a five-year-old girl named Amelia," I said.

Mia's face clouded. She glanced around our little glassed-in closet of a room. Given what I knew about this case so far, I wasn't about to label her paranoid for thinking Undersheriff Brown might have the visitation rooms bugged. I nodded my understanding of her unspoken concern and checked for hidden recording devices. When I sat down again I told her we were all clear, but she looked even more troubled than she had seconds earlier.

"I know you were babysitting her on the evening of the murder," I said. "She was the little girl the neighbor saw in Jimmy Ray's backyard with him."

Mia picked at a hangnail.

"How'd she end up on Jimmy Ray's side of the fence?" I asked.

Mia's eyes lost their focus.

"Come on," I said. "Annie was there that night picking up her daughter wasn't she? If she was the killer, this could be your ticket out of here."

"Did you talk to Annie?"

"Russ did—the investigator I hired."

"What'd she tell him?"

"Never mind that. Tell me what happened."

She slouched back in her chair. Gazed at the little table between us.

"Look," I said, "ever since she was arrested on possession, there's been a buccal swab with Annie's DNA on it floating around in the justice system somewhere. Maybe it's with the sheriff's office or sitting in a KBI evidence locker, who knows? Point is, one way or another, someone will eventually test Annie's DNA against the old stain on the grip end of that axe handle. If Annie killed Jimmy Ray, you might as well tell me now, before the DA has enough evidence to prove the case against her without you." I gave her a moment, then said, "Before the DA has a chance to offer Annie a deal to testify against you."

She leaned forward, stabbed the table with a finger. "As my lawyer, you have to keep me informed of all the major developments in my case. That's in the agreement you signed with me."

"I know what's in the agreement. I wrote it."

"Good. Then tell me what Annie said happened."

"She denies killing Jimmie Ray."

Mia's eyes grew distant while she processed the information. "What else did she say?"

"Said someone else was driving her car that night. Whoever it was picked up Amelia from your house. Is that what happened?"

"Yeah, someone picked up Amelia."

"No shit. Who?"

She shut her eyes and let her head droop.

"I can't do my job if you keep information from me."

"I'm not stopping you from doing your job."

"The hell you aren't. You're keeping me in the dark. Who are you protecting?"

"Maybe myself. Maybe Ricky Butler took Jimmy's head off and I'm too afraid to tell anyone."

I laughed. "Is that supposed to be a joke?"

"What's so funny?"

I looked at her with one eye. "You really haven't heard?"

"Heard what?"

"Ricky Butler's dead."

Her mouth fell open.

"A lot of things have changed since I saw you on Thursday. You haven't heard anything in here?"

She shook her head. "No. What happened?"

"Butler was murdered four days ago."

I told her how Ricky Butler was found in a rural farmhouse in Harvey County with another murder victim by the name of Lucky Andrews. She said she wasn't familiar with the location and didn't know anything about a Lucky Andrews.

"Do the cops have any suspects?" Mia asked.

"That's part of what brings me here. The KBI is handling the Butler and Andrews' double homicide. I know the lead investigator well. Her name is Caroline Gordon. We can trust her. She gave me something to show you."

"Why didn't she come herself?"

"She doesn't want to give Brown or anyone connected to him reason to think you might know anything that could help solve Butler's murder. She doesn't want to put a target on your back."

"She thinks Brown had something to do with Butler being murdered?"

"She's not ruling anything out. She gave me a video for you to watch."

I took out my phone and found the video, which showed Lucky Andrews and Butler being killed. If Caroline had footage of Geronimo, she was still hiding it from me for some reason. I hit play and handed Mia the phone.

She watched slumped over, clutching my phone with one hand and her side with the other. She stared silently at the screen. When the video ended, she was pale and looked like she might throw up.

"I'm sorry you had to see that," I said. "Are you alright?"

She leaned forward, handed me the phone. "I'm fine."

"Can I get you some water, or a bucket?"

"I said I'm fine."

I gave her a moment.

When her color returned, she said, "Remember me telling you about the guy called Youngblood who took those photos of me that Annie had?"

"Yeah."

"That's him on the video dressed in drag. He was also the photographer in the Trump mask."

"How do you recognize him?"

"His legs. Best set of legs on a man I've ever seen. And that's his voice. It's him."

"Have you ever seen his face before now?"

"No. But that's him. I'm certain of it."

"But you don't know his name?"

She shook her head. "Not unless it's actually Youngblood, which I doubt."

"Is there anything else you can tell me about him?"

She thought about that. "This might sound stupid, but he seemed kind of . . ."

She slumped back in her chair, hugging herself.

"He seemed kind of what?"

"It's stupid. Doesn't make any sense."

"Just say it. The world is full of stupid shit that doesn't make sense."

"He seemed kind of . . . I dunno . . . almost religious in a way, y'know? The way he turned down what was being offered to him by the men."

"Meaning sex with you."

"Yeah. It's like he had a moral objection to what was going on."

I nodded, trying to process the information. "He had a moral objection to what the men were doing to you, yet he was recording it."

"See what I mean? It doesn't make sense."

"I get what you're saying, but trust your gut on this. What makes you think he had a moral objection to what was happening?"

She shook her head and shrugged. "Things he said, I guess. Like he was disgusted by what was going on. Like he wasn't a part of what was happening. Like he was above it all and thought he was better than us."

"Are you saying he was judgmental?"

"Yeah, that's what I'm trying to say."

"Can you think of something he said that made you think that?"

Her eyes narrowed. "We took a break at one point and the guys were wandering around the hotel room and going in and out of the restroom and one of them asked Youngblood if watching us made him feel like joining in. Youngblood said we were less interesting to him that dogs humping in a ditch."

"How did the men respond to that?"

"They laughed and Brown made a big deal out of offering Youngblood a turn with me, but Youngblood turned his back on Brown. Brown said that anyone that would pass up a hot piece like me must be a fag. He said stuff like that a lot that night. He was such an asshole."

"To be clear, you're talking about Undersheriff Clint Brown?"

"Actually, I didn't know it was him at the time. I figured it out later."

"How'd you do that?"

"Wasn't hard. He started showing up at my house the day after we made the video. Asking me to go places with him. He followed me to bars and he would be at my car sometimes after work behind Ricky's club."

"Did you ever go anywhere with Brown?"

"No. I told him he had to go through Ricky."

"How'd Brown take that?"

"Not well. He threw the flowers he tried to give to me on the hood of my car and called me the 'c' word."

"He brought you flowers?"

She nodded. "And they say romance is dead."

I stifled a laugh, cleared my throat, and got back to business. "I'm playing devil's advocate here, okay? How do you really know Brown was one of the men in the masks?"

"Well, the timing of when he started stalking me was a lot of it, but also, his legs." She laughed. "Maybe I have a thing for legs. Not his though. His were really, really short and . . . not attractive at all. I guess it was the general shape of his whole body and the way he moved that made me realize it was him as much as anything. He kind of waddled, y'know? I noticed that when he was walking around the room naked."

"Waddling?"

She nodded.

"Kind of like a penguin?" I said.

She shrugged. "I guess. Or a duck."

That put a smile on my face. "Was there video surveillance behind Ricky's club when Brown threw the flowers on your car?"

"No. Ricky didn't want surveillance back there. He was doing more illegal shit back there than anyone else."

I nodded.

She said, "Okay, what else?"

"Excuse me?"

"You said a lot of things have changed since Thursday. Tell me about the other big haps."

"Oh, sure. Big haps. How 'bout this? I actually have those photos that Youngblood took. Some of them anyway."

Her eyes grew wide.

"My investigator got them from Annie last night. There are twenty of 'em. Got 'em right here."

I reached into the leather briefcase at my feet and set the photos on the table. She picked up the one on top. Seven photos deep into the pile she said, "This is Brown."

She spun the photo around, and put a finger on the image of a narrow-shouldered, pear-shaped man in the mask of our forty-second president, Bill Collins. Brown had a handful of Mia's hair, using it to haul her head back toward him, making what Shakespeare called "the beast with two backs." There was a birthmark shaped like Israel on his left butt cheek.

I nodded. "Thank you, Mia."

"What do these photos have to do with my case?"

"It's a piece of the puzzle. Might be a piece that could fit into several puzzles, who knows?"

"You have no idea, do you?"

"That'd be correct." I gave her a smile. Before she could stop herself, she smiled back.

I tapped my finger on the photos. "Who set all this up? Tell me about the arrangements."

She made a face like she thought it was a stupid question. "Ricky sent me on a call. Hotel room on south Broadway. One thing led to another, like it always does. Escorts that don't put out on a first date aren't in high demand if you know what I mean."

"Okay, yeah, but . . ."

"You'd like to think I was raped or at least manipulated or taken advantage of, wouldn't you?"

"Doesn't matter what I think."

"You remind me of Youngblood, in a way. You don't want to think of me like that."

"Like what?"

"Like some dirty dog humping in a ditch."

"I'm not judging you. I'm trying to help you."

"The best explanation for why I had sex with those men is that they paid me ten grand."

"That's part of what I'm asking about—the arrangements. Who paid you?"

"Youngblood gave me the money in cash."

"You directly—the money didn't go through Butler?"

"It happens that way sometimes."

"Did that mean anything to you?"

"Cash transaction involving masked men and a vid meant a premium for kink and being discrete was agreed upon. It could be that this was somebody Butler owed money or a favor to."

"So Youngblood actually paid you, but do you know where the money came from?"

"I assumed the men pooled their money, but I have no idea. After it was over, as he was paying me, Youngblood asked if I'd like to go on a tropical vacation sometime."

"With him?"

"No no, I don't think so since he'd shown no interest in me. I assumed he was approaching me on behalf of one of the guys in the group."

"Brown?"

She shrugged. "That'd be my guess, but I don't know."

"Were any of the other men around when he propositioned you?"

"No. Just me and him. The others had left."

"What'd you say?"

"I asked him how much it paid, and that's when it got weird."

"*That's* when it got weird?"

She nodded. "Okay, weirder. He said it paid more than I could imagine and would cost me everything I had."

"Not the best sales pitch I ever heard. Did you ask him what he meant by that?"

"No. Sounded like some kind of creepy-ass religious bullshit to me, like he was trying to warn me off accepting the offer, like if I did accept, I'd lose my everlasting soul or something."

"So, if he's trying to warn you off because he's concerned about your everlasting soul, why make the offer at all?"

"None of what this guy said or did made any sense."

I shrugged. "Or, in this instance, maybe he meant something else."

"Like what?"

"Hear me out, I realize he's probably propositioning you for sex with whoever he's working for, but if he's some kind of religious nut, maybe he's involved in some kind of cult. Maybe he was telling you the cost of discipleship. It almost sounds to me like this guy was mimicking the Bible—your reward would be great, but you'd have to give up life as you know it to take the deal."

She nodded. "Whatever he meant, something about the guy felt all wrong. Like he might snap any second. I told him I wasn't interested."

I asked her several questions that yielded nothing earth shattering before circling back to the heart of her case—the part she was hiding from me.

"Tell me who killed Jimmy Ray."

"You're holding out on me."

"Oh, *I'm* holding out on *you*?"

She shrugged. "Your investigator questioned Annie, and I'm supposed to believe that the only thing he got out of her is that she denied killing Jimmy Ray? I find that hard to believe."

"I guess there is something I haven't told you."

She perked up.

"Youngblood tried to kill Annie last night."

Mia's head jerked back.

"She survived," I said. "Youngblood tried to strangle her at her uncle's house—out in the country, in Brown's jurisdiction—so instead of calling 911, Annie called my investigator, Russ. When Annie found out that Agent Gordon was on her way to the scene of the attack, she took off and we haven't been able to find her. Russ didn't get a lot of time to question her."

"Jesus."

"Now, how 'bout you stop jerking me around and tell me who killed Jimmy Ray."

"I'm not a snitch."

"I'm not a cop."

"The next time you come here you'll try to convince me to be a snitch for the cops or the DA or whoever to save my own ass. That's how it works, isn't it?"

"Sometimes."

She shook her head. "Bigknife predicted that. The way of the white man is to turn us against each other."

I chuckled. "'The way of the white—Bigknife doesn't know me."

"She was in the room next to us the first time you were here."

I ignored Mia's last statement because I realized I'd missed an opening to explore who wielded the axe against Jimmy Ray. "Back up ten seconds. Bigknife said the way of the white man is to turn us against each other? Who's 'us'? Who am I turning against each other? You and your sister? You and Geronimo? Hispanics in general?"

"Nice try."

I spent the next five minutes trying to convince her to tell me who killed Jimmy Ray, to no avail.

A lawyer I knew sat down across from an inmate in the room next to us. The back of his balding head loomed over Mia through the thick safety glass behind her. "'Turn us against each other,'" I said, "is that you talking, or Bigknife?"

"Bigknife."

"Thought I told you not to talk to her."

A half-smile formed on Mia's face. "I didn't, for the most part, but I was stuck in a cell with her. She figured you'd told me to stop talking to her and predicted you'd remind me to keep my mouth shut around other people each time we met."

"So what? She knows sound legal advice when she hears it and doesn't want it to shut down her game."

"What's her game exactly?"

"Jailhouse snitch. She's always pumping you for info, right? She's the fuckin' snitch. She's probably spent more time in a courtroom than half the bar in this state. What else did she say?"

The half-smile disappeared.

"Come on. What else did she say?"

"She predicts that you'll ask me where she got her law degree." Mia laughed. "Well, I doubt you'll do that now."

"Bigknife has obviously been in the system for a long time."

Mia's smile was back, bigger than before. "She predicted you'd say that as well. She says you're so rooted in your system of privilege that the sound of it rolling off your own tongue every day has become nothing more than white noise to your white ears."

White noise to my white ears. My half-white ears? I didn't really know. I laughed. A little at first, but the more I laughed the funnier things seemed and when I tried to stop laughing things got out of control. My attempts to quell whatever was going on inside of me resulted in the eruption of sounds like a series of muted sneezes, which I also found hilarious.

When the storm inside me finally subsided I wiped the tears from my eyes and focused on Mia. Her face was pleasant.

"I thought that would piss you off," she said. "It did me."

I waved my hand dismissively.

"What's so funny?"

I leaned back in my chair as far as the wall behind me would allow, oddly satisfied. My stomach muscles ached. "Inside joke. You wouldn't get it."

Her eyes gleamed with curiosity. "You're Hispanic aren't you?"

"Hell, Mia, it might turn out that way, but who gives a damn?"

"Might turn out that way?"

"Long story. What's it matter if I'm Hispanic?"

She shrugged. "Proves Bigknife's full of shit and got what she deserved."

"Explain that."

"I took your advice about Bigknife. Ignored her best I could for as long as I could, but she wouldn't shut up. The more I ignored her the more she talked. Then she started talking shit on you. That's when I lost it and punched her fuckin' face and got put in this red jumpsuit."

*   *   *

I walked back to Manny's law firm after my meeting with Mia. When I walked through the front door Rashonda peered at me over the top of her leopard-print reading glasses and informed me in the brisk manner of a schoolmarm that a client was waiting for me in my office. I pulled out my phone and saw it was ten till four.

"My appointment isn't for another forty minutes."

Rashonda shrugged and stuck her nose back in a ledger spread open on her desk.

"I don't want clients sitting in my office alone." I pointed to the seats along the wall next to the statue of Prudence. "She couldn't wait out here? In the waiting room?"

Rashonda took off her glasses like now I'd finally done it. "First of all she's a he. And he claims you told him to go on back to your office once he got here. Said he just talked to you on the phone." She put her glasses back on and looked down at the ledger, mumbling under her breath. "Not my place to call the man a liar."

The client I was expecting at four-thirty happened to be a woman. I looked down the hall like that could somehow answer the question swirling around in my head. "Who the hell's back there, Rashonda?"

She flipped a page in the ledger, eyes peeking over her glasses at me again. "Shirt says, Alex. The one that came in for the divorce last week when you was puttin' it to your old lady."

Geronimo.

I took in a deep breath. You know things are bad when a surprise visit from a cartel hitman registers relief. Rashonda was still eyeballing me, her last comment still hanging in the air.

"About the other day," I said, "sorry about that."

Rashonda leaned way back in her chair, whipping the glasses off her face and flinging them so that they spun like the rotor of a helicopter onto the ledger as she did. "Why?"

"Why what?"

"Why are you sorry?"

"Because we offended you."

"I been reflectin' on that for a few days now. On why I took that so personal. Came to the conclusion that I've become a lonely ole prude."

My mouth popped open. I shut it. Rashonda had the floor.

"Man gotta keep the home fires stoked anyway he can," she said. "I can respect that. Just don't let Manny hear you. He'd kick your ass outta here for that. He ain't ever gonna understand why people would go and do the humpty-hump in a place a business."

I nodded. "Thanks for the advice. We'll, um, be more discrete."

She flicked the apology away with her hand. "Better go take care of your client."

I found Geronimo sitting in front of my desk in the same disguise he'd worn the first time he was here—thick-rimmed glasses and an asphalt-colored shirt with the name ALEX stenciled in blue on the breast pocket. I plopped down in the executive chair behind my desk and locked eyes with him.

He said, "Kage Walker."

"Nice to see you, too."

He smiled. "Of course it is. Kage Walker."

"That the name of the man who killed Butler?"

He shook his head. "No. But I'm told that's the name of the man Dean Curtis has used for that sort of thing in the past."

I sat up in my chair. "The past?"

He nodded.

"How far back in the past? We talking thirty years?"

"It's possible."

"You think this could be the guy that killed my mother?" Then, I added, "And Paco Correa?"

"Again, it's possible. Walker is in his early fifties, but that puts him in his early twenties in '93 and my source doesn't think he was in the game that long ago. The guy's a real professional and sells exactly what a billionaire like Curtis needs more than anything. There won't be a provable connection between Dean Curtis and Kage Walker that a prosecutor could exploit if Walker ever fucked up and got himself charged with murder. The best evidence Walker might have that Curtis was ever a customer is the amount of money Walker was paid for his services. Walker won't kill a cockroach for less than six figures."

"How do you know this?"

"I told you. One of my sources." He shrugged. "Trust me, you don't want to know more than that, but use your imagination. Whatever you come up with will probably come pretty close to the truth."

My stomach felt heavy. I figured someone in the Trevino Cartel had done their due diligence on Dean Curtis long before I suspected he'd become a dark force in my life. This case had always swirled around sex trafficking and it looked more and more like Curtis was right in the middle of it. He fit the profile. He had a lot of time on his hands and the resources to indulge every depravity he fancied with an abiding faith that his money could buy him total privacy and a clean slate in case of a breach. It was the kind of power few people can handle without it changing them for the worse. Curtis might be a big-time consumer of cartel-trafficked girls or maybe even some kind of business partner to the cartel. He could even be a rival. Whatever the situation, the cartel either feared him or respected him enough to make every effort to find out where he buried the bodies, literally as well as figuratively.

I said, "How do you know Kage Walker's not the one who killed Butler and went after Annie Black?"

"I saw the guy leaving the tranny's house. Walker doesn't match that description. Walker looks like a, how'd my guy put it?—like one of those old middle-weight MMA fighters. White dude with cauliflower ears and a nose smashed flat. Maybe five nine, hundred eighty-five pounds. Still put together well, even for a guy half his age. Some think he used to be in the military—special forces. My guy thinks that part's bullshit."

"Why?"

"Because Walker put that out there himself. If he really was a Special Forces guy turned hired hitman, he'd know the importance of being a ghost. He wouldn't want people to know anything about his past. My guy thinks Walker leaked that information to throw people off about his identity."

"Or maybe he's not that smart. Maybe he just has a huge ego and likes people thinking he's a special kind of badass." I shrugged. "Or, it could be a marketing ploy."

"You're a lawyer. You think too much."

"Right now I'm thinking I need Kage Walker's real name."

He leaned back in his chair. Laced his fingers across his stomach. "I don't know his real name. My source got a little nervous. Thought maybe I was asking too many questions. Thought maybe I might be able to find the guy, kill the guy, if I knew his name."

"Your source have some reason he doesn't want Walker taken out?"

Geronimo smiled. "I thought the same thing. Finally decided quality hit men are hard to find. My guy might need to use him some day."

I figured his source was another cartel guy and cartel guys can change course quickly. One day you're in the club, next day you and your whole family are headless in barrels. A cautionary tale, but I was already in too deep. One of the devil's minions was sitting right across from me, feeling as at home in my office as he would in his own brother's house, talking to me like I was his best friend.

"I'll get Walker's real name for you." Geronimo stood, walked to the door and turned around. "No one can hide from me for long."

He was supposed to get back with me if his girlfriend, Carmen, Mia's sister, knew of anyone with a motive to kill Jimmy Ray. I wondered if he'd even broached the subject with her. "You got anything for me from Carmen?"

"No."

"I don't think Carmen killed Jimmy Ray. Neither does anyone else. Tell her we think Annie Black did it. See how she reacts. Tell her I think her sister will spend the rest of her life in prison if no one comes forward."

"I'll pass that along." He pointed a finger at me. "You need to watch yourself. Kage Walker is no joke, and he might be coming after you."

"Thanks for the heads-up."

Geronimo put his tongue in his lower lip, looking like he was about say more but instead nodded and disappeared through the door.

20

YOUNGBLOOD'S REAL NAME was Elias Matusak. He pulled
off an empty highway near South Haven and parked an old
pickup on the broken asphalt of a roadside motel in the late-
afternoon sun. The limp body of his wheelman lay on its side
next to him. Elias scanned the empty lot, then the motel.
Twenty rooms long with missing doors, broken windows, and
peeling paint. A rusty old Coke machine was on its back,
gutted, the top half of it in the parking stall in front of the
office. Elias opened the driver's door, leaned across the cab
and hooked his arms under the man's shoulders and pulled
him across the seat while slipping out of the truck. Elias sat
the man upright in the driver's seat, then pushed him over so
that it looked like he was taking a nap, or was dead, which he
was. The empty syringe and the hypo on the floorboard would
tell the authorities what he wanted them to believe—just
another drug overdose.

He lifted his T-shirt and used it to wipe away sweat, then
looked up the road, expecting the first sign of the long-armed
wrath of Dean Curtis to appear in the distance. If a tracker was
hidden somewhere on or in the truck, he couldn't find it. As
he squinted against the sun, he couldn't shake the feeling there
was a tracker and he'd missed it. Worse, he couldn't shake the
feeling that Dean Curtis was the prophet of God he claimed to
be.

Ten hours earlier he'd left Annie Black alive. And he'd
killed the wheelman who had a burner phone he knew was

being tracked by Curtis. Elias had kept the phone on the dashboard while he drove, circling the country home of a lawyer named Benjamin Joel who was to be their next target, thinking about his next move. When the call came to tell him where to find the rifle he was supposed to use to kill the lawyer, Elias buzzed the window down and chucked the phone into a ditch and headed south, fulfilling Dean Curtis's prophesy that betrayal was nigh.

Elias hadn't seen this coming—that he would be the one to defect and betray Curtis. He was surprised to find that he wasn't seized with remorse and didn't want to hang himself like Judas Iscariot, which he took as a sign that Curtis was a false prophet, which caused Elias to question all revelation, new and ancient. He squatted on his haunches in the parking lot and prayed and heard no voice but his own which he took as proof of his dual nature—he was both fully God and fully man, and as a man he was trapped in his own creation. Now he wanted to hang himself, but for quite a different reason. He didn't have any rope so he stood and unsheathed the knife on the wheelman's belt and set the blade on his own throat and closed his eyes and summoned the will to cut until he heard the Jake Brake of a tractor-trailer rattling in the distance. He was distracted long enough that he came to believe the world he'd created was groaning in distress at what he was about to do. This he took as a revelation of the great burden of purpose that was upon him.

He took the blade from his throat and slipped the sheath off the dead man's belt, then walked toward a creek lined with giant cottonwoods where he waited prone on the bank peering back at the truck through the brush to get a look at the man who would be coming after him.

Thirty-five minutes later a van pulled into the parking lot and parked next to the truck with the dead wheelman in it. A middle-aged man with cauliflower ears and a shaved head which had long ago been reshaped by beatings stepped out of the van and walked around the truck and looked into the cab. The man pivoted casually and looked in all directions, then flipped open the fuel door and unscrewed the gas cap. He climbed into the van with it and left. The tracker had been hidden inside the gas cap. Elias hadn't thought of that.

He slid down the embankment and crossed the creek and walked under a canopy of trees along the creek until he came upon the smell of death and a trailer home with a yard full of swaybacked couches and rusted cars and appliances and flies droning around a bloated, dead horse. None of the vehicles were operational and the front door was unlocked. In the fridge he found beer and pink lemonade and sat on a recliner and drank the lemonade from a pitcher until he heard a vehicle pull up and the engine shut off. When a man came through the door, Elias stabbed him in the throat and guided him to the floor face-first on his groceries as a geyser of blood from the man's carotid artery covered Elias's face and neck. When the man stopped moving, Elias picked the keys out of the blood, found a plastic sack in the kitchen and took it to the restroom where he stripped and put his clothes in the sack. Then he cleaned his combat boots in the sink, showered, and walked naked into the man's bedroom where he dressed in jeans and a T-shirt that fit him well enough.

He left with the sack of bloody clothes and a .22 Ruger pistol he found in the nightstand and took the man's Chrysler LeBaron south on backroads into Oklahoma. After four hours of driving and backtracking and stealing gas he found the double-wide trailer of a man named Roland Ballard he'd done time with in the James Crabtree Correctional Center. Ballard's homestead was nestled in a wooded stretch of country at the end of a long, ungraded road that pitched the Chrysler to and fro and left it coated with a layer of red dirt and a missing muffler. Elias had spent the night here alone with Ballard three years earlier, a week after Ballard had been paroled. The pale blue paint of the double-wide had faded and the white trim had yellowed. A satellite dish was now attached to the roof above the bedroom. Elias worried someone else had moved in, then noticed, as he was driving in, that there were no vehicles parked anywhere around, which made him wonder if anyone still lived here at all.

But the weeds and the grass looked like they'd been knocked down with a dull blade in the recent past. Maybe two or three weeks ago, he thought.

He pulled into an empty lot that was shaded by tall elms in the late-evening sun. Drove through the yard around the trailer to the back door. No vehicles back there either. Before he could put the Chrysler in park, Ballard's one-eyed German Shepard mix came out from under a deck and barked and snarled at the Chrysler. Elias regarded it through the half-open window on the driver's side as a man might endure the barbs of an angry ex-lover in public.

When the dog would not go away, he got out with the pistol as the old dog growled and backed up woodenly, defecating involuntarily. It'd been a big dog three years ago, but now it weighed maybe thirty pounds and its ribs were showing.

Elias glared at the dog, willing it to recognize its creator. It stopped growling and averted its eyes.

Elias glanced at Ballard's double-wide, then looked at the dog again. "You want out of here? I'll make this easy for you."

He shot Ballard's dog twice in the head with the pistol and scooped it up and carried it fifty yards to the lagoon, petting its limp body as he walked. He prayed for it at the water's edge, dropped it in, and watched it float away. He looked into the dark woods and walked trancelike around the lagoon, entered the woods and tried to find what he'd told himself three years ago was the grave of a medium-sized animal. Now that the veil had been lifted and he was aware of the dual nature of his deity, he knew what was in the ground and it was no animal. Roland Ballard would've never bothered to bury anything he didn't need to hide. He could've known this about Ballard before but the veil blocked so much. When Elias couldn't find the grave he walked deeper into the woods until he came upon a different grave. Fresh. Dug less than a week ago, he thought. Then he knew he was standing in a graveyard because he heard a cacophony of voices crying out and when he covered his ears and looked back, he could no longer see the lagoon or the Chrysler or the trailer, but he saw a third grave, this one sunken and covered with downed limbs that looked like they'd snapped off in a storm. The grass had overtaken most of the dirt and was thin and he figured it'd been dug and refilled months ago, but the limbs had been laid over it more recently. There were drag paths in the grass. He decided to look for a shovel.

He walked to the tin shed behind the double-wide and banged open its bent doors on broken sliders, kicking up a nest of wasps. First thing he saw was an eight-foot-tall wooden cross made from railroad ties leaned over a riding lawnmower which he took as a beacon from the Father. He ignored the wasps and stepped inside and knelt. Felt the cross with his hands, then put his cheek to the oily wood and closed his eyes. When he opened them again, he noticed that there were wheels built into the base of the cross. He thought about that for a minute—how in prison Ballard had talked about hauling a cross like this through neighborhoods, looking for young boys. People would think he was spreading the gospel. Elias hid the Chrysler in the woods and went to the back door of the trailer and picked the lock and found Ballard's shotgun under the bed where it had been three years ago. He levered the gun open, saw it was loaded, closed it back up. Took it to the front room and sat on the couch facing the front door. And there he waited for Roland Ballard.

*　*　*

It was dark when Ballard got home. He slung the front door open and its spring stretched and whanged as he came in and flicked on the light. He flinched at the sight of Elias sitting with a shotgun across his knee. He flinched again when the door snapped shut on its spring.

Ballard stood there rawboned and sunburnt with grime so deeply embedded in his skin that it looked like a stain.

"I talked to your mother on the phone," Ballard said. "Three years ago when you never came back."

"She passed."

Ballard nodded. "That explains that."

"What?"

"The disconnected phone."

"You kept calling?"

"Thought you and I had a good time. Thought we could take it all the way. Do what we talked about."

"I've changed," Elias said.

Sweat trickled down Ballard's temple. "Your mother said you went crazy. Said you'd run off and joined some kind of a cult."

"I moved on."

"Moved on from what?"

"My life before. Things have fallen into place. I now realize who I am."

"And who might that be?"

Elias's eyes glowed. "I am."

"You am what?"

The glow became a squint. "You don't see it?"

"See what, you crazy fuck?"

Ballard reached for the door behind him.

Elias leveled the shotgun at him.

Ballard froze. Eyed the distance between them. "You come for the guns and money in the safe."

"Yes."

"You need the combination."

Elias nodded.

"Then what? You kill me?"

"You'll kill yourself."

"What?"

"I said, you'll kill yourself."

"I heard you, but that don't make no sense."

"Makes perfect sense. I came to save you, but you'll choose death in the end."

"Break into my house and hold me at gunpoint, but you're here to save me. Do you have any idea how crazy you are?"

"I have to get your attention. Make sure you hear my offer and consider it, with everything on the line. This is the only way forward for you. It was always written this way."

"Religious talk. You think you're a prophet or something?"

"More than a prophet."

"Oh, so that makes you what then? God?"

Elias nodded.

"God is stealing guns and money." Ballard tried to smile. Gave up. "How is it, if you're God, that you don't know the combination to the safe?"

"There are limitations to my present form."

"I suppose I'm too stupid to get that."

"Unfortunately."

"And whose fault is that if you were the one that made me?"

Elias stood, waved the shotgun toward the bedroom. "Open the safe, then I'll make the offer."

"Are you going to let me live?"

"You will be given that option."

Ballard walked to the bedroom and worked the combination to the safe with Elias standing in the doorway behind him. Ballard opened the door to the safe and scooted back so Elias could see. Three rifles, two shotguns, a pistol, ammo, and a small stack of money.

"What now?" Ballard said.

"Drop your pants."

"Oh I see. You want to dominate me. Is that what gets you off now?"

"Drop your pants."

"Fuck this shit, man. Just shoot me."

Elias widened his stance. Braced for the shotgun's kick.

Ballard's eyes snapped shut and he raised his hands. "No, no, no." Three seconds later he was breathing heavily. He opened his eyes.

"Drop 'em," Elias said. "Underwear and all."

Ballard unbuckled his belt and undid the buttons on his fly, then pushed his jeans and underwear to the floor.

"How many boys are buried out back?" Elias asked.

"Twelve. Stick around. We'll do thirteen together."

"I'll rid the world of those thoughts."

Ballard's sunburnt face glowed hotter. "Just take the guns and the money."

"I will."

"Where's this going?"

Elias took the knife on his hip out of its sheath and tossed it on the floor at Ballard's feet.

"Where's this going?"

"If thy right eye offend thee, pluck it out and throw it away from you."

"You want me to cut out my right eye?"

"Your pants are down for a reason. Pick up the knife and cut." He watched Ballard. Watched it dawn on his face what was being asked of him.

"You'll kill me if I don't."

Elias nodded. "I'm not asking you to do anything I haven't done to myself."

"You mutilated yourself?"

"I purified myself."

"Just kill me you goddamned psychopathic sonofabitch."

Elias shot Ballard in the face. Blew bloody bits of his head onto the guns and the wall behind the safe. Ballard lay half headless on the floor, pants around his ankles.

Elias made the sign of the cross, then looked at the clock on the wall. He needed to get to the lawyer's house.

21

AT 7:00 A.M. on Wednesday, my day started with one of my cell phones blowing up on me twice in thirty seconds. The first eruption was premeditated and my own doing—the alarm I'd set the night before. The second was Russ calling me.

"You up?"

"No. But I'm awake."

"You sure about that?"

"No."

"How fast can you get to The Beacon?"

A restaurant in downtown Wichita.

I looked at Keri in the grey light of morning, curled up in a ball, faced away, sheets pulled tight around the swell of her hip.

"Depends," I said. "Why?"

"Breakfast."

Keri flipped around and threw her arm around my belly. Her eyes were open and it was quiet enough in the room for her to hear every word.

"Breakfast?" I said.

"Yeah," Russ said. "With Jake Brackeen."

Jake was the man Pops hired twenty-eight years ago to find my father. The jolt from hearing this news burned off the fog in my head. Keri popped up on an elbow and looked at me.

"You're having breakfast with Jake Brackeen?" I said to Russ.

"Now you're awake."

"How'd this come about?"

"Okay, so I'm not exactly having breakfast with him. Not yet anyway, but I am watching him walk into The Beacon as we speak. He lives in College Hill. I sat off his house and followed him."

"I'll be there in forty-five minutes," I said. "Follow him if he leaves. Let me know if he does."

Ten minutes later I was starting my truck and popping the button on the garage door opener hooked to my visor. As the door clattered up behind me, I buzzed the windows down.

When the garage door was up, I glanced in the rearview mirror and put my hand on the gear shift. Heard distant gunfire, multiple rounds, so I ducked. Glass wasn't shattering around me so I peeked out the back window. Didn't see anything that concerned me anywhere, including across the field to a line of trees along my neighbor's land. The shots seemed to have come from that general direction. Could be someone hunting squirrel or rabbit or coyote but I doubted it. Wrong time of day, already too hot, and I'd never known anyone to hunt on that property. Given what I'd been through in the past and who might want me dead now, I didn't like it. I killed the engine and punched the remote to bring down the garage door, then went into the kitchen and called my neighbor.

He'd heard the shots too and had already called 911. He promised to let me know what was going on the second he found out.

I called Russ to tell him I'd be a few minutes late and why. He understood, and said Brackeen was already drinking coffee with a woman at a table so he might need to approach him without me if this was going to take long.

Twenty minutes later I still hadn't heard anything from the neighbor so I decided to stay close to my family for the morning trek into town to drop the kids off at school. Keri drove my pickup with me in the passenger's seat. I put my Glock in the glove compartment and carried a shotgun with a blanket over it. The kids asked what was going on from the back seat. I told them that some folks were trespassing on the neighbor's land and discharging firearms for some unknown reason. Leo didn't see how that was a big deal, explaining that we lived in the country and that he heard shooting all the time, which wasn't exactly true. Lindy stared out her window, solemn and pensive. I knew the look. Darkness and violence had touched my children in their youth, as it had me. She was summoning the strength to live like something other than a hunted animal trembling under cover. I asked her if anything was wrong. She didn't answer. When I repeated the question, she insisted nothing was wrong. We were all pretending everything was okay and Leo was the only one of us that was any good at it.

Before we got to Worthington, the phone I'd used to call the neighbor buzzed. It was Sheriff Roberts—the local sheriff. He knew me from the past and referred to me as "judge" out of habit, then told me he and my neighbor were standing over a dead body, apparently shot. The dead man had no ID on him and law enforcement hadn't found any abandoned vehicles in the area which suggested the man had been dropped off. But it was early in the investigation. Cruisers had been dispatched to area roads and were actively looking for the killer. As the deputy explained the situation, I could feel my neck turning hot.

"It looks to me like the dead man had a perch all set up with a line of sight directly through your neighbor's trees and through the gap in your trees to your garage door. And there's a serious sniper rifle lying here next to him. Now, I understand from your neighbor that you both heard shots this morning."

"That's right," I said. "Ten minutes after seven."

"And where were you when you heard the shots?"

"I'd just opened the garage door and was sitting in my truck. Never even got it in gear."

"You know anyone who wants you dead?"

"I am a lawyer," I said. "So it would be odd if I didn't."

I wasn't ready to trust yet another area cop with accusations involving a local billionaire and one of their brothers in blue, but my words were glib and I regretted them the instant they rolled off my tongue.

"Good to hear you haven't lost your sense of humor, Judge, but you might have trouble finding anything funny in what I'm about to say. From what you told me, and from where I'm standing right now, it looks to me like this guy was about to have a bead on you when he was attacked from behind."

Keri took her eyes from the road to glance my way. I felt sick to my stomach.

"What do you think is goin' on here?" the sheriff asked.

"I'd tell you if I knew."

"I don't think you would."

"Can't help what you think."

"I'm calling the KBI in on this one. I think this is somehow connected to the death of Detective Mallory and that trial of yours from two years ago. It was pretty quiet around here after you went into hiding and now that you're back, this starts up again. I don't think the fact that your sister went missing during the trial is a coincidence either. Your brother-in-law paid me a visit, you aware of that?"

"I'm not surprised."

"He assured me that the story your sister told the KBI was bullshit. Says your sister wouldn't't've had any reason to hide from him."

"My sister wasn't the first woman Rod ever beat up. And he's an ex-brother-in-law at this point."

"I'm sure that's all true, but my point remains. I'm calling in the KBI."

"Reckon they'll be here shortly then."

"Reckon so."

I ended the call. The kids bombarded me with questions. I told them the sheriff hadn't figured out what happened yet, which was true. But it was an evasive answer and the kids knew it.

Keri parked along the curb in a line of vehicles in front of the Catholic Christian Academy. The kids piled out. We watched them meet up with other children and make their way toward the entrance. I told Keri what I'd learned. Familiar vehicles carrying familiar kids came and went around us.

Keri puffed her cheeks. "Did the sheriff say who the dead guy was?"

"Said there was no ID on him. They have no idea who he is."

"Well, if it turns out to be that hitman you told me about, the one that works for Dean Curtis—"

"Kage Walker."

"Yeah. If it turns out to be him, then maybe Geronimo killed him." She sighed. "Or Pops. It could've been Pops."

I shook my head. "Can't imagine Pops sitting in my neighbor's trees all night waiting for snipers."

"Maybe he put up trail cams at spots he thought we were most vulnerable. Saw a visual of the guy through that app he has on his phone for hunting, then went out there and took the guy out."

I shook my head.

"I'm spit balling here. If you got any better ideas, I'd like to hear them."

"Pops would've only needed one shot."

"He's seventy-five now."

"His ten percent is better than most marksmen's hundred percent, especially in a real-world scenario. And a situation like this—just fish in a barrel for the old man. Like I said, would've taken him one shot."

Keri thought about that. "If Pops takes the guy out from three hundred yards with one shot, might be too obvious who did it, y'know. Maybe he didn't want it to look like the work of a marine sniper with two hundred eighty-three kills under his belt."

"He would've called me. Warned me. I would've never come that close to dying if Pops did this."

"We're a block from his house. Let's just go there now. Make sure it wasn't him."

I grabbed my phone and called Pops. He picked up on the second ring.

"Pops, where you at right now?"

"Donut shop."

"You don't eat donuts."

"I drink coffee. Talk to people. Some of them eat donuts."

"How long you been there?"

"Oh I don't know. Since six-thirty I guess."

"Talking to your friends."

"Yeah, talking to my friends. You have a stroke or something? What's goin' on?"

I told him the story. He said *I told you so* in so many words and urged me to drop my inquiry into my parents' deaths and withdraw from Mia's case, then said he'd support me in whatever way he could regardless of what I did. It wasn't a good time to tell him we'd found Jake Brackeen, so I thanked him for the advice and ended the call.

Keri and I sat staring out the windshield in what was now the lone vehicle idling at the curb.

"Guess we're back to thinking this might be Geronimo's work," Keri said.

"Well . . . he was trying to get Kage Walker's real name for me. Maybe he actually found the guy and followed him. Saw what was going down and decided to protect the lawyer he'd paid a couple hundred grand to defend his girlfriend's sister."

"Yeah, I like that."

"I like it if it's Kage Walker that's dead out there."

"And if it's not," Keri said.

I shook my head. "Then . . . no clue."

An acute awareness of my own mortality rushed through me. The thought of leaving my children alone in this world settled like a weight inside my chest.

Keri pulled away from the curb and took us down the street. She looked full of the same energy that was thumping through me—mad enough to kill and scared enough to run. Since we didn't know exactly who to go after or run from or where to take cover, it felt a lot like panic.

When we hit the city limits on our way back to our home, Keri suggested I call Caroline Gordon to see if we could get a look at my would-be assassin sooner rather than later.

I nodded and changed the subject. Caroline would call soon enough. "You're not going to ask me to back off trying to figure out what happened to my mother?"

"Someone's already decided it's better for them if you're dead, so I think we're way past that. And there's something else."

"What?"

"I think you're doing the right thing and I'm behind you one hundred percent. If you decided that finding out what happened to your parents wasn't worth the risk, what would that say about you?"

"That I love you and my children more than anything else in the world. That I had patience, showed restraint, was prudent, and trusted there would be a reckoning. Not on my time, but God's. That I would forego my anger, my ego, my sense of justice and desire for revenge and accept peace in my time."

We sat listening to the sound of the road and the wind.

I studied Keri's face. It looked like she was about to cry. I said, "I've come to the conclusion that you and Pops were right. I should've dropped this whole thing. But it's too late now, like you said."

Keri glanced at me. Looked back at the road. "You giving those photos to Caroline didn't change things. You were right. Once you'd stumbled on to this, you became a threat to them. These assholes were coming after you no matter what. What happened this morning was a blessing, because it made our situation perfectly clear. We have two choices. Run and hope they don't find us, or stay and try to nail them before they kill us."

I opened the glove compartment and pulled out one of my cell phones.

"You calling Caroline?"

"Not yet."

I called the last number I had for Geronimo. He didn't answer so I called Russ to tell him what we knew. When I ran out of answers for his questions about this morning's dead guy, he told me he'd talked with Jake Brackeen at the restaurant. Brackeen was having breakfast with a woman and didn't want to talk in front of her, but agreed to meet us for lunch at Crossroads Bar & Grill at noon today. I told Russ I'd be there.

When we pulled into our driveway, the phone dedicated to Caroline chimed. I needed to talk with her as much as she needed to talk with me. I took the call.

"I need to meet you at your house ASAP," Caroline said. "Get the lay of the land."

"Just pulled into my drive. I'll put on a pot of coffee and wait for you."

Thirty minutes later, I met her at the front door and handed her a Styrofoam cup of joe. We walked straight through the house to the garage where my pickup was parked. I showed her the sight line through a gap in my trees to the neighbor's property. On the driveway, we watched a clot of sheriff's officers across the field four hundred yards away, their movements mostly obscured by trees.

"Sheriff Roberts thinks you might know who killed that man over there."

"No idea."

"He doesn't think it's murder. Thinks it's ..." She shrugged. "You know . . . home defense."

I shook my head.

She took that in and nodded at my house. "I see you have security cameras."

"Yeah."

"How long you had those?"

I thought, *since after me and my family were kidnapped two years ago*, then shrugged, and said, "Couple years."

She took a drink. "The Vaughn Rummell murder trial was a couple years ago. Your sister went missing a couple years ago. Someone killed Detective Mallory a couple years ago."

"How could I forget? You can watch the surveillance video from last night and this morning if you want."

"I will later." She squinted against the hot, August wind, watching the activity in the distant trees. "I can't take you over to the crime scene right now, especially with the sheriff thinking you might know who did this, or be behind it somehow."

"I figured as much."

"Don't you wanna know who's dead in those trees?"

"Sure I do."

"You mind telling me who you think it could be?"

"Why do I get the feeling you're investigating me?"

"Only in the interest of being thorough, you understand."

"I understand a lot of things."

She looked in her cup. "Hot coffee in this kind of heat—I must be addicted." She laughed. "This is good stuff. Where'd you get it?"

"Glad you like it. Spice Merchant on Douglass in Wichita." I swirled my hand over my stomach. "It's low acid. Easier on the tummy."

"Have to check that out."

"I grind my own beans."

She nodded. "You're snootier than you look."

"I'm full of surprises."

"You're full of shit."

"Who isn't?"

She smiled. "If this turns out to be an attempt on your life, which it seems to be, any chance you'll disappear again?"

"I won't rule it out."

Caroline sipped her coffee and stared at the activity across the tilled field. "If you and Keri decide to go that route again, you know you can trust me to keep your whereabouts a secret. At least keep in touch with me. I'm trying to help you."

"We'll keep that in mind."

"Sheriff Roberts doesn't know what I know, so he's got this figured as a continuation of that cartel violence that hit here during the Rummell trial."

"Yeah I know."

"How do you know that?"

"He told me."

"I see." She looked behind us into the garage, then back across the field. "Anyway, it'd look bad for me if I took you over there. You're a half-ass suspect in the guy's death. At least in the sheriff's mind."

"You told me that already. I told you I understand. What's on your mind?"

"I know you're worried about leaks from the Harvey County Sheriff's Office on Butler's murder, but from talking to Sheriff Roberts, I don't think he has any clue what happened up there. That could change, but right now he's got no idea that the man dead in those trees is probably a hitman sent by Dean Curtis or Undersheriff Brown."

She gave me a chance to respond, but I didn't.

"You know . . . ." She let the thought die on her lips.

"Know what?"

"This attack wasn't exactly a surprise, now was it?"

"Sure as hell was to me."

Her eyes were on me. Probing. "You were bracing yourself for something like this. That's what you told me two days ago in your office."

"From the looks of things, maybe I should've braced myself a little better."

A huff of air blew through her nostrils. "You mean to tell me that you didn't have any idea this was coming, and you didn't have anybody in those trees?"

"It's weird, I know, but that's the situation. What can I say?"

"Maybe your grandfather took the guy out. Sheriff has that idea swimming around in his head. Says your grandfather is a war hero and the kind of guy who'd do anything to protect you."

"I'm sure you'll look into that."

"Count on it."

I met her gaze. "I know how this looks, and I don't have any answers for you. The sheriff's not the only one to think maybe Pops had something to do with this. Keri and I had the same idea. As it turns out, he was at the donut shop all morning."

She tossed the last swallow of coffee back and handed me the cup. "Donut shop? Where's that?"

"Downtown Worthington."

"How's their coffee?"

"Pops seems to like it."

"You like it?"

"Meh."

She called me snooty again and took off walking toward the crime scene in the distance, then stopped and faced me. Strands of hair that had come loose from her ponytail lashed her face. She raised her voice above the wind. "You must be a pretty special guy."

"I like to think so."

She raked hair out of her eyes but it was no use. "Never met anyone with a guardian angel before."

"Maybe it's you," I yelled, then winked at her. "I'll understand if you don't want to confirm that."

She ignored that. "I'll be back to watch your surveillance footage. And I'll send photos of the dead guy to your phone in a few minutes."

"Thank you."

"If you know who it is, tell me."

"Was."

"What?" she yelled.

"I'll let you know."

She shook her head like something was lost in translation and walked away. I watched her clomp across the field toward the neighbor's trees.

Fifteen minutes later I was frying eggs in the kitchen when the phone in my pocket dinged. It was a text from Caroline. No words, just photos. I looked at the first one—a man on his stomach, his back riddled with bullet holes, two of them in his shaved head. The second photo was of his face. He was an overly tan white man with cauliflower ears and a flat nose.

The image of the dead man disappeared as the phone rang in my hand. I accepted Caroline's call. I wanted to tell her this guy probably went by the moniker, Kage Walker, but I couldn't tell her Geronimo was my source so I told her something true and misleading. I said I'd never seen the man before. She wasn't surprised and told me she'd let me know when she had an ID on him. She also said that the sheriff would agree to assign two deputies to protect me and my family until the danger passed. I asked who would be assigned and she told me. I'd known both deputies for years. I trusted them. I asked Caroline to thank the sheriff for me.

Keri darted into the kitchen as I ended the call, hair wet from a shower. "Eggs are burning."

So they were. Suddenly I could hear them crackling a little too loud in the skillet. Keri beat me to the spatula and flipped the eggs onto plates I'd set out.

I showed her one of the photos Caroline sent me.

Her eyes danced as she inspected it. "Kage Walker?"

"Probably."

"Did you tell Gordon what we know?"

"What we think we know?" I shook my head and handed her a plate of extra crispy eggs. "She'll know who this is soon enough. She doesn't need to know that we already know, or how we know."

I called Pops and asked him to come out to the house as an added measure of security. Keri would need the extra hand when picking up the kids from school if my meeting with Jake Brackeen ran long. Then I sent the photos of my would-be assassin to Russ, who called and told me he would call a buddy of his who ran a big-time security firm in Texas. Professional bodyguards—the whole nine yards. He said they were pricey, but he thought he could get me a deal I could afford. He said his buddy owed him a huge favor. I didn't argue with him, but guessed I couldn't pay for this kind of service even with a healthy discount. But it wouldn't hurt to check into it. I didn't know how long the sheriff would let his deputies protect us, or how effective they'd be, but I needed to explore my options.

22

I WAS DRIVING north on the turnpike on my way to lunch with Russ and Jake Brackeen when Keri called.

"Where you at?"

"On the turnpike passing a semi, why?"

"Got a call you need to take."

"Who is it?"

"Guy claiming Dean Curtis sent him to kill you yesterday."

"What? Wait—yesterday?"

"That's what he said."

"Don't suppose he gave you a name."

"Of course not."

"Did he say why he's calling?"

"No. He's seriously strange."

"Sounds like it. Patch him through."

The phone clicked.

"Who is this?" I said.

"The man who saved your life this morning."

"Saved my life how?"

"I took out the man hired to kill you, before he could take you out."

"You killed that guy on my neighbor's property?"

"Yes."

"Why?"

"Because I need you alive to tell the story I cannot. Because I'm on the run, and even if I wasn't, I am a clanging cymbal. A useless noise. The world is not yet prepared to listen to me. But it will listen to you."

"You lost me, partner. What story do you want me tell the world? How Dean Curtis hired you to kill me, or how you killed the man hired to kill me?"

"I was not hired to kill you. I was sent to kill you. After I defected, the man I killed was hired."

"You said you defected. Defected from what?"

"A human trafficking ring. I was in Curtis's innermost circle. We see a part of him he hides from the world, including others in the ring, those on the outside."

"Curtis is the leader of a human trafficking ring? That's hard to believe. How have I not heard of this before?"

"What—you were not consulted?" He laughed. "The world is not constrained by the limits of your imagination. I think you know this about the world—that anything is possible."

Delusional and hyper-religious as this guy sounded, he had a point. Jeffrey Dahmer ate people. How many wires had been crossed in that guy's head for him to do that? And for what? He wasn't hungry. It was for sexual gratification, of all things. But Dahmer was one person while Curtis was supposedly the leader of a fair-sized group of wackos. Harder to believe? Maybe, maybe not. In the late seventies, over nine hundred members of a cult called the Peoples Temple committed mass suicide under the direction of their leader, Jim Jones. You live long enough, see enough shit, you forget sometimes how truly strange and evil the world really is.

"Tell me about Curtis's group," I said.

"They are small in number—smaller now that I am gone— and composed of two distinct groups, those with a façade of legitimacy and respectability hiding in plain sight, and those invisible to the outside world—his inner circle. Those closest to Curtis have no family on the outside. No one misses them. No one missed me. No one wonders what happened to us."

"How many are in this . . . this inner circle?"

"Four women. Just two men—eunuchs, which used to include me."

"Eunuchs? Are you telling me—"

"Matthew, chapter five, verse thirty."

"What?"

"If thy right hand offend thee, cut it off, and cast it from thee: for it is profitable for thee that one of thy members should perish, and not that thy whole body should be cast into hell."

"Shit, guess that's why we can't have nice things."

"For that I'll have your tongue when this is over."

"Hey, I didn't mean to offend you. You have to admit this is all a bit strange for a Wednesday."

Silence. Guess the "Wednesday" joke didn't fly either. This guy had less sense of humor than a pile of bear shit.

Finally, I asked, "How many are in the ring but not in Curtis's inner circle?"

"I cannot answer your question because the ring—such as it is—is actually a series of rings, like links in a chain, set up in small groups, so that each person in the group only knows the identity of the people in their own group. There are exceptions for those required to forge bonds with other groups."

"So it's set up like a clandestine cell system, like terrorists use, to resist penetration into the operation by law enforcement?"

"Yes, but the links in the chain—the cells—don't usually have a common leader, or even a common ideology like a terrorist group. The only thing binding each cell together is their common goal—trafficking woman and children for sex and money."

"A snake with many heads."

"Take off a head, another one grows back because of demand for the product, because of man's sinful nature. I can speak to how and why these loosely affiliated cells work together, in general terms, but beyond that, there's not much I can tell you."

"Then tell me everything you can about your cell—the inner circle."

"Curtis calls the women his wives. Not under man's law, but God's, you see. At least that's the false theology Curtis peddled to us last year when one of the women told him she wanted to leave because she thought she was sinning against God. He told us he was God's prophet, that it was God's will that the women help him spread his seed, that it was God's will that I and the other male not breed because our seed was defective, full of sin, and could only perpetuate countless abominations. I fell for that line of crap at the time, but I see now that Curtis is not a prophet, but a pretender. An atheist and a con man with a keen eye for weak people and what they're willing to believe to get what they think they need. This was revealed to me yesterday in prayer when I received a wondrous revelation of who I am."

"And who is that?"

"I will not reveal that to you now. The greatest prophet born of woman would never recognize me, but soon, you will, and you will have no choice but to believe."

What Mia told me yesterday about a man we called Youngblood sprang to mind—she recognized him as the guy caught on video killing Butler. He'd been the cameraman in her video with Undersheriff Brown and two other men. He had propositioned her about a tropical vacation afterward. He told her it paid more than she could imagine and would cost her everything she had. Mia thought that sounded like "creepy-ass religious bullshit," and now I was getting the same vibe from this guy. I wondered if I was talking to Youngblood.

"What does that mean?" I asked.

"All you need to know now is that Dean Curtis is having sex with young women, some of them underage, which is why he'll deny what I'm telling you and do anything within his power to keep all of this secret."

"You're telling me Dean Curtis has created some kind of a harem, and that you and the other guy in his inner circle are eunuchs? Meaning your genitals have been removed?"

"Yes. His followers tend to fit a specific profile—young, mentally deficient drug addicts with little or no family and a yen for fairy tales. The ones who remain believe he is the conduit of a new revelation that man is no longer capable of sex without perverting it into something it was never meant to be. Curtis claims that the correction God calls for is the lifelong abstinence of Curtis's male followers."

"But God is cool with Curtis having sex."

"Predictable, isn't it—that God would tell him exactly what he wants to hear—that he'd be the only one permitted to have sex with the women, that I and the other man have our defective seed quarantined while helping him spread his?"

"What are the names of the others in your group?"

"I do not know any of their real names. One of them escaped last month. A woman."

"Why does Curtis want me dead?"

"Thought you could tell me."

"All I know is that a guy named Ricky Butler who was murdered five days ago thought Curtis and Undersheriff Brown had something to do with killing my mother twenty-eight years ago."

Silence.

"Do you know anything about how my mother was killed or who killed her?" I asked, figuring it was a long shot, but the whole world seemed so absurd at the moment, what the hell did I know?

"No."

"Know anything about a guy named Paco Correa?"

"Never heard of him."

"Do you know who killed Butler?" I said.

"Yes."

"Was it you?"

"Yes."

Now, finally, I knew I was talking to Youngblood.

"Why did Curtis want Ricky Butler dead?" I asked.

"Not sure, but I know Butler found women for him, including the four that became his wives."

"Curtis sent you to kill Annie Black too," I said.

"Yes."

"Why?"

"I don't know." His voice had no inflection.

"Do you care?" I asked.

"I didn't then."

"Do you know a guy named Clint Brown?"

"I know of him. He and Curtis talk. He's the undersheriff."

"What else do you know about him?"

"He's useful to Curtis because of his job in law enforcement, but I don't know anything specific. I just know how the world works."

I heard what sounded like a door slamming on his end, then rhythmic breathing, like he was walking. I changed lanes.

"I need to go now," Youngblood said.

"Wait! Ever hear of a man named Jimmy Ray?"

"Yeah, he's the man your client is accused of killing."

"What do you know about him?"

"I saw him at Curtis's mansion several times. I'm ending this call—"

"Hold on, dammit, this is important! Tell me everything you know about Jimmy Ray."

"Curtis took Jimmy Ray to his island with him once."

"His island? He has an island?"

"He owns a two-hundred-fifty-acre island in the Caribbean. Took Jimmy Ray there on his jet and got him hammered. Got a blackmail video of Jimmy with an underage girl."

"How underage?"

"Fourteen, maybe fifteen."

"Why was Curtis blackmailing Jimmy Ray?"

"I don't know, but once Curtis had the video, Jimmy Ray wasn't about to cause Curtis any problems."

"What sort of problems?"

"All I know is that Jimmy Ray was Curtis's inside man for the Wichita Police Department, which was useful but it also made Curtis very nervous. So did Undersheriff Brown."

"Why?"

"They both had information that could hurt Curtis, but I don't know anything specific. I just know how the world works. This conversation is over—"

"Wait! You want me to tell this story to the world, I need to know that what you're telling me is true. How do you know these things?"

"I was a chamberlain. I managed the household. I saw things—day in and day out—involving Curtis with young women. Some of them looked underage to me, like I said."

"You saw things? Like what? What did you actually see? Did you see him having sex with these women? These girls?"

"No. I saw them come and go. A steady supply of them. They didn't stay long. One of the wives would show them around the mansion. In the massage room they were shown how Curtis liked to be touched. Whenever Curtis would go in, he was alone with them."

"The wives groomed these girls. Prepped them for Curtis."

"Yeah, that was one of their jobs."

"I find it hard to believe that a man with as much to lose as Curtis let you see this much."

"You don't know Curtis. He brainwashed us, didn't give a damn what any of us saw. In fact, he got off on it—that he could control people like that. That we would see and do evil every day and think it was normal. No, not just normal, but good, whatever that meant to him. There was no real standard."

"How did he brainwash you and the others?"

"Controlled our every hour. Withheld food and water and deprived us of sleep if we displeased him. Could be an uninspired prayer at the dinner table, or a lack of enthusiasm in bed. But there were rewards and praise if we did good. Like if I'd killed you."

"After you defected, you said Curtis hired a man to kill me. How do you know this?"

"Logic inference—the man I shot this morning wasn't in the inner circle."

"Do you know who he was?"

"No."

"How'd you find that guy out there in all those trees?"

"I sat off the spot I planned to kill you from and waited for him."

"How did Curtis know you'd defected?"

"He was tracking me through a burner cell with the Life360 app downloaded on it. When he called I didn't answer. I tossed the phone in a ditch and ran. But I came back. Waited for the new guy. Watched him set up his perch in the dark. I waited until your garage door started to rise before I shot him so you could hear. So you would know how close you came to dying. So you would know the words I say are true."

I could hear him breathing, harder than before. Then I heard bumping, like maybe he'd dropped the phone.

I said, "Are you still there? I need more information—"

I heard what sounded like a gunshot on Youngblood's end. Then another. Then footfalls and scuffling sounds—like he was running with the phone in his pocket.

"What's going on?" I yelled.

No answer. More scuffling noises. I listened. The noises ended but the call was still active.

"What's going on?" I yelled.

No answer. Then more scuffling noises. I listened. Finally, the sounds stopped again.

"What's going on?" I yelled again.

"Same as this morning," he said, between breaths.

I heard an engine start up. "You just shot someone?"

"More than that, I'm afraid."

"Who'd you kill?"

"Don't have a name, but it's another hired killer. I can only tell you who I saved."

"Who?"

"A man named Jake Brackeen. I was supposed to kill him after I killed you. For some reason Curtis wants him dead too. I suggest you figure out what it is."

The call ended.

Adrenaline thrummed through me. In fifteen minutes I was to meet Brackeen for lunch, which probably meant Youngblood was near Brackeen's house or Crossroads Bar & Grill or somewhere in between.

I took the south Wichita exit, scrambling to call Russ as I did.

* * *

When Russ answered, I said, "Where are you?"

"Here at the bar waiting for you to get your ass over here. What's wrong?"

I realized I'd almost yelled into the phone. I lowered my voice. "Is Brackeen there yet?"

"No, what's the matter?"

I started to explain, but Russ cut me off.

"Brackeen's calling now."

"Take the call," I said.

Russ did, and the phone went silent.

I rolled through the toll plaza, the K-Tag on my windshield notching another entry on my bill somewhere, then accelerated into the traffic on the canal route, the road cutting through the heart of the city. When Russ came back his voice was as calm as before.

"He's on his way," Russ said.

"That's all he said?"

"Pretty much, why? What's going on?"

I told him.

"Where did this happen?"

"I don't know."

"He said he was just leaving his house."

"Somewhere close to his house, then. He didn't say anything about hearing gunshots?"

"No. You need to call Agent Gordon right now."

"Warn Brackeen. Tell him what's going on."

"On it." He ended the call.

I called Caroline and told her the situation.

23

ELIAS DROVE OUT of College Hill in Ballard's old pickup past an automated license plate reader as he did. He knew a little black camera on a pole with a solar panel above it guarded every road into and out of the stately old neighborhood and fed tag numbers into the police department's database. He'd researched the troublesome little cameras and knew cloud servers and vehicular fingerprint technology and algorithms were involved, recording the makes and models and colors of the vehicles passing by and storing the information in a database for use later if the need arose. He knew Ballard's truck might even trigger the software program's hot list, in which case the program would immediately alert law enforcement of the hit.

Elias hadn't planned to kill Brackeen in College Hill because of the complications posed by the ALPRs, but knew his successors didn't have the luxury of waiting for the perfect time to perform the perfect hit now that Elias had gone rogue. Which meant Elias hadn't had the luxury of waiting around for the perfect time to thwart the hit.

He turned south and headed under a raised highway and was acutely aware of his limitations as a man and the temptation to lose faith in the truth of what had been revealed to him by the Father. He prayed for strength to complete his mission and in the silent war between his ears demons were gathering around and when he felt himself slipping into oblivion he recited the Lord's Prayer and hung on until the storm passed and he found himself on the road in front of the Calvary Cemetery which he took as a beacon from the Father.

A few blocks later he headed west and saw a homeless young man in an army jacket sitting cross-legged on a sidewalk in front of a dollar store. He parked behind the store and approached the man on foot, calling him brother and holding out one of Ballard's hundred dollar bills. Army Jacket's eyes grew large as he stood. He hesitated to reach for the money and when he finally did, he did so in a way that made it look like he thought Elias might be a mirage.

"What's your name?" Elias asked.

"Tommy."

"I need a favor from you, Tommy."

Tommy put the bill in his pocket. Traffic was loud. A semi downshifted and a lone siren wailed in the distance.

Elias said, "I need you to bear my cross."

"What?" Tommy said.

"I'll show you."

Tommy followed Elias behind the store and they looked into the bed of Ballard's pickup at the cross made from railroad ties that Elias had brought from Ballard's shed.

"It stinks," Tommy said.

"So do you."

If Tommy heard the insult, he didn't show it. "It looks heavy."

"It is."

"What do you want me to do?"

Elias pointed in the direction of the cemetery. "Carry this to Calvary."

"Where?—It's too heavy."

"It's on wheels."

"Is this for the hunnerd bucks?"

"It's for me."

Tommy squinted at the strangeness of the answer.

Elias reached into his pocket and pulled out another hundred dollars and held it up. "Roll the cross toward the Calvary Cemetery. You know where that is?" Elias pointed again.

Tommy grabbed the hundred bucks and nodded.

Elias reached into his pocket and pulled out the keys to the truck and tossed them to Tommy but he didn't see because he was pocketing the money. The keys glanced off his chest and dropped to the asphalt.

Tommy stared at the keys, then up at Elias.

"Put those in your pocket," Elias said.

"Why?"

"Pick up the keys."

Tommy did.

"Now put them in your pocket."

He did.

"If you make it to the cemetery, leave the cross standing on the sidewalk by the entrance and come back for the truck. It's yours, but not before you do what I said. I'll be watching."

Tommy nodded.

Elias let the tailgate down and jumped into the bed and hefted the cross and pushed its wheels over the edge of the tailgate onto the asphalt where he balanced the cross upright on its built-in base. "If anyone asks about me, tell them I'm the one they've been waiting for."

"Someone's waiting for you?"

Elias dropped off the tailgate. "Everyone is, whether they know it or not." Then he got into the cab of the truck and took out a grocery sack full of something and walked toward the front of the store without looking back. He marched west away from the cemetery and College Hill until he came upon a thrift shop. It was a stand-alone building with big glass windows. A bell above the front door jingled when he went in. An elderly woman behind the counter smiled at him as a police cruiser blew by outside with its lights flashing. If anyone else was in the store, Elias couldn't see them.

"Can I help you, sir?"

"Need clothes for a job interview."

The woman smiled and nodded. It was a knowing smile, but she didn't know shit.

Elias smiled back. "Need a proper suit."

"A suit? Okay, what kind of job we talkin' 'bout here?"

"Construction."

"Construction? Sure you need a suit for that?"

"For the interview."

"Yes, but—that's what I mean. You sure you need a suit to interview for a construction job?"

"Yes."

The woman tried to smile but it died on her face. He could tell she was sizing him up now—ill-fitting jeans and a black shirt with stains of some kind. Carrying a big grocery sack with paper handles. Elias knew he looked homeless. That's what he was.

"How 'bout we look for some proper work clothes?" she said.

"How 'bout you show me the suits?"

The woman nodded. "Okay, sir. Suits are over there." She pointed and said, "Way in the back. The back wall. See it?"

He looked. "I don't see the suits."

"They're on the back wall."

"You said that."

"Yes."

Silence.

"Sir, what seems to be the problem?"

"I don't see the suits."

"They're on the . . . along the . . . there's stuff in the way so you can't see them."

"I can see that."

"Just go all the way to the wall."

Elias grimaced a little. "I intend to."

"Sir?"

"Ma'am."

"Sir?"

Elias noticed the women wore a crucifix on a chain around her skinny neck. "You Catholic?"

"Excuse me?—No."

Elias pointed. "Your crucifix."

She clasped it with her bony fingers.

"What denomination are you?" Elias said.

"Oh. Methodist. I'm a Methodist. This store is run by the church."

"The Methodist Church?"

"Yes."

"That's an odd name for a church, isn't it?"

"Oh, I don't . . . how do you mean?"

"What could be so great about your method?"

"Excuse me?"

"What's so vital about the church's method that it became the name of the church?" Elias unfocused his eyes. "Methodist."

"I . . . don't know."

"You don't know?"

She shook her head.

"How can you not know?"

Silence.

"Yet this is the name of your church?"

The woman nodded.

"Is this a Christian church?"

"Of course."

"Of course." Elias smiled. "Jesus is your savior?"

"Yes."

"You could name your church after him."

"It's not up to me. I'm not in charge of naming it."

"But you're in charge of joining it."

The woman nodded. "A lot of good people there."

"A lot of good people. With a particular method of doing what exactly?"

She didn't respond.

"In any case, someone must've been awful proud of it. The method, that is. Seems off, doesn't it? Seems like a problem."

"I don't know."

"But that's not your problem, is it? Can't be too proud of something you don't know shit about."

The woman licked her lips and looked through the glass outside. No one on the sidewalk or in the parking lot. Cars passing by on the roadway in the summer sun. She looked toward the back of the store. No one there either.

"Ma'am?"

"Yes. Um, yes." She touched the loose, soft skin on her throat with her fingers. "What?"

"You really don't give a shit about me, do you?"

"I think you need to leave."

"I think I need a suit."

She glanced at the back wall and cleared her throat. "I'll take you—I'll um, take you back there."

"I'd appreciate it."

The woman came out from behind the counter through a swinging gate and walked toward the back. Elias followed, looking for a way to avoid this, His will—but being God and being stuck in this temporal body, there was none. When they got to the back wall the woman made for some metallic double doors next to a rack of suits but he seized her from behind before she got to them and snapped her neck, covering her mouth and lowering her limp body to the floor with a consoling shush, silently absolving her of a lifetime of sin as he did. He walked to the front door with his sack. Locked the door, turned off the lights and flipped the sign on the glass from open to closed. A police cruiser sped through traffic with lights and siren, headed away from College Hill. Elias stood transfixed, watching. They were already looking for Ballard's pickup.

When the cruiser was out of sight, he turned his back to the street and studied the store. No movement. The ceiling fan over the register made a gentle ticking sound. Somewhere a door slammed and someone laughed. Barely audible. He heard voices that weren't there before. He went through the swinging gate and knelt behind the counter, found the woman's purse, took out her car keys and put them in his sack. Then he pulled out the Kimber .45 semiautomatic he'd taken from Ballard's safe.

He walked toward the back carrying the sack and the Kimber and went through the metallic doors into a room full of furniture and toys and tables with stacks of clothes on them. A man and a woman were on their knees sorting through boxes of paperbacks, turned away, lost in conversation. He shot them in the back of their heads, dropped the Kimber in the sack and went out the back door to find the elderly woman's car.

24

WHEN I STEPPED into the bar, Russ was behind the cash register, pointing me to the corner table where a man in a loose-fitting silk shirt and khaki pants was seated with his back against the wall. He was missing part of one ear and his ruddy complexion was yellow in places and his face sagged as if it were melting. I figured him for mid-seventies.

He watched me pick a path through tables full of customers. A Manilla folder was on the table in front of him. When he stood and shook my hand, I saw a revolver in a pancake holster on the waistband of his khakis. I was carrying too.

"I'm Jake Brackeen," he said, his voice hoarse. "You look like him. Paco Correa, I mean."

He was seized by a fit of coughing. When he recovered, we sat and he smiled like he felt sorry for me. "Your grandfather told me you'd be calling on me. Don't worry," he indicated his throat, "it's not Covid. I have throat cancer."

Russ arrived holding a plate of food in each hand, balancing a third on his forearm. He put the plates on the table and left.

"Cancer," I said to Brackeen. "Sorry to hear it."

He waved that off. "Enjoyed every cigarette I ever smoked," he said. A waitress placed glasses of water in front of us as Russ returned with a file of his own and sat.

When the waitress left, Brackeen said, "What can you tell me about this guy Dean Curtis supposedly sent to kill me? Do you know who he is? Russ here tells me you have an agent in the KBI that you trust."

I nodded. "Caroline Gordon. I just spoke to her and she's on her way here to talk to you. And no, we don't know who the guy is who might've came to kill you."

"Did she tell you anything new?"

"She said the PD found a man dead in a Buick on your street, south of your house. No ID. Shot twice in the head. Surprised you didn't hear it."

He pointed at one of his hearing aids. "I don't hear shit without my ears in, and they weren't in until right before I left."

Brackeen licked his cracked lips. "You want to know about Paco Correa. Might as well get this show on the road." He pulled a piece of paper out of his breast pocket and pushed it across the table at me. "Four days after your grandfather hired me twenty-eight years ago, I found three of Paco's friends who were willing to talk. You know, 'off the record.'"

He made air quotes with his fingers when he said *off the record*. "Like Paco, they were here illegally. They didn't trust cops, but they were pissed and wanted to see something done, so they told me what they heard, mostly from Paco. I have no idea where you can find them now or if they're even alive."

I picked up the paper. Two men, one woman, names written in cursive. No other identifying information. I didn't recognize the names.

Brackeen shrugged. "They didn't give me much. Wouldn't even give me their birthdays."

"What'd they tell you?" Russ asked.

"That Paco and Ben's mother, Paula, were selling cocaine in the early nineties. They made the mistake of selling half a kilo to an undercover cop." Brackeen paused and studied my face like he was giving me time to get used to the idea that my mother was a drug dealer. "Paco and Paula believed they were looking at serious prison time. And of course, if convicted, Paco would be deported after serving his sentence."

"I knew my mother was an addict," I said. "Never knew she was a dealer."

"How could you? There's still no record of their arrest or the undercover buy. I have a friend in the sheriff's office who confirmed that for me after I spoke to Russ this morning." His eyes volleyed from me to Russ and back. "Back in '93, after I spoke with Paco's friends I made a formal records request from the Sedgwick County Sheriff's Office and the Wichita Police Department. Asked for any and all arrest records of anyone named Paco Correa. Also asked for the arrest records of Paula Joel. Both searches came back: *no records found.* Only thing I got out of it was my name on somebody's blacklist."

He let that sink in. I knew what he meant. Twenty-eight years ago he'd told Pops that someone had put a gun to his head and told him to stop asking questions about Paco Correa.

Brackeen continued. "Paco's friends said the undercover was Deputy Clint Brown. Said he had a partner but didn't know his name, but the only partner Brown had in '92 and '93 was Reserve Deputy Dean Curtis."

"Were any other cops involved in the undercover buy?" Russ asked.

"I don't know, but I kind of doubt it. What happened after Brown busted Paco and Paula has been a secret too long for there to have been very many cops involved."

"What happened?" I asked. "After they were busted?"

Brackeen pointed at the paper with the names on it. "What all of these people told me, is that Paco turned CI for Brown, the idea being, as it usually is, for Paco and Paula to stay out of prison. Supposedly, Brown seized small amounts of money and illegal drugs here and there based on Paco's information. Nothing too big in the overall scheme of things. He just hit street level guys."

"Any record of those busts? Arrests? Seizures of drugs or guns?" Russ asked.

"No," Brackeen said. "Not according to my friend at the SO. If what Paco's friends say is true, Brown's dirty."

"You think Brown was pocketing money from small-time drug dealers?" I said.

"Yeah, probably, but that wasn't the end game."

"Let's skip to the end, then," Russ said.

Brackeen nodded. "Brown told Paco he was real interested in a case involving a young girl who'd been smuggled into the United States from Mexico and was found raped and murdered at a local flop house in the hood."

"The hood? Where exactly?" Russ said.

"Grove Street, Wichita. New Salem neighborhood. I have the exact address in here."

Brackeen pulled a yellowed newspaper article out of the Manila folder and laid it before us. It was a *Wichita Eagle* story with the headline: MISSING TWELVE-YEAR-OLD GIRL FOUND RAPED AND MURDERED IN NEW SALEM. Above the article was the paper's masthead with the date, June 12, 1993. I did the math—forty-one days before I found my mother dead. The story recounted the brutal murder of Maria Alvarez, a twelve-year-old girl who'd been missing from her home in Juárez, Mexico for almost six months. There were no suspects.

Brackeen talked while we read. "Brown threatened to pin that on Paco unless he provided information about the human trafficking problem that was making itself known at the time. Brown said he wanted to nail the traffickers to the fucking wall, then made Paco a simple offer, one that wouldn't necessarily nail any traffickers at all. If Paco provided enough intel to save even one woman or child from the cartels, the coke charge would go away." Brackeen made like he was washing his hands, then opened his palms to us. "All is forgiven. Paco wouldn't even have to testify against anyone."

Brackeen snapped his fingers like he'd just remembered something. "The middle person on that list, what's his name?"

"Jose Gutiérrez," I said.

"Yeah, ol' Jose told me Paco thought this was what Brown was after the whole time."

"Saving women and children from a human trafficking ring?" Russ said. "Paco must've been into that for Brown to even think that could work."

Even though I'd never known the man, the thought of my putative father selling innocent people into sex slavery sent a wave of shame and horror through me. I wondered if it was true and if so, whether my mother knew.

Brackeen gave me a sympathetic smile. "I don't know for sure if Paco was involved in human trafficking himself, but he was in a position to get the information from somewhere, so it's possible, but his friends said Paco was against that so I kinda doubt it."

"Against raping women and children," I said, more to myself than to Brackeen and Russ. "Way to take a stand, Paco."

Brackeen shrugged. "His friends might've been lying for him or didn't know the truth."

"Or they were involved in it too," Russ said.

"Possible," Brackeen said. "But here's what I'm getting at. What Clint Brown was doing here, on the face of it anyway, was using Paco to go after human traffickers, or at a minimum, to save a few lives. That sounds like a worthwhile law enforcement goal, right? Use some low-level who-gives-a-shit coke case as a tool to save a woman or child from sex slavery." He tapped a fingernail on the table. "Except Paco saw through it—kind of."

"What do you mean 'kind of'?" I asked.

"Somehow Paco knew about a place in El Paso near the border where ten or fifteen young women and children were being temporarily warehoused by smugglers."

"How would he know that if he wasn't into it up to his neck?" I said.

"Right," Brackeen said, nodding, "I don't know and neither did his friends, or at least they said they didn't, but the point is that he might've had information. Maybe good information, and Brown, our future undersheriff, wasn't real interested in it."

"Why?—because the girls weren't in his jurisdiction?" Russ said.

Brackeen nodded again. "That'd be my guess. Not enough kudos for Brown to get involved. You see where this is going. Brown told Paco he wanted to know about stash houses in his jurisdiction. In Sedgwick County, not some place in El Paso.

Problem was, Paco didn't know of any, and if there were any, it's unlikely there'd be as many as ten to fifteen women and children being kept there, even temporarily. We're probably too far away from the border for a warehousing operation that extensive."

"You said Paco saw through it, kind of," I said. "What did you mean by that?"

"You have the benefit of hindsight. Paco Correa didn't. He thought Brown was one of those people who didn't want to share the spotlight with his superiors, let alone some A-hole cops in El Paso. He thought Brown was . . . I don't know, looking for the best way to kick-start his career. Maybe he gets a prettier girlfriend out of the deal, or at least one who's crazy about polishing his knob on a more regular basis. Paco simply misread Brown. Thought he was a simple guy with simple ambitions. So Paco played Brown's game by Brown's rules. All three of the people listed on that paper told me Paco somehow figured out that there were a few girls headed this way and where they were going to be kept." Brackeen shrugged. "He might've even diverted them there, who knows? Whatever the situation, he tipped Brown about it."

"How'd that turn out?" I said.

"The information was good. Brown and his partner—I'm thinking it was Curtis—pulled four girls out of an abandoned farmhouse north of Clearwater in late June of '93. Shot a cartel guy in the process—a Mexican national here illegally. One guy got away. Brackeen held up four fingers. "Four living, breathing girls—undocumented and prepubescent, not one of 'em into her teens—were pulled out of that fucking house."

Brackeen took a drink of water and cleared his throat. He was shaken up, even after all these years. "But there's still no record of that bust ever occurring either. Or the shooting."

"Your friend at the SO checked that for you this morning too?" I said.

Brackeen nodded. "No record I could find in '93. No record now."

"No record the guy who was shot was ever in the country?" Russ said. "Do you think Brown killed him? Dumped the body somewhere?"

Brackeen picked up his sandwich, looked at it and set it down. "I do. So did Paco, I'm told. No one ever saw the guy again as far as the three people on that list ever knew. As far as Paco knew, too. Maybe the guy showed up later, after I stopped digging into this, but I doubt it. Hell, we don't even know the guy's name. You see the problem? It's like he never existed."

Russ's mouth was open a little, his eyes fixed on nothing in particular.

"Were any of the girls ever found?" I said.

"What girls?" Brackeen said coldly. "They were smuggled across the border then sold into prostitution. Maybe the smugglers told the girls' families they died in transit. Dollars to donuts nobody came looking for the girls. God only knows what happened to them."

All this was hearsay or rank speculation, so errors could abound. That's why hearsay and speculation aren't admissible in court, but they were rungs in the ladder of this investigation. Rungs we needed to climb in our search for reliable evidence, something admissible in a court of law.

Brackeen's jaw tightened. "After that, Clint Brown modified his deal with Paco."

"How so?" I said.

"Brown said four girls wasn't enough. He wanted to know about other stash houses in the area. Problem was, even if Paco would've been willing to keep dealing with him, whatever source of information he had had was dried up. He had nothing to give Brown. My sense is that Paco wasn't well connected to any criminal underworld. Anyone selling half kilos isn't that well connected. If Paco's friends are right about him not being involved in human trafficking or smuggling himself, my guess is that he came across someone in his world that slipped with some information or maybe he went looking for the information when Brown made him that deal, which might've looked pretty suspicious to the traffickers after one of their guys and four of their victims went missing. Anyway, Paco tried to exploit what he'd learned to get himself clear of that drug charge but ended up being exploited by Brown."

Brackeen nodded toward me. "About then, Brown approached your mother."

"For information?" I said.

"No. For sex, according to Paco's friends."

My muscles tensed.

Brackeen noticed. "Don't ask me how Paco or his friends learned that. I'm just telling you what I was told. I don't know what went down between Brown and your mother, and I don't have any idea what happened to Paco, but I know who might."

"Who?"

"Emily Knudson." He handed me a sheet of paper from his folder. "In her mid-fifties. Got her address for you too. She's a widower to a cop who was on duty with Brown and Curtis the night Paco Correa went missing from a bar called The Rabbit Hole."

"The Rabbit Hole?" I said.

"Biker bar in the country, northwest of here," Russ said. "It's out of business now."

"That's right," Brackeen said. "Someone from the bar called 911 the night Paco went missing."

Russ laughed. "Someone from The Rabbit Hole actually called the cops?"

Brackeen smiled. "Yeah I know. Hard to believe. This was before cell phones. Call came from the bar's landline, but the caller wouldn't identify himself. Guy sounded drunk as hell and said he heard gunshots when he was out back taking a piss, then hung up."

"Out back taking a piss," I said. "And he offered that gem to the dispatcher? Sounds like a lovely place."

"You have no idea," Brackeen said. "Anyway, Deputy Charlie Knudson went there without backup because his backup was nowhere to be found."

"I'm guessin' that was Brown and Curtis," I said.

"Yep," Brackeen said. "But the call turned out to be no big deal. That's what the records show anyway. By the time Deputy Knudson got to the bar, no one claimed to have heard shit."

"What's all that have to do with Paco and my mother?" I said.

"I told you. Gutiérrez told me that night at The Rabbit Hole was the last time anyone saw Paco, and he was dating your mother at the time."

"The guy who called 911 didn't give his name, but do you have any idea who it was?" Russ said.

Brackeen pursed his lips. "I think it was Gutiérrez, even though he said he didn't."

"Why do you think that?" I said.

Brackeen shrugged. "Gut instinct. A hint of shame in his eyes maybe. I think he ran from the scene and left his friend to die after making the call."

"You have a recording of the call?" Russ said.

"Yeah. I only talked to Gutiérrez the one time. I think that might be his voice on the recording. I have Knudson's incident report as well. Last report he ever wrote."

Brackeen got a CD and a police report from the folder and slid them to me. "I made copies for you. There isn't much to Knudson's report. Dispatcher sent him to The Rabbit Hole. When he got there nobody had seen or heard a damn thing, or had any idea who called 911, which is typical for places like that."

As we scanned the report, Brackeen kept talking. "Knudson was killed on duty the day after he took that call. Ambushed while sitting at a stop sign on a country road. His regular patrol. There were never any suspects."

I said, "I think I know why you never talked to Mrs. Knudson."

Brackeen looked me in the eye. "It's like I told your grandfather all those years ago. A man in a mask caught me in my alley while I was taking out the trash one night. Put a gun to my head and asked me why I was asking around about Paco Correa. I told him I had a client who wanted to keep Paco away from his grandchildren. The man told me my client had nothing to worry about. Told me I needed to put down the shovel and stop digging my own grave. That's when I gave your grandfather his money back and told him he should let things be."

I held up the paper with three names on it. "Not as much help as I'd hoped for."

Brackeen shrugged.

I tried to shake off my disappointment, reminding myself what Pops had hired Brackeen to do almost thirty years ago—figure out if Paco was coming to take me and my sister away from him. By all accounts, Brackeen had done what he was hired to do.

"How'd this mess of shit get stirred up again?" Brackeen asked.

Russ held up a hand. "My fault. Six days ago I played Brown against a guy that owned an escort service—"

"Ricky Butler?" Brackeen said.

Russ nodded. "Yeah, I went to Brown's house. Told him Butler claimed Brown had raped an escort, told him Butler had made a vague threat to go after him because of it."

"Why the hell'd you do a fool thing like that?" Brackeen said.

"To make trouble for Butler because he's a fucking piece of shit."

"What's that got to do with what happened in '93?"

I raised my hand. "I went with Russ to Brown's house that day. It's a long story but the gist of it is this: We knew Butler claimed to know something about some cops murdering Paco and a woman in Worthington in '93, which is where my mother died. We didn't know who the cops were or whether the story had any truth to it, but when I saw where Undersheriff Brown was living, I knew I'd been by the place as a small child with my mother."

Brackeen nodded. "Sounds like Brown told Dean Curtis about you and Russ showing up. Told Curtis who you were— Paula Joel's kid, grown up and a dead ringer for Paco Correa. Brown would've also told Curtis about Butler's accusations.

That would have fired up Curtis's paranoia. He'd figure the two of you were using Butler and Brown to work a game of some kind—trying to dig up bones he didn't want dug up."

"We shook the dice, didn't really have any idea what we were getting into," Russ said. "But here we are."

Brackeen frowned. "Including me. Thanks for that."

"I'm sorry we put you and your family in danger," I said. "I thought you might not want to talk to us."

Brackeen made a face. "Might as well go down swinging, and since I'm too old for swinging, what I mean is I'll go down talking. Or shooting. Maybe both." He chuckled and started to say something, but was again seized by a fit of coughs.

He paused to catch his breath, then took a drink. "I'm thrice divorced and my only child died a year ago. Doc tells me this throat-cancer thing isn't going to end well. I got nothing left to lose." He squinted. "I actually appreciate the chance to do right by those girls Brown found north of Clearwater. They were probably murdered. Hell, I don't know what happened to them. God only knows."

"There's nothing you could have done," Russ said. "You'd have been killed."

"We're all going to die sometime, and then what? What will still be important after that?" Brackeen's face, matching his voice, was somber. "It's easy for me now. I'm no longer afraid of death like I was years ago because I'm tired, and I have so little left to lose in this life. I'm ready to leave it. I can see what matters and what doesn't and I can tell you that there are only a handful of things that matter in the end and none of them will be a surprise to you. None of them are secret. We want what we want and we tell ourselves things are complicated, but they are not. The things that truly matter are written on our hearts. If I've learned anything new at all, something that wasn't so obvious, it's this: I would rather see a world in which the strong die for the weak, than one in which the weak die for the strong. I never became the man I was supposed to be, but I can help you."

"We appreciate that. What else you got in the folder?" Russ said.

Brackeen handed the folder to Russ. "Those are for you— copies of the records I got from the Worthington Police Department back in '93. Since Paula Joel's death was ruled an overdose right away, the case was subject to the open records act almost immediately." His eyes found mine. "There are photos of your mother in there. Autopsy photos. And photos of her at the scene there in the mobile home. Just sayin'."

Russ glanced my way.

"Go ahead, have a look," I said. "I already saw it in living color."

Russ opened the folder. First photo was of the outside of the mobile home. Second one took me back to the day I stood in that living room for the last time, transfixed by the sight of my mother's dead body on the couch. A familiar tightness formed in my chest as I looked at my mother in the picture, but its grip no longer had the power it once had. Russ flipped through the photos. Stopped when he got to a close-up of a silver crucifix on a broken chain lying on the lime-green carpet. The jewelry meant nothing to me.

"Do you recognize the necklace?" Russ asked.

"No. Never seen it before."

"Neither has your grandfather," Brackeen said.

"If you thought my mother died of an overdose, why do you have these?" I asked Brackeen.

"Given Paco's disappearance and what his friends told me, I thought I should look into it at least. But, as you know, that gun in my face got me off the case." He looked at Russ. "That cross mean something to you?"

"Maybe," Russ said. He opened the file he'd brought, pulled out a packet of papers and handed them to me. "You can keep these."

It was a copy of a *Disculture* magazine article he'd printed off the Internet, titled, "The Talented Mr. Curtis."

Russ pulled out a copy of an actual *Disculture* magazine and flipped to the same article and pointed to the headshot of Dean Curtis in a collared knit shirt. The photo was a particularly flattering one, highlighting the rugged good looks of a man in his prime. Mid-thirties, thick brown hair, steely eyes, and a deeply suntanned, weathered face. Russ put his finger on the magazine photo of the silver crucifix visible at Curtis's throat.

"What year is that magazine?" I said.

"March first of '92," Russ said.

Brackeen coughed. "Where'd you get it?"

"I found the article online, of course, but the photos of Curtis with all these famous people—and I was mostly interested in the men—were too pixilated to print out well, so I found this issue on eBay and ordered it. UPS delivered this today."

Russ flipped two pages deep into the article and pointed at another photo, this one of Dean Curtis dressed in jeans, loafers, and another knit shirt with the crucifix hanging outside the collar again. In the photo, he was standing next to a man in a suit speaking at a podium. "Here is the president of Harvard, tickling Curtis's balls—telling everyone how very special Curtis is for volunteering his time as a reserve deputy in Kansas even though he's a billionaire, as if that somehow makes him more altruistic than every other reserve who volunteers time. This photo was taken at the ceremony dedicating campus office space to Curtis."

"They gave him an office on campus? How much fucking money did he give them?" Brackeen said.

Russ's brows went up. "Fifty mil."

"What was the money for?" I said.

Russ moved his finger quickly through a long paragraph, then read aloud. "To um, 'create the Curtis Program for Mathematical Biology and Evolutionary Dynamics' it says."

"What the hell is that?" Brackeen said.

A waitress interrupted our conversation by hollering at Russ from behind the bar—something wasn't working right with the register. There was a line of customers waiting to pay.

Russ glanced back and nodded at the waitress, then used his finger to search the article again. "Yeah, um, looks like they'll be searching for nature's algorithms."

He looked up and smiled, then pointed at the caption on the photo. "Here's what's important now—"

"I see it," I said. "That cross on his neck looks like the cross on the floor of my mother's mobile home. Same cord chain and everything."

Russ nodded. "According to the caption here, this photo was taken in January of '92."

"It could've broken off his neck while choking out my mother."

Russ put his tongue in his cheek. "Yeah, maybe."

The waitress called out to Russ again. He ignored her for a few seconds while he studied me, then stood and left us for the bar.

I scanned the article, which was written by a women named Heather Wood. Her article painted Dean Curtis as a sort of mysterious Gatsby-like figure—a high-flying bachelor financier with a lavish lifestyle and questionable business ethics. Besides his mansion here in Wichita, the article listed other notable assets: a nine-story town house on Manhattan's Upper East Side; a sprawling twenty-million-dollar ranch in New Mexico; a two-hundred-fifty-acre island in the Caribbean; an eight-million-dollar house in Palm Beach; a fleet of aircraft; and a yacht as long as a football field.

Ms. Wood wrote that Curtis stood to inherit a fortune from his father, which would be added to the billions he'd made on his own. According to Curtis, he made his money by playing the currency markets. But there were rumors of Ponzi schemes and a long account of shady dealings too numerous to read at the moment. All Curtis said in response to Ms. Woods' invitation to address her concerns, was that he considers himself an advisor to billionaires and keeps his clients and his deals secret.

Other parts of his life weren't so secret. There were photos of him with future presidents from both major parties, British royalty, and Hollywood elites, several of which over the three decades since the article was written had faced various and assorted sex scandals, everything from sexual harassment to rape. In one of the photos, Curtis was posing with movie mogul Harvey Fogle and several scantily clad young women. Years later, Fogle was sent to prison for the systematic rape of several of the country's most famous actresses.

"Can I see that when you're done?" Brackeen said.

I pushed the magazine at him.

He put on reading glasses and looked over the tops of them at me. "I don't suppose there's any hint in here that Curtis might be involved in sex trafficking."

"Not from what I saw, other than some of the people he hangs out with."

Russ returned to his seat. "What do you think about the necklace?"

"It's got promise," I said. I looked up and saw Caroline through the front window making her way to the door.

"Crosses like that are a dime a dozen," Russ said. "It could be nothing."

Brackeen said, "Forgive me for asking this, Ben, and maybe it's none of my business, but what makes you think Curtis, or anyone for that matter, strangled your mother. What about all the evidence of overdose?"

Caroline came over to our table, popped me in the arm with the back of her hand and nodded toward the front door. "You have a second?"

"Sure," I said, getting to my feet. "Thank you for meeting with us, Mr. Brackeen. Caroline can tell you what you need to know when she comes back." I turned to Caroline. "Can you get Mr. Brackeen some kind of security? Police presence in or around his house?"

"No thanks," Brackeen said.

We looked at him.

"Took me by surprise back in '93." He touched his revolver. "But I'm ready for them this time."

Caroline gave Russ a look. *Stay here with Brackeen.*

Russ nodded and said to Caroline, "I'll stay with Mr. Brackeen until you get back, but your first order of business is to find and protect a woman named of Emily Knudson. Ben will explain."

I nodded. "He's right. That needs to happen as soon as possible."

"Okay," said Caroline. "You can explain in the car."

"Where we going?"

"Nowhere in particular," she said. "It's just that moving targets are harder to hit."

When I got to the door, my stomach growled and I realized I hadn't touched my food. I thought about going back and getting it but Caroline was walking so fast she was practically running. I'd grab a bite later.

25

CAROLINE PUT ON her sunglasses as we stepped outside. I followed her to a grey Crown Victoria in the parking lot, both of us scanning the area as we did.

We piled into her car and headed north past the grain elevator away from the city. Traffic was light, bordering on nonexistent.

She said, "The man killed on your neighbor's property is Paul Keefer, AKA, Kage Walker. That name mean anything to you?"

Kage Walker was the man Geronimo told me Curtis hired as a hitman in the past, except Geronimo didn't know his real name was Paul Keefer.

"No," I said, using Slick-Willie lawyer logic to tell myself I hadn't actually just lied to Caroline, which would've been a felony. She'd asked if the man's name meant anything to me. It didn't. An imprecise question deserved an imprecise answer. His name could've been Humpty Dumpty. The name meant nothing. I was just glad Youngblood had killed him before he could kill me.

"You sure about that?" Caroline said.

"Yeah, I'm sure."

She gave me a long look. "I've got a source that tells me Kage Walker was a hired hitman for the Trevino Cartel on occasion."

Geronimo's cartel. This is why Caroline separated me from Russ and Brackeen. She wanted to have another crack at me about what happened two years ago.

"What's this Kage Walker guy doing hits for the Trevino Cartel have to do with me? If you're suggesting the Trevino Cartel wants me dead, that doesn't make any sense."

"I agree," Caroline said. "Kage Walker is a mercenary. He'd whack his own mother if the price was right. I don't think a cartel hired him to kill you. I think it was Dean Curtis."

"Okay, so what're you asking me?"

"Do you have any connections with the Trevino Cartel?"

Other than Geronimo, no. Shit, this question was as clear as the answer. I didn't want to lie. Didn't want to commit a felony either. But I damn sure didn't want to answer her question.

"Connections?" I asked. "People assume one cartel attacked another two years ago during Rummells' trial, right? It caused so much turmoil that I declared a mistrial. If the Trevino Cartel was involved, then they caused the mistrial and in that sense I guess we're connected. You worked the Rummell case, so you'd be connected too."

"Fuckin' lawyers." She shot me a quick glare. "I'll try one more time. Do you have any ongoing connection with the Trevino Cartel unrelated to the damn trial two years ago?"

"No further comment," I said. That's what I came up with. Brilliant.

"Why not?"

I shook my head. "Got my reasons."

"I'll be damned. You're pleading the Fifth."

"Call it that if you want."

She smiled. Glanced in the rearview mirror. "Still don't trust me, do you?"

"I trust you as much as I trust very few people, but not a hundred percent. Don't take it personal. I don't trust myself a hundred percent."

"From what I can tell, I don't think you did anything wrong. Illegal, maybe, but not wrong. Things were bad back then. I get that. All the people I thought were going after you two years ago ended up dead. Not a big problem for me. But how about we go another route this time? Maybe you trust me enough to let me help you."

I thought about pressing her for information. See if she knew anything about my alliance with Geronimo. But if I wasn't going to talk, I figured she wouldn't either, so I changed the subject.

"I need to tell you about this woman who needs protection—Emily Knudson."

She nodded. "Alright."

I summarized what I'd learned from Brackeen, particularly as it pertained to Knudson, who, according to Brackeen, lived in nearby El Dorado, Kansas. When I finished, Caroline got the El Dorado police chief on the phone and made the pitch Russ and I had asked for.

She ended the call and said, "The chief knows Knudson. He's sending a couple officers to find her. They think she's at work. They'll stay with her until I can get there late this afternoon."

"I appreciate it."

"There's something else I need to ask you. Got nothing to do with anything that happened two years ago. Are you done lawyering up?"

"Depends. Ask your question."

"The Wichita PD is looking for a white 2006 Dodge Ram pickup with Oklahoma plates in connection with the College Hill shooting. Tag comes back to a Roland Ballard. That name mean anything to you?"

"No. You have a picture of him?"

She swiped her phone and handed it to me. "Here's his prison mug."

Below Ballard's mugshot was a sign that read:

ROLAND T. BALLARD

JULY 7, 2015

CRABTREE CORRECTIONAL CENTER

"Ballard didn't kill Ricky Butler," she said. "I can tell you that much."

I agreed. Ballard's face was horse-like, long and angular. Nothing like the man who killed Butler on video.

"Is Ballard still in prison?" I asked.

She shook her head. "No. Out on parole."

"What was he in for?"

"Burglaries. Thefts. Meth Possession. He's not supposed to leave Oklahoma without approval of his parole officer, which he didn't have. The Okies are sending deputies to his place to see who, if anybody, is there."

Caroline's phone rang. She answered and I watched her for a reaction. Couldn't tell if she was getting good news or bad, but her body language told me it was important. She asked whoever was on the other end to send her a copy of something. After a few seconds I could tell that wasn't going to happen.

When the call ended, she glanced in the rearview mirror, flipped a U-turn, and romped on the accelerator.

"What is it?" I asked.

"Someone on Brackeen's street might have caught Youngblood on a surveillance camera. You and I know what he looks like from the video of Butler's murder. You're going with me."

"Am I?"

She shrugged. "You could open the door and jump. I wouldn't, but that's just me."

*　*　*

Caroline parked the Crown Vic in front of a big two-story frame house on North Pershing Street. A police officer was talking to a sweaty middle-aged woman in leggings and a tank top in the driveway. We climbed out of the Crown Vic under a canopy of giant elms that lined both sides of the street. Beams of sunlight poked through gaps in the canopy. Down the street a lawn mower started up and a sprinkler sputtered over new grass near the woman's front porch. The neighborhood's homey vibe was marred by police cruisers and the medical examiner's van and the clot of cops surrounding the Buick at the curb three doors down.

I followed Caroline up the long driveway while watching the activity at the Buick which was faced away from us, parked at the curb with a view of Jake Brackeen's front door. An officer was taking photos of something inside the Buick.

"You Agent Gordon?" the cop said as we approached.

"Yes, sir," Caroline said, looking at the woman in leggings. "You must be Evelyn Todd."

Evelyn nodded.

Caroline smiled. "I was told you have video of our suspect on your phone. Mind if we have a look?"

Evelyn handed Caroline her phone. "Only place you can see the guy is when he's directly in front of the camera zipping across my yard." She indicated her front door which was largely concealed from the street by a legion of plantings on a heavy wooden railing and in baskets hanging from the eaves.

Caroline held the phone so we both could watch the video.

The officer said, "It's cued to the exact moment he crosses the yard. Blink and you'll miss it."

Caroline hit play. The cop was right about how quickly the man zipped by. He was headed in the direction of the Buick and had roughly the same build as Youngblood.

"Son of a bitch is fast," Caroline said. "What do you think? That him?"

"Let's see it again."

Caroline reversed it and we gave it another look. Same problem as before—too quick—so she backed it up again and paused it when the guy ran into view. He looked fit, wearing a dark shirt and blue jeans. He had a phone to his ear.

"Hard to tell for sure, but I think it's Youngblood," I said.

"Youngblood?" said the cop. "Who's that? Name I heard was Ballard."

"This isn't Ballard," Caroline said. "Youngblood's what we're calling the guy we think killed the guy in the Buick since we don't know his real name."

I glanced down the street at the Buick. "He had to have been talking to me on the phone when he came through here."

The cop stared at me. "You were talking to this Youngblood guy as he was on his way to kill the guy in the Buick?"

"I think so," I said.

He made a face. "You think so? If you were talking to him, you must know him somehow."

"Not his real name."

The cop frowned. "Roland Ballard doesn't ring a bell?"

"Yeah, it does," I said. "Ballard owns the truck Youngblood was driving."

I could see by the look on his face that I was starting to annoy him.

Caroline pointed at the other houses along the street. "Any other surveillance cameras nearby that might've caught this guy?"

The cop nodded. "We've spotted a few, but Evelyn is the only homeowner we've been able to contact so far. We're working on it."

We watched a man and a woman from the ME's office pull a body out of the Buick and place it on a stretcher. Evelyn gasped.

"Were any of the cameras the police have spotted in a position to've picked up the actual shooting?" Caroline asked the cop.

"Doubt it. I didn't see any surveillance cameras over that way that could've picked it up."

"Is my video helpful?" Evelyn asked.

Caroline smiled and handed the phone to the cop. "Sure. It's a piece of the puzzle. Thank you for giving us this, and for your cooperation."

When we got to the Crown Vic, Caroline told me we weren't heading back to the bar for her meeting with Brackeen just yet.

* * *

On our way out of the neighborhood, Caroline pointed out the license plate reader that had captured the white Dodge pickup's exit from College Hill after the shooting.

We turned left onto South Hillside just as Ballard's pickup had. Coming out from under the East Kellogg overpass I noticed a cross made from railroad ties lying on the sidewalk in front of a QuikTrip convenience store.

"What's up with that?" I said, pointing at the cross. "Thing has wheels on it."

"You haven't seen those before?"

"No. What are they?"

"Crosses on wheels."

"No shit."

She smiled. "People haul them up and down busy streets, along interstate highways. Evangelicals getting out the good news. The crosses I've seen before weren't nearly that big, just a couple of two-by-fours on rollers."

"Holy rollers," I said, laughing.

Caroline wrinkled her nose.

I looked back at the cross as we kept going, remembering something Youngblood had said—*the greatest prophet born of woman would never recognize me. But soon, you will, and you will have no choice but to believe.* I pulled out my phone and Googled the phrase, "the greatest prophet born of woman."

We stopped at a red light behind a line of vehicles. Caroline drummed her fingers on the steering wheel, looking around as I read. We took off again, slowly. First five entries of my search all said the same thing. *The greatest prophet born of woman* was what Jesus had called John the Baptist.

I thought about that. A cross. Jesus was crucified on a cross.

"Turn around," I said. "Go back to QuikTrip."

"Why?"

"I think Youngblood might believe he's the Second Coming of Christ. At least that's what he believed this morning."

"So what?"

"So turn the car around, lady."

She made a face—annoyed, slightly offended. "What makes you think he thinks he's the Second Coming?"

"Something he said to me. I think he's traded one delusion for another."

"What? This guy is juggling delusions?"

"In Curtis's cult Youngblood thought Curtis was a prophet. Then he saw Curtis for what he is, a narcissistic con man. Now Youngblood apparently sees himself as a Christ figure of some kind. At least that's how he talks. Just turn around and go back to the QT, I'll explain later."

"You think Youngblood was hauling that big-ass cross around and what? Dropped it there? That was his idea of a brilliant getaway, do it in slow-motion? That what you think?"

"I don't know, maybe. Guy thinks he's Christ, it might not be about logic with him, you know what I'm saying?"

"Yeah, because if it was about logic, he wouldn't go anywhere near a QuikTrip."

"High prices?"

She stared at me. "Surveillance cameras, dumbass."

"He has a knack for getting caught on camera, in case you haven't noticed. Are you gonna turn around, or do I need to jump out and run back there?"

"Relax, I'm working on it. Don't think anyone's gonna steal the cross or erase the video in the next three minutes."

She changed lanes and turned into the entrance of a strip mall of mostly boarded-up businesses and made for the exit. The mall was one long building that took up the whole block. Two cars were parked in front of a massage parlor which looked to be the only store in the mall still operating.

As Caroline was about to get back on the road headed north, I noticed a man in a ragged army jacket walking out from behind the end store in the mall—what used to be a pharmacy.

"Stop," I said.

Caroline hit the brakes. Looked at me. "What?"

I pointed to where the man had been. "Guy in an old army jacket saw me and ducked back behind the building."

"Homeless guy maybe—cops have been trying to clear them out of this area for a while."

"It could've been a homeless guy. His clothes looked pretty beat up."

"So why'd you have me stop?" Then she read the look on my face. "What? You think it was Youngblood?"

"Maybe. I didn't get a good look, but he was young and looked to be in decent shape. He didn't like seeing me at all, or maybe it was your Crown Vic he didn't like seeing—thing puts out a heavy cop vibe."

"Youngblood wasn't in an army jacket."

I thought about that. "Could've thrown it on to change his look. Why else would anyone wear a jacket in this heat?"

Caroline put the car in reverse and backed into a parking spot in front of the defunct pharmacy. She called a police officer she knew and gave him our location. Told him she was checking out a suspicious person behind the mall roughly matching the description of the College Hill shooter.

When the call ended, she climbed out of the car, so I did too.

"Where you going?" she asked.

"With you."

She reached into the backseat and pulled out a ballistic vest with the letters KBI in bold yellow print on both sides. I stood on the sidewalk and watched for anyone coming around the corner as she put it on. She looked up at me and nodded at the Crown Vic.

"How about you get back in there?"

I felt like a kid who'd climbed out of bed and wandered into the adult party. "Think I'll hang here. Get some fresh air."

"I could order you back in the car."

"You could."

"Jesus, Ben. Get in the damn car."

"No."

"Suit yourself. Don't get shot. I don't have a vest for you."

"Fair enough."

"Other than the army jacket," she said, "did you see what he was wearing?"

"Looked like blue jeans, I think."

"Dark shirt?"

"Couldn't see his shirt."

Caroline pulled her Glock out of its holster. "Could've been Youngblood, right?"

"Could've been, or just a homeless dude like you said. How about we wait for the uniforms?"

"How about you get in the car?"

"Hell of an echo in this neighborhood."

She trotted to the corner of the defunct pharmacy and peeked around it. For a moment I thought she was going to take my advice and wait for backup, then she darted around the corner. I jogged over there in time to see her reach the back of the building. She peered around its far end. Yelled at someone to stop, then took off.

I drew my pistol and bolted to where I'd last seen her. Peeked around the corner. Saw Caroline in full sprint away from me, chasing after Army Jacket. He reached a chain-link fence and tried to scale it, almost made it, but snagged his foot and landed face down in the grass on the far side. In that moment I knew this wasn't Youngblood, but it was too late for Caroline to disengage because the guy stood and squared up on her. She screamed for him to put his hands in the air.

He reached into his coat.

Caroline fired. *Bapbapbap.*

One bullet hit a fence wire and ricocheted off somewhere. Two hit the man in the chest. He dropped like someone had cut the power.

*   *   *

Caroline scaled the fence and dropped to her knees next to the man. Checked for a pulse.

I ran up behind her, looking around as I did to make sure we were alone. The man was on his back, arms splayed out, palms up. The army jacket was unbuttoned, his dark shirt now visible. Blood flowed through two holes in the shirt near the man's heart. Caroline pressed her hands on the wounds. Blood oozed between her fingers.

"Shit, shit, shit." She looked up at me. "Give me your shirt."

I started to holster my pistol so I could take off the shirt when a man's voice behind me yelled, "Drop the gun!"

A cold chill ran through me. I dropped the gun in the grass.

"He's with me, don't shoot," yelled Caroline.

I raised my hands in the air.

"He's with you?" said the man behind me.

Caroline worked to plug the man's wounds with her hands. "That's what I said. Call for an ambulance."

I looked behind me—a uniformed cop. He had his gun out, glancing around. His name tag read, SGT. TRILLO. I remembered the guy. He'd been involved in Jimmy Ray's murder investigation. "Any more threats back here?" he asked.

I looked around, still didn't see anything. "No."

Trillo continued to scan the area as he called dispatch for an ambulance on his shoulder mic. I pulled my shirt off and dropped it over the fence to Caroline. She took it and pressed it to the man's chest.

"He have a gun on him?" Trillo asked.

"I don't know," Caroline said. "He was reaching for something in his jacket."

"I saw it all. That's what happened," I said.

Trillo climbed the fence, dropped to the other side.

Caroline pressed down on the man with her hands and knees, bringing her full weight to bear on the wounds, my shirt soaking up blood.

Trillo dropped to his knees. Pressed two fingers on the man's neck. "Pulse is fading," he said. "He's pretty much gone. Let's see if he was reaching for a gun." Trillo patted around on the army jacket, trying to keep out of Caroline's way.

She gave me an anguished look. "It's not Youngblood."

I nodded. "I know. I'm sorry."

"Sonofabitch," she said.

"Only thing he's got in his jacket is definitely not a gun," Trillo said. He pulled a ring of keys out of the man's right pocket. Sorted through them, and showed us one with the Dodge Ram emblem on it. A plastic key tag on the ring read:

TRUKTOWN

OKLAHOMA CITY

Caroline looked as confused as I was.

"I think you got him," said Trillo. "Guy pretty much fits the description of the College Hill shooter, and he has a key to a Dodge Ram that probably came from Oklahoma. It all fits."

That's when a call came in over Trillo's shoulder mic. They'd located Roland Ballard's Dodge Ram pickup abandoned behind a vacant building on Lincoln Street, six blocks away—what used to be Wyman's Furniture Store.

* * *

The ambulance arrived ten minutes later. The paramedics told us what we already knew. The man was dead. The ID they pulled from his back pocket said he was Tommy Garner. They loaded Tommy on a stretcher and took him away, leaving Caroline to clean herself with towels and wet wipes they'd given her, but blood had stained her pants and ballistic vest.

Caroline and I walked with Sergeant Trillo to the front of the strip mall.

"The officers checking out Ballard's truck tell me it has a TrukTown dealer sticker on it," Trillo said. "It'd be one hell of a coincidence if the key I took off that man didn't crank the engine."

When we reached our vehicles, Trillo gave me a gray T-shirt out of a gym bag in his trunk. He was tall and built like me and his shirt fit well. He offered to give us a ride, but Caroline said she was okay to drive. Told me the same thing when I asked her to let me drive, adding that letting me drive her duty car would violate bureau policy.

I kept a close eye on her as we followed Trillo through traffic. Her pupils were dilated and she was sweating profusely, obviously wrestling with the strain of having killed a man.

"What happened wasn't your fault," I said.

"Really? Whose was it then? I pulled the trigger."

"You had to. Couldn't be avoided, by you anyway?"

"Can we not talk about it right now?"

I felt sick for Caroline. The men I'd killed two years ago had it coming. They'd turned their world into a death match and lost. I had no regrets. Killing them didn't seem to bother me at all. At least on a moral level. Maybe that was a problem. It probably was, but I wasn't losing any sleep over not losing any sleep so I counted it as a win. But this situation seemed different. In that last second before the shots rang out I feared Caroline was about to kill a hopelessly confused homeless man. While I was certain he wasn't the man we knew as Youngblood, I held out hope he was an accomplice of Youngblood's. A wheelman perhaps. I wondered what the license plate reader showed. Seems like we would've been told if it showed two people in Ballard's pickup, but maybe not. Maybe the guy was in on the College Hill killing and had it coming after all. I hoped for Caroline's sake that was the case. I wondered if something like that would help her get through this. I decided that it couldn't hurt.

We pulled in behind Wyman's Furniture. It looked like it'd been out of business for at least a decade, drab scaling stucco, cracked front window, nothing but an empty shell. We parked next to Trillo who'd parked next to two other police cruisers.

There were two uniforms standing by the open driver's side door of Ballard's pickup watching us as we approached. An officer wearing rubber gloves with a name tag on his shirt that read, HAWKINS, held out his hand. Trillo handed him the keys. Hawkins leaned in, slid the key into the ignition, and cranked the engine. It started. He shut it down again.

Trillo smiled at us. Caroline shook her head and looked at me.

"Maybe he was an accomplice," I said. "A wheelman would have the keys, right?"

"LPR photos show only one person in the truck," Trillo said. Then he shrugged. "Unless one of them was ducking down. I guess that's possible. What makes you think this guy wasn't the shooter?"

Caroline looked at me.

I said, "I was talking to the shooter on the phone during the shooting. Caroline and I have seen the shooter's face on another video. Guy Caroline shot wasn't the College Hill shooter."

Caroline looked around. "No surveillance cameras back here?"

"No," Hawkins said.

I glanced around. Given the fences and the trees surrounding the back lot, it was unlikely that anything that happened back here would have been captured by any cameras from nearby businesses.

"Any cameras from other stores on Lincoln out front that might've caught something?" Caroline asked.

"No," Hawkins said. "We checked already."

Caroline peeked into the cab of the pickup and walked away toward Lincoln Street. I watched her go, then decided to follow. Caught up to her when she stopped on the sidewalk out front. She stood there looking east, then west. Hawkins came up behind us.

"Agent Gordon, we really did check those places for video. Their surveillance doesn't extend this far. There's nothing, I promise."

She didn't take her eyes off traffic and the businesses along Lincoln. "Thanks."

"Sure," Hawkins said. He watched her. "Is there something else you're looking for?"

"I don't know."

He gave me a look—concerned, perplexed. Then he left us.

"You okay?" I said.

She didn't look at me. She was looking west up the street. "You ever shoot a man, Ben?"

I steeled my face.

She turned and saw the look. "Pleading the Fifth again?"

"What? Can't hear you for all the traffic. You'll be on administrative leave for a while, huh?"

Her look told me she knew I'd heard her just fine. "Yeah, admin leave. That's what cops get after they shoot someone."

"Shit," I said.

"Yeah, shit. I need to call Ted."

Her supervisor. I remembered his last name was Novacek.

"You gonna call from here?" I wiped sweat out of my eyes. "Out here in this heat?"

She didn't answer. Her eyes were still fixed on something to the west. I followed her gaze. Only thing I could see of the slightest interest was a guy trying to see through the window of a thrift shop with his hands cupped around his eyes. He stepped back and jerked on the handle of the door. It didn't open. He peered through the glass again.

"Kinda weird," Caroline said.

"What?"

"He was looking in the window a minute ago, then he went around back with a phone to his ear, now there he is again."

The guy pulled away from the glass and hit it with the heel of his hand, then stormed off and hopped into a topless Jeep with boxes stacked in the back seat.

"Pissed he can't unload his junk," I said. "Checked the back to see if there was a place to leave it, didn't find a good one."

Caroline ignored me. She took off walking toward the thrift shop.

I hurried to catch up, then fell in beside her. The guy backed the Jeep out and left. As we made our way toward the thrift shop, I noticed he was in line at a Wendy's drive-through. He had a phone to his ear again.

A few minutes later we reached the thrift shop. The storefront window ran the length of the building and the sign on the door read, CLOSED. We peered through the glass. The lights were off and we didn't see anyone inside. We turned to leave when the man in the Jeep pulled into a parking space in front of the store and hopped out. We stood there as he came toward us.

He stared at Caroline, then slowed and stopped. "What's goin' on?"

"What do you mean?" Caroline asked.

"You're with the KBI. And your vest has blood on it."

"It's been a rough day," Caroline said. "Who are you?"

The man pointed at the thrift shop. "I saw you looking in the store."

"That's funny," Caroline said. "I saw you looking in there too. Then you went to the back of the store. I got curious about what you were doing back there."

The man gave her a questioning look. "My aunt works here. I talked to her maybe an hour ago on the phone and she said she'd be here until six, but I show up to drop off some stuff and the place is locked up and the KBI's nosing around. Why are you here?"

Caroline shrugged. "Already told you. I wondered what you were doing behind the store. Now I know. You wanted to drop off your stuff." She looked at the boxes in the Jeep.

"The doors are locked, front and back. My aunt's car isn't here either which is . . . well, it's just weird."

"You know for sure she drove?" I asked. "Maybe she got a ride."

The man looked at me, like, who the fuck are you? Then he surprised me with an answer. "Yeah, maybe. But that would be unusual for her."

"Does your aunt work here alone?" Caroline asked.

"No. There's usually a couple other employees I think, but it's like they're not here either."

"You said your aunt's car wasn't here, but are there any other vehicles in back?" I tasked.

"A couple, yeah. Why are you so interested—"

"Her coworkers' cars maybe?" Caroline shrugged. "Maybe your aunt took them to lunch."

"She knew I was coming and now she's not here and she's not answering her phone. It's not like Auntie Harper to not answer her phone for this long."

The man's phone trilled. He pulled it out and looked at it. "Hang on a sec, it's my mom. Maybe she knows what's going on." He put the phone to his ear. "Did you get ahold of Uncle Kent?" His eyes darted around as he listened to the answer. "Okay, I'll wait for him. I'm at the store now. It's probably nothing, Mom. Maybe she just took everyone to lunch and forgot her phone." He listened. Shook his head. "I know it's not like her but maybe that's what happened, I dunno. She's not getting any younger, maybe she forgot it. Left it in the store or something."

He was trying to be strong for his mom, but his eyes looked worried. He finally ended the call and said, "My mom got ahold of Harper's husband. Harper isn't answering any of our calls. Her husband says an app he has says her phone is still in the store. He works here too. He's on his way with a key. You never really answered me. What's the KBI doing here? You're wearing a blood-stained bulletproof vest for Christ's sake and I noticed there's lots of cops in the area. Lots of lights and sirens too. What the hell's going on?"

Caroline hesitated. "We're looking for a suspect in a shooting. The guy ditched the truck he was driving just down the street—less than two hundred yards from here."

"Jesus!" the man said.

"I never got your name," Caroline said.

"Brandon Conwell."

"Brandon, I think everything's probably just fine with your aunt, but I also think it wouldn't hurt to make sure everything's alright inside the store."

Caroline called Sergeant Trillo. He and Officer Hawkins showed up in under five minutes. Auntie Harper's husband— a vibrant white-haired man in his eighties named Kent— showed up a minute later in a pickup with a lot of questions and a key to the front door that he gave Trillo.

"Sir, how did your wife get to work this morning?" Caroline asked Kent.

"Her car. A Toyota Tercel," Kent said. "Why?"

"Just trying to piece everything together," Caroline said.

Trillo pointed. "If all of you will just go stand over there away from the glass, we'll check the place out."

He was being cautious and wanted us out of the line of fire. We eased away from the front door, off to one side.

Trillo said to Hawkins, "Guns out. College Hill killer was right down the street not too long ago."

Hawkins drew his pistol as Trillo unlocked the door, pulled out his Glock 17, and followed Hawkins in. Kent and I peeked through the glass. Saw the officers crouched, moving cautiously through racks of clothing on their way to the back.

Caroline took a call from someone with the El Dorado PD. I gathered that Emily Knudson was alive and well at the dentist office where she worked. Caroline persuaded whoever was on the phone to escort Mrs. Knudson home when she got off work and stay with her until someone, presumably from the KBI, could meet her there at six o'clock.

Three minutes later Trillo and Hawkins came out with grave looks on their faces. Police sirens kicked on somewhere in the city.

Trillo looked at Kent, who was standing next to Brandon.

"Can you tell me what your wife was wearing when she went to work today?" Trillo asked.

Kent's hand went to his chest. "Blue blouse with sunflowers on it."

Trillo pressed his lips into a hard line, fighting to maintain his composure. "I'm sorry, sir, we found her in there. She's . . . she's gone."

"Gone?" Kent looked confused.

"There's been a shooting—"

Kent's knees gave way and he dropped. Brandon caught him. Didn't keep him from going to the ground, but sat him against the side of the building. Officer Hawkins stepped to them, maybe to help in some way, but what could he do? He stood over them, frowning, while Kent's mouth went slack, like a thousand thoughts and emotions had hit him at once and struck him dumbfounded. When he finally sobbed, Hawkins looked out at the traffic on Lincoln trying not to look like he was shaken up.

Trillo motioned for me and Caroline to step away with him. When we did, he said quietly, "Three people have been murdered in there. Two shot in the head, and the old guy's wife looked like somebody snapped her neck."

The police were checking their automated license plate readers for a hit on the missing Tercel when Caroline and I left the thrift shop on foot and made our way back to the Crown Vic. Before we got back to the car, Russ texted us to meet them at Brackeen's house. Brackeen had grown tired of waiting on us at the bar.

*　*　*

Caroline insisted on driving again. She called her boss, Ted Novacek, from the Crown Vic on our way to College Hill. My attempt to listen to Caroline's part of the conversation was interrupted by a call from Keri.

"Youngblood's on the phone again," Keri said.

I told Caroline that Youngblood was on the line again. Caroline told Ted and ended her call as Keri transferred Youngblood's call to my phone. I put it on speaker.

"You cannot see that I am working through you, but I am," Youngblood said.

"You're right, I'm not seeing it," I said.

"You will, and I'm about to use you again. Tell the cops that Roland Ballard was the one kidnapping all those boys in Oklahoma. Ballard was a serial killer."

Was.

Caroline's eyes widened. The missing boys had been in the news a lot over the last two years.

"How do you know this?" I asked. "And who's Roland Ballard?"

"Just tell the cops what I told you. I'm sure you've been in close contact, no?"

Caroline and I shared a look.

"Where's this Ballard guy?" I said.

"In the outer darkness."

"Outer darkness—think I've heard that one before. You mean he's dead and in hell."

"Gone from Earth and separated from God, yes. His body is in his trailer, and in the woods behind the trailer are many graves. A prop he used to troll neighborhoods for his victims might be at Calvary Cemetery near College Hill—it's a cross on wheels made from railroad ties."

We were on Hillside approaching the QuikTrip. The cross lying on the sidewalk came into view.

"I don't understand," I said. "You said this cross might be at the cemetery. What do you mean, 'might be,' and if it's there, how did it get there?"

"I paid a man named Tommy to leave it there. And like Simon of Cyrene, the man wanted nothing to do with bearing the cross at first, so I don't know if he got the job done, but I suspect if he did what I paid him to do, he ran into some trouble."

Heat crawled up my neck.

Youngblood said, "I never told you I believed I was the Christ, but being the sharpy you are, I suspect you put two and two together. I counted on you telling the cops I was a wacko who thought he was the Messiah. And I thought maybe those cameras on light poles in College Hill might pick up the cross in the bed of Ballard's pickup."

He'd seen the automated license plate readers in College Hill and used them against us. Or tried to anyway. He was crazy, but also cunning. Caroline's glare was fixed on the road. Muscles in her jaw knotted.

I said, "What are you saying?—you used this guy Tommy as a diversion to get away?"

"Yes, but that's not all. Now you see how I can use you for my own purpose. I can do anything through you. You have no say in the matter—in the end result I mean. Your intentions and the choices you make cannot stop me from fulfilling my Father's destiny. I will use you again. That's not what you want to hear, but that's what I'll do."

"Crazy fucker," Caroline said under her breath.

Youngblood said, "I wonder how far Tommy made it down the street with the cross. I hope the police didn't hurt him."

Anger swelled in me. Tommy must've sensed something was wrong when he saw cops swarming the area, so he left the cross on the sidewalk in front of the QT, but didn't want to give up the key to the truck until he knew he'd be in trouble for having it if he got stopped. He might've had a hunch the truck had been stolen. He might've decided to lay low for a while. See if the truck was still behind Wyman's later. Who knows what he thought? Tommy looked homeless, and with those vacant eyes I saw just before he was shot, he didn't strike me as a high functioning individual, which is how Youngblood was able to use him so easily. Youngblood may've fancied himself God, but he exploited weakness like the devil.

I could hear him breathing on the other end. I wanted to ask him if he'd killed those people in the thrift store but didn't want him to think about that and end up ditching the stolen Tercel. If he still had it, it might get him caught.

Youngblood said, "You figure out how to go after Dean Curtis yet? Or how to defend yourself against him?"

"I'm working on it."

"You know what to do," he said.

"Oh? And what's that?"

"You're a lawyer—use that silver tongue of yours to speak the truth for once."

"I don't follow. Speak the truth to whom about what?"

"To the world about Dean Curtis. Think about how to expose him—see if you don't come up with a plan. While it is true that you were chosen for this, it is also true that you have chosen this for yourself."

"You're full of shit. I chose nothing. Neither did you."

"You chose everything."

The call ended. I looked at the phone in disbelief.

"He's crazier than you described him," Caroline said.

I looked out the side window as I thought about Youngblood's final words. "I chose to represent Mia Delarosa," I said, mostly to myself.

"What?"

I looked at Caroline. "I chose to represent Mia. Maybe that's what he meant."

"Who knows what that crazy sonofabitch meant?"

"I actually have an idea about how to go after Curtis while at the same time making it harder for him to come after me."

Caroline rolled her eyes and shook her head. "I hope your idea wasn't inspired by Youngblood."

"No, of course not. But I was thinking about it when he called."

"Let's hear it."

"I file a motion for a bond reduction in Mia's case—"

"Yeah, sure, that'll fly. I hope your big idea doesn't require winning that motion because Judge Abernathy won't go for it. He likes high bonds on murder cases, everyone knows that. Also, how do you figure filing a motion for bond reduction in Mia's case is a way to go after Curtis? I don't get that."

"Hear me out before you start shooting holes in my idea, since it's just that—an idea. It's not like a fully formed plan or anything. I'll bounce it off you if you don't mind."

She glanced at me, then turned into College Hill. "I'm listening."

"The judge denied Mia's motion to lower bond a couple months ago, but now we've got new information for him to consider. And I could give him an option he hasn't been presented with in Mia's case. I think I should, at a minimum, ask the court to order that Mia be held in a different jail pending trial."

"One not run by Undersheriff Brown," Caroline said, nodding. "Makes sense so far."

"Yeah, and here's the best part. In support of the motion, I could file an affidavit laying out the human trafficking case against Brown, Curtis, and Jimmy Ray, explaining what we've learned through our sources."

"Our sources? You mean Youngblood, Brackeen, and Ricky Butler?"

"Yeah, but I'll need your help. Did you have permission from your boss to give me the video of Butler's murder?"

"No, why?"

"Shit."

"What's the matter?"

"To make any of what we've learned from our sources believable at all, I'll need to use Butler's murder video as an exhibit in court. Let the judge see for himself that Butler thought Brown sent Youngblood to kill him before deciding it was actually Curtis."

"You want me to get permission from my boss to allow you to use Butler's murder video in Mia's court case? If I thought I could get that from him, I would've done it before I gave it to you to show Mia. You have the video. I guess you could just use it. I can't stop you. Neither can Ted."

"I don't want to get you into any more trouble than you already are."

"I appreciate that, but there's no way around it. Trust me, Ted won't allow it."

"Talk him into it. At least try."

Caroline shook her head. "I'll try, but to what end? Do you really think the judge will believe a word of what Youngblood told you? Of what three witnesses told Brackeen thirty years ago? You think the judge would order Mia held in some other jail based on that information?"

"Might be enough there to make him nervous enough to do that, yeah."

"You really think so?"

"Yeah, I do. Look, take everything we learned from our sources, combine that with the Butler murder video, then add in the assassination attempt on me this morning. Throw in what just happened at Brackeen's house and everything we're dealing with right now. I figure anyone with at least two brain cells to rub together will think there's a damn good chance that Brown, Curtis, and Jimmy Ray have been involved in human trafficking for decades, and that Brown and Curtis will stop at nothing to keep the truth from coming out."

Caroline turned right onto South Clifton Avenue, gunned it to East Lewis Street and turned left. "For the sake of argument, let's say Ted gives you his blessing to use the video and you get Mia transferred to some other jail. You said you had an idea for going after Curtis. What is it?"

"The press is following this case so they'll have a field day with this, and if they drop the ball, we'll leak the motion to them, so lots of mud will get on Curtis and Brown. But's that's just stage one of what I'm hoping will happen. If a woman did defect from Curtis's cult like Youngblood says, maybe she sees the news coverage and comes forward. If so, then we'll have something. A live witness willing to tell all. Maybe some of Paco's friends are still alive and will come forward. Maybe we'll learn more about what happened to Paco, and to my mother."

"Stage two feels like you're throwing dice."

"Can't win if you don't play."

"You know what I think comes right after stage one?"

"What?"

"Brown and Curtis hire an army of lawyers to sue your ass for defamation."

"They'll lose if they do. I'll have to be careful about how the press gets wind of my motion, but as an attorney acting on behalf of my client in criminal court, I'll have full immunity from a defamation suit."

Caroline squinted. "Okay, you're the attorney, I'll take your word for that, but what about this? Without the testimony of Youngblood, won't everything he told you be hearsay?"

"Yes."

"And those people Brackeen spoke to almost thirty years ago—Paco's friends—won't everything they told Brackeen be hearsay too?"

"Absolutely. Most of what we know—what we think we know—is inadmissible at trial. But this won't be a trial. It'll be a pre-trial release hearing, and a hearing regarding the threat to Mia's safety if she continues to be held in a jail run by Clint Brown. In these kinds of hearings, the judge has a lot of discretion to consider evidence that wouldn't be admissible at trial. That's the beauty of this idea."

"But the judge could enforce the rules of evidence if he wants?"

I shrugged. "Yeah, he has discretion to do that, sure. But I've never seen that done in a bond hearing before."

She thought about it. "The press would eat this up."

"That's the idea."

"And it'll look bad if Mia or you or any potential witnesses end up dead," she said, almost to herself.

"That's right. My motions will bring all kinds of heat and light to the game. Something for the judge to consider."

Caroline gave me a sidelong glance. "I'm warming to your idea, but Ted's not going to go for this. KBI brass above Ted won't like it either. You might just have to use Butler's murder vid without KBI approval. If so, I'll take the heat. I can handle it."

"Tell Ted he should make the video public anyway. At least part of it. Tell him he needs to publish the portion of the video with Youngblood's face on it as soon as possible so the public can help us figure out who he is."

"He might do that, but that won't get you his blessing to use the video the way you want. He won't want people thinking he's siding with an axe murderer. The most important thing to Ted is Ted. Dean Curtis pisses a big stream in this state. If Ted helps us and Curtis is left standing when this is over, Ted's career will take a big hit. He won't want Curtis knowing he authorized my sharing the video with you. I think you'll just have to go for it without Ted. The hell with it. Use it however you want if you think your plan will work."

"It's still just an idea." I shook my head. "I don't want to get you fired."

Caroline turned onto Brackeen's street. "I'm going on administrative leave for the shooting anyway, remember? Ted is giving me until midnight to get this case turned over to Agent Washington."

I remembered Eric Washington. He'd been in my home on a couple of occasions applying for search warrants when I was a judge. Good cop. We'd shared a few beers when we weren't working. I suddenly realized I probably wouldn't be seeing Caroline for a while. No telling how long, at least in her capacity as a KBI agent.

"I'm sorry about today," I said. "Everything's going to work out fine."

"I killed a man. Nothing will ever be the same."

"The man you shot—Tommy—he should've listened to your order to stop and put his hands up. Instead he puts his hand in a pocket. You had no choice but to shoot."

She stifled a sob. "He wanted to give me those keys."

"You can't wait to see what he'd pull out in a situation like that. Good shooter could take you out. You'll be cleared—"

"I think I'm done with this job whether they clear me or not."

"Take it easy," I said. "Youngblood is responsible for that homeless man's death, not you."

Caroline pulled to the curb in front of Brackeen's house and put the Crown Vic in park. Russ's Malibu was parked in the driveway and Russ was leaning against it with his arms crossed, watching us, waiting to take me back to my pickup still at Crossroads Bar & Grill.

"I pulled the trigger," Caroline said. "So it's on me. It's my fault. That's how it works. Use the video if you want. I mean it. My career is over anyway."

"No it's not."

"Yes it is. After today I'm quitting."

*　*　*

Halfway back to the bar curiosity got the best of me. I convinced Russ to head for the town of El Dorado to see if we could question Mrs. Knudson ourselves. He convinced me we should wait until she got off work. In this situation, he felt like Mrs. Knudson was more likely to open up to us and speak freely in her own home. I agreed. This was sensitive stuff. We wanted to know if her husband had told her anything about what happened at The Rabbit Hole biker bar the night Paco Correa went missing twenty-eight years ago—the night before her husband, Deputy Charlie Knudson, was murdered in the line of duty. Worst thing that could happen is we'd get turned away. At least that's what we thought.

26

AFTER QUESTIONING BRACKEEN, Caroline thanked him for his time and stepped outside onto the front porch. A young girl went by on a bicycle and a UPS driver jogged down a neighbor's driveway to his delivery truck as Brackeen's door closed behind Caroline. She stood on the porch and watched a tow truck three doors down being hooked up to the Buick where the murder occurred.

A plainclothes detective she knew named Riggins was also watching, standing next to the Buick in slacks and a tie. He noticed her on Brackeen's porch and waved. She waved back, then remembered that she'd ignored the vibration of two incoming texts while talking with Brackeen. The last text had been from Riggins. When he saw her car parked in front of Brackeen's house he'd gotten her number from Sergeant Trillo. Riggins wanted her to give him a call ASAP.

The other text was from Agent Eric Washington and it came with an attachment. She opened it and found herself staring into the vacant eyes of an Oklahoma prison inmate, who, according to the placard below the man's face, was Elias Matusak, but she knew him as Youngblood. Crazy fuck.

She called Washington, who answered with, "You get the mugshot I sent? I think that's the guy you're calling Youngblood. What do you think?"

"No doubt about it, that's him."

"Matusak spent two years in Crabtree as Roland Ballard's cellmate."

"Good work, Eric."

"Easy work. Once we had the Ballard connection, I called the prison and got mugshots of all his cellmates. When I saw Matusak, I knew he was our guy. The Okies are telling me they're finding graves in the woods behind Ballard's trailer just like Matusak said. The press is already involved. It'll be all over the Internet by the end of the day if it isn't already."

"Jesus, what are we getting into?"

"You okay?"

"I'm fine."

"It's okay if you're not. I wouldn't be."

"I said I'm good," she said.

"Okay. I think Bingham's been assigned to your case."

Her agent-involved shooting case. "Yeah. Ted said Bingham would hit town around seven-thirty." Agent Bingham would be taking her firearm as part of the investigation. It should've already happened, but the agency had been getting slammed with relatively high-profile, labor-intensive cases throughout the state for the last three months. Caroline's cases were just the tip of the iceberg.

"When you're cleared," Washington said, "we need you back on your cases as soon as possible."

Caroline didn't answer. She still wanted to quit and crawl into a hole. Maybe she'd marry Brad, a pediatrician she was dating who'd asked her to marry him last week. She could move to the suburbs and work out seven days a week, get into mid-level marketing, white picket fence, laundry on Sundays. She shuddered, like she'd peeked over the edge of a cliff.

"If you're okay with that," Washington said after a few seconds of silence had gone by.

"Why wouldn't I be?" She didn't want to let him down, or seem weak. Time to shut her mouth, keep what she was thinking to herself. It had been a mistake to tell Ben she was quitting.

"Hey, I understand if you need some time—"

"Christ, Eric, I said I'm okay."

Washington was silent for a moment. Then he said, "Listen, Caroline, I know you have a lot on your plate, but there's been some developments on this case in the last hour. There's no way I'll get to El Dorado today to talk to Emily Knudson. It'll have to be tomorrow."

He told her the Okie cops found a Chrysler LeBaron registered to a South Haven man named Jud Jameson behind Ballard's double-wide. Jameson was found stabbed to death in his home, and thirty minutes ago a Sumner County sheriff's deputy had found another man dead in a pickup at an abandoned hotel less than a mile from Jameson's home. Washington thought the dead guy in the truck at the hotel had probably been killed the way Ricky Butler was—blood choke to put him down, then a lethal injection of Fentanyl to make it look like an accidental overdose or a suicide.

While she listened, Riggins came toward her. He got to her about the time the call with Washington ended.

"Sorry about what happened today," Riggins said. "Trillo said you had no choice."

Trillo didn't see the shooting, she thought, and there was always a choice. If she'd waited for backup, things would've played out differently. Tommy might've gotten away, which would've been fine. He hadn't done anything wrong as far as she knew. Or she could've waited to see what Tommy was reaching for in his jacket. She knew that last thought went against her training but there it was, the second-guessing that followed the haunting visual of the shooting that kept playing in her mind, seeing that half-second over and over. She closed her eyes and willed it to go away, something she'd done several times during her interview with Brackeen.

"People don't understand how it is out here," Riggins said. "Remember that. I know you were shot a couple years ago. You never know what's behind door number one. You know that better than most."

Caroline gestured toward the Buick. "Do you know yet if the guy I shot was here in College Hill earlier?" She thought the answer was no, but hoped she was wrong.

Riggins shook his head. "No. A couple of officers remember seeing a guy in an army jacket heading east on Lincoln lugging a cross and we've watched video from several doorbell cams here in the neighborhood. Only one guy got away in Ballard's truck and it wasn't that guy, Tommy."

"It was Elias Matusak."

Riggins eyebrows went up.

"That's your shooter's name," Caroline said. "He probably killed the people in the thrift shop too. And we're pretty sure he killed Roland Ballard—the guy whose truck Matusak used. Not that Ballard is innocent. It's likely he kidnapped and killed those boys in Oklahoma they've been looking for. Looks like he was a serial killer, but who knows, it might've been Matusak." She shrugged. "I'll send you Agent Washington's contact info. He's taking over the case from me."

"Jesus, what a fucking mess. Ballard and Matusak." Then, he nodded at Brackeen's house. "I've heard bits and pieces about all this from a bunch of different cops, but none of us really knows what the hell is going on."

The public was about to find out Elias Matusak was wanted in connection with the College Hill shooting, so she hadn't given away anything critical to the investigation, but she didn't want to get into a long discussion with Riggins about Jimmy Ray's murder either, or anything involving Ben. She pulled out her phone and sent Riggins Washington's phone number. "Call Agent Washington. First name Eric. He probably knows more about your shooter than I do at this point. I think I'm done."

She stepped off the porch, recognizing the ambiguity in what she'd said. Done for the day? Done with being a cop? Maybe her subconscious was trying to tell her something about her life's choices. But she realized she wasn't going to take Brad's ring, not because she didn't love him or think he'd be a fine husband, but because she was afraid of losing herself. Which had pretty much happened today anyway. At least that's the way it felt.

She knew her relationship with Brad was a stupid thing to think of now, but her mind was jumping from one thing to another and it had come up with Brad and his proposal—a future that didn't include the KBI. Her old identity was gone—the girl cop who hadn't killed an innocent man. The girl cop who'd never made that kind of mistake. She felt herself grasping for Brad and a life with him. Instinct maybe. A desperate survival instinct she didn't want to acknowledge, grasping for a man to save that part of herself that could still be had. She could still be Brad's wife.

She felt pathetic, but couldn't stop.

Why *not* get married to Brad and start a family? No mid-level marketing necessary, and she liked working out. What was so bad about laundry on Sundays? Brad was her age. They could grow old together. He had a good sense of humor and no obvious baggage—no ex-wives, no kids. A solid guy. If she wasn't married to Brad in another year, two at the most, she probably never would be. He'd be married to someone else because he was exactly the kind of guy so many women wanted—decent looking, a condo in Vail, by all accounts, monogamous and faithful. He had new money, and would eventually have old money, earned money, to give the kids he would have. He also made no secret about being the kind of guy who wanted a family. She hadn't wanted to admit it, even to herself, and she would never say it out loud, but she wanted children too, in time, with the right guy, and "right guys" without baggage weren't growing on trees around here. All of this reminded her of something her dad used to say: How life was about timing and how, for example, when you missed the first green light in a series, you usually ended up missing them all. Her dad used to say that about all kinds of things, including actual traffic lights, but now she was applying it to her relationship with Brad and to a lesser degree to her biological clock. Which wasn't ticking too loudly at the moment, but in another five years it would be. She didn't want to hear it ticking a year or two in the future while thinking about another woman with Brad, having his kids, making love to him on vacation in Vail. Sweet, gentle, doctor-Brad-with-a-condo was all hers if she wanted him. A life with him had been offered and she'd said, *not yet*, which, it occurred to her now, seemed more offensive than a simple *no* because it had put his life on hold so she could retain her treasured independence and play cop and accidentally kill a homeless man. Maybe she should do the world a favor and quit the KBI, marry Brad. Maybe now was the time to gun the accelerator and make it through that first green light, the one that makes it possible to hit all the other lights green with a slightly vapid but contented smile on her face. Where was it written she had to wake up every morning and crawl through a sewer to be fulfilled?

She gestured toward Brackeen's front door, "He's all yours," she said to Riggins.

"Okay, but Mia Delarosa's attorney was with you earlier. Mind telling me how all this affects that case? That's my case, too."

He was pumping her for information about Jimmy Ray's murder and Ben's involvement. Nothing wrong with what he was doing, and she didn't know the answer to his question, but it would lead to further discussion she didn't want to have. She'd never heard anything bad about Riggins, but she wasn't ready to trust him completely yet. "Would if I could but I don't have any idea. Like I said, call Washington." She walked past him to the Crown Vic.

He watched her go, then came after her. "Hey."

Caroline kept walking. Got all the way to her car and opened the door before she looked back at Riggins who was still on Brackeen's lawn. "Who does the lawyer think killed Jimmy Ray?" he called to her.

Caroline laughed. "Don't let the DA hear you ask that. According to him, the answer is Mia Delarosa."

"You know what I mean. Who was Mia's accomplice? Who does the lawyer think brought the axe down on that piece of shit?"

"How should I know what Ben Joel thinks?"

"You were with him all day. Maybe he said something about who he thinks killed Jimmy Ray."

Caroline shook her head. "We had other things on our minds today."

"I know about the Harvey County case and the video that showed Rick Butler being killed. I know what Butler said about Dean Curtis and Undersheriff Brown. And I know Joel's name was mentioned in the video."

"Sheriff's office in Harvey County leaks like a sieve, huh?"

"What's the connection between what went down here today and Jimmy Ray's murder?" Riggins asked.

"Je-sus, Riggo. Who said there was one?"

"Well, nobody, it's just I don't believe in coincidences." He shrugged. "And I have my own information."

"Then you've got more than I have."

"Jimmy Ray was a dirty cop. Looks like Brown was dirty too. Is still dirty. Since Mia was there when Jimmy Ray was killed, and you had Mia's lawyer with you earlier, it's likely there's a connection between Jimmy Ray's murder and everything else that's been going on."

Persistence was the hallmark of a good detective and Riggins had it in spades. He was a hard charger. That was his reputation. Caroline decided to put him on the defensive.

"You said you had your own information. Tell me what you know."

Riggins smiled. "Quid pro quo. You first."

"Call Washington. I'm on administrative leave."

"Not yet, you're not. You just interviewed Brackeen. What's he going to tell me?"

"I don't know that he'll tell you anything."

Riggins' eyebrows went up. "Why wouldn't he?"

"He had a bad experience with some dirty cops a long time ago." She shrugged. "Ever since, he's been real choosy about who he opens up to."

"What's that have to do with me?"

"You're a cop."

"So are you."

"Not for the Wichita Police Department I'm not."

"Oh I get it," Riggins said. "I work for the same agency Jimmy Ray worked for before he retired. Guilt by association. Brackeen thinks I'm dirty?"

Caroline shook her head. "I don't know what Brackeen thinks. Talk to him, find out for yourself. I'm tired."

Caroline dropped into her car and shut the door. When she looked out the window, Riggins was already on his way to Brackeen's door. She started the Crown Vic and went down the street, hitting speed dial for Ben so she could brief him about what Washington had told her.

She had just enough time to go home to take a long hot shower. Then it would be time to meet Agent Bingham at the Wichita Police Department where she'd turn over her duty pistol and be interviewed and given a time and date of when to see the bureau's psychologist. As she drove, her thoughts began to whip around worse than before. She cancelled the call to Ben before he picked up and pulled the car to the curb.

She saw Tommy's face over and over, right before she shot him. And right after. He winced differently each time, so that part was garbled and she couldn't tell what had really happened in that split second. The action played on in slow-motion and she tried to blink it away, but the replay went on and on. She didn't think she would be able to come back from this. Maybe she shouldn't. Something felt broken in her head. She'd never experienced anything like this before in her life and she no longer trusted herself to handle her firearm or her emotions in a tight situation. If that didn't change, she was done as a KBI agent.

Her phone went off and she about jumped through the roof. It was Ben. He'd seen her number come up on his phone and was calling her back. She let it go to voicemail and wept as her car idled at the curb.

27

CAROLINE CALLED, THEN ended the call before I could say anything. I called her back, left a voicemail for her to get back with me if she hadn't called by mistake. It was almost six o'clock and I was sitting in the passenger seat of Russ's Malibu heading north on the turnpike on our way to El Dorado to speak with Emily Knudson. Try, anyway, if we could get past her police protection detail.

Before leaving Wichita, I tried to set up a meeting with Mia, but the jail was in lockdown again. "Security reasons," was all the deputy on the phone would say, but chances are that was bullshit. Brown might have shut down the whole jail to keep me from meeting with my client. If you could swing it, that's what you'd do to your enemy in a conflict like this—cut the lines of communication. I wanted to tell Mia everything that had happened today, to tell her my idea for getting her out of Brown's jail and how we could use the video of Butler's murder as an exhibit to add substance to our claim that Brown posed a danger to her. I also wanted to explain how using the video might get our greatest ally, Caroline, fired from the KBI. But all of that was part of a bait and switch operation. What I really wanted was to pressure her into telling me who killed Jimmy Ray. I needed to flip over as many puzzle pieces as fast as possible to see if I could figure out where they fit in the overall picture, if they fit anywhere at all. That's why we were blazing a trail to Emily Knudson's house—to find out if her husband told her what happened at The Rabbit Hole twenty-eight years ago, the day before he was murdered in the line of duty.

My phone dinged with a text from Caroline. She'd sent me Agent Washington's contact information. Then she called to tell me no one from the KBI would be available to interview Emily Knudson until tomorrow, and why. Someone—in all likelihood Youngblood—had killed two men near South Haven and, she said, "By the way, his real name is Elias Matusak. Call Washington to get the details. It's his case now. It's up to him to decide what you need to know."

"Do me one favor before you bow out," I said.

"What's that?"

"Russ and I are on our way to Knudson's house right now. See if you can grease the skids with the El Dorado PD for us. Tell them we're coming. Encourage them to let us speak with her. She's in danger, and needs to know why the hell the KBI thinks she needs protection. You might also speak to Emily and let her know this has to do with the murder of her husband so she can begin to prepare herself for what we'll be asking her."

"There's a young cop with her at her house. She lives alone. I'll tell the cop that the KBI can't get anybody there until tomorrow, and that I've asked you and Russ to speak with her for us about her husband's murder. Then I'll ask him to put her on the line so I can explain all of this to her."

"Thank you," I said.

"But you have to tell Washington what she says."

"Of course. Thank you."

I told Russ what Caroline had said as seven pearly-white storage tanks, each the size of a city block and shaped liked a can of tuna, came into view along I-35. A smell like rotten eggs followed an instant later. The curse of a refinery town. A girl I dated in college called this place Smell-Dorado.

We found Emily Knudson's single-story ranch home in a neighborhood full of them. The houses might have been nice at one time, but now most of them were weathered and in disrepair. Driveways and curbs on her street were filled with cars, trucks, and shiny adult toys—RVs the size of Greyhound buses, jet skis, fifty-thousand-dollar boats. Rich people with fun stuff my mother never had—that's what I saw in neighborhoods like this as a kid. What I saw now were childlike priorities and the fruits of quite a few bad banking decisions.

In contrast to the rest of the neighborhood, Emily Knudson's driveway was empty. A steel pole came out of the concrete where a basketball goal used to be. Her yard had gone over to weeds. The only car parked at the curb in front of her house was a police cruiser. Russ parked in the driveway in front of the garage. We went to the front door and knocked. A police officer in his early twenties answered.

"I'm Ben Joel and this is Russ Osborne. We're here to see Emily Knudson. Ten minutes ago I asked KBI Agent Gordon to let you know we were coming."

The officer nodded and let us in.

Emily was standing in her living room, watching us file in with her arms crossed and a pinched expression on her face. She was a stout woman in her mid-fifties dressed in green scrubs.

"Who are you, exactly?" She gave the cop a quick glance then looked at me. "Trevor said you weren't with the KBI, but he couldn't tell me who you're with."

Trevor? El Dorado was a small town. Maybe she knew the cop personally.

"No ma'am," I said. "We're not with the KBI but we're working closely with them right now. Did you talk with Agent Gordon on the phone?"

"No, I was in the restroom when she called."

She shot glances at Russ and me, and the bulge my Glock made in the shirt at my hip. I detected fear in her eyes and in her voice. It made me think Brackeen's hunch was correct—that Emily's husband told her something Brown and Curtis didn't want to get out, probably something having to do with the murder of Paco Correa behind The Rabbit Hole twenty-eight years ago. The look on Trevor's face gave me the impression he thought Emily was acting a little bit paranoid. I wasn't so sure. If she knew from her husband of a murder that'd happened behind that bar nearly three decades ago—a murder there was no record of—she probably had an idea of the danger she was in. If her husband had confided in her about a murder being swept under the rug, he was probably suspicious of the other two cops on his shift, Curtis and Brown. Police corruption—how else could there be no record of Paco's murder, and why else had Officer Charlie Knudson been murdered the next day? I didn't believe these were coincidences. If Emily suspected her husband had been murdered by Curtis and Brown, her fear made sense. So too her insistence on knowing who the hell we were and why we were here. We weren't getting anything out of her until we convinced her this wasn't a ploy by Curtis and Brown to find out what she knew and if she'd told anyone.

"You never answered my question. What kind of cops are you?" Emily asked. "I don't see any badges, just those guns under your shirts."

"We're not cops," Russ said. "But I used to—"

"Then what are you? I don't understand why you're here if you're not cops." She glanced at Trevor, who was standing by the front window. "What'd you get me into?"

"Agent Gordon wants you to speak with them." Trevor shrugged. "What can I say? That's all I know, Mrs. Knudson."

I glanced at Trevor. "Do you and Emily know each other?"

Trevor smiled. "She's cleaned my teeth since I was a kid."

Emily ignored the exchange. Fixed her glare on me. "If you're not a cop, what are you?"

"An attorney."

"What kind of attorney?"

"Defense attorney."

"That's weird isn't it? That the KBI would send in a defense attorney to do its job."

I held my hands up in what I hoped was a calming gesture. "I agree, but hear me out. I can explain. Agent Gordon—the agent who called Trevor and told him we were coming on the KBI's behalf—shot and killed a man in the line of duty several hours ago. Being the wife of a sheriff's deputy, you might know that this automatically triggers admin leave and an internal investigation, so she can't be here. Because of everything that's hitting the fan right now, there aren't any other KBI agents who know what's going on available to talk to you. But you're still in danger and you need to be told. That's why we're here . . . because we're involved in this case up to our necks and know the situation better than anybody."

"How are you involved?" Emily asked.

"For starters," I said, "someone tried to kill me this morning. Then, around noon, someone tried to kill an investigator my grandfather hired to find my father twenty-eight years ago."

"Twenty-eight years ago?" Emily said. "The year my husband was murdered?"

"That's right," I said.

Something played in her face. She was intrigued, and seemed to be thinking about what to say next. "What was your father's name?"

I took a deep breath. "Paco Correa. At least I think he's my father, near as I can tell anyway. I recently learned his name."

The name didn't cause any reaction in her that I could see and neither did the picture of him I showed her. She said she'd never seen him before and that I looked like him, then asked if he was still alive.

"Almost certainly not, from what I can tell," I said. "Likely he was murdered behind a bar called The Rabbit Hole on July tenth of '93. The day before your husband was murdered."

A little cry escaped her lips. Tears glistened her eyes.

I looked down as she gathered herself, saw a box of tissues on the coffee table. Handed her one, then took a moment to gaze around the room. The walls were covered with framed photos of her family. It looked to me like she and Charlie had a daughter. Judging by the clothes, hair styles, and Emily's age in the photos, the framing of pictures to hang on walls had pretty much ended when Charlie died.

When Emily regained her composure, I outlined what had brought me here. Told her how representing Mia had led to a confrontation with a guy in the sex trade business named Ricky Butler, and how Butler pegged me as a dead ringer for a man I'd never heard of before named Paco Correa. I explained that that meant nothing to me at the time, until Butler paired it with statements about the murder of a woman in a Worthington trailer park at the hands of some dirty cops. Which brought me to the backstory—me as a child finding my mother dead in a Worthington trailer park on July twenty-third of '93 and the coroner ruling her death an accidental overdose. I told Emily about the video evidence of Butler's murder and how he had implicated Curtis and Brown in my mother's death, that Russ and I had visited Undersheriff Brown at his country home and about my hazy, childhood memory of the place, and the look of fear and recognition in Brown's eyes when he saw me and heard my name. I told her about the madman named Elias Matusak who would probably be in the news in the near future—if he wasn't already—predicting that there would be a well-publicized manhunt for him. I told her how Matusak had saved my life then called and told me he'd been part of Curtis's cult and how Brown and Butler and the man my client was accused of killing funneled women and children to Curtis for illicit purposes.

When I finished, her neck and face were bright red. "You're here because you want to know how your mother died."

"Yeah, and if she was murdered, who killed her."

"And your father? What's his name again?"

"Paco Correa. Which is part of the puzzle too."

She nodded thoughtfully. "The puzzle. I'm not seeing exactly how your client fits in to all of this."

"The truth is," I said. "I'm not exactly sure how this all fits together, if it does, other than to show a long history of Brown and Curtis dressing as wolves in sheeps' clothing."

Russ said, "These jerks have been rolling the dice for a long time. What's happening now, all of this coming to light, was bound to happen eventually. It's been a hell of a run though."

Emily's eyes darted to Russ. "These kind of people make their own luck." Then, to me she said, "What makes you think I know anything that can help you?"

"That investigator my grandfather hired twenty-eight years ago knows Charlie was dispatched to The Rabbit Hole the night Paco Correa went missing. He was suspicious of the timing of your husband's murder, and suggested you may know something."

"This is the investigator someone tried to kill today?"

"Yes."

She appeared confused. "If he thought I might've known something in '93, why didn't he talk to me then?"

"Someone put a gun to his head twenty-eight years ago," Russ said. "Told him to stop asking questions about Paco Correa."

Her eyes danced as she thought about that.

"But he's talking now," I said to give her a little push. "A few hours ago he told us that your husband was dispatched to The Rabbit Hole the day before he was murdered."

She wet her lips. "This investigator—he thinks maybe my husband told me some secrets before he was murdered."

"That's right—secrets about Curtis and Brown. That's why we're here," Russ said.

She grew still, except for her hands, which held a balled up tissue and fidgeted with the draw string on her pant scrubs. "They came and saw me, you know? The day after Charlie was murdered."

"Who, Brown and Curtis?" I said.

She nodded. "They offered their condolences. Asked if I needed anything. I could feel them reading me. Looking for a reaction that told them what they should do about me. They were alone with me and my daughter in my house. Not this house. We were in Wichita at the time. Curtis said if anyone was ever in heaven it was Charlie. He kept saying that I could call anytime and that no ask was too big." Her eyes grew wet again. "The voice in my head was screaming, *he's trying to bribe you,* then the next moment they're looking at me in a way that made me think they were going to kill me. Not right then, but later. I imagined them killing me like rich men do. One of them would talk to a guy who knew a guy. Curtis and Brown—they'd be eating at a fancy restaurant or on vacation when it happened."

She grabbed another tissue and dabbed her eyes.

I tipped my head toward the wall. "I see you and Charlie have a daughter."

"Yeah, she lives in Fayetteville with her husband. They're both doctors."

"Oh wow, that's impressive," I said.

She pursed her lips into a frown. "Kylan doesn't know what I know. Is she in any danger?"

"What is it you know?" Russ asked.

She ignored Russ's question. She was fixated on the safety of her only child. "They won't go after her will they?"

"It's possible," I said. "I'd know better if I knew what Charlie told you about that night?"

She ignored the question again. "Kylan doesn't know anything."

"They won't care," Russ said. "They'll use her to get to you. Tell us what you know. We'll help you whatever way we can. We'll get Kylan some protection. You too."

Russ and I watched that sink in. Trevor had been looking out the window periodically—keeping tabs on the street. I wondered what he thought about all this. His face gave nothing away. Dean Curtis was famous. Not like a president or a pop star, but if Trevor followed business or politics, he'd know who Curtis was. And certainly around here Curtis was a big deal. Maybe Trevor had a great poker face, or maybe he wasn't into politics or news or the wider world around him. Some people are like that.

Emily looked reluctant. She wasn't ready to tell us what we wanted to know just yet, so I came at her from another direction.

"From what you just told us," I said, "Brown and Curtis weren't sure if you knew anything back in '93. You thought they were trying to gage your reactions."

"Yeah, they couldn't just come out and ask, now could they?"

"Not without giving the game away," I said.

She gave me a long look. Seemed like she was making a calculation—trust me, or not. Maybe she was thinking about Curtis and Brown—go after them, or not. Finally, she said, "Given everything you've told me, you think Curtis has decided to get rid of anybody that could cause him and Brown a problem?"

"Things have happened very recently to bring up the past, so we have to assume that, yeah. That's the pattern we saw today. With me, then Brackeen. Brackeen was the PI my grandfather hired twenty-eight years ago to find Paco to protect me from him. My grandfather was afraid Paco would take me away from him. If he could prove he was my father, he'd have the legal right."

She nodded, then seemed distracted by something new. "There's something you need to know before we go any further. Before I tell you what Charlie told me happened."

"Okay," I said.

"Dean Curtis paid for Kylan's college and medical school. All of it. Room. Board. Tuition. Books. A hefty allowance." She glared at us, looking for a reaction. Condemnation maybe. I tried to give her nothing.

"He even bought her a car," she said. "Paid for the insurance. Bought the tag, paid the taxes. Everything."

"Good," I said.

"Good?"

"Yeah," I said. "Seems like you believe Curtis and Brown murdered your husband. If that's what happened, I'd like to see you with a whole lot more of Curtis's money."

"I wouldn't want it. It's cursed."

"The money?"

"Yeah—it's blood money."

"I understand," I said.

"I don't think you do." She looked away. "Would you have taken that money, Mr. Joel?"

She was wrong; I did understand. Emily hated herself for accepting the money. She was ashamed.

"Depends," I said.

She dried her eyes with the tissue again. "Depends on what I know, right? Depends on whether or not I took hush money."

She'd kept a secret surrounding her husband's murder for almost thirty years and I could see the heavy toll it had taken. Her eyes were heavily bagged and frown lines cut deep ravines around her mouth.

"You couldn't have gone after these guys back then," Russ said. "Not by yourself."

I nodded. "Russ is right. But now we can, Emily. Together, maybe we can take them down."

"People like Dean Curtis don't get taken down," she said.

Russ shook his head. "Not true. Nixon went down, and lots of others. The truth takes people like Curtis down."

"We're in the lion's den now," I said. "And the lion is wide awake, scared, and angry as hell. He's already on the attack and won't stop until we're dead. Whether or not we can take him down isn't even the relevant question anymore. The question is whether or not we fight back."

"Will I have to testify?" she asked.

"Maybe," I said. "What do you know that can help us?"

She honed in on me. "Were you close with you mother?"

"No."

She took a deep breath and gestured to a pair of club chairs across the coffee table from her. Russ and I sat.

"The night my husband was dispatched to that bar—The Rabbit Hole—he couldn't sleep when he got home. Was tossing and turning in bed, which wasn't like him. I asked him what was wrong.

"He told me he'd been dispatched to a bar out in the county where someone had heard gunshots out back. He couldn't get any backup, so he answered the call by himself which was a bad idea and against policy, but what could he do? When he got there, it was pretty much a mob scene of drunk and belligerent derelicts, and no one knew anything about any gunshots and he never found anybody who would admit to making the call. When he went around back where the gunshots were supposed to have come from, his supervisor, Clint Brown, came walking out of the gloom. He wasn't even in uniform. He told Charlie that he answered the call already and that it was nothing. He told Charlie to hit the road. Patrol the countryside. Brown said he'd been checking things out behind the bar to make sure there wasn't anything to the call. Charlie asked him why he wasn't in uniform and hadn't answered dispatch. Brown got annoyed and curt with Charlie and ordered him to do what he was told to do. Go on patrol.

"Brown was his supervisor, so Charlie went back to his cruiser. But before he got in, he heard gunshots, so he pulled his gun and ran to the back of the bar again. He didn't see anyone, so he made his way through some trees down a hill to see where the shots might be coming from. He saw light coming from a cabin at the bottom of the hill. A shack or a shed might be a better way to describe it, I dunno. Charlie said it was extremely small with only one room. He saw a man lying in the doorway of the cabin, dead. Brown was standing over the guy and Dean Curtis was behind Brown looking over his shoulder. When Brown and Curtis laid eyes on Charlie . . ."

Emily shook her head. "That's when Charlie told me he got a real bad feeling. They both came over and talked to him. Brown told him not to call for backup. I mean, that was the first thing out of his mouth, y'know. No ambulance. No one securing the scene. Nothing like that. They told Charlie they were working an undercover drug operation and there were dirty deputies on the force. Brown told Charlie that calling dispatch would alert the dirty cops to the investigation. He told Charlie he wasn't supposed to have seen this, which I remember Charlie saying was probably the only thing Brown told him that wasn't a lie that night. Brown assured him everything was okay though, and that he trusted him, that he wasn't one of the cops they were trying to take down. Brown and Curtis told Charlie that he would be brought in on the operation eventually, but that it was critical that he leave quietly and not mention this to anyone."

Emily squeezed the tissues in her hands into a tight ball and looked at me. "I left something out. It might be about your mother."

"Go ahead," I said. "I'm ready for it."

She sighed. "Charlie told me he saw a woman inside the shack. When Curtis and Brown came over to talk to him, Charlie could see through the open door all the way to the back where there was another door. Charlie was as shaken as I'd ever seen him that night, you have to understand. He said he saw a woman on a mattress on the floor. She'd been crying. Mascara all over her face, and she had a fat lip. She got to her feet, gave Curtis and Brown a fearful look as they were talking to Charlie, then slipped out the back wearing only a bra and panties. When Charlie left he looked for the woman, but didn't see her anywhere in the dark. He told me he'd been thinking about it all night, and had come to the conclusion that he'd forced himself to believe what Brown had told him out there. But the more he replayed the scene in his head, the more convinced he became that he'd interrupted a rape and the woman was scared for her life. Charlie said he must've known this in his gut the whole time, because he didn't say a word to the two men as he watched the woman escape out the back undressed the way she was. And if she'd been raped or assaulted, then it was likely the dead guy had been murdered."

"Did Charlie know the woman's name?" I asked.

"No."

"What about the dead guy?" Russ asked.

She shook her head. "All Charlie knew was that none of this looked right. He was young, but not stupid. And he'd always trusted Brown. He *wanted* to trust Brown, because Brown had taken him under his wing, and, of course he was intimidated and slightly awestruck by Dean Curtis and all his money and power. They went places together, all three of them. Nice restaurants, probably to a few places they shouldn't have gone. Charlie said they ended up at strip clubs several times. They'd invited him and he didn't want to say no and lose their friendship."

Her eyes checked our faces for a reaction. "I'm not naïve. Curtis paid the tab for all their escapades. If I'm honest, I know Charlie loved every minute of feeling like an insider. I think all of that is what got Charlie home that night without saying anything to anybody else on the force. He wasn't a bad man. Before he got home, before he got away from Brown and Curtis, I believe he'd convinced himself that Brown and Curtis were involved in a secret undercover operation out there. But the feeling that something wasn't right wouldn't go away. He didn't know what to do. Risk blowing an undercover sting that was meant to root out corruption, or keep quiet and risk hiding corruption. Of course, Brown must've sensed how close Charlie was to putting two and two together because Brown called him first thing that morning. They did a good job of confusing him. And me. I didn't want to believe it either. After Charlie was killed I told myself . . . I told myself my grief was making me crazy. Told myself there probably was an undercover investigation and what Charlie had seen wasn't anything illegal. Maybe that's what they were gaging when they came by to talk to me. Whether or not Charlie had mentioned their secret investigation. But now that I think about it, I'm sure there was more to it than that."

I said, "Did Charlie ever say anything about the dead man in the doorway? Like, what they might've done with his body?"

"That's part of what was bothering him. It just didn't make sense. He told me there would have to be other cops involved. And a coroner. Probably an ambulance for the woman who looked like she'd been assaulted, probably raped. Brown never said a word about how any of that was being handled. Legitimate cops in the line of duty couldn't just dump a body anywhere. Couldn't just sweep a rape under the rug. When Brown called that morning, Charlie asked him where the man's body ended up."

"Were you there with Charlie during the phone call?" I said.

"No. I was in the shower at the time. Charlie told me about it after the call ended."

"What did Brown say about the body?" Russ said.

"He said the feds were involved. That they took possession of the body."

"Did Charlie ask about the woman?" I said.

Emily's face clouded. "Yeah. He told Brown he saw the woman in the shack. Told him the impression he got was that she might've been raped or something. He asked Brown what'd happened to her. Brown told him the feds found her hiding in the woods behind the bar early the next morning and were having her examined by a nurse trained to assess sexual assault cases. Then they would put her in witness protection."

"Did Charlie buy that?"

"He did, initially. He kind of fell back under Brown's spell, but that didn't last long. By lunch he was back to having serious doubts."

"Did he tell anyone but you?"

"I don't think so." She looked at Russ, then me. "That's everything I know."

"Thank you," I said. "We've hired a professional security firm from Texas. They should be here day after tomorrow. They'll be protecting my family, and I'd like them to protect you and your daughter until this is over. I'd also like it if you went with us for now. Russ will put you up in a nice hotel and keep you safe until the security people from Texas get here."

"Is all of that really necessary? I'd like to stay in my own home."

"Mrs. Knudson," Trevor said, "I don't think my captain will let an officer stay here all night. Also, from what I've heard, it might take more than one of us to keep you safe." He took in all of us with a sweeping glance. "There's something else you all need to know before you go outside."

"What's that?" Russ asked.

"I've seen a Dodge Charger with California tags roll by out front four times. Guy driving seems real interested in the place."

Emily gave a frightened look toward the window. "If I went with you, where would you take me?" she asked me.

"Russ can put you up in a hotel under a fake name, or you can stay at my place. I live in Sumner County. Deputies are guarding my place until the security firm we've hired can get here."

"What are we gonna do about her work?" Russ said.

The question was for me, and I didn't have an answer because I was operating on the fly, but Emily took me off the hook.

"I've got a lot of vacation time built up at the office. They've been trying to get me to take it for years. I think I finally will."

"Thank you," I said.

"What are you going to do with the information I told you?" she asked.

"I might want to put it in a motion and file it in Mia's case. I might even file it as soon as tomorrow, depending on several factors. If I do, it's likely to be national news because Dean Curtis's name will appear in the motion along with Brown's. The idea is to smoke out some witnesses we hope are out there. Hopefully, someone will stand up against these guys with us. If that doesn't work, it might cause Curtis or Brown to try to come after us, which might force them to make a mistake. I know it's risky, which is why I'd like to get you out of harm's way and keep you safe. The motion is going to be like poking a hornets' nest. Will you be okay with that?"

She nodded and took in a deep breath. "Yes. What kind of motion are you filing?"

"A motion to get my client out of Undersheriff Brown's jail."

She thought about that for a moment. "Oh shit," she said. "That'll reach Dean Curtis right away, won't it?"

"Yes." I smiled a little. "So oh shit is right. God knows where it'll end up when it hits the fan."

28

BEFORE SHE PACKED, Emily made a Facetime call to her daughter, Kylan. At Emily's request, I sat on the couch next to her in case she asked me to help explain the situation and the danger Kylan might be in.

When Kylan appeared on the phone's screen she was on the move. I caught glimpses of a kitchen in the background as she went through a doorway to what looked like a garage— bicycles hanging on hooks, a pegboard full of tools. She told Emily she didn't have time for a Facetime call because she was about to leave for a hair appointment, then seemed to sense something was wrong.

"Mom, are you okay?"

"Ky, there's no other way to say this other than to just say it, so here goes. I've just received information about who may have murdered your father."

That stopped Kylan in her tracks.

"Kylan?" Emily said.

Kylan's voice came, shaken. "I never thought this day would come."

"Me either, sweetie. There are a lot of things I need to explain. It's important that you forget your appointment, get back in the house, lock the doors, and listen. What I have to say is going to take a while."

After Kylan went inside, Emily explained the situation and finally convinced Kylan to take leave with her husband from their medical practices to hide until this was over.

When the call ended, it was well past seven and I felt as tired as Emily looked.

She went to pack, leaving us alone in the living room. I went to the restroom to get away from Trevor and Russ to check my phones in private. Found that Geronimo had returned my earlier call. I'd wanted to know if he'd killed Kage Walker, but now I knew he hadn't, so I called him back and told him in a hushed voice about the attempt on my life. Told him there was a lot going on but I couldn't talk at the moment, that I'd give him an update soon.

Russ had stepped outside for a smoke when I got back to the living room. I called Keri and told her I would be heading home shortly. She and the kids were holed up in the house with two sheriff's deputies on security detail. Pops was there too. He would sleep in the spare bedroom, at least for tonight. When I realized my family hadn't eaten yet, I told Keri I'd grab Mexican takeout on the way home.

Russ came through the front door as I ended the call. He said his buddy and two other men from the security firm were flying into Wichita in the firm's Gulfstream tomorrow. They'd be here by noon. I asked him what it would cost. He told me his friend was a good man who'd heard my story and had already hinted about doing this job for free. I didn't like the feeling of needing charity, but I was about to stick my finger in the eye of a powerful man with an endless supply of money. I was in no position to turn away help.

We headed south on I-35 as the sun set. I phoned in an order to Connie's Mexico Cafe in Wichita. It was dark by the time we reached the cafe, and I'd convinced Emily that the best and safest place for her was a spare bedroom in my basement. I'd also convinced Russ that we wanted no part of a nighttime drop-off at my truck, which had been sitting in the Crossroads Bar & Grill parking lot for hours. We'd be easy prey for anyone waiting for me to show up.

South of Wichita on the turnpike, I called Keri to give her a heads-up about our guests. She was watching one of several versions of the six o'clock news she'd recorded from various stations and asked if I'd seen any of them. I hadn't. The discovery of human remains of young children in the woods behind Roland Ballard's double-wide had made national news as we'd expected. Elias Matusak was prominently featured as a suspect in several Kansas murders. He was also linked to the Oklahoma serial killings along with Ballard, who, it was reported, had been found murdered in the double-wide. Both men's mugshots were being splashed all over the television and social media. Matusak was said to be armed and dangerous. Dangerous was an understatement.

We were heading west on U.S. 160 through Worthington when Keri called to tell me that the deputies guarding our place were on the front porch talking with a detective from Oklahoma who had arrived to question me. She didn't catch the detective's name, but told me he was a small man with a shaved head. I asked her if it was Danny DeVito and she told me I'd better have food with me or I was dead meat.

Dead meat. I grinned. But a detective. Perfect. My long day had just gotten longer.

When the call ended I dove into the bags and containers of food looking for my order so I could eat before having to deal with some detective for no reason I could think of, but a subtle feeling that something wasn't right gave me pause. Why wouldn't the Okie detective call first? He could've gotten my number from Agent Washington or anyone in the local sheriff's department.

I was about to ask Russ if he thought what the Okie did felt weird to him when he said, "Did I hear right—there's a detective from Oklahoma at your place waiting to interview you?"

"Yeah. Why wouldn't he call first? He drives all the way from Oklahoma on the off chance I'm home?"

Russ shrugged. "I dunno, maybe a little strange under the circumstances. Maybe he wanted to get out from behind his desk. Did Keri give you a name? I know a few cops down there. I could call, ask around about this guy."

"Hold off on that. Let me try something."

Keri had installed an app on my phone that allowed me to see a live feed from our security cameras. I swiped the screen, hit the security company's icon, and found the live view of the front porch. The two local deputies were talking to a plainclothes detective who wore a bulletproof vest over a shirt and tie and a badge hanging on a lanyard. He openly carried a pistol on his hip. I didn't recognize him. I watched a moment, then closed the app.

Russ said, "Maybe he thinks you might put him off, which is hard for most people to do if he's standing right there in the flesh but it's very likely something lawyers do almost without conscious thought, especially on a phone call."

I smiled. "Lawyers do that?"

"You oughta know. Lawyers make everything difficult. Nothing's routine, nothing is easy. No offense, but you guys pull out the legalese and drag everyone through the mud just to do it."

"That's bullshit, we do it for money."

Russ laughed. "Point is, this guy might think if he shows up on your doorstep, he gets the interview done now instead of sometime next Christmas."

I speed dialed Keri, but she didn't pick up. I tried twice more. Still no answer. On the fourth call, a sick feeling crept through me. Nothing subtle about it. I opened the security camera app again and was shook to my core.

Both deputies were down—one on his back with hands around his own throat kicking wildly and the one named Ed was lying in a heap. The door was open, no one else in sight.

"The deputies are down," I cried out. "That detective's not in the video—if that's what he is."

Russ pulled his phone out as he circled a roundabout in the center of town. He stayed on U.S. 160. Gunned the Malibu down a straightaway.

My phone lit up with a call from Leo. In a hushed voice he said something I couldn't hear because Russ was talking to a 911 dispatcher. Russ asked me for my address. I almost yelled it out. Russ repeated it into the phone. I was finally able to hear bits and pieces of what Leo was saying. There'd been shooting upstairs. He and Lindy had locked themselves in the basement bathroom. Lindy was on one of Keri's phones with 911.

"Where are Pops and Keri?" I asked Leo.

"Pops was down here watching TV with us when he heard the shooting. Keri was upstairs."

Russ shot through a red light and across train tracks, then up a hill in a residential area.

I realized I'd been all but shouting so I took it down a notch. "Is there any shooting going on right now?"

"No, it stopped," Leo whispered. "Where are you?"

"I'll be there in another six or eight minutes."

Russ glanced back at me. He wasn't on the phone anymore.

"Drop me off in front of my house and keep moving," I said to Russ.

The red and blues of a cop car streaked by left to right in the distance before us, heading north on Oil Field Road in the direction of my home. Twenty seconds later Russ blew through a stop sign, turning right and pushing hard to catch up to the flashing lights on the horizon.

A few minutes later we whipped left off Oil Field Road and skidded in the loose dirt of Seventieth Avenue almost ending up in a ditch. Our headlights illuminated a thin mist of dust floating above the road as the Malibu's engine whined to pick up speed on the straightaway toward my property which looked like the site of a small carnival in the distance.

"Alright Leo," I said. "I'll be there in another minute, but police are at the house now. Can you hear anything?"

"People are walking around upstairs. Lindy told 911 where we were. They told us to stay put and stay quiet and said the deputies were here."

"Okay, okay, good."

"They're here," he said. "The cops are here knocking on the door. Oh, Lindy just let them in."

"You can see them?"

"Yes, they just opened the door."

"Good Leo, good. Give one of them the phone. I need to talk to them."

A man said something I couldn't make out, then a voice I recognized came on the phone.

"Ben, this is Dallas. Where are you?"

Dallas had been a highway patrolman in my county for twenty years.

"On Seventieth," I said. "Be there in less than a minute."

"What kind of car you in?"

"Grey Malibu. There are three of us."

"Okay, I'll meet you out front, you shouldn't come in here."

"Are Keri and my grandfather okay?"

"You shouldn't come in here, Ben."

My heart skipped several beats. "Are they okay?"

"No, the assailant's been neutralized, but your wife and grandfather have been shot. That's all I know."

I kept talking, but he didn't hear me. He was yelling at someone. I realized he was yelling information to the other cops on the scene, telling them we were coming up Seventieth in a Malibu.

Realizing what was going on, Russ stopped in the road twenty-five yards from the entrance to my driveway and said, "Tell them we're on the road outside the house. They can come to us."

I didn't respond. I bolted from the car and ran. Got as far as the driveway where I was met by a deputy in the gloom pointing a pistol at me, yelling for me to stop and put my hands in the air. I did and told him who I was, but it didn't matter. He was young and sounded panicked. A female deputy came out of the driveway with her pistol drawn and walked toward the Malibu. I continued to follow the young cop's orders to keep from getting shot. He got me to my knees, cuffed me, and planted me face first in the gravel about the time an ambulance came. He took my Glock, stood me up, and walked me to the ditch as the ambulance passed, its wail drowning out all other sounds. When it turned into my driveway, the siren stopped and a highway patrolman— Dallas—came walking, then running, toward us.

When he got close enough to see my face, he said to the young deputy, "What the fuck are you doing? You don't recognize this guy? That's Ben Joel. This is his house, you fucking idiot."

"How the fuck would I know that?" the deputy said.

"He's one of the people you guys are supposed to be protecting." Dallas looked up the road at the Malibu. The female deputy was ordering Russ and Emily out of the car at gunpoint. "Ah, Jesus H. Christ," he muttered. Then he yelled, "Chrystal, leave them alone and get back here. They're with the guy who lives here."

Chrystal looked back at us, then holstered her pistol.

Dallas turned to me as the deputy unlocked my cuffs. "Your kids are safe," Dallas said. "In the basement with a deputy. I'll get them out here with you in a second, but then I have to get you guys out of here. I don't know what the hell's going on, but I'm told it's not safe for you to be here. We need to secure you, and this scene right away."

"Is my wife going to be okay? Pops? How bad is it?"

"I dunno, Ben. I just don't know. Look, I'm sorry. All I know is that I'm supposed to get you all out of here."

I kept on. "Were they conscious? I mean, you were inside, right?"

"Your grandfather's fine, I'm pretty sure."

"But not Keri?"

He shook his head. "No, and neither are the deputies or the assailant."

"What did you see?" I said.

He took in a deep breath and shook his head. "The assailant was wearing Kevlar. His body is in the living room. He took a shotgun blast to the chest. The Kevlar stopped that but he was shot in the head too. I think your grandfather got him with a pistol. That would be my guess from what I saw and what I heard the deputies saying, but other than that, my job was to go in for the kids."

"Keri—is she alive—"

"I dunno, look—"

"Goddammit, Dallas, just tell me."

"Listen, Ben, I was in. I was out. I don't want to guess at this."

"You didn't see her?"

He shook his head. "Ben, I don't know."

I felt lightheaded. "You damn well know if you saw her or not. What did you see?"

Through the vehicles and the flashing lights I caught a glimpse of EMTs wheeling out someone on a stretcher. I couldn't see who. Dallas followed my eyes and looked back. I tried to get past him, but he caught me. He and the young deputy held me back.

"No, Ben," Dallas said. "I can take you to the hospital, but I was told to get you out of here." He looked around. "We're sitting ducks out here, man. You getting shot isn't going to help your kids, so goddammit listen to me. There's nothing you can do here to help. You have to let them take care of her."

"What did you see?"

He shook his head and took a quick look around him. "She was face down when I saw her, laying on the shotgun. There was a spent casing on the floor beside her, so I think she got off a shot and hit the son of a bitch as he came through the door. But . . . the Kevlar." Dallas had tears in his eyes. "On the way out, I heard one of the deputies say she was shot in the chest."

I have a vague recollection of Dallas ushering me to the back of his trooper's car where I sat with my children, huddled together. He took us to Wesley Medical Center, where I found that Keri was pronounced dead on arrival. I have no memory of the next half hour. None at all.

29

I STAYED ALONE with Keri in the little room the nurses put her in, doing things people do when they lose a loved one unexpectedly in the prime of their life. What else could I do but endure the agony and tell her I loved her while caressing her cheek and letting a small strand of her hair glide through my fingers? Everything I did had the weight of something I would never do again, that what I was doing was a final parting, a last goodbye.

As I stood there processing this new, terrible reality I was vaguely aware of the steady drumbeat of the world around me. Sounds from the hallway. The emergency room wasn't far away and there was a lot of activity. Every so often a door would open behind me. I assumed a nurse was peeking in to see if I was okay or maybe they needed to clear the room but wanted to give me a little more time. Eventually Pops came up next to me and put his hand on my shoulder. He'd been shot, but the bullet had only grazed his shoulder. He'd been cleared to go home, which is where he intended take me and the kids—his home on B Street in Worthington. This time we'd have two deputies from the sheriff's office assigned and two officers from the Worthington Police Department watching over us until people from the private security firm got here tomorrow.

"You already call Mindy?" Pops said.

Mindy was Keri's foster mom, the only family Keri had, other than us.

I nodded.

Pops grunted, the grunt saying he knew how hard that must've been. Then he said, "I talked to Ed's wife. She's devastated."

Ed was one of the deputies who'd been killed by the fake Oklahoma detective. The other deputy, Grant, had also been killed.

"Has anyone told you how this went down at the house?" Pops asked.

"Bits and pieces."

Pops nodded. "From what I gather, Ed was suspicious of the guy claiming to be a detective. He told dispatch what was going on and was in the process of making a call to check out the guy's credentials. The guy realized the jig was up and started to walk back to his car. That probably would've been it, but Grant made the mistake of trying to stop the guy. The son of a bitch stabbed Grant in the throat before Grant knew what hit him, then shot Ed in the face. Happened so fast Ed didn't pull his gun." Pops stroked Keri's hand. "Keri hit that bastard hard with the shotgun as he came through the door though. That probably saved the rest of us."

I hooked a lock of Keri's hair behind her ear and could feel the bottom drop out again—the ever-deepening abyss. You don't feel the whole loss at once. It comes in waves. I closed my eyes and let the pain wash over me as Pops told me the rest of what happened.

"The guy was sitting on the floor, leaned against the wall near the front door firing at her when I got to the top of the stairs. But it was too late. Then he damn near got me too. I must've fired six rounds into his vest before I finally got him in the head."

Pops put his hand on my shoulder again. "I loved her like a daughter. She's with Him now." His voiced cracked. I'd never heard his voice do that before. "You might be doubting that there's anything good on the other side, any place for her to go, but there is and it's a good place."

"I'm just numb."

"I know. I am too." He hesitated, then said, "You're right to go after Brown and Curtis. You were always right about that. You were never supposed to let what these guys did to your mother go. I was wrong before."

"Doesn't feel like it."

"In the years I have left, I think I was hoping for the path of least resistance. That happens, you know? When you get tired, it gets easier to just give in. Let shit stand that you should oppose with all your being." He cleared his throat. "And that's not what we're called on to do. If there's nothing out there beyond what you see here in this life, then what you're feeling right now—the loss, your love for Keri, the injustice of it all— is just meaningless. Her sacrifice meant nothing if there is no God. She will have died in vain as she lived in vain. As we all will have lived and died in vain at the end of the day. If there is no God, there is no reckoning, no justice, and everything is absurd. Everything is permitted and evil gets a pass."

"Everything is permitted, except what's prohibited by an arbitrary pact among men."

His eyebrows went up. "Sounds like something I heard Father Garrahy say one time. He said if people were the source of law, then law is neither right nor wrong. All one can claim it to be is a codified collection of opinions made and enforced by those in power, no more just or unjust than a collection of opposing opinions, and as arbitrary as a pact among wolves."

"I was sitting next to you in church when Father Garrahy said that, or something like it. Guess it stuck with both of us."

Pops nodded toward the door. "The kids are in the chapel upstairs with Caroline and a guy named Ted Novacek. I think he's her supervisor. They want to talk to you before you leave. They're with the woman who was with you and Russ. Go meet with them and let's get the kids home."

I found my children sitting next to Caroline inside the small chapel provided by the hospital. I wrapped my arms around them and held them close. Emily and Ted were sitting together in a pew at the back of the room. They stood and filed out with Caroline to give us privacy, but I wasn't there long.

Pops was right. I needed to get the kids home, but first I had to talk with Caroline and Ted.

I left Leo and Lindy with Pops in the chapel and found the agents huddled with Emily in the hallway. Ted, a broad-shouldered middle-aged man with a square jaw and slicked back hair saw me first. He expressed his condolences while the others nodded with something like pity in their eyes. Then Ted awkwardly pivoted to the subject of the man who killed Keri.

"His name is Kevin Gans," Ted said. "He's from New York. Did five years in Rikers for aggravated robbery. That name mean anything to you?"

"No. I'm thinking he was in Curtis's inner circle with Matusak though. Curtis may not have had enough time to vet another hitman and got desperate. My surveillance camera is in plain sight. A professional wouldn't have allowed his face to be caught on camera like that."

Caroline shared a look with Ted, then said, "In a way, the coroner just corroborated your conclusion about Gans being in Curtis's group. Gans was emasculated."

Ted made a face. "No twig, no berries."

"Matusak told you earlier there'd been two men in the inner circle, both eunuchs, right?" Caroline said to me.

"That's right."

Caroline shrugged. "Gans was likely the other male in the group."

"We're going to do a press release," Ted said. "Put Gans's mug out there and ask anyone with information about him to call."

Caroline shrugged. "Maybe Matusak sees it and calls your office about Gans. If this guy was the other male in Curtis's group, Matusak will know."

Ted looked at me. "We know you can't agree to have your office phone tapped by law enforcement, but we'd like you to install an app on your phone so that you can record Matusak if he calls again."

"Sure. I can do that." I turned to Caroline. "Thanks for stopping by. It means a lot. I know you've got a lot on your plate right now."

Caroline waved off my thanks and gave me a hug.

"I'll do what I can to fast-track the agent-involved-shooting process," Ted said. "See if I can't get Caroline back in a week or two. You need anything, Ben, call me or Agent Washington."

"I'll do that," I said.

"We're here for you," Ted said. "I mean it, anything you need, call us. Same goes for you, Mrs. Knudson. If you'll allow it, I'll have you in witness protection tonight."

Emily nodded, then looked at me, a hint of concern on her face.

"I didn't know we had that," Caroline said.

"We do now," Ted said. "I just created it. Ben, we can put you and your family in it as well."

"I appreciate that, Ted, but I've got it covered."

"I figured you did, but if you change your mind, let me know." Ted regarded me with a stern look on his face. He meant to convince me that he was on my side, and in theory, he probably was, but I didn't know if that would actually do me any good. You never knew with brown-nosing middle-management types. The kind that care more about their careers than the job. It crossed my mind that Ted could be in with Brown and Curtis, and wouldn't that be something?—him in charge of my safety. Emily's safety. Before my thought got any traction, Ted pulled an envelope out of his pocket and handed it to me.

"What's this?" I said.

"A copy of the video of Rick Butler's murder. You have my express permission to use it in any way you see fit."

Then Ted said something in Russian and walked away. It was a phrase I'd heard Pops say on occasion. It was the only Russian I knew. It was likely the only Russian Pops knew too.

"Ted was a Russian translator for the Army," Caroline said. "We never know what he's saying when he does that. It's kind of weird actually."

I put the envelope in my pocket. "He said, 'not one step back.'"

Caroline looked a question at me.

"Stalin's order to the Red Army during the Nazi invasion. Maybe Ted Novacek's not such a bad guy after all."

30

Thursday, August 19

AT SIX THE next morning I was wide awake watching the ceiling fan spin above my childhood bed, my mind like a runaway engine that wouldn't shut off. I was still fully dressed, except for my shoes. I rolled over and watched my kids sleeping on an air mattress on the floor for a while in the grey light. I still had them. Things were terrible, but it could have been worse. A *lot* worse. I left for the little galley kitchen where I found Pops pouring coffee. When he saw me he poured another mug and handed it over.

"Sleep at all?" he asked.

"Not much."

"It won't get any better for a while." He leaned back against the countertop, watching me. "Want some advice?"

"No."

He smiled. "When you're back in your house, whenever that is, sleep on her side of the bed. Where she slept."

"That helps?"

"That's what I did when your grandmother died." He shrugged. "I think it helped. Felt like it anyway."

"Like taking Advil when your leg gets cut off?"

He sighed. "Probably. But every little bit helps."

"Okay. I'll try it."

"What are you gonna do today?"

"I dunno. Thought maybe I'd call the funeral home."

"I can do that for you."

"I should probably do it."

"There aren't any rules about who does it."

I faked a little smile.

"Let me do this for you," he said. "Shelley next door can come sit with the kids for a couple hours if that's what you're worried about."

I drank, wincing because the coffee was scalding hot.

He nodded at my mug. "You like the coffee?"

"Yeah."

"Know where I got it?"

"The grocery store?"

"Yeah, a regular ol' grocery, not the specialty place you go to. Beans were already ground up and everything."

I looked down at my mug. Plumes of steam twisted in the air above it. "As long as it stays hot enough that I can't taste it, it'll be fine."

"Don't you got something else you oughta be doing today besides talking to a funeral director?"

"I guess. Need to see what Chief Bell has in evidence from Mom's death in '93."

Pops drank. No wincing. Still tougher than me.

I said, "There is one other thing I have to do today."

"What's that?"

I told him about the motion I was filing in hopes of getting Mia out on bond or held in some other jail away from the long reach of Undersheriff Brown.

Pops stared into his mug. "That'll stir things up a mite I reckon'."

* * *

Just before eight a.m. I called the school to tell the principal that the kids wouldn't be there today and why, but that wasn't necessary. She knew what'd happened and offered her prayers and support. Then I called the Worthington Police Department and asked to speak to Chief Bell. He wasn't there so I showered, got dressed in yesterday's clothes, then ate corned beef hash and eggs with Pops and the kids.

The chief finally returned my call at 8:45. I asked him if the department still had the evidence he'd collected from the scene of my mother's "unattended death" back in '93. He said they did, that he'd just been on the phone with an agent named Washington about that very topic twenty minutes earlier and that Washington and my PI—Russ—would be at the station in about thirty minutes if I wanted to come too. I told him I did. He said he'd been briefed about what was going on, and wanted to apologize to me if he'd messed anything up in '93. I told him it wasn't his fault and no one could have seen what was coming, which he said was true about everything going on in this country these days.

After the call ended, I found Lindy and Leo in the living room curled up on either end of the couch, both staring absently at the TV. *The Family Feud* was on. Lindy sniffled. I sat between them.

After a while, Lindy said, "I liked Keri. I never told her that. And I acted like I hated her sometimes."

"Keri knew you liked her," I said.

Lindy sat up. Her eyes looked tired. "How'd she know that?"

"Because she put herself in your position, and knew how she would feel if she were you. She knew you missed your mother."

"We got Keri killed," said Leo.

I shook my head. "No we didn't."

Lindy looked up at me. "You didn't want to come back here, but Leo and I did. We begged to come back about every day."

"Keri wanted to come back too," I said. "We all did."

"Would you have come back if we hadn't kept asking for it?"

I nodded. "Yeah, and look, the people responsible for what happened today aren't the same ones who had us kidnapped two years ago."

That probably didn't matter to them, which left me wondering why I'd said it in the first place, which made me think that deep down, somehow it made a difference, at least to me. When Keri and I made the decision to come back and take on Mia's case, we were concerned about retaliation from the Mendez-Rodriguez cartel, but there was no way to anticipate getting tangled up with Brown and Curtis like this.

Leo sat up. "We didn't think you ever wanted to come back."

"Keri and I decided it was best." I watched their faces as their little minds parsed my words. "It was our decision—Keri and I made it together. Obviously, it didn't turn out so well but no one can see the future. We can look back and play the what-if game, looking for something we did wrong, for something we should've done differently, so that none of this would've happened. No one wins that game. The people who sent the man who killed Keri only think about themselves. I don't want us to ever be like that. So, what you two are doing is natural, and healthy, but only for a while. Eventually you'll have to let it go and move on. This wasn't your fault."

"Are we going back to Idaho?" said Leo.

"Not right now."

Leo tilted his head. "Maybe later?"

"Maybe. Might go somewhere besides Idaho, who knows?"

Lindy put her head on my chest. "I'm sorry, Daddy."

I pulled Leo to me and held them both tight. "Me too."

* * *

Ten minutes later I strapped my holstered Glock inside the waistband of my jeans and left out the back door. I was surprised to find a police captain named Funderburk there talking to one of the young officers guarding the place. Funderburk had been sent by the chief to give me a ride, even though the station was only about a block away. We sped to Eighth Street, went left past the Catholic school playground and across C Street to within half a block of Main Street, where he darted left down an alley past the fire station to the back of the police station where he swung into an open bay.

The overhead door shut us in as we piled out of the cruiser, climbed a flight of stairs, and went into a hallway where we were greeted by Chief Bell, a wiry man in his sixties with a deeply grooved face, shriveled like a raisin from years in the sun. Funderburk went left down the hallway and I followed Chief Bell in the opposite direction to the outer evidence room where Russ and a rangy black man in khaki cargo pants, Eric Washington, were looking over the shoulders of a female officer who was pecking at a keyboard, eyes locked on a computer monitor. I remembered the woman's name was Janet Fisk, the department's long-time evidence custodian.

Washington turned to me and nodded. "Mr. Joel, I'm sorry for your loss."

"Thank you," I said.

"Doesn't look like there was much evidence collected from the scene in '93," Fisk said.

I looked at the short list of inventory she'd pulled up on the screen: hard copy photographs; a syringe; a pipe; and a silver crucifix (engraved RIP PC) on a broken eighteen-inch cord jewelry chain. In the photos I'd seen, none had shown the engraving on the crucifix.

I made eye contact with Russ. "Rest in peace, Paco Correa."

Russ shrugged. "Probably a good guess, since it looks like Paco was murdered about a week or so prior to your mother being found."

"Could be that she'd just been to a jeweler before she died." Washington pointed at the monitor. "Why is there an asterisk next to the listing for the crucifix?"

I hadn't seen the asterisk, but now I did.

"Means we've returned that item to the owner," Fisk said.

Russ shot me a look. "The owner—Ben's grandfather?"

Fisk punched a couple of buttons. "On September thirteenth of '93, then-Detective Tom Bell returned the jewelry to a man named Dalton Campbell." She punched a few more keys and brought up a document entitled, RELEASE OF PROPERTY. It had been scanned into the computerized logging system years ago. "Campbell signed for it, and prior to that Leonard Joel approved the release of the item to him."

Russ looked back and forth between me and Chief Bell. "Leonard Joel's your grandfather, right?"

"Yes."

Russ nodded. "Who's Dalton Campbell?"

I shook my head. "No idea."

"I don't know Campbell either," Bell said, "but now that I see this, I kind of remember calling Ben's grandfather for permission to return the jewelry to this guy who called here claiming he may've lost a crucifix in Ms. Joel's trailer and asking if we'd by chance found one there. Leonard must've okayed it, so it looks like this Campbell guy showed up and signed for it, but I have no memory of that."

Russ's gaze went from Bell to Fisk. "You have an address for Dalton Campbell?"

Fisk scrolled to the top of the document and pointed to the screen. "Right there. Wichita address. I'll print this out for you before you leave, but let's look at something real quick while you're here." She scrolled to the bottom of the document again and squinted at the handwritten scribbling below the signatures, then looked back at Chief Bell. "That's your chicken scratch, Chief. Can you make out what it says?"

Bell looked, then chuckled to himself as he bent closer to the screen and put on his reading glasses. "Says, 'Dalton Campbell partied at Paula Joel's trailer few weeks ago. Realized he'd lost his crucifix. Thought maybe he'd lost it at Joel's trailer, but wasn't sure. When heard she'd died, he thought he might better check with us to see if we had it.'"

Washington's eyes narrowed. "That's weird."

Bell laughed. "I must've thought it was weird too, or else I wouldn't've written a note that long. On the other hand, I was probably thinking this must be the guy's stuff if he knows about it and came looking for it like he did."

I said, "Pops probably figured the same thing, or if he knew about the engraving, he would've figured, like we did, that PC stood for Paco Correa and he wanted no part of it."

"RIP PC," Russ said, almost to himself. "The engraving could mean, rest in peace, Paco Correa, or, Paul Curtis."

"Paul Curtis?" Washington said.

Russ glanced around at us. "Dean Curtis's brother killed himself in a Los Angeles hotel called the Chateau Marmont in 1991. His name was Paul Curtis."

To Bell, Washington said, "No way you checked for prints on the syringe or the pipe back in '93, right?"

Bell shook his head. "No, and in my experience there'd have been about zero chance of getting a usable print off those things, even back then when they would've been fresh. Probably too late now, but—" He pointed at the glue box against the wall, an airtight Plexiglas fuming chamber where superglue and other chemicals were boiled to enhance fingerprints. "But in the spirit of being thorough, we can run 'em through the chamber now if you want."

"Might as well, and let's have a look at the evidence while we're here," Washington said. "After that, I know what I'm doing."

"Looking for Dalton Campbell?" Russ said.

Washington nodded. "Damn straight."

31

BEFORE TAKING ME to the Crossroads Bar & Grill parking lot where my truck was parked, Russ swung me by my house for a change of clothes and to pick up the laptop and other equipment Keri had kept at the house. My plan was to keep it light and not linger in the living room where Keri had been shot, but I couldn't escape the haunting aura I felt as I stepped through the kitchen into the dining room. Someone, almost certainly Keri, had added a leaf to the dinner table upon which sat napkins and glasses full of room temperature water— yesterday's preparation for a meal we'd never share. In the master bath, one of her bras hung on the door, and a little bottle of cobalt-blue nail polish sat on the edge of the tub. A vision of her painting her toes took me back to a place I never wanted to leave. I stood there for a long time, until a floorboard in my bedroom creaked behind me. I turned. It was Russ. He nodded and walked away without a word.

Russ parked behind an abandoned warehouse one block from the parking lot of the Crossroads Bar & Grill, then left me in his Malibu while he walked to my truck with the key I'd given him.

Fifteen minutes later he parked my truck behind the Malibu. We exited our vehicles and met between them.

He gave me my key. "No bombs, no trackers. I checked. Are you going to write this motion you told me about at your home or office?"

"Office," I said. "I need to touch base with Manny and Rashonda. And I need Rashonda's help."

"I'll follow you."

We parked in front of my office and walked in together. Rashonda's jaw dropped a little when we came through the door.

"Howdy," I said. I never say that. I wasn't myself.

"I'm so sorry, Mr. Joel."

"Thank you." It felt inadequate, but what else can you say? I looked down the hallway at a closed door. "Is Manny in?"

"No. I'm not sure if he's coming in today or not. I could call him if you want."

"That's okay. I might call him in a little bit."

I went to my office while Russ stayed in the reception room with Rashonda.

As I sat behind my desk and tried to figure out why I was there, Rashonda appeared in the doorway.

"I'm just . . . I'm so sorry," she said.

"Thank you . . . thank you, again." Still inadequate and I was still lost. This was going to take time.

"If you need anything . . . anything at all, let me know."

"I appreciate that. I know this office-sharing arrangement I have with Manny wasn't meant for you to give me a lot of help, but I need help. I'd like to hire you—for more than just answering phone calls, or interaction with clients. I need an assistant. A secretary. Like, right now."

"No need to hire me. I'll just help you."

"I really want to hire you, Rashonda."

She shook her head. "I won't take your money. You said you needed something right now. What is it?"

"I won't let you do the work if I don't pay you for it. That's just not right."

"Jeez. Okay, so pay me. What do you want me to do?"

"I need a motion e-filed. I'll have it written sometime this afternoon."

She shrugged. "No problem. You write it. I'll file it. Take me five minutes."

"Taking me on might end up being a lot of work, and even if that doesn't wind up being the case, anybody working for me ought to consider asking for hazard pay."

"Manny told me this morning to help you if you asked, and he's the boss. And he pays me pretty good."

"I'll pay half of what he's paying you. And if Manny still wants to pay you your full salary on top of that, fine with me. I won't take no for an answer."

She shook her head in frustration. "Let me know when you get that motion written. I'll be up front."

Before she got away, another idea hit me.

"Rashonda?"

She turned. "Yeah."

"You have a motion for a special process server on your computer?"

"Of course."

"Can you make one up for me on Mia's case? I need to have a subpoena served, and I don't trust the sheriff's office to do it."

"Who do you want appointed?"

Rashonda stepped back as Russ appeared in the doorway.

I pointed at Russ. "Him."

Russ held out his hand. Rashonda shook it and said, "I'm Rashonda."

"Russ. Nice to meet you."

I was about to make another request when Rashonda turned back to me. "You want a proposed order granting your motion for a special process server sent to the prosecutor?"

I nodded. "You read my mind."

These things were routine. With any luck, the order appointing Russ to serve my subpoenas would be signed by the judge before I was done drafting my motion.

She said, "Let me know if you need anything else," then left us.

Russ watched after her. "I'll be up front with her. Oh, by the way, I just got a text from Mason. He and two of his men will be here around two o'clock. They're flying in on the company's Gulfstream V."

"A Gulfstream V? Jesus, you sure he's doing this for free?"

"Hundred percent. Mason's a man of his word."

"Why's he doing this? It'll probably end up costing him a small fortune."

Russ wrinkled his nose. "Cause Mason and I are tight, and I told him about the guys we're dealing with, and knowing Mason, he probably thought, y'know what? Fuck those guys. That's how Mason thinks."

"My kinda guy."

"Mine too." He shut the door and I went to work.

*   *   *

An hour and a half into writing the motion, Geronimo called. He'd seen the news and said he'd understand if I needed to get off the case. I told him he couldn't get me off the case now if he wanted to and that I didn't have time to talk because I was working on something important in Mia's case. He asked what it was. I told him he'd probably find out this evening if he watched the news, which didn't fly with him. Which figured.

"Tell me," he said.

So I went on offense.

"When do I get to talk to Carmen?"

"You don't."

"Did she kill Jimmy Ray, or was it you?"

"I'm going to pretend that's the grief talking."

"Pretend all you want, but I still need to sit down with Carmen before trial."

"Is the trial still set for October fifteenth?"

"As it stands now, yeah."

"We'll talk later." Then he hung up on me.

*   *   *

Within the motion to get Mia out of the jail run by Undersheriff Brown, it was critical that I outline Dean Curtis's and Brown's criminal activity over the span of the last thirty years, up to and including the events of yesterday. This document was going to be among the most important things I would ever write, and almost certainly, the most widely read by the press. I wanted it to hum with clarity and emotion. I had visions of it setting off a chain reaction that began with key witnesses stepping forward and ended with Curtis and Brown strapped to a gurney with a lethal dose of potassium chloride running through their veins. I wanted the motion to be worthy of Keri, my mother, Paco Correa, Charlie Knudson and all the victims whose lives were cut short or ruined by these narcissistic animals. But I was tired, emotional, unfocused, and putting too much pressure on myself. To say the words didn't come easily was an understatement. At times, I had a hell of a time writing anything at all. But I kept at it until I had the shittiest first draft of anything I'd ever written, which is saying something.

By one o'clock, I had a third draft roughed out, but still wasn't pleased with it. The editing was difficult. At one point, I got stuck reworking the same sentence for twenty minutes. At two o'clock I changed the font and printed a hard copy of the thing so I could read it in a different format. At that point the writing didn't seem half bad, which I realized was probably something like a mirage.

I went to the office kitchen and grabbed a Dr. Pepper to reset my mind for the final push. Normally, I would have set the motion aside for a couple of days and circled back when I was fresh, but I needed to get the information in the motion on file and into the public domain so that it could make a big splash on the six o'clock news and provide cover for Mia and my family. I was about to test the age-old adage—sunlight is the best disinfectant. Moreover, I figured there was a good chance that Undersheriff Brown was on Dean Curtis's hit list at this point. If there was any truth to what I'd learned in the last two days, Brown could probably cut a deal with prosecutors and take down Curtis hard. Simply stated, I needed to get this motion on file before Curtis had Brown killed, undercutting the stated purpose of the motion—to get Mia out of Brown's jail.

When I returned to my desk, I pored over the motion yet again. After a few minor changes, I emailed it to Rashonda, buzzed her on the intercom, and asked her to spend no more than half an hour editing it, then I put my feet on the desk, leaned back in my executive's chair, and fell asleep.

Twenty minutes later my computer dinged with an email. I roused myself from a strange dream about running through the woods, and opened Rashonda's email. She'd caught several typos and made suggestions to improve the motion in three spots. I incorporated all but one of her suggestions, then called her on the intercom and asked her if the proposed order appointing Russ as special process server had been signed by the judge. She checked and said it had. I sent the final version of the motion back to her and told her to file it right away.

I was coming out from behind my desk when Russ and a black man with a short beard strolled into the room. Former Delta Force operator Mason Westwood may not have looked like anything special to most people—mid-forties, dressed in khaki slacks and a white short-sleeve button-up shirt, just under six feet tall, maybe 180 pounds—but he moved with the same calm, efficient glide I still saw in Pops and his eyes somehow looked incapable of expressing surprise. Before we could introduce ourselves, Russ's phone was chiming.

Russ glanced at the screen, then at me. "It's Agent Washington." He took the call. "What's up, Eric?"

He listened as his eyes swept around the room. Finally, he said to me, "Eric wants to know if you filed your motion yet?"

"Rashonda's doing it now."

"Being filed as we speak," he said to Eric, then listened. I couldn't hear everything Eric said, but I heard enough to know it had something to do with Dalton Campbell and the crucifix he'd claimed from the Worthington PD evidence locker back in '93. When the call ended, Russ said, "Campbell died of prostate cancer thirteen years ago."

He'd spoken to Eric for over two minutes so there must be a lot more to it than that. I waited for the rest of it.

"Eric tracked down Campbell's ex-wife in Haysville. Said her eyes about popped out of her head when he showed her a picture of the crucifix and asked her if her ex-husband ever owned one like it. She told him, 'fuck no, sonofabitch never owned a crucifix or been to church in his life.' But then she said that Dalton did have one hell of a story involving a crucifix that she'd never believed. Said Dalton came home one night from a bar with twenty-five hundred dollars he didn't have on him when he'd left. She found the money going through his pockets the next morning and confronted him about it. She was upset with him because she thought he was selling coke again. Anyway, she went on to tell Eric about how she was all up in her then-husband's grill about the money and he gave her some bullshit story about how he'd met a guy in a bar who asked him to go to the cop shop in Worthington and pretend to be looking for a crucifix they may've found in some woman's trailer home who'd recently died. Dalton told her he was supposed to tell the cops he thought maybe he'd lost it there a few weeks earlier, but wasn't sure. He told her this guy paid him twenty-five hundred up front, and promised twenty-five hundred more if he came back to the bar with the crucifix the next night. Eric asked her when this occurred. She placed it in the early nineties. Eric asked the lady if it could've been '93. She thought about that for a moment, then said that's exactly when it was because their divorce was finalized a few months later in January of '94."

"I wouldn't've bought a story like that either," Mason said.

"Me either," Russ said. "Especially since Campbell had been to prison for selling cocaine in '85."

I said, "Did she say whether or not Campbell ever got the crucifix and the other twenty-five hundred?"

Russ shook his head. "She doesn't know because she kicked his ass outta the house that morning, but there is some good news." He glanced at Mason before returning his eyes to me. "Eric said that when the LAPD found Curtis's brother dead in the Chateau Marmont in May of '91, he was wearing a crucifix. The two photos of the crucifix the LAPD took during inventory of Paul Curtis's property show that it looks identical to the one that used to be in evidence here, right down to the cord chain it's attached to. Only difference is, there was no engraving."

"I take it the LAPD doesn't still have the crucifix in evidence," I said, "or we wouldn't be talking about this."

Russ nodded. "That's right. LAPD released it to Dean Curtis on December twenty-first of '91. You think that's enough to convince a prosecutor to charge Curtis with your mother's murder?"

"Way too thin," I said. "Most of what's in my motion wouldn't be admissible at a trial."

"What if a prosecutor flipped Brown?" Russ said. "Offered him a deal?"

I nodded. "I bet Dean Curtis already thought of that. Brown better watch his ass."

"If Brown were dead, wouldn't that make the motion you're filing irrelevant?"

"Yeah, the prosecutor would have a great argument that it was moot. But the genie's already out of the bottle now, or is about to be anyway."

Russ nodded. "Eric says he has a contact in the press who will go looking for the motion in the public access portal shortly."

"Good," I said, "that'll move things along." I said to Mason, "I'll need to meet with my client at the jail for five or ten minutes to tell her what's going on. Then we can leave. You ready to meet my family?"

He nodded. "Yessir."

Rashonda appeared in the doorway. "The motion has been filed. And I just got off the phone with the clerk's office. The hearing will be set two weeks from today at nine in the morning."

"Thanks, Rashonda, just one more thing."

"Sure."

"Prepare subpoenas for Clint Brown and Dean Curtis."

She nodded.

"No way either one of those guys will ever testify," Russ said.

"Oh, they'll hire attorneys and ask Judge Abernathy to quash the subpoenas alright. And if their attorneys lose that motion, both men will do what men like them always do."

"Hide behind the Fifth?" Russ said. "That won't look so good for them."

I nodded. "Understatement of the year. Only ten people at a time are allowed in Abernathy's courtroom right now because of Covid restrictions. He's still playing it pretty cautious because his wife is immunocompromised. With all the news organizations that will want to attend, he may decide he needs to broadcast this hearing on YouTube."

Mason made face, like *what the hell?*

"Courtrooms have to remain open to the public, even during a pandemic," I explained. "Broadcasting hearings on YouTube is a fix that courts around the country have come up with to maintain transparency. The Constitution abhors secret proceedings."

"Sounds like these two guys are going to abhor public proceedings even more," Mason said.

Russ laughed and slapped him on the back. "That's the whole idea, buddy."

*   *   *

I could tell by the look on Mia's face that she knew about Keri. The jail has televisions in its dayrooms, and news of the attempt on my life and Keri's murder had been widely reported. Of course, there'd been no connection to Brown or Curtis mentioned in the reporting, but that was about to change.

When we sat down across from each other in one of the jail's little glass conference rooms, Mia's hand went to her forehead and she told me how sorry she was and that this was all her fault.

"If you want to take the blame for this, you'll have to get in line," I said. "My kids think it was their fault and I've been blaming myself."

She shook her head. "No—"

"Exactly. Don't tell me you're responsible for my wife's murder again, okay? That's not right."

She straightened at my tone.

I sighed and slumped in my chair. "Sorry I snapped at you. It's been rough. I think I'm about to lose it."

She frowned and her eyes were wet. "Are you here to tell me you're getting off the case?"

"No, I'm here to give you a copy of this."

I set the motion in front of her.

She picked it up and read. Fifteen seconds later she looked up. "You had no clue your mother may have been murdered before you took my case?"

"None."

She went back to reading about everything I'd learned from Jake Brackeen, Elias Matusak, Emily Knudson and the KBI—all of it. When she reached the second to last page, she teared up reading the account of Keri's murder, then stood and stepped around the table. She wanted me to stand, and when I did, she wrapped her arms around me and buried her face in my chest. I could feel her shaking. Her warmth was comforting, but I was too tired and numb to cry.

When she pulled back, she put her hand on the wet spot her tears had made on my shirt and apologized for putting it there, then told me I looked like I'd already lost twenty pounds.

I smiled faintly. "Not that much. You stay alive until I get you out of here, okay?"

"You stay alive long enough to get me out of here."

She cupped my cheek with her hand and looked up at me with something like gratitude in her eyes. I didn't feel worthy of it, which made me uncomfortable.

32

WITHIN AN HOUR of filing the motion Rashonda was inundated with calls from the press, and when they couldn't reach me that way they started calling Pops' landline. I told Pops he should probably take the phone off the hook, then asked him to set his DVR to record every local and national news program he could find.

After dinner, I sat on the couch in his living room with my sister, Ashley, and expanded on what Pops' told her about our situation while I worked the remote, looking for coverage of anything that had to do with Mia's case, including the serial killings in Oklahoma. Reporters covering the story seemed to be working from the same checklist, saying the situation was fluid with a lot of moving parts and unanswered questions. So far, so good. I'd gotten the exposure I needed from the press with one exception: the billionaire/undersheriff angle was only covered locally. Still—a good start. Dean Curtis couldn't be reached for comment, but Clint Brown got in front of local news cameras in his uniform with a clinched jaw and vowed to sue me. While the sheriff—an obese man in his seventies— had the good sense to stay off camera, he made the mistake of putting out a written statement expressing his unwavering confidence and trust in his undersheriff. All of this put a little smile on my face.

Ash noticed. "You're not worried about being sued?"

I shook my head. "Nah, this is perfect."

"Perfect, huh?"

"Yeah. The undersheriff going off half-cocked like that didn't surprise me, but I thought maybe the sheriff would at least hedge his bets. He could manage this mess by shipping Mia off to another jail or placing Brown on paid administrative leave. If he did either of those things, the judge would probably dismiss my motion as moot. If I were the sheriff, I'd make one or both of those moves before the national press decides to take an interest."

Ash wasn't convinced. "This story—the Brown and Curtis part—is going to blow up big time, Ben. These guys, including the sheriff, obviously aren't the type to shy away from a fight. Brown is going balls to the wall here. Curtis will too. Deny, deny, deny. The press will eat it up."

Ash's eyes were bloodshot. Years of substance abuse had taken its toll, showing now more than ever. She'd put on at least thirty pounds since being kidnapped two years ago. She was sober at the moment, but the odor of alcohol seemed to be coming through her pores. She was thirty-seven, two years younger than me, but could easily pass for fifty. The revelations about our mother and a man named Paco Correa were the last thing she needed. Pops had already told her he didn't think we had the same father. In the two hours I'd spent with her I could tell that really bothered her. She was my half-sister. She said all the right things and was doing her best to be there for me, but I knew Ash. There was a wedge between us that wasn't there before.

I nodded. "I hope you're right about the press eating this up, but I'm a little worried because the national press hasn't touched it yet. Makes me think Curtis is pulling some strings behind the scenes."

"Maybe they're just having a hard time believing what you're accusing him of. You think Curtis and Brown really killed Mom?"

"I wouldn't have put everything on the line if I didn't."

"You think they'll ever be held responsible?"

"Your guess is as good as mine."

Ash shook her head. "I don't think they ever will. The world doesn't work that way, brother."

"Bigger men have fallen harder. They're scared now. I can feel it."

"I'm scared too. You feel that?"

I tried to comfort her with a sympathetic smile but it didn't work.

"How do you think things would have been different if Mom had lived?" she said.

"I dunno. Might've been worse for us if she'd been around longer."

"That's pretty pessimistic."

"Actually, I was looking on the bright side."

"How so?"

"Things could've been worse, that's all."

She scowled. "You think so?"

"I'm sure of it."

"Because Mom was a bad person?"

"I didn't say that."

"You said we were better off without her. Same thing."

Ash was right. It was close to the same thing—what lawyers call a distinction without a difference.

She stood from the couch and stepped to the big window that normally offered a view of B Street. The curtain was closed and needed to stay that way for security purposes. But she stood there anyway, her back to me, staring at the curtain. "You don't know what Mom went through."

"I know some of it. I was there, remember. So were you."

"But you don't know the whole story."

"No one ever really knows the whole story in another person's life. You don't get to see all their cards."

"You ever think that maybe I know exactly what was going on in her life. Because I'm an addict, just like her."

"You want help, Ash? All you have to do is ask. We've been through this before."

"You don't understand."

"You're right. I don't."

She turned and pooched out her lips in thought. "Addicts have trouble letting go of the past."

"Okay, I'll buy that, but where's this going?"

"You want to help me, let's talk about the future."

"The future? Alright fine. Let's talk about the future."

She smiled. "How will things be different if these guys—Curtis and Brown—end up in prison?"

"Different how? For whom?"

"For us."

I shook my head. "No difference I guess. Kind of money Curtis has, he can come after me from anywhere, including prison."

"That's right. You need to prepare for the fact that none of this makes any real difference to us. You heard what they said on the news. Dean Curtis is one of the fifty richest people in the world. Only way we'll be safe from him is if he's dead. You ever think about that?"

"What are you saying? That we should have him killed?"

"He'd be impossible to get to, so, no. But maybe we do the next best thing."

"What's the next best thing?"

She shrugged. "Sue him."

"Sue Dean Curtis? For killing Mom?"

"Yeah, and Brown too. Why not?"

I thought about that. "For starters, the statute of limitations for a wrongful death suit ran out a long time ago."

"There's a statute of limitations for murder?"

"No, of course not, but you're not a prosecutor filing criminal charges for the state, you're talking about bringing a civil lawsuit. Statute of limitations for wrongful death actions in this state is two years."

"Jesus Christ, Ben, you're an attorney. There's a fuckin' loophole for everything else in the law, I'd think there'd be one for suing the motherfucker who hid the fact that he murdered our mother twenty-eight years ago."

Her hands shook, like maybe she needed a drink. She balled them together to quell the tremor.

"Okay, Sis. Something to think about."

She sat next to me on the couch again, closer this time, leaning into me and putting her quivering hand on mine. "Think about this. If you have his money, he won't be able to use it to go after you and the kids? Like you said, a guy with that kind of money is a threat even if he's in prison."

"*We*, you mean."

"What?"

"If *we* have his money, you mean, right? I assume you'll want some of it."

She took her hand off mine. "I guess. Sure."

"Even if we are able to prove Curtis killed Mom, and if there happens to be a loophole in the statute of limitations that allows us a determination on the merits of a wrongful death action, *we* wouldn't end up with *all* his money. You understand that, right?"

"It'd be a hell of a lot easier to hide with a big chunk of his money in our bank accounts though, wouldn't it?" She nodded toward the window. "Those guards out there gotta be expensive. How you gonna pay for all that, Benny?"

"They're working for free, out of the goodness of their hearts."

"Really?"

I nodded. From the look on her face, I wasn't sure she believed me.

"You picked a fight with a man that basically has an unlimited supply of money," she said. "You're going to need—your kids are going to need—bodyguards for a long time. How you gonna pay for that?"

"Get enough of Curtis's money to pay for bodyguards, problem solved. That's your argument?"

"Yeah. And I don't see what's wrong with it."

"Just thinking about me and the kids, right?"

"I don't know if you know this, but I don't mean shit. And you know *why* I don't mean shit?"

I shook my head. "I don't have the slightest idea what you mean by that, but it sounds wrong anyway."

"I don't mean shit, because I got no money."

"You'll always mean shit to me, Ash."

She blew out a huff of air. "Ha ha, very funny."

"Probably not, but I get your point. Go after his money."

"Money is his weapon, so fuck yeah, we should go after it."

"Know what I think, Ash?"

"What?"

"I think you've been thinking of a way to sell this to me all day."

"How am I doing?"

"Not bad, Sis. Not too bad."

33

RUSS CALLED FRIDAY afternoon and told me he was sitting off Clint Brown's house in the country, watching it from a distance with binoculars. Said he'd been at his post since sunrise waiting for Brown to leave. Russ wanted to follow him to see what he was up to. Logic dictated that Brown had sensitive matters to discuss in person with Curtis, so I understood the play. If Brown was smart, he'd meet with Curtis at the sheriff's office—a semi-public place on the other side of metal detectors. Phones were a risky way to discuss organized crime and the inevitable fallout that occurred when shit hit the fan. Anyone could be listening or recording the conversation, even once-trusted allies. If Russ got made following Brown or surveilling his house, there was a good chance he would be detained by the sheriff's department for questioning, or worse. The subpoena he had for Brown in his hip pocket would come in handy if that happened, assuming the cops detaining him were straight. If they weren't, the subpoena could still give them pause. But so far, nothing had happened. No one came or left out the front gate, and no one came for Russ. The two deputies guarding the gate had been there since at least seven a.m. My guards were working for free. The taxpayers of Sedgwick County were paying for Brown's.

I told Russ I'd rather he look for Annie than continue his surveillance of Brown. I told him when our call was over, he ought drive to the front gate and see if the deputies would let him in to personally serve the subpoena. Admittedly, the odds of that happening were slim, but it was worth a try, and besides, he could always serve the subpoena by giving it to one of the deputies. Nothing was as legally solid as personal service, but service via an armed guard at the gate of Brown's residence counted as legal service too, although it left open the possibility—slight here if the guards were clean, great if they were dirty—that Brown could claim he never received the subpoena. Russ said he'd go that route on Tuesday if he didn't have the subpoena personally served by then, but in the meantime, he didn't want to give up his excuse for keeping an eye on Brown, not that he legally needed one, but I understood his point. My instinct told me to let him do the job his way.

Friday evening, Dean Curtis finally made national news. Close-ups of the motion I filed were made visible and talking heads recounted the allegations with their usual over-dramatizations. One network went further, unloading on *Disculture* magazine for burying their reporter's 1992 exposé about how Curtis and his unnamed associates had sexually trafficked three underage girls who had come forward and told their stories. Also buried was the story of how Curtis had confided to a prominent but recently discredited Harvard biologist about his dream of seeding the human race with his DNA by impregnating women at his various properties throughout the world. Apparently, Curtis was fascinated with transhumanism—a modern day form of eugenics that promoted genetic engineering, artificial intelligence, and controlled breeding as a way to improve the human race. According to the coverage now, Curtis had gotten wind of the exposé and deployed a coterie of high-powered lawyers to threaten *Disculture* with a lawsuit if they ran the story, and if that wasn't enough to discourage the magazine from running it, Curtis visited the editor-in-chief personally at his office and made a six-figure donation to his favorite charity that same day. The following morning, the editor-in-chief found the severed head of a cat screwed to his front door by an ear. Though *Disculture* maintained that the allegations of sexual abuse and Curtis's dream of spreading his seed didn't meet their legal standards for reporting, the media coverage now suggested the magazine had been intimidated into stripping the article of any mention of the biologist and the girls' statements and titling it, "The Talented Mr. Curtis," as opposed to "Lifestyles of the Filthy Rich", the original title proposed by their reporter.

A couple months after the altered *Disculture* article was published, a similar exposé by a reporter at *The New York Chronicle* was axed following a similar pattern of events. Curtis learned of the story, deployed the lawyers, donated to a charity favored by the newspaper's editor, and in case the lawyers weren't intimidating enough, a live 30-06 bullet was found in the morning on the driver's seat of the editor's car, which had been parked all night in his locked garage at home.

It appeared the tide was turning on Dean Curtis and several powerful men in his orbit. Photos of politicians and billionaires and Hollywood elites standing arm and arm with the white-haired predator in exotic locations flashed across TV screens across the country, casting them in the harsh light of the sprawling scandal with a look of assurance on their faces that they were anointed by fate to live a life without limitations. One of the stations brought the story back to the present by showing a photo of me and Keri on our wedding day two years earlier, which caught me off guard, making me shake my head as if I were snapping out of a daydream. They must've found the photo on one of our friends' social media accounts. Journalists hadn't forgotten Keri, and they'd read the motion I'd filed and knew Matusak said Curtis had sent him to kill me. That should turn up the heat on Curtis.

I turned off the TV and sat there on the couch alone in the living room, listening to Pops talk with Father Phan in the adjoining room until the reverend poked his head through the archway and asked if it was okay to join me. He was Vietnamese but had been an American citizen for thirty years, now pushing sixty. He wore glasses with coke-bottle thick lenses. I managed a nod and he sat next to me and talked about

Keri's wake and the funeral mass, then asked if I wished to give a confession.

"Not right now, Father, thank you."

"Have you had a moment with the Lord since Keri passed?"

"If He was here, I didn't notice." Maybe I shouldn't have said that, but I wasn't in the mood for this conversation.

"Join me in prayer, Ben."

I shook my head. "Doesn't feel right. All that stuff seems like superstition to me right now."

"Many in the church, some of them saints, lost faith in their darkest hour. In our journey to the Father of souls, our way lies past a dragon."

I found myself nodding to be polite, but his words felt like an argument from a litigant to me.

He put his hand on my shoulder. When I looked at him he wore a little smile. "I can see by the look on your face that you are trying to pretend my words are of some comfort to you now."

"Yeah, Father, I'm sorry."

"As am I. You need time. I will pray for Keri and you and your family and the justice you seek." He stood from the couch and walked through the archway into the dining room and let himself out.

* * *

The visitation at the funeral home on Saturday evening was private for security reasons. Mindy, Keri's foster mother, came up from Oklahoma on Saturday night and ate dinner with us. Afterward, we were all taken to the funeral home by Mason and his men. Mindy was a seventy-three-year-old widow with two adult daughters who, she said, wouldn't be able to make it to any of the services, which didn't surprise me because I knew Keri hadn't been close to her foster sisters who were much older than she. We had a long talk when we got back to the house. It was cathartic and exhausting at the same time.

Sunday morning I called Russ for an update regarding the search for Annie. He told me not to worry about it. He said he would find her and that he would get those subpoenas served by Tuesday, one way or another, that if anything important went down, he'd be sure to call. Rashonda gave me a similar message when I phoned her. Elias Matusak hadn't called, nor had anyone else I hoped might be useful in bringing down Curtis. The only people calling were reporters, and that, Rashonda said, was something that happened every ten or twenty minutes throughout the day. I apologized and promised to make it up to her somehow. She told me not to worry about it. Said I should concentrate on protecting my family. She didn't say, "And staying alive," but I heard it in her voice.

When I got off the phone, Mason's men took us across the neighbor's back yard, then through the side door of St. Anthony's for mass. Afterward, we lunched in the dining room on food that friends had brought over. Pops and I played board games with the kids for a while, then I went to my room and slept. When I woke, it was early evening. I opened my laptop and searched the Internet for news. Nothing new was being reported regarding Curtis. The big stories had taken over: the United States' bungled exit from its twenty-year war in Afghanistan and a hurricane battering Mexico's east coast.

On Monday evening two hours before the wake, Mason called and told me to peek out the front window. When I did, I saw a reporter I recognized from a major network walking toward the front door. Behind him was a van with his network's logo prominently featured on its side. Across the street I caught glimpse of one of Mason's snipers keeping an eye on things from his perch on the roof of a red-bricked public school building. The chief of police had granted Mason permission to plant two snipers in the neighborhood during the wake and the funeral. The local sheriff had deputized them to make things official. I was told the second sniper was positioned on the roof of St. Anthony's Catholic Academy behind us. I watched the reporter gesticulate wildly in

Mason's face, to no avail. He turned around, stalked away, back to his van.

Half an hour before the wake, the streets in the neighborhood were bloated with parked cars. Clots of people made their way down the sidewalks to St. Anthony's. There was a heavy police presence and news organizations had set up cameras on the playground across the street from the church. Ten minutes before the wake would begin, Mason whisked us across our neighbor's back yard, through a small parking lot, and into the side entrance of the church.

* * *

The next morning Pops left with Mason at nine a.m. to greet people entering the church for the funeral mass and point out to Mason and Chief Bell anyone he didn't recognize. At a quarter to ten, the rest of us repeated the same trek as the day before. We sat in the same spot in the sanctuary as we had at the wake, which were the same seats Pops and Ash and I sat in twenty-eight years earlier during my mother's funeral. The same place we'd sat with the kids five years ago during my first wife's, Natalie's, funeral.

There were more people in the church than I'd ever seen before and the air conditioner couldn't keep up. Within minutes I'd sweated through my shirt. Lindy scooched into me and leaned her head on my shoulder. Leo and Ashley stared forward with glassy eyes. I could hear the collective shuffle of people behind me—their ambient reverence. I didn't like them where I couldn't see them. It was becoming a problem for me. Lindy looked up at me with concern in her eyes. She wasn't sweating at all. I glanced behind us and saw many familiar faces. One of them nodded. I nodded back and faced the front again, closing my eyes, now drenched in sweat. When I opened them again, the scene before me struck me in a way it never had before. We lived in a world in which a statue of the God I worshiped was nailed to a cross on the wall above an altar. Perhaps that should have horrified me before now. When the priest came out I closed my eyes and whispered goodbye to Keri.

34

RUSS SAT IN a cornfield with the heels of his boots dug into the dirt and binoculars to his eyes. He was watching two deputies in a patrol car parked at Brown's front gate. They'd backed into the drive and were facing the gravel road. Through their windshield, Russ saw faint movement, like maybe they were talking. After a while, they stepped out, stretched, and spoke to each other over the top of the car with travel mugs in their hands. The one on the driver's side was a lanky young redheaded man Russ had never seen before. The other one had been at the front gate on guard duty a lot over the last few days. He was one of those guys who had lifted weights for so many years that his muscles caused him to walk like he had little suitcases strapped to his limbs. Russ watched them climb back into the cruiser, then dropped the binoculars from his eyes and glanced at his phone. Keri's funeral was starting and he realized he would miss it without having decided whether or not he would attend. It was a head-in-the-sand way to decide something, but whatever the process, he told himself, it was the right outcome. The last funeral he attended had sent him into a tailspin, a three-day bender that landed him in the hospital with alcohol poisoning. His partner's funeral had brought back the loss of his son in a way that wasn't conducive to his sobriety. Besides, he'd promised to get the subpoenas served today, one way or another.

He went to his Malibu and drove it to the front gate like Ben had suggested four days earlier—what a colossal waste of time this surveillance had been. As he pulled into the drive he buzzed his windows down. The deputies stepped out of the cruiser and approached him cautiously.

"Put your hands on the wheel where I can see them," the redhead said with his hand on the grip of the pistol in his gun belt.

Russ gripped the steering wheel—ten and two. "I'm here to serve a subpoena, fellas. Got it right there on the seat beside me."

Muscles made his way to the passenger side of the car. "Keep those hands on the wheel."

"No problem." Russ made eye contact with the redhead. "The door's unlocked if you want to open it. I'll keep my hands right here. Don't need a misunderstanding that ends with you shooting an innocent process server."

The redhead opened the driver's door. Russ stepped out and put his hands on the roof of the Malibu. The redhead patted him down as Muscles opened the passenger door, reached in, and came out with the subpoena. He inspected it for a moment. "Hey, Virgil, it's a subpoena for Brown in that Delarosa case."

The redhead finished patting down Russ. "He's clean." Then to Muscles: "What'd you say?"

Muscles came around the car and showed the paper to Virgil. "Subpoena for Brown in the Delarosa case."

The redhead looked at Russ, "No shit?"

Russ nodded. "No shit."

"We'll be sure to give it to him for ya," Muscles said.

"I'd like to be the one to give it to him if you don't mind."

"We do mind," Muscles said, stepping closer to Russ. "You can leave now."

Russ scratched his cheek and looked off in the distance like he was thinking about how to phrase what he was about to say. "You know I'm not the reason you guys are out here guarding the gate, right? Neither is the guy I'm working for, Ben Joel."

"We don't ask a lot of questions," Virgil said.

Russ considered that with a look of bemusement on his face. "Let me come at this another way, then, Virgil. Maybe you give Brown a call. Tell him his old friend, Russ Osborne, is here to see him."

"You're Russell Osborne?" Muscles said.

Russ nodded.

Muscles tilted his head. "Used to work undercover for ATF?"

"That's me."

He handed Russ the subpoena. "Can I see some ID?"

Russ pulled out his DL and showed it to Muscles.

Muscles nodded, pulled a remote out of his breast pocket and hit a button. The gate started opening. "Brown's a piece of shit. Go serve his ass." Then to Virgil, "Call Brown. Tell him Oz is here to see him. Don't mention the subpoena."

Virgil did what he was told as Russ got in his Malibu and put it in gear. When Virgil got off the phone, he said to Muscles, "Brown said for us to kick that sonofabitch off his property."

"Too late," Muscles said. "If Brown doesn't like how we do our job, maybe he should hire his own fucking security." He waved Russ through the gate with a grin. He and Virgil watched the Malibu drive toward the house.

* * *

Brown answered the door in gym shorts and a T-shirt, holding a Glock in his right hand. Russ handed him the subpoena and told him he'd been served.

Brown looked at it. "State versus Delarosa? What's Joel expect me to say that'll help his client?"

"No idea. Not my department."

"Tell him I'm suing the shit out of him for this."

"You might want to read up on that. I'm told that won't fly."

"Fuck you."

"Appreciate the offer, but that's your style, not mine." Russ looked around, like he was concerned for his safety, but in an exaggerated, mocking way. "How long you think Dean Curtis can tolerate the threat you pose to him?"

Brown shook his head. "Don't know what you're talking about."

"You're probably right. I'm sure your friendship with Curtis is rock solid. That's what you two are, right? Friends?"

Brown's face flushed. "Joel will be disbarred for this."

"For what? Subpoenaing you? Exposing you? Knocking your dick in the dirt? I don't think so. But you know what will happen? People you and Curtis have hurt will start coming out of the woodwork. You think what's happening now is ugly, partner, you ain't seen nothing yet."

Brown's face clouded.

Russ suppressed a smile. "You and I both know Curtis has his finger on the button of what some people call a doomsday weapon—video of you and God knows who else doing something you shouldn't. Maybe raping underage girls. That's just a guess. Personally, I wouldn't know. He'll probably use the threat of mutually assured destruction to call in favors like he has his whole life. Favors from men he can't get to any other way, some of whom have their hands on the levers of power. But not from a pissant like you. You, he'll kill. But I see by the pistol in your hand and the armed guards at your gate that you already know that."

"Get the fuck off my property."

Russ turned and stepped off the porch, and with his back to Brown yelled out, "You should get a lawyer and come forward. Cut a deal, while you can. Deals tend to go away if information is too late to help law enforcement. But I don't need to tell you that."

When Russ got to the driver's side door, he reached for the handle and froze, pretending to be lost in thought, before locking eyes with Brown, still glaring at him from the doorway. "When Curtis sees no other way out, that's exactly what he's gonna do—feed you and the others to the wolves." He glanced around the property again. "In the meantime, I'd get back inside if I was you, boy."

Brown leveled the Glock at Russ.

Russ winked at him, ducked into the Malibu, and drove away.

An hour later Russ walked into the downtown office of Curtis & Company Inc. and left the subpoena for Dean Curtis with one of his personal assistants, recording his conversation with the assistant as added proof of service. Later still, after he was refused entry into Curtis's gated mansion, he tacked a copy of the subpoena on the gate, then took a photo of it.

35

TWO DAYS AFTER Keri's funeral the district attorney, Blaine Swartzmiller, called my office. I knew Blaine from law school. We'd run in the same circles—went to the same parties, drank at the same bars, played a few rounds of golf together. I counted him as a friend, albeit not a close one. We hadn't kept in touch, so when he called I figured it was about Mia's case. I figured he was feeling some heat from Curtis and Brown's attorneys to not object to Mia's transfer to another jail. Perhaps it seems counterintuitive to a non-lawyer for their attorneys to do that, but it made perfect sense to me. If the state agreed to Mia's transfer, there'd be no hearing and no obligation to testify under subpoena at the hearing. Brown and Curtis would avoid the public humiliation of being forced on the witness stand and put in a situation in which their best option was to plead the Fifth.

Judge Abernathy had scheduled an impromptu remote (Zoom) hearing tomorrow morning to discuss that matter. *Discuss the matter*—that's what Abernathy's email said. Everyone knew what he really meant—this was an informal settlement conference of sorts. My guess was—if necessary— he'd lean hard on the state to concede my motion to move Mia to another jail so he didn't have to deal with any of this shit. The murder case against Mia was relatively straightforward. The issue of whether or not she was safe in the undersheriff's jail was full of extraordinary, high-profile complications that he would rather sidestep. One prudent decision by the DA, and the complications would go away like a bad dream. Rashonda patched Blaine through to my cell phone. I muted the TV and leaned back in Pops' recliner.

"How you holding up?" he asked.

"As good as can be expected."

"I don't know what to say. I'm sorry."

"Thanks for calling."

"Keri's service was . . . nice. It was a nice service."

I'd seen Blaine sitting in the back of the church, but we'd never made eye contact. "Yeah, it was nice," I said.

"I'm sorry—Jesus, I keep saying that—this is awkward as hell and I apologize for that, but I'm actually calling about the Delarosa case. I hate to call you so soon after the funeral on business, but—"

"It's okay. What's up?" As if I didn't know.

"Did you know that Curtis hired Benowitz to represent him. Brown hired Monet."

Monet's first name was Steve. I'd tried cases against him when I was a prosecutor. His reputation as one of the best attorneys in the state was well deserved. His signature look sprang to mind: three-piece pinstriped navy blue suit; slicked-back hair; perfectly round, wire-rimmed glasses that made him look even more like John Lennon than he already did. The image I had of Curtis's attorney, Jerry Benowitz, came from TV. He was perhaps the most famous lawyer on the planet, former Harvard law professor turned TV pundit, a curly-haired septuagenarian with a bulbous blue nose.

"I saw that. Welcome to the big leagues."

"Monet and Benowitz are up my ass about conceding your motion to transfer Delarosa to another jail on the grounds that the DA's office doesn't have the resources to pour a bunch of time into a wholly unnecessary pretrial hearing. You got 'em worried, Ben. Curtis and Brown don't want anything to do with getting called to the stand and lawyering up about a thousand times. Be a public relations disaster for them."

"Ask the attorneys to put their requests in writing," I said. "You'll need it as cover when they throw you under the bus for conceding the motion."

"I did. Got two letters stating that none of the allegations you made in your motion about their clients were true, therefore, Brown posed no threat to Delarosa—she'd be as safe and secure in Brown's jail as any other inmate, according to them. The letter from Monet also expressed concern about the message I'd be sending to the public about the propriety of law enforcement in this county if I conceded the motion. However, both letters concluded with the same assurance— their clients understood the benefit of not objecting to Delarosa's transfer to another jail in order to avoid the sideshow you're trying to gin up. They promised to respect any decision I made about how to proceed. Guess that's what they think passes for cover."

I laughed. "Maybe you should break them of sucking eggs and oppose the motion. See how much respect flows your way."

"You'd like that wouldn't you?"

"Damn right I would."

Blaine understood the situation perfectly. Sure I wanted Mia out of Brown's jail, but I wanted a contested hearing even more. I wanted to get Brown and Curtis on the witness stand, which wouldn't be possible if Blaine conceded the motion for any reason.

"You know what I'd like?" Blaine said. Then he answered his own question. "The name of the person who killed Jimmy Ray."

I sighed. "I'm working on it."

"Your client won't tell you, or she won't deal?"

Both, I thought. "I'm working on it. That's all I can say."

"Then all I can say is that my gut tells me to concede your motion. I think Brown and Curtis are dirty. Depending on how things play out in the press, if my office opposes this motion we might end up looking as dumb as the OJ prosecutors."

As long as I'd known Blaine, he'd always had political aspirations. Month by month, year by year, he'd won big cases and put bad men behind bars. He'd made all the right moves and connections and won two terms as the DA. Word was he was eyeing the governor's mansion in the next election cycle. Job one for him right now was to protect his political career. I needed to give him a reason to contest my motion. I needed his office to fight me in court, like King Kong versus Godzilla. Brown and Curtis would be Tokyo and we'd step all over them. They'd be bloody, on fire, and in ruins by the time we were done.

"If you concede my motion on the ground that your office doesn't have time to fuck with this, Brown and Curtis will be happy you took them off the hook for testifying, but then they'll turn around and blame you for denying them a chance to clear their names. They'll say you threw law enforcement under the bus when the going got tough."

"I have the letter—"

"When all this is over and the threat of having to testify has passed, they'll blame you privately and publically. Nobody will give a damn about that bullshit letter you said yourself doesn't provide cover."

"I'm just trying to do the right thing by you and your client, and by my clients . . . the taxpayers. My job is to seek justice. I'm calling as a friend for Chrissake. Maybe it's best for everyone if I just concede the motion. Your client could be in another county's jail by this afternoon."

"Do what you have to do. Do what you think is right and let the chips fall where they may."

Blaine laughed. "You make it sound so simple, but I've read your motion. You're on shaky ground here. I'm not sure what the right thing is, or even if Abernathy will hear evidence on this matter. Hell, he might be content to hear argument and rule."

"Maybe, but that's what hearings are for. Don't short-circuit the process before I can get these guys in court. Concede nothing."

Now it was Blaine's turn to sigh. "When Benowitz called again this morning, I kind of hinted to him that I wouldn't object to your client being transferred to another jail. He's trying to decide whether he needs to file a motion to quash your subpoena. Judge Abernathy called me too. Wanted to know how big a headache this was going to be. I let him know I was leaning toward not objecting to your motion. He was pleased. But I'll think about it some more. You'll find out what I've decided during Abernathy's Zoom hearing tomorrow."

"Thanks, Blaine," I said, deciding to tease him a little. "You'll make a fine governor someday."

"Not if this case goes sideways on me I won't. Get me the name of Jimmy Ray's other killer so we can both get out from under this case."

"What are you offering?"

"Nothing yet. Let me know when your client is serious about settling this case, and I'll extend a plea offer. A fair one. More than fair if she'll tell me who killed Jimmy Ray and why. If there are mitigating factors and the reason for killing Ray is compelling, I'd be inclined to grant her a deal that gives her most of her life back. Looks like Jimmy Ray was a real dirt bag. She probably did the world a favor."

"My client is adamant about not cooperating with the state right now. I'll let you know if that changes. I know you'll do the right thing tomorrow."

"No you don't, and neither do I."

* * *

The next morning I set up my laptop on Pops' dining room table for the Zoom hearing. For a year and a half, judges had been encouraged to hold remote hearings to keep people out of the courthouses and stop the spread of Covid-19. Zoom worked great for simple proceedings that didn't require the admission of evidence, like this one. The results were mixed for more complex matters, like a contested evidentiary hearing on the motion I'd filed. Abernathy didn't have the patience for all the complications that Zoom evidentiary hearings inherently brought with them, so I knew if he was inclined to hear evidence on my motion, and the DA's office opposed it, we'd be in his courtroom next Thursday morning. If he kept his courtroom closed to the general public as he had since the pandemic began, I figured his practice of livestreaming the proceedings on YouTube—to maintain the transparency—would continue. If he switched course and allowed the public to attend in person, dozens of media outlets would want in. They'd want to bring in their cameras. The media's lawyers would be involved and they'd all write letters and call and request meetings. Abernathy wasn't about to give himself another headache he didn't need.

I logged into the Zoom link I'd been given by Abernathy's assistant. My face appeared on the computer's screen along with four others: ADA Claire Riddle—thirty-something, high cheekbones, straight red hair, minimal make-up; Jerry Benowitz; Steve Monet; and Judge Abernathy. Five faces in boxes on a screen—looked like the opening sequence to *The Brady Bunch*. I'd logged in five minutes early, but was still the last one to the party. In the upper left hand corner I noticed the matter was being recorded and livestreamed on YouTube. I didn't think that was necessary for an informal hearing like this one, but that was Abernathy's call. Given the mystery playing out in the public surrounding Brown and Curtis, Abernathy must've thought it prudent to error on the side of transparency. Given what he'd been told by Blaine, he probably figured this was the only hearing on my motion the public was going to get—a brief announcement by the state not objecting to my client's transfer to a different jail.

Judge Abernathy—a bear of a man in his late-fifties with a full beard and shoulder-length grey hair—called the case, "This is State versus Mia Delarosa, 21 CR 1504. Attorneys, announce your appearances for the record please."

After the attorneys announced their appearances and who they represented, Abernathy got down to business. "As you all know, Mr. Joel's motion is set to be heard in my courtroom next Thursday, unless the parties have come to some agreement. Mr. Joel, Ms. Riddle, is this going to be a contested matter?"

I shrugged.

Ms. Riddle nodded her head. "Yes, Your Honor."

Benowitz and Monet looked stunned. Then they just looked pissed. Their clients were one step closer to being forced on the stand. One step closer to the public relations disaster they were hoping to avoid.

Abernathy looked more confused than mad, like maybe he'd misunderstood what Riddle had said. He cleared his throat. "To be clear, Ms. Riddle, you'd prefer Ms. Delarosa stay incarcerated in the Sedgwick County Jail pending trial in this matter. Is that what you're telling the court?"

"That's correct."

Abernathy didn't like the answer. He squinted, then looked down, like he was searching for the right words—something proper for a judge who was neutral, and who didn't mind working a few extra hours. Finally, he looked up. "Why does the DA's office care which jail Ms. Delarosa is in, as long as it's one close by?"

Riddle was ready for the question and answered quickly. "Because we received a letter from Mr. Monet stating that Undersheriff Brown was concerned that if the DA conceded the defendant's motion, we'd be sending a false message about the propriety of law enforcement in this community to the public. Mr. Monet makes an excellent point. Since the jury pool in this county is a subset of the public, and since Undersheriff Brown is obviously willing to come forward and answer Mr. Joel's questions—at least that's how we read the letter—we oppose the motion."

I suppressed a smile. Abernathy no doubt regretted his decision to make the hearing public. What could he do now but keep proper judicial decorum and remain neutral? Monet and Benowitz didn't dare say a word. Not now, with the whole world watching on the Internet. Now wasn't the time for them to give ADA Riddle a tongue lashing for not agreeing to have Mia moved to another jail without a hearing, without Brown and Curtis having to testify. After all, she took her orders from the DA. It was Blaine they wanted to lay into. He'd refused to do Monet and Benowitz's work for them. If that didn't change, Monet and Benowitz would have to file motions to quash—nullify by judicial action—their client's subpoenas. If that didn't work, their clients would have to suffer the humiliation of hiding behind the Fifth Amendment in the public square to avoid testifying or risk incriminating themselves by answering my questions. But the hearing was still six days away. No time to panic or show their hand or say something stupid. There was still plenty of time to get at the DA in private. If Benowitz and Monet couldn't convince Blaine to change his mind, there were still ways for Curtis and Brown to get to him the old fashioned way—blackmail, bribes, threats. I was grateful for Blaine's help so far and hoped he would stay strong. If he came out the other side of this case with his career ruined I didn't know how I would ever repay him. As Abernathy concluded the hearing, the image of Monet and Benowitz rendered mute struck me as a thing of beauty. As their angry faces disappeared from my screen, I couldn't help but smile at the victory, however small. However temporary.

* * *

That night I lay awake in bed, my mind racing through all the complexities of the motion and how it would play out—would I get the sonsofbitches on the stand or not? Then I had an epiphany that made me laugh out loud in the dark. How had I not seen this before? What would happen on Thursday morning now seemed as inevitable as the sunrise. Brown and Curtis's best play wasn't to threaten Blaine or hide behind the Fifth Amendment or ask the court to quash the subpoenas. Their best play was to play the Covid card. They'd claim symptoms at the last minute, maybe even send their attorneys to court with notes from doctors—positive for Covid-19. King's X motherfucker. The court had been dealing with this sort of thing—dare I call it a tactic—since the beginning of the pandemic. Abernathy would suspect the judicial system was being manipulated, but what lengths would he take to find out for sure when he was looking for a way to avoid the hearing in the first place? Of course Abernathy wouldn't want to reward this behavior, and to be fair to my client, would probably order that Mia be immediately moved to another jail. On the surface, it would be a win for my client, and that was fine, but it was Brown and Curtis who'd be most relieved because they would save face. The next morning I told Russ about my epiphany.

"Fifty bucks says they play the Covid card on Thursday morning," I said. Russ wouldn't take the bet. He thought I was probably right.

He called back six hours later.

"I got information makes me think you'll get Curtis on the stand, one way or another, whether or not he plays the Covid card. I'd put money on it, if you're still in a gambling mood."

"I'm listening."

"At my request, Rashonda's been forwarding calls from reporters to me. I rope-a-dope them for a while, don't give them anything, and when they're done asking questions, I solicit their help. Ask them to call me anytime they think they have information that might help our cause. I may have something. Just got a call from a reporter working for *TMI*."

"*TMI*?"

"Stands for Too Much Information, naturally. It's a media outlet that dishes dirt on famous people on their website. I didn't have much use for *TMI*, until maybe now."

"What'd the reporter say?"

"Told me Curtis is scheduled to attend a private fundraiser for Senator Mack Anderson's presidential campaign at a five-star restaurant in Chicago this Wednesday—the night before the court hearing. Place called Cuisine. The reporter says they've got someone on the wait staff willing to risk her job to snap some photos of Curtis. Senator Anderson will be there, has the place to himself until three in the morning. *TMI* is gonna pay this waitress ten grand up front, twenty if she gets any photos of Curtis, and fifty grand if she gets one of him hobnobbing with Senator Anderson. The reporter's been following Mia's case, knows that Curtis is subpoenaed for court in Wichita the morning after the party. She figured if he attends the fundraiser in Chicago and stays until the wee hours of the morning, there's a good chance he already has plans to skip court. She agreed to send me whatever photos she has of Curtis as soon as she gets them. If Curtis's attorney plays the Covid card like we think, I'm willing to bet you can use the photos to convince the court he's thumbing his nose at the judicial process. It's hard to think of anything that would piss Abernathy off more than that. I think you'll get Curtis on the stand. Maybe not Thursday morning, but it'll happen."

"He's arrogant enough to pull something like this, isn't he?"

"I got fifty bucks that says he is, and that we'll have photographic evidence you can use to get Curtis on the stand. Only sticking point—can the waitress get a pic without getting caught? How 'bout it? We got a bet?"

"No. I won't bet against the waitress. If she gets caught she might be at the bottom of Lake Michigan before the sun comes up Thursday morning. Also, my gut tells me Curtis is about to step in it. I'll be right there to rub his nose in it when he does."

36

Thursday, September 9

FIVE DAYS LATER at 8:45 in the morning I sat alone in Judge Abernathy's courtroom waiting on detention officers to bring in Mia. As far as I knew, no one had gotten to Blaine. The motion to get her out of Brown's jail was still slated to start at nine, along with the motions to quash Curtis and Brown's subpoenas. One way or another, I hoped to have Mia out of Brown's jail by noon.

The courtroom was eerily quiet. Abandoned-building quiet. Many in the court system were still working from home, even as most of the world ditched the masks and attempted a return to life as it was before the pandemic. But courts took extra care because, unlike a restaurant or a ball game, a courtroom wasn't usually a place people flocked to voluntarily. Defendants and people subpoenaed to court or summonsed for jury duty were ordered to be here under threat of contempt, which could lead to incarceration if the orders weren't followed. These people hadn't assumed any of the risks associated with Covid-19, so most of the safety measures recommended by the CDC and encouraged by the Kansas Supreme Court were still very much in effect. To the extent judges and their staff were in the building at all, most of them stayed holed-up in their offices. There was a sort of well-lit-ghost-town vibe to the place—some futuristic vision of a postapocalyptic civilization. Because the courtroom had been closed to the general public for a year and a half, there were video cameras set up that were linked and would livestream the proceedings through YouTube for public viewing, a necessary measure that maintained the transparency our republic required. Adding to the postapocalyptic aura was the legion of newly erected Plexiglas walls—between the witness stand and the jury box, between each seat in the gallery and the jury box, between counsel tables, and between the judge's bench and the court reporter's station. There was even a clear acrylic wall between me and where my client would be sitting in a few minutes. A little rectangular hole had been cut for passing notes.

The Plexiglas afforded those in the courtroom the luxury of foregoing masks, but the glare coming off all the acrylic was problematic. From my seat at counsel table, I couldn't see the witness stand or the back left corner of the jury box without moving to my left and shielding my eyes from the glare like a centerfielder battling the sun. Someone had hauled in two extra tables and placed them to my left where the clerk usually sat in close proximity to the judge. The tables formed a semi-circle before the judge's bench. Mia and I would be situated between the prosecutor on our right, and Benowitz and Monet on our left.

Neither Brown nor Curtis had played the Covid card yet, but I still figured it was coming. If Brown claimed to have Covid, there wasn't much I could do to get him on the stand today. If Curtis made that play, I was ready for him. The waitress working Senator Anderson's campaign fundraiser had come through for *TMI*, and *TMI* had come through for us. Russ had texted me a digital photo of Curtis bellied up to a bar in a tuxedo, red-faced, laughing, his arm around a young woman in a high-dollar evening dress. Both had half-empty glasses of wine in front of them. The photo was taken only seven hours earlier.

I sat there watching the clock, on edge, waiting for time to pass, which caused my mind to wander and make strange associations. With twenty-seven-thousand dollars' worth of Plexiglas screwed into the woodwork, the courtroom reminded me of Superman's fortress of solitude with its crystalized pillars—alien, cold, silent—like my life since the funeral. I counted it as time to get my head straight, but more often than not it felt like I was drifting away from the world, the only things tethering me to it were my two children and Mia's murder case. I had a lot of time on my hands because there hadn't been any major developments in Mia's case or my own personal search for the truth about my parents' deaths. Russ hadn't found Annie, Geronimo hadn't produced Carmen, and Mia hadn't broken her silence about the killer. Elias Matusak was still a fugitive and hadn't made contact with me, nor had anyone else with any information.

The only progress on Mia's case since Keri's funeral came from a search warrant for Annie's DNA that Agent Washington executed on Annie's trailer. He came away with a toothbrush, two hairbrushes, and several tubes of lipstick. Someone—most likely Caroline—had finally convinced the DNA analyst in Mia's case, Cass Witham (aka Mama Cass, Caroline's trusted friend), to compare any DNA found on the items collected by Washington to the discolored—presumably older—bloodstain on the grip end of the axe used to kill Jimmy Ray. More importantly, Mama Cass told Agent Washington she'd thought of a way to do the comparison on the sly, keeping her work for the KBI a secret from Detective Riggins and the prosecutors, no small feat in an accredited and highly regulated lab. It was a questionable move for the KBI and for Cass, but they felt the move was justified because they didn't know who they could trust.

If there was any good news, it was that Caroline didn't quit her job. She'd been cleared by Blaine of any criminal charges stemming from the shooting death of the homeless man, and had been placed back on active duty yesterday.

At 8:55 the deputies brought Mia into the courtroom wearing a jail-issued jumpsuit, still the red version because of her trouble with Bigknife Wilson. Conventional wisdom holds that jail garb is the uniform of a criminal. Defense attorneys usually take great pains to get their clients out of that uniform and into civilian clothes for jury trials and highly publicized court appearances such as this one. But I chose to leave her in the jumpsuit to play up the optics for a press looking to promote this kind of story—oppressors versus the oppressed. The white-privileged billionaire predator playboy and the dirty white cop versus an incarcerated young Mexican girl and her tragically widowered attorney, the bastard son of a drug-dealing illegal alien.

At 8:58 the clerk came in and sat in the front row of the jury box next to a TV tray with a laptop computer on it. Seconds later the attorneys came in. Claire Riddle sat to my right. Monet, Benowitz, and the local attorney appointed to "supervise" Benowitz (because Benowitz wasn't licensed to practice law in Kansas) sat to my left. No Clint Brown, no Dean Curtis. Their attorneys had smug smiles on their faces. When Benowitz finally glanced at me, I winked at him. He rolled his eyes and chuckled to himself. I looked behind me in time to see Russ taking his seat in the gallery directly behind me. I'd gotten permission from the court for him to be in the courtroom.

The clerk in the jury box said, "Livestream is up in three, two, one." She clicked a button on her computer and nodded at us with a pinched expression on her face.

Judge Abernathy came into the courtroom and one of the deputies bellowed, "All rise."

Everyone stood. Abernathy sat, told us to be seated, then called the case and listened as each attorney stood in turn and announced their appearance. I went second, after Riddle. Monet went last. When he sat, Abernathy glared at him, then Benowitz.

"Where are your clients?" Abernathy said.

Benowitz and Monet stood in unison.

Monet held a piece of paper in the air. "Unfortunately, Undersheriff Brown is unable to be here today without violating CDC guidelines and the court's own rules because he's ill with Covid. Tested positive late last night. I'm aware how this might look to a cynic, so I insisted Clint do everything he could to get a letter from his doctor. It took some doing, but we got that done. Here's the letter if you want to see it. Since my client is having some trouble breathing and has a splitting headache, the doctor says testifying, even remotely by Zoom, would be harmful to his health."

"Bring me the letter," Abernathy said, putting a cloth mask over his mouth and nose.

Monet donned a mask and walked the letter to the bench. Abernathy looked at it, then up at Benowitz. "I assume Mr. Curtis is home sick with Covid too."

Benowitz nodded and opened his mouth to speak, but Abernathy cut him off.

"Where's his doctor's note?"

"Unfortunately, my client's symptoms didn't come on until very early this morning, so we didn't have time to get to a doctor." Benowitz shrugged, like what are you gonna do? "Mr. Curtis texted me about thirty minutes ago. Can't taste or smell a thing. Has a headache and nausea. I'm afraid he's not going to be able to testify either, by Zoom, or otherwise."

"Of course not," Abernathy said.

Benowitz made a face, like he was trying to figure out if the judge's comment was meant sarcastically. It could've gone either way.

Abernathy faced me and held up the doctor's letter. "Mr. Joel, did you want to have a look at this?"

I shook my head. "No. I'm not surprised."

Monet shot me a look. "What's that supposed to mean?"

"Mr. Monet," Abernathy said, handing the letter to him. "Take your letter and have a seat. And direct your comments to the court, not counsel."

"Your Honor," Monet said, "he's implying—"

"He's implying that he's not surprised Covid has spread to your clients," Abernathy said. "That's what I heard. Now go have a seat."

Abernathy watched Monet return to his seat and peel off his mask. Then Abernathy spoke with his still on. "With Brown and Curtis unavailable, my inclination is to grant Mr. Joel's—"

I stood.

Abernathy stopped talking, looked at me, and took off his mask. He was annoyed. "What is it, Mr. Joel?"

"If Mr. Curtis really doesn't feel well," I said, "I think I might know why. Might not have anything to do with Covid."

"What are you talking about?" Benowitz said.

I held up my phone. "If you'll allow it, Your Honor, I can show you what I'm talking about."

"What is it you want to show me?" Abernathy asked.

"A photo of Dean Curtis taken a few hours ago."

Benowitz stood up quickly. "I object, Your Honor, I haven't seen—"

Abernathy shook his head. "Save it, Mr. Benowitz, this isn't a trial." Then to me. "Show us the photo."

I pulled it up on my phone. Flashed it around the room for the others. Maybe they could see it, maybe they couldn't. "This is a photo of Curtis taken several hours ago at a five-star restaurant in Chicago called Cuisine. Fundraising event for Senator Anderson's presidential campaign. As you can see from the photo, Mr. Curtis appears to be having one helluva good time."

"Where'd you get that?" Benowitz said.

"Mr. Benowitz," Abernathy said sharply. "What did I just say to Mr. Monet? Address the court, not counsel." Abernathy motioned for me to come to the bench while putting his mask back on. "Let me see that."

I put on my mask and went to the bench and handed my phone to Abernathy.

He glared down at the photo. "How'd you get this?"

"Media outlet called *TMI* sent it to my investigator this morning. Couple hours ago. Like I said, the announcements by Mr. Monet and Mr. Benowitz weren't a surprise. Saw that coming a mile away."

Abernathy nodded and handed me the phone. "Show this to the other attorneys."

They put on their masks and I walked my phone around the well of the courtroom showing them the photo.

I ended with the local attorney "supervising" Benowitz. His name was Charlie O'Meara. As he was looking at the photo, Abernathy gestured toward Benowitz and said, "You still want to supervise this guy, Charlie? Your license to practice law might be on the line."

Benowitz shot up out of his chair and ripped off his mask. "Your Honor, that's highly improper. You can't believe I meant to deceive the court."

"So it's just your client doing that then?" Abernathy said, his mask off again. "Is that what you're saying?"

Benowitz's jaw actually dropped. "Before you jump to any conclusions, Your Honor, at least allow me the opportunity to consult with my client. I'm sure there's a rational explanation you're not seeing. With the court's indulgence, I can step into the hallway and call him now."

Abernathy arched his brows. "Sounds like a good idea, counselor."

Benowitz went into the hall, returned a minute later, and said, "My client was indeed in Chicago last night. Had a couple glasses of wine at the fundraiser. Nothing wrong with that. He has his own jet, of course, and fully intended to be here this morning. Started feeling bad on the flight back to Wichita. Nothing has changed, Your Honor. He still feels terrible, and it's still a violation of the court's own policy to order him here today. Due to my age, I myself am at high risk for severe Covid complications. Ordering Mr. Curtis here puts my life in jeopardy."

"You have nothing to worry about," Abernathy said. "Court services has the rapid test kits for Covid downstairs. If your client tests positive, he won't be testifying today. Simple as that."

"Whether he has Covid or not, it won't change the fact that he doesn't feel well," Benowitz said.

Abernathy shrugged. "If it's alcohol and lack of sleep that's making him feel bad, that's on him."

Benowitz scoffed. "He could still have Covid, even if he tests negative—"

"We've got all these Plexiglas barriers in here and you're free to wear a mask. Wear two masks if you like. Have Curtis wear a couple masks if you think that'll help. When can he be here to take the test?"

Benowitz shook his head with a look on his face that said, *unbelievable.*

Abernathy noticed. "Watch yourself, counselor. When can your client be here?"

Benowitz looked at his watch. "In about an hour I'm told."

Abernathy fixed his glare on me. "Besides Curtis and Brown, are there any other witnesses you plan to call to the stand?"

I removed my mask and stood. "Yes, Your Honor, I have four of them. Emily Knudson, Jake Brackeen, Agent Gordon, and my investigator, Russell Osborne." I turned and pointed at Russ when I said his name. He actually waved at the judge.

Abernathy made a face. "A total of six witnesses? I'm starting to wonder if we'll be through today. I've got prelims in other cases scheduled all day tomorrow."

Monet stood. "Your Honor, I'll make this easy for you. If you'll enforce the rules of evidence, as is your prerogative in a hearing like this, we'll be through in no time at all because everything his witnesses have to say about my client and Mr. Curtis is hearsay—"

Abernathy cut him off. "You know the rules of evidence don't apply to today's hearing."

"You have the discretion to enforce them," Benowitz said. "And we're asking that you do just that, because none of what Mr. Joel wrote in his motion would be admissible in a trial, or most any other kind of court hearing for that matter. Mr. Joel is utilizing your courtroom and the rules regarding pretrial release hearings to make an end run around the rules of evidence to blatantly defame our clients while hiding behind the immunity he enjoys as a criminal defense attorney."

"What's your complaint?" Abernathy said. "That he's doing a damn good job of lawyering?"

I raised my hand.

Abernathy audibly sighed. "What is it, Mr. Joel?"

"May I make a suggestion?"

"Fine."

"I'd like you to order Clint Brown to take the court's rapid Covid test too."

Monet, who had just sat, shot out of his chair like a jack-in-the-box. "That's . . . that's outrageous, Your Honor."

"Not really," Abernathy said, "given what's transpired here today so far."

"We have a note from a doctor—"

"Then get him here," Abernathy said. "Let's get him under oath too."

Monet made a face. "Get who under oath? Dr. Llewelyn?"

"That's right," Abernathy said. "Why not?"

Monet laughed. "Your Honor, you can't be serious. Dr. Llewelyn can't just . . . I mean, I imagine he's a busy man."

"I imagine he is," Abernathy said. "So I'll give you two options. Get the doctor here, or get your client downstairs to take the test."

"Or what?" Monet said.

Abernathy shrugged. "Or Clint Brown might be sitting behind bars in his own jail this morning."

Monet shook his head. "You can't do that, Your Honor."

"Try me." Abernathy leaned forward. "Call your clients right now. Tell them to get here ASAP or they're going to jail. When you've made the calls, I'll hear argument on the motions to quash."

Benowitz and Monet looked at each other.

Finally, Benowitz said, "For the record, you're ordering a man with Covid, and another with symptoms, to come to the courthouse."

"I'm ordering you to tell your clients to come to the courthouse right now. Court service officers will meet them outside in their personal protective gear to administer the tests." Abernathy pointed at Benowitz, then Monet. "Make the calls right now, gentlemen, I don't have all day."

They pulled out their phones and made calls. When they were through, Abernathy leaned back in his chair and said, "Mr. Benowitz, present your motion to quash the subpoena. Then I'll hear from Mr. Monet, then Mr. Joel."

The judge was silent as they argued their motions, which were cut from the same cloth in both form and substance. Each attorney began their presentation with condolences to me for my loss, an empty gesture meant to humanize their clients to the viewing audience before making the case that subpoenaing Curtis and Brown was nothing more than a publicity stunt that was placing an unnecessary burden on their clients. They took turns calling what I was doing a witch hunt and a fishing expedition. Predictably, they took exception to everything in my motion pertaining to their clients' involvement in murder, rape, and human trafficking, arguing that my motion was full of unguarded emotions, rank speculation, and hearsay, focusing in particular on the statements of Elias Matusak, making the point that the information alleged to have come from him was self-impeaching on account of his status as a fugitive and suspected serial killer. Each attorney took care to explain—more for the viewing audience, than the court—that no matter what happened here today, if their clients were called to the stand, each would exercise their constitutional right to remain silent, not because either of them were guilty of any crime, but because the Fifth Amendment protected innocent people like their clients when *"reasonable cause to fear a real danger of incrimination existed."* These were the kind of arguments that non-lawyers called doublespeak, or, in grittier circles, bullshit.

Monet went second, and when he sat down, Judge Abernathy looked at his watch as if to say, *It takes you two bloviating wind bags forty-five minutes to tell me these guys are pleading the Fifth?* When he looked up from his watch, it appeared as if he might have something to say, but he didn't, other than to ask for my response.

I cleared my throat and stood, remaining at the table next to Mia per Abernathy's rules. "Unlike criminal defendants, witnesses pleading the Fifth are not allowed to avoid testifying altogether, as Your Honor well knows. Dean Curtis and Undersheriff Brown are obviously witnesses in this proceeding, not criminal defendants, so the proper procedure is for them to be called to the stand and questioned. With a specific question on the table, this court, and any appellate court, will then be in a better position to determine the reasonableness of any assertion of their rights to remain silent on the grounds that their answers might incriminate them."

Benowitz stood. "His plan is to pummel my client with questions everyone knows he can't answer, Your Honor."

"Can't or won't?" I said.

Abernathy shook his head, "Careful, Mr. Joel." Then he turned to Benowitz, Monet, and O'Meara. "A witness cannot make a blanket assertion of his right to remain silent, and we are not in front of a jury, so Mr. Joel will be allowed to call your clients to the stand and ask his questions. Any assertion of the right to remain silent, if challenged by Mr. Joel, will be taken up on a question-by-question basis. Of course, whether or not Curtis and Brown take the stand this morning depends on the results of their Covid tests."

Benowitz said, "This is akin to a bail hearing, Your Honor. It would be highly unusual for a court to hear this amount of testimony—"

Abernathy's eyes narrowed. "So what? It's a highly unusual case."

Benowitz shook that off, kept rolling. "You have a lot of discretion at your disposal in a matter such as this, Your Honor. There are a thousand questions Mr. Joel could ask my client and the undersheriff. If you don't shut this down, we'll be here, not only all day, but the rest of the month."

Abernathy gave Ms. Riddle a flat, unflinching look—*this is all the DA's fault for not conceding the motion, haven't you seen enough*—before turning back to Benowitz. "You think I don't know that?"

Monet stood. "Your Honor, if I may? Perhaps you could take our motions to quash under advisement until Mr. Joel's other witnesses have testified."

"I thought of all that, Mr. Monet," Abernathy said. "I'm not about to tell Mr. Joel how to proceed on a contested motion."

Suddenly, Abernathy seemed distracted by something.

"It's your courtroom, Your Honor," Benowitz said. "You don't need to apologize for using the tools at your disposal to stop this wholly unnecessary and gratuitous grandstanding."

"Then I won't apologize for telling you and Mr. Monet to sit down."

"Excuse me?" Benowitz said.

Abernathy had his phone out. Whatever he was looking at caused him to smile "You heard me. Both of you sit down."

They did, with looks of disbelief, then defiance, on their faces.

The judge glared at the prosecutor one last time, as if willing her to finally see the havoc she wrought by opposing the motion wasn't worth it. When she didn't stand or respond in any way to the cue, he said, "Mr. Curtis's and Mr. Brown's motion to quash the subpoenas are denied. And oh, by the way, I just got a text from court services. The tests are done. Clint Brown has been sent home because he tested positive for Covid. Mr. Curtis tested negative. He's being escorted by court service officers to the courtroom right now." He turned to me. "Mr. Joel, I've read your motion and don't need it summarized or read to me, so you may call your first witness."

I stood. Before I could say a word, the courtroom door clicked open behind me. I turned as Dean Curtis came through it in a silk button-up shirt and jeans. Two court service officers in disposable medical gowns came in behind him. None of them were wearing masks. Curtis stopped when he noticed all eyes were on him and shot looks around the room. He didn't look like a man with a splitting headache and nausea. He didn't even look tired. When he looked at me, I said, "I call Dean Curtis to the stand."

Abernathy pointed at the witness chair. "Mr. Curtis, come forward and be sworn in."

"Are you serious?" Curtis said.

"Very," Abernathy said. "Now come forward—"

Curtis cleared his throat. "What about the motion . . . to, uh, set aside the subpoena?"

"Already heard it," Abernathy said. "You lost."

Curtis looked at Benowitz who nodded and said, "Your Honor, may I have a word with my client before he takes the stand?"

Abernathy was still looking at Curtis when he gestured toward Benowitz. "Certainly, but make it quick. Court started at nine, Mr. Curtis. You're very late."

Curtis walked through a swinging gate toward his attorney. He was fit, six foot tall, with thick white hair and that deep tan I saw in photos of him. Even with all he must have endured over the last two weeks, he still carried an aloof bearing about him.

"Yeah, well, I'm not feeling real well," Curtis said.

"Heard all about that," Abernathy said. "I'd drop it if I were you. You look like you feel just fine."

Curtis smirked, then huddled with his attorney.

Thirty seconds later Benowtiz stood. "Please note my objection, Your Honor, but my client is ready to comply with the court's order."

"Objection noted. Mr. Curtis, come forward and be sworn in."

37

CURTIS STRODE TO the witness chair and raised his right hand and swore to God he'd tell the truth.

I noticed Mia eyeballing me—watching me watch him with a questioning look on her face. I gave her a knowing nod in an attempt to make her think I had my emotions in check, even though I wasn't sure that was true. The courtroom is a place of restraint, and I was burning to get my hands around Curtis's throat.

In the witness chair, Curtis stared straight ahead at nothing in particular, like he was bored. Throughout my career, there'd always been nerves to manage, and on some level, emotions, but never like this. I felt a little dizzy so I reminded myself to breathe. I took in a deep breath but it didn't help.

"You may question the witness," Abernathy said to me.

I stood. "Please state your name for the record."

"Dean Curtis," he said, with the weary patience a parent might have for a young child. Being a master manipulator, and because I had become a sympathetic figure to the public, he must've known how important it was to suppress his contempt for me. Despite efforts to conceal his anger, his cheeks turned a deep shade of red. He'd lost control of his life in this moment to the likes of me—orphaned trailer trash of a heroin junkie. His temper was warming up. That was good. I wanted to stoke it, bring it to full flame. See if I couldn't provoke Curtis's massive ego to override prudence and sound legal advice. To come out from behind his rights and answer questions.

I had four legal pads full of them.

The questions were divided into subjects covering the genesis of Brown and Curtis's human trafficking operation in the early nineties to last night's political fundraiser and everything in between, with particular focus on how the conspiracy and the exposure Mia's case brought to it continued to be a threat to my client and me. I'd carefully crafted the questions, most of which Curtis would never answer. My original plan was to start at the beginning, then march through the major events chronologically. Curtis would plead the Fifth and be convicted in the court of public opinion of rape, child molestation, murder, and human trafficking. Most of what I'd be asking about was detailed in my motion already. The world already had that information and would learn nothing new by me asking questions of Curtis, other than to see for themselves that Curtis had a lot to hide. What the public hadn't yet seen was the video of Butler incriminating Brown and Curtis before he was murdered by Matusak. That's where I decided to start, before Judge Abernathy grew even more irritated than he already was and pulled the plug on me.

I held up the thumb drive containing the video of Ricky Butler's murder. "Your Honor, before I go any further, it would be helpful if I showed Mr. Curtis and this court the video of Rick Butler's murder, marked Defendant's Exhibit A. I ask that it be admitted into evidence now."

Benowitz, Monet, and Riddle took turns objecting on every legal ground under the sun and lost. Mostly because the rules of evidence didn't apply, but also because Abernathy wanted to keep things moving at a brisk pace. Abernathy knew the KBI had given me the video and I was an officer of the court. At a bail hearing, that was enough for him. Benowitz and Monet shook their heads at each other as they sat, as if silently acknowledging the kangaroo nature of Abernathy's courtroom.

The bailiff took the thumb drive from me and handed it to the clerk. Abernathy told her to use the table of contents I'd provided to start the video from the point in time Butler appears. He didn't want to see Lucky Andrews being murdered if he didn't have to.

The clerk inserted the drive and the courtroom's large-screen TV flickered to life.

The scene was Lucky Andrews' basement, awash in a glowing green light because of the party bulbs hanging from the ceiling. I'd been told by the clerk two days earlier that Abernathy's IT crew had set things up so that any video played on the TV would livestream directly to YouTube. The viewing public would see this video better than if they were sitting in the front row of the gallery.

"*Get on your knees*," Elias Matusak could be heard saying.

Abernathy watched with a look of grim reluctance on his face. Within seconds, Butler was on his knees wheezing and yelling his dead lover's name. Then he said, "*I never told anyone Brown raped one of my girls.*"

"*Brown didn't send me,*" Matusak said.

Abernathy stole a glance in the direction of Steve Monet. There was an empty chair next to him where I wished Brown was sitting. Monet averted his eyes from the judge and took a drink of water.

"*The one who sent me believes Brown raped your girl. Just like you been tellin' people,*" Matusak said.

"Permission to pause the video, Your Honor?" I said.

Abernathy nodded at the clerk. She froze the screen.

"Do you recognize the man there on his knees?" I asked Curtis.

He drew his cheeks in like he was sucking on a cough drop, looking at the pitiful form of Ricky Butler, the man that, according to Matusak, had provided a steady flow of trafficked women to Curtis, Brown, and Jimmy Ray. I figured there was a pretty good chance that Butler was present at The Rabbit Hole twenty-eight years ago when Paco Correa was murdered and my mother was raped. I'd wondered if Butler made the 911 call from the bar's landline until I listened to the audio of the call I'd gotten from Brackeen. The caller had a slight Hispanic accent. I played the call for Mia and she agreed it wasn't Butler, but other than that had no idea who the caller could have been.

"I plead the Fifth," Curtis finally said.

"Do you know who it was that Brown was supposed to have raped?"

The redness in Curtis's cheeks crawled down his neck into his collar. "Five."

"Was it a woman named Annie Black?"

"Fifth."

"Do you recognize the voice of the man talking off screen?"

Curtis adjusted himself in the witness chair. "Fifth."

"We can resume the video," I said.

Abernathy nodded at the clerk, who hit the play button. Within seconds Butler was on all fours and Matusak—dressed in drag—stepped into the frame and told Butler he was going to die because he had a big mouth. Lucky Andrews coughed and Matusak left the frame.

"*Dean Curtis sent you,*" Butler said, knowing he was being recorded, knowing he was going to die. He knew because he'd paid Lucky top dollar to film his encounters with her. Third time I watched the film, I noticed Butler sneak a glance at the camera hidden in the skull-shaped bong. Whatever kind of video he'd planned to make, he knew he was about to star in his very own snuff film. Heavy irony for someone who'd peddled flesh his whole life.

Dean Curtis shook his head as he watched. Fat-ass Ricky Butler had hurt him. Bad.

Butler continued. "*You don't have to choke me out. Just give me the needle. I won't fight you.*"

"*Wouldn't be much of a fight,*" Matusak said.

"*Wouldn't have to be,*" Butler said. "*Bruise me up and you got a murder investigation on your hands.*"

I noticed that Claire Riddle wasn't watching the video. Like all of us, she'd already seen it. She was watching Dean Curtis, probably trying to read his reactions.

"*This'll look like two sodomites overdosing on smack no matter what you do,*" Matusak said.

Matusak got on one knee behind Butler. "*You know how I'm going to kill you?*"

Butler said, "*Same way Brown and Curtis—*"

I stood again and the clerk paused the video on instinct, but not before Matusak had jumped Butler from behind and wrapped his arm around Butler's neck. The scene was frozen on the big screen. Abernathy nodded at me, letting me know I was free to ask a question of the witness.

I asked, "Do you recognize the man dressed in drag?"

Curtis looked at the TV and shook his head, following the gene-deep instinct built into every human to lie in a tight spot. Then he caught himself. "I plead the Fifth."

"Did you send him to kill Butler?"

"Five," Curtis said, feigning boredom.

"Where'd he get the idea to kill Butler using a blood choke, then an injection of Fentanyl?"

Curtis threw out his arms. "I'm pleading the Fifth here."

"Before becoming a volunteer reserve deputy for the Sedgwick County Sheriff's Office, did you ever receive any training from the Kansas Law Enforcement Training Center on the use of neck restraints?"

"Plead the Fifth."

I reached into my briefcase and got a document Agent Washington had pulled from KLETC's archives. It was a certificate acknowledging Dean Curtis's successful completion of the training required to become a reserve sheriff's deputy. It was signed by then-Deputy and training center instructor Clint Brown, dated February of 1991. I offered the document into evidence, along with a binder of course materials that went with the training, which included written instruction on the proper use of vascular neck restraints. Over the objection of every other attorney in the room, Judge Abernathy accepted the documents into evidence.

"The man in drag on the screen," I said to Curtis, "did you send him to kill a woman by the name of Annie Black?"

His eyebrows flew up. "Five."

"Did you order, or otherwise ask the man dressed in drag to kill me?"

He clinched his teeth and took the Fifth yet again. His temper was starting to boil over.

"When this man in the video failed to kill Annie Black and went rogue on you, did you contract or otherwise send a man by the name of Paul Keefer—pseudonym Kage Walker—to kill me?"

He shook his head, shot a hateful look at his attorney, then pled the Fifth. That hateful look was pure gold. It would play well on YouTube. It would be source material for a thousand memes.

"Later that day, did you send a man named Kevin Gans to my home to kill me, who instead, ended up killing my wife and the two deputies guarding my house?"

Curtis laughed bitterly, raised his voice. "Still pleading the Fifth."

"This man on the screen, the one in drag, Elias Matusak is his name, he was in your inner circle, right?"

"Inner circle? What the hell do you mean?"

"He was one of your followers, wasn't he?"

Benowitz stood, "Objection, leading—"

I cut him off. "Matusak had his penis surgically removed for you, didn't he?"

Before the judge could rule, Curtis smirked and looked up at the judge. "This guy's losing it."

My jaw tightened. I'd held my composure a long time, but my anger swelled to a new high. The judge was talking but nothing he said registered because I'd slipped into a day dream—me bolting through the well of the courtroom and ripping this man apart.

An urgent whisper brought me back.

"Ben."

It was Mia. She reached around the Plexiglas and put her hand on my arm. I looked down at her and saw that she had tears in her eyes. All of the sudden I did too.

"Ms. Targos," Abernathy said while he eyed me with a concerned look on his face, "go ahead and resume the video please. Why don't you have a seat and cool off, Mr. Joel?"

I sat as the clerk hit the play button.

We watched Matusak seize Butler from behind and in a flash the bong shaped like a skull with the hidden camera had been knocked over and we were left with a shot of the stairs and the sounds of a man struggling for his life, saying something about Ben Joel and a murdered woman in Worthington. It was hard to understand, but you could make it out.

"Ms. Targos," Abernathy said. "Play that again, from the point of the attack on."

She reversed the video. Abernathy watched and listened intently to Butler getting choked out again. I didn't watch this time, and neither did Curtis. He stared down at the microphone in front of him, intermittently shaking his head. When the video ended, Curtis glared at me, waiting for the next question. I held his glare as Abernathy gave me permission to proceed.

I nodded and stood. "Mr. Curtis, have you ever heard of Strictly Confidential Escorts?"

He shrugged. "I've heard of that, sure."

"But you're pleading the Fifth to whether or not you know the proprietor, the man we just watched being murdered in a farmhouse basement?"

"That's what happened, yeah. I plead the Fifth to whether or not I know anyone on the video."

"Move on to something else, Mr. Joel, or you're through," Abernathy said.

"Yes, Your Honor." My window of time for asking questions was closing rapidly, so I circled the most important set of questions left on my notepad. The ones likely to garner the most news coverage, the ones most likely to draw witnesses out of hiding.

"Do you know any presidents of the United States on a first name basis?" I asked.

Curtis's eyes found Benowitz, who was shaking his head. Curtis reacted by pursing his lips and pleading the Fifth, a nonverbal cue I took to mean that he would've answered the question if his attorney hadn't encouraged him not to.

Abernathy leaned forward and put his elbows on the bench as I asked Curtis if he'd ever owned a silver crucifix on a cord-style eighteen-inch jewelry chain. Instead of pleading the Fifth, Curtis made a face, like he was dumbfounded. So I had the bailiff pass around copies of a photo of the crucifix found by the Worthington Police Department in my mother's trailer on July twenty-third of '93. If he denied ever owning such a necklace, I had Russ's March of '92 edition of *Disculture* magazine in my briefcase which had a shot of Curtis wearing just such a necklace.

When the bailiff finally showed Curtis the photo of the necklace found on my mother's floor, he shrugged. "Sir, what was your question again?"

"You ever own a necklace like that one?"

He made a face—dumbfounded again, then looked up at the judge like answering that question was beneath him.

"Lose the attitude, Mr. Curtis," Abernathy said. "Either answer the question, or take the Fifth."

"I don't know if I've ever owned a necklace like that," Curtis said. A mistake. A big one.

Benowitz stood.

"You don't know?" I said.

"I'm worth over ten billion dollars, Mr. Joel—"

"Hold on Dean," interrupted Benowitz, but his client couldn't take it anymore.

"Ten billion dollars! So, I have a lot of assets. I probably wouldn't recognize half the things I own, and you want to know if I owned a necklace like this one?" He held up the photo so we could all see. So anyone watching on YouTube could see. "I own a chain of jewelry stores, Mr. Joel, so if I was to answer your question, I'd guess I owned thousands of necklaces. I'd be willing to bet hundreds of them look a lot like this one."

"Your Honor," Benowitz said, "I need to have a word with my client."

Curtis threw out his hands. "I don't need to talk to my lawyer. Let's get this charade over with." He looked up at Abernathy. "I'll keep pleading the Fifth if that will help you speed things up."

"Watch your mouth, Mr. Curtis," Abernathy said. "You don't want to talk to your attorney. Alright, fine." Abernathy nodded at me. "Ask your next question, Mr. Joel."

"Ever own a necklace with a silver crucifix on it, engraved RIP PC, just like the one in the photograph you're holding?"

Curtis laughed bitterly and shook his head. "I can't believe this."

"What?" I said.

"I plead the Fifth."

"Do you have any siblings?"

"One brother. He's deceased."

"Paul Curtis?"

"Yeah."

"How'd he die?"

"Tragically. He committed suicide in May of '91."

"At the Chateau Marmont in Los Angeles, California?"

"Yes. That's public record."

"Speaking of public record," I said, holding up a copy of the release-of-property form he'd signed for the LAPD, "your brother's silver crucifix necklace was released to you by the LAPD back in December of 1991, correct?"

Benowitz was up again. "Your Honor! It's imperative that I have a word with my client—"

"Sit down, Jerry!" Curtis bellowed.

Abernathy attempted to admonish Curtis for the outburst, but Curtis kept talking, raising his voice over the judge's. "I've been following my lawyer's advice, and it's done nothing but make me look like I've got something to hide. And I don't. I didn't kill anybody and I'm not a pedophile."

Curtis pointed a finger at me, ignoring Abernathy's threats to hold him in contempt. "When this is all over, I'm going to sue you for everything you have."

Abernathy had given up on trying to shout Curtis down when Curtis threatened to sue me. Perhaps that's what gave Curtis pause—the pure, unadulterated desperation he must've heard in his own voice. He gathered himself, dropped the arm with the accusatory finger into his lap. Beads of sweat had multiplied on his forehead. He glanced at the judge, then turned back to me and cleared his throat. "I'm sorry for what you've gone through, Mr. Joel, I really am, but I'm not responsible for any of it. There's no excuse for what you're trying to do to me and Undersheriff Brown."

"Mr. Curtis," Abernathy said, "that's enough—"

"Of course I went to LA and got my brother's property. If that piece of paper you're holding says the LAPD gave me a necklace or a crucifix or whatever, then they gave me the damn thing." He looked up at Abernathy, who'd lost control of his courtroom, but seemed content to watch Curtis hang himself.

"This is all public record by the way," continued Curtis, "so I don't know why I'm being forced to sit here and tell everyone what they already know."

Curtis and Abernathy were locked in a staring contest, until Curtis broke away and took inventory of the room. If I were in his position, I'd have felt like the newest exhibit at the zoo. Benowitz was still standing. His hands were in his pockets and he wore a look of acceptance on his face—*I guess you're on your own now, buddy.*

As Curtis scanned the room, I could see that his easy, aloof bearing had been replaced by the fearful aggression of a cornered animal. I stayed silent in hopes he would fill the vacuum before Abernathy reestablished order.

Curtis licked his lips and granted my wish.

"I read your motion and know where you're going with this. It's not the same necklace that was found in your mother's trailer. It's a coincidence that your mother's boyfriend and my brother have the same initials, and that our family members had the same taste in jewelry. That's all it is. A coincidence." Curtis shot looks around the room. "Why's that so hard to comprehend?"

"Do you know a person by the name of Dalton Campbell?" I said.

Curtis smiled—a man grasping for control of his own bearing. "Of course not, Mr. Joel. And no, I didn't hire him or anyone else to go down to the PD in Worthington to get your mother's or Paco Correa's necklace out of evidence."

I hadn't put anything about the crucifix being released to Dalton Campbell in my motion, but I also knew that Benowitz had called Chief Bell and Campbell's ex-wife and knew through them everything that we knew about the fate of the crucifix found on my mother's floor, so it wasn't exactly a Perry Mason gotcha moment. But at least I had him talking and mad as hell. I looked at the list of questions on my legal pad, thinking about my next move.

"Not so easy now that I'm fighting back, is it?" Curtis said.

"Mr. Curtis," Abernathy said, "one more outburst from you, and I'll hold you in contempt of court. And I'm talking incarceration, not a fine, so get control of yourself. That means you are not to speak unless you are either pleading the Fifth or answering a question or requesting to have a word with your attorney. Understand?"

"Of course, Your Honor. I apologize." Curtis's words would appear proper on the official transcript, but they oozed of bitter disrespect.

Abernathy sighed and looked at his watch. Just when I thought he was about to declare that he'd heard enough, he said, "Ten more minutes, Mr. Joel, then I need a break."

I nodded and moved to another topic as fast as I could. "You own a seventy-acre island in the Virgin Islands, correct?"

"Public record," Curtis said.

Abernathy slammed his fist on the table. "Answer the question, or plead the—"

"I plead the Fifth."

"To the fact that you own this island?" I said.

Benowitz was up yet again. "What's the point of this, Your Honor?"

Abernathy nodded. "What is the point of this, Mr. Joel?"

"As you know from my motion, we have information leading us to believe that Jimmy Ray—the man my client is accused of murdering—has been to this island on several occasions with Mr. Curtis, and so has Undersheriff Brown. This island has been where Curtis provides a forum for men he wishes to control. It's a set up. The men are given what they think is a safe atmosphere to comingle with underage girls. Turns out it's anything but. I'm sure not every man that's ever been on that island partook of forbidden fruit, but some of them did. And those that did got themselves caught on video having intercourse with women and/or children who were not their wives. I have reason to believe that my client was invited to be one of the girls, one of the playthings on Curtis's island . . . ."

Curtis was shaking his head the whole time I was talking.

"Flight manifests for Curtis's private jet indicate that President Collins and several other heads of state and even Jerry Benowitz himself, were among the VIPs that have visited this island."

Over the last two weeks, the press had finally done their job and made sure everyone knew about the flight manifests.

Bemused, Judge Abernathy said, "I guess that's the point of it, Mr. Benowitz." Then he turned to the prosecutor. "Ms. Riddle, haven't you heard enough? I'm racking my brain here, trying to understand why you continue to insist on contesting this motion?"

"I would need to confer with the DA to withdraw my opposition," she said.

Abernathy let out a loud breath, his focus still on Riddle. "Can you explain to me how continuing this hearing helps your cause? I was surprised when your office chose to contest this motion, and having seen how this is playing out here today, I'm baffled Mr. Swartzmiller himself hasn't run screaming into the courtroom by now to stop the bleeding."

I wasn't. I owed Blaine big time. What happened here had no doubt hurt his political career. It probably wouldn't do wonders for Claire Riddle's reputation either, though she could defend herself by reminding people she was simply following her boss's orders. Whatever the public would eventually think of the two of them, the result we hoped to produce had come to fruition. Together, we'd forced Curtis into this perfect storm of public reckoning. If this didn't bring hesitant victims and witnesses out of hiding, nothing would. I owed Swartzmiller and Riddle more than I could ever repay them for playing like fools during their fifteen minutes of fame.

"You know what?" Abernathy said. "I think I've finally had enough of this. I can't imagine leaving Ms. Delarosa in that jail after what I've heard, so I'm calling it right now. Mr. Joel, there's a lot of evidence against your client, so I'm not lowering her bond, but I will order her immediate transfer from Sedgwick County to the Sumner County Detention Center. Defendant will be held in the Sumner County Jail pending trial on October fifteenth, assuming she doesn't make bond. Ms. Riddle, send me the paperwork. This hearing is concluded."

Abernathy stood and the bailiff called out, "All rise."

Everyone not already on their feet stood and watched the big black robe disappear through the door behind the bench. Seconds later, the clerk said, "Livestream is down."

Mia looked at me through the Plexiglas and thanked me. Behind her Claire Riddle stood, as Benowitz and Monet walked through the well and confronted her about the unmitigated public relations disaster she had just put their clients through for no reason they could fathom. She didn't want to hear it, and was stuffing papers into her briefcase for departure. She didn't look at them, didn't speak to them.

Beyond the bickering attorneys, Agent Gordon opened the door to the courtroom and motioned for me to join her in the hallway.

I was still at the table when a voice said, "I've been in tough spots before." I faced forward and stared into the glacier-blue eyes of Dean Curtis. He was standing, four feet in front of us.

"Not this tough," I said.

Russ hopped the waist-high railing that separated the gallery from the parties and stood next to me.

The bailiff and one of the deputies in the courtroom saw what was happening and darted across the well. They clutched Curtis's upper arms to keep him from coming across the table at me.

"You're right," Curtis said, as the two men hauled him backwards. "But you have no idea . . ." He stopped short of uttering an outright threat and smiled as his attorney stepped between us and implored him to shut up. Curtis maintained eye contact with me over the diminutive Benowitz, smiling to let me know I hadn't got the best of him.

But we were all about to learn that I had.

38

WHEN JAILERS TOOK Mia away, Russ and I left Curtis and the attorneys bickering among themselves in the courtroom. Agent Gordon approached us the second we stepped into the hallway.

"It's possible we got Curtis for the murder of your mother," Caroline said. "Someone called in."

"Who?" I asked, my mind racing through the possibilities.

"The jeweler who put the engraving on the crucifix for Curtis the week before Christmas of '91. Guy named Gavin Sober."

Russ popped me in the arm with the back of his hand. "Holy shit, your plan may've worked." Then he said to Caroline, "You talk to this guy?"

She shook her head. "Washington did. He's on his way to meet with Sober and get his statement in writing."

"Where's Sober now?" I asked.

"I'll find out from Washington. All I know right now is that the poor guy's been in hiding for two weeks. Ever since you filed that motion. He was watching the hearing on the Internet, decided to call the KBI hotline when you started asking Curtis questions about the crucifix."

"What's the story?" I asked.

Caroline put her tongue in her cheek. "After reading news accounts of your motion, especially the part involving Curtis's deceased brother's necklace, Sober copied your motion from the public portal and realized the timing of things. Put together his own timeline of events. In May of '91 Curtis's brother killed himself in the Chateau Marmont in LA. On December twenty-first of that year, Dean Curtis got his brothers crucifix from the LAPD. Two days later Sober engraved it for Curtis—RIP PC. He remembered it because Curtis was famous and because Curtis talked about his brother's death and how his brother was wearing the necklace when he died. The second time Curtis came into the store was the last week of August, 1993."

"The week after I found my mother dead."

Caroline nodded. "Curtis bought up thirty-thousand-dollars' worth of jewelry. As he was checking out, he made a comment to Sober about how he appreciated discretion from the people he did business with. Said he rewarded those who kept their mouths shut, and punished those who didn't, then added with a smile, 'Economically speaking, of course.' Sober thought it was a weird thing to say, but Curtis was weird, so he didn't think anything of it at the time. Just thought Curtis was asking him to not brag all over town about the spending spree. But when he saw your motion a couple weeks ago, he put it all together. The comment had nothing to do with the spending spree in '93 and everything to do with engraving the crucifix in '91. Curtis had just killed your mother, discovered soon after that he'd lost the crucifix and thought he might've lost it somewhere in your mother's house when he killed her.

"Curtis was laying the groundwork with Sober on what to do if the cops ever came around asking about engraving a crucifix for Curtis. Shut the fuck up, and you'll be rewarded financially. Talk, and there'll be hell to pay.

"That's how Sober sees the message now. He thinks Curtis knew exactly how his comments would be viewed back in '93—weird, but harmless, like Curtis himself, until you filed that motion and he realized Curtis's words had been a very serious personal threat."

"And when Sober saw that," I said, "he went into hiding."

Caroline honed in on me. "Damn right, I would've done the same thing. Sober said chills ran down his spine today as he watched you question Curtis about the engraving he'd done for Curtis thirty years ago. Said he was probably a dead man whether he came forward or not, so he might as well do the right thing."

Two men in their late thirties stepped off the elevator and walked toward us. Their badges were out, flipped over the pockets of their suit coats prominently displaying the letters, FBI. They breezed by us without a look or a word and went through the doors into the courtroom.

We shuffled after them and peered through the windows in the doors. The tall agent pulled out a pair of handcuffs. Benowitz was saying something, but the agent appeared to pay him no mind as he cuffed Dean Curtis's hands behind his back.

The agents walked Curtis out of the courtroom, past us, and to the elevators. We stood there watching as Benowitz, Monet, and O'Meara came out of the courtroom and sidled up next to us, watching too.

Curtis looked back at us, eyes alive with hatred, as if to say, *This isn't over.*

"Did you know they'd be coming to arrest him?" Benowitz said to me.

I shook my head. "No. What did they arrest him for?"

"Sex trafficking of minors is what they said. They're taking him to the Southern District of New York." When Curtis disappeared into the elevator with the agents, Benowitz continued. "You did a good job in there today. Good luck with the jury trial. Hope you can walk your client."

He, Monet and O'Meara headed toward the elevators. When they were out of earshot I turned to Caroline. "You have any idea what's going on?"

She shook her head. "No clue."

39

AFTER THE HEARING, Mia was immediately transferred to the Sumner County Detention Center. It was located on the outskirts of Worthington, so I had my bodyguard and driver, Mason, make a stop at the jail when we got back to town early that evening. The visitation room was three times the size of the one in Sedgwick County and Mia was already back in a standard-issue orange jumpsuit. She'd heard about Dean Curtis's arrest and wanted to know more, but all I could tell her was what Jerry Benowitz told me.

She shook her head in disbelief. "I saw you on TV walking down the sidewalk outside the courthouse, ignoring all those reporters who were chasing you with their questions. How come you wouldn't talk to them?"

"The mob is already on our side, at least for now. And I don't want to overplay my hand with the judge."

She smiled faintly. "Damn, you really stirred up some shit."

"That was the plan, and by the way, there's more."

I told her about the jeweler who'd engraved the crucifix for Curtis. She was thrilled at the news, then her face clouded. "They're gonna kill him."

"I doubt it. The KBI already has him in protective—"

"Not the jeweler. Dean Curtis—they're gonna kill Dean Curtis."

"Who's they, Mia?"

She made a face, like it was obvious what she meant, which it was, but I wanted to find out if she knew anything beyond the obvious. Finally, she shrugged and spelled it out for me. "Former presidents, British royalty, other heads of state, or . . . shit, for all I know, maybe some other billionaires. They're saying now on TV that one of the guys that used to run the FBI, the head guy, I guess, visited the island one time too."

I hadn't heard any reports about any former FBI directors visiting Curtis's island, but planned to binge-watch the news tonight over beer and pizza with Pops. Given the nature of this case, watching the news came under the heading of necessary research.

Mia studied my face as I digested this new information. "Take your pick," she said. "They all want him dead, and the people we're talkin' 'bout are the best in the world at getting what they want."

I nodded. Nothing about the way feds had swooped in and whisked Dean Curtis off to New York felt right to me. Common sense dictated that none of the men who'd been to pedo-island wanted to be associated with Curtis at the moment, but who among them had a dark secret worth killing over and a way to move the levers of power? Surely, not all of them. Probably not even most of them, but it only took one. After years of abusing women and children in multiple jurisdictions, it was hard to believe that reports of Curtis's crimes hadn't made their way to a prosecutor's desk somewhere before today. So why now, before he can even step foot outside Abernathy's courtroom, is he suddenly arrested? Maybe the timing of the arrest was one part coincidence and two parts reaction to public outcry, but I tended to agree with Mia. Dean Curtis had finally found himself too far from shore. Someone in the system had a sacred cow to protect and had made the call: *This ends now.*

Mia watched me think things through.

Finally, she said, "Why do you think Brown and those other men wore masks of the presidents when they were with me?"

"Other than to protect their identities?"

"Yeah. Other than that."

"Dunno," I said, just to hear what she would come up with.

"Seeing all this come out the way it has, with a couple ex-presidents visiting Curtis's pedo-island, now I think the masks were something of an inside joke," she said.

"Not sure I get what you're saying."

"I was a minor-league product." She shrugged. "Remember how I told you about Youngblood—I guess his real name is Matusak—approaching me after making the video?"

I nodded. "He wanted to know if you were interested in a tropical vacation."

"Yeah. The video wasn't made for blackmail purposes. I mean, I don't think that was its primary purpose originally."

I thought about that. "Could be. Curtis most likely had all the blackmail material he needed on Brown already. And with the masks on, it's not much of a tool for blackmail against any of the men in the video."

Mia licked her lips. "Wanna hear my theory?"

"Of course."

"Curtis was scouting for talent. He wanted good little whores who couldn't get enough sex. Submissive girls who enjoy being with a lot of men and didn't have to fake it. Couldn't be many of those since a lot of the guys were old and fat and gross and needed meds to get it up. Anyway, the video was my tryout for the majors—Curtis's island—where VIPs like President Collins played. Same thing happened to Annie. Saying yes to a visit to the island was the final test."

"You're saying Brown knew you were there for a tryout of sorts. And he was being ironic or whatever by wearing the Slick Willie mask. That was his idea of a joke?"

"Yeah."

"Not a bad theory. I like it." She liked hearing that. This girl didn't belong in prison. She was smart and had backbone. She belonged out in the world helping other women who'd been hurt by predators. If I could keep her out of prison, she could be a blessing to them.

"You said no to them," I said. "Missed your chance at the majors."

"I'm glad I said no."

"Me too, but they wanted you there, which tells us something."

"What's that?"

I shrugged. "You're a young woman, not a child. Safe to say not every man who visited pedo-island was into children."

"Probably. I guess I would've been a delicacy for powerful men of more conventional tastes—and been used as a tool for compromising them."

She watched my face to gauge my reaction, then said, "After what happened today, I think Dean Curtis is a dead man."

I would've liked to think he'd be safe in a federal holding facility, but I nodded in agreement with Mia because my gut told me she was right.

*   *   *

I climbed into the passenger's seat of Mason's rental—a full-sized black Chevy Tahoe. Before we'd turned out of the jail parking lot, my cell was vibrating with a call from Rashonda. She transferred a call to me from a woman claiming to be with one of the country's so-called innocence projects. The woman said she was a lawyer and told me her outfit had started two fundraisers for Mia online, already raising over seventy-five thousand dollars for her defense. The second fundraiser had already topped ninety grand and was dedicated to her bail. She thanked me for everything I had already done for Mia and told me how sorry she was for my loss. She wanted me to know that they were happy to provide me support in whatever way I needed free of charge, and that the money they'd raised for Mia's defense fund could be used to pay the bodyguards I'd hired for the protection of me and my family. She also suggested that the funds could be used to hire security for Mia when she was eventually released on bail. She gave me her contact information and told me she'd be happy to electronically transfer the money already collected to my trust account, or, if I'd rather, she would cut a check and overnight it to me. I thanked her and transferred her back to Rashonda to hash out the details.

When the call ended, we were one block from Pops' home—my family's well-guarded, makeshift home away from home.

"Looks like I might be able to pay you after all," I said to Mason.

He shook his head. "I don't want your money."

"The woman I just talked to on the phone told me her organization raised over a hundred and fifty grand for Mia's defense, so I can pay you. You should take it."

"I don't want money. I want you. I want you to work for us."

I stared at him. "What are you talking about?"

Mason turned right onto Eighth Street. "That woman you were on the phone with is Cathy Brisbane. She works with us sometimes. The fundraisers and the money are real. The money dedicated to Mia's defense is meant to cover your attorney fees, expert witness fees, et cetera. Use the money as you see fit. I want to see that you are paid well for your services."

Which didn't come close to answering the question I'd asked. Maybe this guy was a lawyer as well as a bodyguard.

Mason turned left into the paved alley and blew past Pops' garage toward Seventh Street, looking between the houses as he did.

"You want me to work for you. Doing what?"

"Lawyering, mostly. All over the country. I'm in the market for a lawyer who isn't easily intimidated and knows how to handle himself in a tight spot if necessary."

"What makes you think I can handle myself in a tight spot? What's that even mean?" I said, as another question hit me. "And lawyering? What kind of lawyering?"

He turned right on Seventh Street, went half a block, and stopped at the stop sign without answering any of my questions. We were facing the Worthington Police Station and the fire department, a single structure that took up the whole block.

"Maybe you didn't hear me," I said, knowing he had. "You want me to move to Texas and be your firm's attorney or something?"

Mason still didn't answer. He was in bodyguard mode. He turned right, heading back to Eighth Street, then turned right, circling Pops' house. Finally he said, "Nothing like that." He parked in front of Pops' house. We exited and strode to the door past one of Mason's men. The house was empty. I knew from a text that one of the other men had escorted Pops and the kids on an excursion for pizza.

We went to the dining room and sat down. "You want a lawyer. Me? For what?"

He pressed his lips into a line. "First of all, I want to shoot straight with you. Our meeting was no accident. We've been trying to find you for a while."

We? My chest tightened. "Who is we?"

"It's complicated. In March, Russ went to work for your friend, the bondsman, to see if he had any idea where you were hiding. Russ works with us from time to time and called to tell us he thought he'd found exactly what we were looking for in a lawyer. Only problem was, he, uh, didn't know where you were. We wanted to find you, so we could talk to you, maybe recruit you. Or at least try to."

"That doesn't make sense. I called Russ. He didn't call me."

Mason smiled, a bit condescendingly.

"Recruit me for what?" I said.

"For what you're doing right now. To represent Mia Delarosa and eventually, maybe even Annie Black . . . on her possession case. If things worked out on those fronts, I wanted to make you an offer—"

"You sent Geronimo. He didn't show up on his own." My stomach lurched at the revelation.

He looked away for a moment, then back at me. "That was Russ's idea. Not sure if it was the best idea he'd ever had, but

Geronimo owed him a favor. Getting Geronimo to hire you to represent Delarosa was that favor."

I remembered back to my initial meeting with Geronimo at the lake in Missouri when he'd insisted I use his investigator and I insisted on hiring my own. Turns out, they were one and the same.

"Geronimo all but ordered me to use his investigator," I said. "But that was going to be Russ, wasn't it?"

"That's right, but you balked. That was a problem for us, until you went out and hired Russ on your own. A major stroke of luck for us. Solved a lot of problems. Russ went to work for your friend, Tony Cornejo. Got close with Tony in hopes of finding out where you'd run off to. Russ worked on him in subtle ways, but Tony was tight lipped, so that didn't work." He paused to see if I could put the rest of it together.

"Then I called Tony," I said, "wanting the name of a good PI who wasn't Geronimo's man and he gave me Russ's name. Tony didn't realize Russ knew Geronimo, or what was really going on. That the whole time, Russ was using him to find me." My head was swimming, trying to keep up with all of this, but I was starting to get it. "Why all the subterfuge? Why'd you go through Geronimo of all people to get me on Mia's case?"

"That was a close call, one of those six of one, half a dozen deals, but we figured he could be more persuasive than Russ, cause, who the fuck was Russ to you? You'd never met him before. And with Geronimo, saying 'no' could be hazardous to your health."

"Geronimo wouldn't hurt me. Not over refusing to use his PI or represent Mia, he wouldn't. I know that."

Mason shrugged. "We didn't know that. We figured you'd be more deferential to Geronimo's demands than you were, given his reputation for violence. But mostly, we figured it was more plausible for him to approach you with this, given that he's in a relationship with Mia's sister. It was more likely you'd take the case than if a stranger approached you out of the blue. We wanted you to deal with Russ through your connection with Geronimo."

"That's . . . almost ridiculous," I said. "You made everything one hell of a lot more complicated than it needed to be."

"We know that now. But it worked out in the end."

"Wait a minute," I said, remembering something about my initial meeting with Geronimo in Missouri. "Geronimo didn't tell me about his relationship with Mia's sister at first. He kept that from me. I had to drag it out of him and Mia later."

"We knew about Carmen and Geronimo, but we didn't know he was determined to keep this from you when Russ sent him to meet with you. Turns out, Geronimo was more than a little nervous that Carmen might be somehow involved in Jimmy Ray's murder, so he hid his connection to Mia from you as long as he could. Not the smartest thing he'd ever done because of course you'd figure it out, but Geronimo does what Geronimo does." Mason shrugged again. "Guess when you saw the money, you didn't need to know the real connection he had to Mia."

"What connection do you have to Mia, and who the fuck *are* you anyway—a rogue arm of the FBI or something?"

He frowned. "In answer to your first question, I have no connection to Mia. And, no, I'm not a rogue arm of the FBI or the CIA or anything like that." He shrugged. "I might be a rogue arm of my own security firm, but that's it. When I'm not running my security business, I do this."

"You do this? What is *this*, exactly?"

He squinted, looking inward. "I'm part of an invisible force in the world that gives things a nudge in the right direction. Kind of like you did two years ago when the Mendez-Rodriguez Cartel kidnapped your sister to compromise you when you were the judge on a triple homicide trial. You were invisible then. The public has no idea what you did to make things come out right, and you get no credit for it. Our operation is something like that. People like you don't grow on trees."

My stomach felt heavy. "I was the judge in the case you're talking about, that's all. Other than that, I have no idea what you're talking about."

He gave a knowing smile. "You can deny what you did behind the scenes all you want. That's fine, and prudent, but don't worry, your secrets are safe with us."

I shrugged, trying to stay cool, but I was still reeling. "What secrets?"

Mason's eyes narrowed in concentration. "I'll tell you how we know what we know. Just over a year ago, before Russ quit ATF, he was undercover and came across a guy who told him you killed four cartel men during a kidnapping attempt on your family a year earlier. That was two years ago when you were still a judge. The guy said the cartel got away with your sister, but you partnered up with Geronimo and got her back, taking down all the major players in the cartel in the process. Russ thinks what the guy told him is true."

I wondered if "the guy" was Geronimo. I didn't know who else it might be.

As if reading my mind, Mason said, "Geronimo wasn't Russ's source, if that's what you're thinking." Then he seemed to wrestle with another thought. "Guess it won't hurt to tell you it was Harold Reynolds. I think you know him."

Well, shit. I did. Harold "Buster" Reynolds was a dirty cop from Laredo and long-time asset to the Mendez-Rodriguez Cartel. I'd forgotten about Buster. Mason wanted me to know Russ had a credible source.

"You don't have to say anything, and don't worry," Mason said. "We're not about to take any of what we heard to the authorities, whether you come work for us or not."

I stared at him. Decided not to talk about the kidnapping and its aftermath as a pulse banged in my temples.

Finally, I said, "You said you were part of an invisible fucking force for good in the world. If you'd have been satisfied to join the fucking Rotary Club or pick up trash on the side of the road my wife would still be alive."

"I'm sorry. I know that's . . . insufficient. Shit. I'm so sorry. Things just . . . blew up."

I looked at him. His eyes were glistening. Or maybe it was mine.

Pops' old cat walked into the room and looked at us. I stared back at it, and for a long moment nothing was said.

"There was way more bullshit going on here than we'd anticipated," Mason said softly. "Russ was going after Ricky Butler and Mia needed a lawyer and that's as far as we knew it went. All that other stuff," he shook his head, "we had no idea."

"Part of me died with Keri. The best part."

Mason nodded. Looked away.

I said, "I'd tell you to get the fuck out of this house and take your men with you, but I can't do that without putting what's left of my family at great risk. But when this is over, I never want to see you again."

"I understand." He hesitated. "Maybe later we can talk about me hiring you."

"Don't count on it. I still don't know how you found me."

"Your boy, Leo, told some of his friends exactly where he was in the mountains of Idaho. In Worthington, Russ sat in the stands of kids' soccer games with their parents. Munched on popcorn. Made small talk."

He studied me. Took a stab at answering a question he figured was bouncing around in my head. "Leo probably used your phone to call his friends when you weren't looking. You know how kids are. His friends probably asked where he was. He told them. Then he probably erased the call logs to hide what he was doing from you. Just a guess. All we really know is that Leo's friends' parents knew where you were and didn't know you were in hiding. They didn't think anything of talking to the friendly guy eating popcorn at their kid's soccer game."

I heard the back door fly open and my kids coming through it like thundering elephants.

"You put a tracker on us up in Idaho," I said.

"One of the men outside flew up there and did that, yes."

The kids came around the corner into the dining room with boxes of pizza in their hands and dropped them on the table.

"You want some pizza, Mason?" Leo said.

"No," I said. "He doesn't't."

Both kids stiffened, looked at us. It was suddenly quiet enough that I could hear the fridge being opened in the kitchen.

"I'm sorry, Ben." Mason said. "We'll talk when the case is over."

"I said don't count on it."

He waved his hand at the table. "I'll leave you be. You've had a long day."

He let himself out as Pops came out of the kitchen into the dining room with two Busch Lights and held one out to me.

I took it. It was so cold that I thought it might be frozen. I popped the top and took a pull. It was a little slushy. "Thanks."

"I watched you on YouTube," Pops said. "Damnedest thing I've ever seen. Looks like you got 'em on the run, but I want you to know there's a downside to what happened today."

"Just one?" I said.

He smiled, nodding at the kids, who were now seated at the table shoveling pizza into their mouths. "Both of 'em claimed to be ill today, 'bout an hour after they got to school. I made them chicken noodle soup, put them in their room to get some rest thinking the whole time maybe they were just . . ." he shrugged, ". . . upset or something. Anyway, come to find out they did it to get home and watch you on YouTube." He chuckled. "They smuggled that I-Pad you got me for my birthday into their room and watched you in court."

I eyeballed them. They noticed, but seemed to know they weren't in trouble.

"I'm sorry to say it gets worse," Pops said straight-faced. "Your daughter has decided she wants to be a lawyer now."

Lindy kept chewing, smiling a little. Leo was smiling a lot.

"She's too nice a person for that," I said.

"That's what I used to say about you, and now look at ya." He shook his head. "You ever think you'd be a famous defense lawyer like that Jonnie Cochran guy, or Shapiro?"

Now it was my turn to chuckle—funny, not funny. I never wanted to be famous, and I never wanted to be a defense lawyer. But despite what I'd just learned from Mason, I still wanted to defend Mia, even if she'd worked in tandem with another to kill Jimmy Ray. I found myself agreeing with what Geronimo said to me three weeks ago at my friend's cabin on Table Rock Lake—*Mia Delarosa doesn't belong in prison whether she killed that pedophile or not.*

Pops put his hand on my shoulder, then went into the other room.

40

Friday, September 10

AT TEN THE next morning Caroline called and asked where I was.

"At my grandfather's house, working on getting Mia out of jail, why?"

"Getting Mia out of jail? I thought bail was set too high. What the hell did I miss?"

I told her about the fundraisers and the bondsman who was on his way down from Wichita.

"Interesting," she said. "Are you going to be at your house for a while?"

"Another hour, maybe. I want to be at the jail when Mia is released. What's up?"

"We'll talk when I get to your place. This is big. I can be there in thirty-five minutes."

I thought I knew what the big news was. I figured she finally knew whose DNA was on the handle of the axe used to kill Jimmy Ray. For a week, we'd been told to expect the results this morning, and if they were inconclusive, Caroline wouldn't have billed her news as a major development.

She arrived thirty minutes later. We sat across from each other at Pops' dining table. She hesitated before speaking, as if weighing her words, then said, "After yesterday's hearing, I got a call from Cass."

"That's the analyst comparing Annie's DNA to the older bloodstain on the axe handle, right?"

She nodded, but was still at a loss for words.

"And?" I finally said. "Spit it out."

"Annie's DNA isn't on the axe. We know that much for sure."

I shrugged. "Okay, so it's not Annie's blood or DNA or whatever. That's good to know, but I'm not seeing how it's a big deal. There must be more to it."

"There is." She put her elbows on the table and made a steeple with her hands. "There's a lot to this—you know how scientists are—and I'm not sure I totally understand the science, but bottom line, Cass tells me she thinks there's a very high probability that the source of that stain is Annie's biological son."

"Son? She doesn't *have* a son."

Caroline tilted her head. "You sure about that?"

I thought about that, then shook my head. "No, I guess not. She has a daughter, but she's never said anything about a son. Did you run a search for birth records with her as the mother?"

She nodded. "Washington ran those traps for me. Near as he can tell, the records show Annie's only child to be Amelia."

"Then Cass comes up with a son. How can that be?"

"I have no idea, but the day Annie ran off when we were talking to her Uncle Gene in his kitchen, he said something to Russ I think is important. He said, 'You might think you know Annie's story, but you damn sure don't, unless she told you.' Then Gene eyeballed Russ for a while and decided Russ really didn't know." Caroline leaned back and threw out her arms and gave me a close look. "Didn't know what, Ben? Take a wild guess."

"That when Annie's father sent her to Texas, she didn't have a miscarriage or an abortion. She gave birth. Somehow, an off-the-record birth. Is that what you're saying?"

Caroline nodded. "I think it's what Uncle Gene alluded to. How else would Annie have a son? I thought you ought to know what you may've unwittingly been asking Russ to help you do."

Ah, Jesus, I thought. "Nail his own son for murder."

"A son he doesn't know exists. But then again, maybe by now he does. Annie could've told him, who the hell knows? Question is, what are you going to do about this?"

"Tell Russ he's off the case," I said. In my mind I'd already cut him loose, albeit for a much different reason, one Caroline didn't know about.

She nodded. "He knows the DNA results were coming in today. He'll press you for information. You'll have to handle it. If you put him off the case and Annie hasn't told him her secret, he'll assume he's being terminated either because the lab results came back showing Annie's DNA was on the murder weapon, or because Mia told you Annie killed Jimmy Ray." She shrugged. "Or both. Or maybe neither, what do we know? But you fire him and he'll be all over you for an answer as to why."

"No problem, I'm used to deflecting questions. But here's what needs to happen—ASAP. You need to round up some agents in the bureau you trust and have them follow Russ wherever he goes."

"You think he knows where Annie is hiding?"

"It's possible. If he doesn't, I figure he'll keep trying. I know that much. Either way, it would be worth our while to watch him."

"He still work for that bondsman, Cornejo?"

"As far as I know."

"Annie still has a warrant out for her arrest on the possession charge for missing court. You think Russ will bring her in this time?"

I shook my head. "No way. It's too dangerous for her to be in Brown's jail, but also . . ."

"You think he's in love with her."

I nodded. "I always suspected it, but now I'm sure."

"Now? What makes you so sure now?"

"Russ has been going after the men who've been using Annie since I met him. He pitted Brown against Butler. I don't think him crossing paths with her was an accident. Also, Mason told me something I didn't know last evening. Russ was eventually going to try to hire me to represent Annie on her possession case." I left out what Mason told me about how he and Russ lured me back here using Geronimo. She didn't need to know that.

Caroline studied my face. "Despite the fact that Annie's DNA isn't on the axe, I still think there's a fairly good chance that she's the one who axed Jimmy Ray. The absence of her DNA on the murder weapon doesn't necessarily mean she isn't the killer. I still think Jimmy Ray went after Annie's little girl and Annie and Mia hatched a plan to take him out. I think they're in it together."

I'd had the same thought a hundred times. And Caroline was right, DNA couldn't tell us who the killer was. It was important information, but at the end of the day, DNA was just another piece of the puzzle. And this piece pointed to Annie's son—a son we hadn't known existed.

Casually, Caroline said, "Is that what Mia says—that she and Annie put this guy down?"

I smiled. "Nice try."

Caroline shrugged. "Tell Mia we know Annie's biological son is the killer. Sell it—make it sound like you're certain of it. If she thinks the truth is coming out anyway, maybe she'll talk. If she thinks we got it all wrong, maybe she straightens us out. Either way, we get to the truth, or closer to it."

"Will do. Anyway, thanks for taking the time to drop by. It was worth it."

She gave me a warm smile. "It looks like you've lost weight. And you didn't have any to lose."

"I'm cinchin' up my belt a little tighter now. I had a pound or two to lose anyway, but thanks for caring."

"Gettin' any sleep?"

"Some." I pointed at the bags under my eyes. "But not near enough. How're you holdin' up?"

"The bureau's shrink cleared me for duty, so I must be fine."

"Is that true—are you fine?"

"It's true enough."

I walked her to the door. When she got outside, she looked back and told me to eat a cheeseburger and go to bed. I told her all of that was on my bucket list.

She rolled her eyes and left.

41

AN HOUR LATER, Mason, Tony Cornejo and I walked Mia out of the Sumner County Jail into the bright light of day. She wore ill-fitting clothes hastily purchased by one of Mason's men from the local Walmart—jeans, T-shirt, tennis shoes. Before climbing into the passenger seat of the Tahoe, she took a moment to gaze across an expanse of pasture adjacent to the jail. Two horses were grazing near an electric fence just across the road. I was glad she got to savor her first moments of freedom since St. Patrick's Day in relative obscurity. By the time the bond paperwork would make its way to the court's file for discovery through the public's portal, the press will have missed its chance to record the momentous occasion for the evening news. The local sheriff and his staff had done a good job of keeping Mia's release under wraps. They'd lost two deputies and understood that being discrete in this case could very well be a matter of life and death.

Mason drove us to Pops' house for the lunch I'd been planning since early this morning when I called a friendly jailer and asked him to pass Mia the message that she needed to call me collect from the dayroom payphone ASAP. When Mia called fifteen minutes later, I reminded her that our conversation was being recorded, explained to her about the fundraisers, then asked her what she wanted for her first meal after being released.

"This is really happening?" she'd said.

"Really really," I'd replied.

"A salad. And steak." Perhaps worried she was being presumptuous, she quickly added that she'd buy it herself.

"Don't be silly," I said. "Working lunches are tax deductible, so it's on me."

We had a lot to talk about. I was going to press her for the name of Jimmy Ray's killer again, this time armed with the new information Agent Gordon had given me about the DNA on the murder weapon.

Mason dropped us off behind Pops' garage. Children in the school yard across the alley were out for recess. I scanned the scene and located Leo and Lindy playing a game of soccer. I knew one of Mason's men was on the school roof overseeing the playground, but I couldn't see him. Pops had the grill going just outside the garage. I could hear the steaks sizzling. As I stepped out of the Tahoe, the smell made my mouth water. After months of jailhouse fare, I couldn't imagine what this was doing to Mia, but I didn't have to. She told us how good it smelled and how nice this all was.

Pops nodded and held up his Busch Light like he was proposing a toast.

Inside, he joined us at the table for a simple meal of steak, baked potatoes, and salad. Having delivered lunch to the rest of our security team, Mason arrived at the table with a plate of food. I didn't like him being there, but Mia needed to meet the guy who would head up her security detail. We all had glasses of iced tea sweating in front of us. Pops also had what was left of his beer. Shakers of salt and pepper were between us, and a half-empty bottle of ranch dressing. That was it. If any of us didn't like ranch dressing, we were out of luck, because that's all Pops ever had on hand.

Mia cut into her steak. "You guys didn't need to go to all this trouble."

Pops smiled. "The day drinking beer and throwing steaks on a grill is too much trouble is the day I want someone to put me down."

She laughed. "Still. You didn't have to do this."

"It's nice to have something to celebrate," I said.

Mia thanked us for everything and told Pops her steak was cooked exactly how she liked it—a line of pink in the middle.

We talked about where she would stay pending trial. With a little convincing from Mason, Mia agreed to stay in the spare bedroom of the widow next door to Pops' house who was thrilled to be a part of the dramatic struggle for justice she'd been watching play out in the media. The location would make for convenient attorney-client conferences, but more importantly, it would make it easier for Mason and his men to protect her. Earlier, Mason told me he'd prefer Mia to be under the same roof as the rest of us, but I vetoed that idea, opting for an arrangement more attorney-client appropriate.

After lunch Mia and I sat across from each other at the dining table and got down to business.

"The KBI tested the dried blood stain on the grip end of the axe and compared it to Annie's DNA. Turns out, Annie's DNA isn't on the axe, but her biological son's is."

Might be true, might not, but I said it as if it were certain. Mia stiffened and leaned back in her chair. She wouldn't look at me.

"The thing is," I said to keep the pressure on, "no one around here seems to know Annie even had a son."

"Is this the part when I'm supposed to tell you who killed Jimmy Ray?"

"It's only a matter of time before we know anyway. I'm your lawyer, Mia. If you don't help me, you're not helping yourself."

She still wouldn't look at me.

I said, "Did you know that my investigator, Russ, dated Annie a long time ago?"

"Dated? Really? How long ago?"

"When they were in Valley Center High School."

Finally, Mia gave me a sidelong glance. "She told me she had a boyfriend that got her pregnant her junior year. She didn't give me a name."

"Russ Osborne. All he was told back in high school was that Annie went off to Texas and had an abortion."

Mia looked down at her hands and said nothing.

"Annie never had that abortion, did she?" I said.

Mia looked at me. "Apparently not."

"What do you know about her son?"

Tears filled Mia's eyes.

I had her on the ropes. "What's his name?" I said.

"Tobias."

"Did Tobias kill Jimmy Ray?"

She shook off the question.

"You're not saying," I said. "What would Tobias say about that? If he tells the truth."

A tear slipped down her cheek. "You'd have to ask him. I won't be part of sending him to prison."

*　　*　　*

Pops introduced Mia to his neighbor and got her settled into her new digs. I checked my phone. Russ had called. I called him back with a sick feeling in the pit of my stomach. This would be the first time I'd talked to him since I discovered that he'd deceived me. By now, he probably knew from Mason that I'd been told the truth about how they'd used Geronimo to get me on Mia's case.

Russ picked up. "Hello."

"Fuck off, Russ. You're fired."

"I'm sorry for what I did. I didn't expect . . . I didn't know about Curtis and Brown. Had no idea they might've . . . shit, in all likelihood, killed your mother. Had no idea I'd be triggering a series of events that put you and your family at risk. I don't know what else to say."

"There's nothing you can say. You brought me into this mess under false pretenses, and now Keri is gone forever. That's something you'll have to live with. It's also something I'll have to live with, but I don't have to live with you around to remind me of what you did."

"I know, and I'm sorry. Shit."

There was a lull in the conversation. A long one. I had no doubt he was sorry, but I also knew he wanted to know about the KBI's lab results. If Annie's DNA was on the murder weapon. The torch he still carried for her was what got me back to Kansas to represent Mia, and it's what kept him on the phone looking for a way to get the information he thought I had.

I breathed through my anger. I still had a client to think about. I wanted to find Annie. Maybe find her adult son, if she really had one—the DNA results were somewhere over ninety-nine percent certain about that, but not a hundred percent. The best way to find Annie and her alleged son was to make Russ think it was only a matter of time before Annie would be wanted for murder.

"Listen, Russ, even though I know you're a lying sonofabitch, I'm obligated to ask on behalf of my client, where's Annie Black?"

"I have no idea."

"I find that hard to believe."

"It's the truth."

I laughed. "You'd like to know if Annie is wanted for murder or just for skipping bail on the possession charge. You also want to know if Mia has finally told me the name of the killer. That's why you're still on the phone. How am I doing?"

Russ didn't answer.

Finally, I said, "Let's just say that the possession charge is the least of Annie's worries," and hung up.

Russ was no longer part of the defense team, but he was perhaps about to do his best work on behalf of my client. He just didn't know it yet.

42

RUSS PULLED THE phone from his ear and set it on the table. He parted the blinds to the front window of the Crossroads Bar & Grill and peered through the slats at the grain elevator in the distance, thinking if he were surveilling this bar, he'd put someone on top of it. A waitress brushed by on her way to a customer in the corner.

"Tammy," Russ called out.

She turned with a question on her face.

"Mind if I borrow your phone?"

She motioned toward his phone on the table. "What's wrong with yours?"

"Would you believe I can't get any service right now?"

"Nope." She set her phone next to his and her voice softened. "Afraid your phone might be tapped?"

"It's been a rough two weeks. I'm just playing it safe."

"Yeah, well, don't get me thrown in the deep end, okay?"

"I won't."

Russ found a number for a friend of his named Cole who worked at the grain elevator and punched it in Tammy's phone. Cole didn't answer, so Russ left a message for him to return the call ASAP. The call came a minute later.

"I didn't recognize the number or I would've answered," Cole said.

"You working today?"

"Until five, yeah. What's up?"

"I need to know if there's anyone on the roof of that elevator."

"What's going—"

"Long story. I'll explain later."

"Okay, whatever, let me take a . . . hmm?"

"What?"

"The monitor to the roof is off. Never seen that before."

"Turn it on. Tell me what you see."

"Okay, the monitor's on now . . . there's a guy on the roof with a pair of binoculars. What the hell's going on?"

Russ ignored the question. "Just one guy?"

"Yeah, a black dude."

Russ figured it was Agent Washington.

"This man, he tall and lanky?" Russ asked.

"Yeah. I think he's looking south toward Crossroads. You there now?"

"Yeah."

"You in some kind of trouble?"

"Not yet. I need you to shut off the monitor. Leave it like you found it."

Russ waited.

"Okay, it's off," Cole said.

"Good."

"You need me to help you get out of there or something?"

Russ eyed Tammy, who was behind the bar talking to another waitress who'd just arrived. "No. I don't think so. I'll let you know if I do."

*　*　*

The call ended. Russ pulled out a burner and speed-dialed the only number that phone had ever called.

"I didn't expect you to call this early," Annie answered. "What's wrong?"

"The DNA report is back."

Silence. Russ watched Tammy deliver a beer to a patron in the corner as he waited for Annie's reaction.

Finally, Annie said, "What's it say?"

"Thought you might tell me."

"What's that's supposed to mean? You're the one that's seen the report."

"No I haven't. Ben fired me. I got nothing from him, but he said your warrant for missing court on the possession charge was the least of your worries."

"Why'd he fire you?"

"He didn't say," Russ said, "but reading the tea leaves, I'd say he feels he can't trust me anymore. Probably thinks I have a conflict of interest because of our past."

"Our past together—he must think you still have feelings for me."

"Yeah, he must, which makes me think they found your DNA on the axe. It also makes me think Ben used the DNA report to get Mia to finally tell him who killed Jimmy Ray—you."

"You recording this?"

"Of course not. Did you do it to protect Amelia?"

"I don't want to do this over the phone."

"Then tell me where you are."

"You're scaring me, Russ. You sound off."

"I *am* off. I've been off for a long damn time."

Silence. Then, "I never stopped thinking about you."

The seismic jolt inside him felt almost physical, like the Earth had moved. He surveyed the interior of the bar for signs that anyone had noticed his reaction. "Then why'd you . . ."

Annie waited. Didn't say a word.

Russ glanced around to make sure no one had come within earshot, then lowered his voice. "After high school, I tried to find you for years, Annie. *Years*."

"I didn't want to be found."

"You knew where I was the whole time and never came back for me. How can you say you never stopped thinking about—"

"You wouldn't've wanted me, Russ."

"You're wrong. I told you I'd never leave you."

"You left me in jail. You found me, took me to jail, and left me there. If I tell you where to find me now, are you gonna do that again?"

Russ closed his eyes, regretting having arrested her before. "No. I'm off both cases. I told Tony to hire someone else to find you like I should've done in the first place."

"The cops might follow you. Tony might follow—"

"The cops are already following me, thinking I know where you are."

"Jesus."

"Yeah."

"I have something to tell you, and I'd really like to do it in person, but maybe I should just do it over the phone."

"Let's do it in person. I've already got a plan worked out to lose the cops." Russ glanced in the direction of Tammy who was behind the bar. She noticed his look, smiled, and went back to wiping the bar top.

"You sure?" Annie said.

"Yeah. I'm sure."

"Ohmigod, Russ. I really want to see you again."

Paralyzed, he sat mute, replaying her words in his mind, *I really want to see you again*. His heart skipped a beat. The heart does stupid shit.

"I know we can never be together like we were before," she said. "But I still want to see you. I have things to say, and I want to do it face to face."

"Will you tell me what's going on?"

"Yes. And it's not what you think."

Russ pulled out a pen and took a napkin from the dispenser. "Tell me where I'm going."

* * *

Russ went to the bar and gave Tammy her phone. "Thanks," he said.

"Anytime. What are you up to tonight?"

"Not really sure yet."

"Private eye stuff?"

"Something like that."

"That's too bad, because if you were free, I thought maybe we could go somewhere. Have a drink or something."

"I'd like that, but right now I need a huge favor."

Tammy smiled. "You want me to smuggle you out of here."

Russ looked her a question.

Tammy shrugged. "You think your phone is tapped and I noticed the way you were looking out that window. Someone's following you."

Russ nodded. "Is your jeep parked out back?"

"Yeah."

Russ reached for his wallet. "I'll make it worth your while."

"Huh-uh," she said. "I want you to owe me."

"What if I don't wanna owe you?"

She put a warm hand on his arm. "Then I guess you'll just have to be my friend."

Russ looked in her round, soft eyes.

She said, "Would that be so bad?"

43

IT WAS A two-hour drive to where Annie was staying just outside of Coldwater. The house was pitch-dark, invisible from the road behind a stand of trees, just as Annie had described it.

When Russ knocked on the back door, she answered. He could barely see her in the darkness. But there she was.

"You lose the cops?" she asked.

Russ nodded. He knew he wasn't dreaming, but the moment had a surreal quality to it. Time wasn't real anymore.

Finally, she moved aside and he climbed the steps into the kitchen. A candle burned on the stove, but other than that, no light, and so quiet that he detected the hum of the refrigerator.

"The house was so dark," Russ said, "I didn't think you had power in here."

"I do. And there's food if you're hungry."

He shook his head, wondering who owned the place and if she was here alone.

"Beer?" she said.

"No thanks."

"You don't drink anymore?"

"I struggle with occasional bouts of sobriety." Russ glanced around. The place was modest and clean, the air close and warm from the summer heat. A rolled-up bag of potato chips sat on a table next to tomato slices on a plate. He could smell something cooking, most likely a roast. "Whose place is this?"

"Does it matter?"

"I guess not. You here alone?"

"No. I'm here with my son."

"Your . . . son?"

She nodded.

A sobering reminder that they were essentially strangers and there were things he would never know about her. He had been her first love, but she'd spent her adult life with other men. The pang of jealousy he felt made him feel like a kid again, but he had no right, so he did his best to take the news in stride. "If he's here, I suppose I ought to meet him."

She shrugged, then stood there silent and unmoving.

"You okay, Annie?"

"No."

She turned away from the light. He thought she was about to cry, so he looked away, then made a show of looking at his watch. "You know what, it's technically still Friday night, so maybe I will take that beer."

She grabbed two cans of Coors Light out of the fridge and handed him one. After they both took a drink, Russ said, "Was that what you wanted to tell me—that you had a son?"

"Yeah, you could say that."

Russ's heart rate picked up a tic and he found himself breathing as if he'd just walked up a long flight of stairs. The anguish he'd felt upon hearing the news that she had a son gave way to a feeling that there was more to it than that, that he was missing something.

"What is it?" he said. "What's wrong, Annie?"

Now she was crying.

He set their beers on the table and held her in his arms as she shook, closing his eyes and breathing in her scent. They were together again, maybe for the last time. When his eyes opened, he saw a man dimly illuminated in the doorway to the dining room and broke away from Annie. She followed his eyes.

The figure stepped forward into the candlelight and stuck out a hand. "Hi, I'm Tobias."

Russ took it. "I'm Russ. Nice to meet you." He let go of Tobias's hand and stepped back. Took in Tobias's face in the flickering light. "You mind me asking how old you are?"

"I'm twenty-eight."

"Born in '93," Annie said.

Russ and Annie's junior year in high school.

Confusion clouded Russ's face as he looked back and forth between Annie and Tobias. "Is he—?"

Annie shook her head. "You're not his father."

Russ pulled a chair out from under the kitchen table and sat, dropping his head between his legs. Tobias went through the back door, started up what sounded like a motorcycle, and left. When Russ gathered himself he looked up at Annie and saw her cupping her mouth with one hand, tears streaming over her fingers.

"Are you sure?" he whispered.

She managed a nod. "I thought the baby was yours, so I ran away from my Uncle Mac's house in Texas. I called a handwritten phone number on a pamphlet a protester in front of the abortion clinic I was going to gave me. Turns out it was the woman's personal number. She didn't know what to do with me or how to help me, but ended up letting me hide at her place for a couple months until I could have the baby. She swore me to secrecy and had a midwife friend of hers handle the delivery at her house. After I had Tobias, I spent many hours just staring at his face, not with a sense of wonder like it's supposed to be. I was searching for your eyes, a familiar facial expression, the way you hold your mouth."

She shook her head. "I knew. Even before the testing. I called my uncle the next day to tell him I had the baby and where I was and that I thought this might be my dad's child— his brother's baby. He came and got me and called my father and told him he needed to get his ass to Texas to deal with the mess he'd made. My father of course denied that it was even possible this could be his child but my uncle didn't believe him and made him stay in a hotel."

"You said there was testing."

She nodded. "Yeah, my uncle arranged paternity testing. Private company—mail-in thing all done in a way to hide the crime. As far as the cops in Abilene ever knew, I'd run off and had the abortion, then came back home. Or to my uncle's anyway. When the results of the paternity test came back a month later, my uncle went to the hotel and almost beat my father to death before coming back for the baby. He took him from me when I was in the shower and left a note in the crib. It was for the best, he said, and I had no choice in the matter. I never got to say goodbye." She bit back tears. "He drove the child to Lubbock and left him in front of a fire station. Made an anonymous call. When Tobias's adoptive mother died eight years ago, there was a story about her in the *Lubbock Avalanche-Journal*. She was a long-time musician in the local orchestra. Part of her story was that she'd adopted this baby that had been abandoned at a local fire station. A friend of mine who lives down there recognized the story and sent it to me."

"You must've looked him up."

She nodded, her face twisted with sorrow. "I shouldn't have. I wish now I hadn't. He's such a good person."

Her hand covered her mouth again, and she sobbed into it.

Watching her, Russ's eyes filled with tears. He wanted to hold her but didn't think he could stand or even remain upright so he bent forward again, dropping his head between his legs. She went to her knees and put a hand on his shoulder. When he looked up, their noses touched and they pressed their wet faces together, lingering that way until finally her mouth found his.

44

Tuesday, September 14

BEFORE TEN A.M. I had finalized diversion agreements with the DA's office for my only two other clients. I wasn't taking any more cases until further notice. Wanting to maintain this productive momentum, I planted myself at my desk in the Wichita office to sketch out a to-do list in hopes that writing the tasks down would keep them from doing jumping jacks inside my brain at all hours of the day and night. Despite my restless mind, I'd managed to spend quality time with the kids over the weekend, some of it on ball diamonds coaching them up for their fall baseball and softball seasons. Both kids had agreed to play with local traveling teams in the last week. Time together in the sunshine did us good, but the presence of Mason and his men were a constant reminder of Keri's murder and the threats we were facing. My inability to calm myself at night left me sleep-deprived and half loopy. The coffee helped, but it was no match for what I was dealing with. As I hovered pen over paper, my brain glitching like out-of-date software, Rashonda buzzed in on the intercom to tell me Claire Riddle was on the line.

I hit the blinking button on the phone and did my own version of Rashonda's catch-phrase greeting. "Ben speaking, state your business."

The voice on the other end laughed in a way that didn't fit with how I pictured the cold-as-ice prosecutor. "You get right to the point in that office, no messing around, I like it."

"I knew you would."

"Guess I better get to the point then. Would you mind coming to the courthouse to meet with me and the district attorney?"

Riddle and my old law school buddy, Blaine, wanted to meet with me. I wondered why Blaine didn't call me himself. "Sure. Sometime this afternoon work for you two?"

"Now would be best." The warmth in her voice was already dissipating.

I looked at my to-do list. I'd gotten as far writing down the words, *replace Russ*.

Riddle said, "We should talk about settling the Delarosa case before the trial date gets any closer. We have a lot to talk about."

"You want Mia to give you the name of the killer in exchange for whatever it is you're offering."

"There's that, but we've got a few other items on the agenda as well."

"You have an agenda?"

"Folks from the FBI and the U.S. Attorney's Office are here right now. The local prosecutor from your home county is on his way. We'd like to sit down with you."

"Sounds like a five-dogs-on-a-cat situation."

"It's not an attack, Mr. Joel. We just want to talk."

"About what exactly? I'd like to know what's on this agenda of yours."

"We want your opinion on a matter, but we also need information, if you're willing to part with it."

"Uh-huh. What matter? What information?"

"How about you come hear us out. We're at a crossroads and want you to be part of a big decision that needs to be made."

"If the feds are there, I'm guessing you all are in the process of coordinating the state and federal prosecution of Curtis and Brown. Not sure you need me for that. But if you want my opinion on something, and the prosecutor from my county is going to be there, this probably involves Keri's murder and my mother's since they were murdered in his jurisdiction."

"You're right about all of that. But first, the DA and I want to sit down with you alone to discuss Mia's case. Like I said, we have much to discuss. There's a lot going on over here, and we want to bring you into the loop."

I dropped the pen on the desk and ran my fingers through my hair, trying to contemplate the possibilities, but Ms. Riddle cut that short.

"You should know that I tried to talk the DA out of what we did last week. What do we care what jail your client rots in awaiting trial? Blaine knew damn well that nothing good for our case against Delarosa would come out of contesting your motion. He was trying to help you. You, not your client."

Maybe it was the exhaustion, but all of the sudden I got the sense of being a pawn, or perhaps more accurately, that my law school buddy's selfless act hadn't been entirely selfless after all. Now Blaine wanted a favor. At least that's what I thought was coming. His assistant was speaking the language of *quid pro quo*—we scratched your back, now you scratch ours. Last Thursday's hearing had been a blow to the reputation of the DA's office and their case against Mia in the short run, but Blaine might be playing a long game here— something to fuel that drive I knew he'd always had for higher office. I decided nothing good could come from voicing my growing suspicions so I kept them to myself.

"Tell Blaine I appreciate the assist."

"Tell him yourself when you get here."

"Where am I going exactly?"

"Blaine's office. Conference room. Right now."

"Ten minutes. And I take my coffee black."

*　*　*

The conference room that abutted the DA's office on the sixth floor had a wall of windows that overlooked the street and the federal courthouse. Claire Riddle was sitting next to Blaine at one end of a long polished table surrounded by hi-backed leather chairs that more or less took up the entire room. Sunlight streamed in from the windows behind two prosecutors, backlighting them, making what struck me as a satirical image of attorneys in heaven. They'd been looking at the screen of a laptop computer when I entered the room. Before either of them noticed me, I noticed how tired Blaine looked. The guy was running on empty. His face brightened a little when he looked up and closed the laptop.

Blaine and Riddle came around the table and shook my hand, then returned to their seats. I took a seat facing them. I found myself squinting against the sun like a disadvantaged gunfighter. Not happening. I moved to a chair next to Blaine.

"You should sit opposite us so we can see each other better," Riddle said.

"I'll sit on this side. You two can move if you want. I'll wait."

Blaine and Riddle exchanged a look. Then Claire got up and closed some blinds. "How's that?"

"Terrific," I said. "But no more musical chairs. I like it over here. You two do what you want."

Riddle went around the table and sat. Pissed. Blaine stayed where he was.

"Thank you for last Thursday," I said to Blaine. "I'm sure that didn't win you any points with the judge or the public."

"The jury pool, you mean?" Blaine said. "That's part of what we want to talk to you about. I think I've got a way out of this mess that resembles justice."

"That'd be a first. But let's hear it."

"What's your fucking problem?" Claire said.

Blaine held up his hands—a calming gesture. "Ben likes to joke around, don't you, Ben?"

"Not really. I'm pretty much all business."

Blaine gave me a look—*cut it out, please.* "Fine, you're all business, but also under a lot of stress right now, right?"

I shrugged. "Sure. Aren't we all?"

Blaine was cookie-cutter good-looking with no pizzazz—no flair—the somewhat older pasty white-guy-next-door modeling suits in a JC Penney catalogue. I wondered if his two-day stubble was meant to give him a sharp masculine edge.

"Fair warning," I said, "so far, as I think you already know, my client has balked at the idea of cooperating with the government."

"Okay, but hear us out," Blaine said. "First thing—we've got the DNA report Agent Gordon shared with you last week. The one suggesting Annie Black has a son and that his DNA is on the axe that killed Jimmy Ray. The KBI briefed us about that this morning. About an hour and a half ago in fact."

I was more than a little surprised. With the approval of KBI brass, and for good reason, Caroline had the testing done without the Wichita PD's knowledge. The victim, Jimmy Ray, was retired WPD. Everyone knew from the motion I'd filed that Matusak had told me Jimmy Ray had been to Curtis's island and was being blackmailed by him, that Jimmy Ray had been Curtis's inside man with the WPD. Since Jimmy was retired when he was murdered, suspicion grew that Curtis had a second man inside the WPD. Since the KBI had made the gutsy decision to keep evidence in Jimmy Ray's murder case from the WPD, and since the WPD would necessarily have to work closely with the DA's office to prosecute the case, I'd assumed the KBI would withhold the information from the DA's office as well. But I was wrong.

Surprise must've shown on my face because Blaine said, "What's the matter?"

"Nothing," I said, still scrambling to put this new development in perspective. If Caroline knew the DNA result had been shared with the DA, I figured I would have at least gotten a heads-up from her, but maybe not. I wasn't really a part of their team. I was a defense attorney representing a woman accused of being an accomplice to murder.

Blaine gave me a reassuring smile. "Don't worry, we understand the need to keep this to ourselves for now. Until we know for sure Curtis doesn't have another cop inside the

PD. I don't see how this information could be useful to Curtis right now, but knowledge is power and the situation is complicated and incredibly fluid."

Claire chimed in. "Since there's no indication the DA's office is dirty, hiding DNA evidence concerning the possible identity of a murderer from us wasn't a smart play by the KBI, politically, or otherwise. You understand that, right?"

"Perfectly," I said, thinking it was a weird thing for her to say.

She smirked. "At some point the surreptitious testing the KBI had done behind the PD's back is going to be controversial as hell and blow up in the press. Blaine is the KBI brass's lifeline. At least when the shit finally hits the fan and the chief of police is calling for KBI heads to roll, the KBI director can say the top law enforcement official in the district—Blaine here—knew of, and approved of, the need to keep the testing a secret from the WPD, at least temporarily."

She twirled a pen in her fingers, a look in her eye telling me she had more to say. "We also know about your investigator's connection to Annie Black."

Word was out. Big fucking deal. If Caroline had followed my advice, she had a lot of KBI agents following Russ. I wasn't surprised they knew the situation, and that word of Russ's past relationship with Annie had spread like wildfire.

"Have you heard from him since last Friday?" Blaine said.

"No. Not since I let him go."

Claire dropped the pen and leaned forward, planting her elbows on the table and making a steeple with her hands. "You know where we could find him?"

"He lives in a little room in back of that bar where he works sometimes—Crossroads Bar & Grill. Other than that, I have no idea where he could be. Look, I think the KBI might have a tail on him. I told Agent Gordon she should do that last Friday. Told her it might lead them to Annie."

Claire laughed bitterly and rocked back in her chair.

The tension vibrating through me kicked up a notch. I felt my eyes narrow. "Are you telling me they didn't tail him?"

Claire huffed. "Oh, they put a tail on him alright."

"He shook 'em," Blaine said. "And now he's gone. No one told you that?"

"No. Did the bureau at least try pinging his phone?"

"Yeah," Blaine groaned. "But he's too smart for something like that. We would ask you to give us numbers for any burners you know he's used in the past, but there's no point. He won't make a stupid mistake like that."

I nodded in automatic agreement. "Damn."

Claire crossed her legs. Disgusted. "'Damn' he says."

"What's your problem, lady?" I said.

"I don't believe you haven't talked to Russ since Friday. I think you intend to ride this wave of public emotion Blaine gave you all the way to trial, and lucky me, I'm gonna be the one left holding the fucking bag, lookin' like some head-up-my-ass dipshit."

Blaine turned to her. "You want off this case, Claire, just say the word."

Her eyes stayed locked on mine, didn't acknowledge Blaine.

"Listen," I said. "My theory has always been that the best thing for Mia's case was for me to find out who wielded that axe and get them charged, so we're pretty much in the same boat here. I'm hoping, when push comes to shove, that whoever took Jimmy Ray down will take Mia off the hook and say she had no idea what was about to happen. None at all."

"For you to come to that conclusion," Blaine said, "you must know who did this."

"It's a hope, not a conclusion. And even if I did know who axed Ray, I couldn't disclose that and you know it, but looking at the logic of it, it stands to reason that it was someone partial to Mia who wouldn't want to see her go down on this if she didn't have to."

Claire said, "Meaning you think the other killer would lie and say Mia wasn't in on any plan to kill Jimmy Ray. That his being killed while your client went down on him came as a *complete shock* to her." She gave a dismissive wave of her hand. "I don't buy that."

"Good job, Ms. Riddle, except for the snarky editorializing. You got the gist of what I hope will happen. I'm working through this just like you. None of us know exactly how this went down because we weren't there."

She shrugged. "Okay, so where is your client's savior and why haven't they come forward to take all the blame?"

"Haven't had to yet, would be my guess."

"One hell of a game of chicken," Blaine said.

Claire's eyes drew down. "It was a two-person operation—planned and executed by your client and the other killer."

I smiled. "Executed. Nice."

She glared at me.

"Premeditated murder," I said. "Maybe you can convince a jury of that, but if that's all there was to it, I wouldn't be here and we wouldn't be talking settlement. Given what went down last Thursday, anybody on that jury is likely to bend over backwards looking for reasonable doubt anywhere they can find it and you know it."

Blaine flipped over some papers that were sitting on the table and slid them at me. "Show your client this."

"What is it?"

"Ellen Bigknife Wilson's statement."

"The bunkmate she punched," Claire added. "Your client told Bigknife that the killing was planned, just like I argued at the prelim."

I flipped through the paperwork. There it was in black and white—the person her public defender and I had warned her about had snitched on her. I read through her written statement. According to Bigknife, Mia told her that she offered Jimmy Ray oral sex and coaxed him into the kitchen chair where he was murdered exactly according the prosecution's theory, all the way down to the detail about Mia propping open the screen door with a brick so there'd be no advance warning to their victim before the axe fell. As far as motive, Bigknife said Mia told her she distracted Jimmy Ray with oral sex so he could be murdered in retaliation for having molested Mia as a child. Nothing in the statement about

Annie. Nothing about Ray being killed in defense of Annie's five-year-old daughter, Amelia. Nothing about the identity of her co-conspirator, the one whose job it was to take Jimmy Ray's head off. By the letter of the law, if what Bigknife was saying was true, my client was guilty of aiding and abetting first-degree premeditated murder, which made her as guilty as if she'd wielded the axe herself, and subject to the exact same penalty—life in prison.

I laughed. "As I recall, Mia punched that loudmouth in the face. That was back when Bigknife was pumping Mia for information she could spoon-feed you to save her own ass." I laughed again—harder this time. Not for show. I was actually enjoying the idea of tearing Bigknife apart on the witness stand. "I can smell your desperation, and if you put Bigknife on the stand, so will the jury."

Claire took that in, didn't respond, but I knew I'd scored a point. She glanced down at Bigknife's statement with pursed lips. Two points.

"What are you giving Bigknife for her testimony?" I said.

"We're dropping our identity theft case against her," Blaine said. "We'll ask the court to modify her probation—"

"The probation she was on when she committed the identity theft charges you're dropping? *That* probation?" I laughed again—third time in less than a minute.

They both nodded. Unhappily.

"What was she on probation for?" I asked.

"Forgery," Claire said reluctantly.

"So you're dropping two crimes of dishonesty in exchange for her testimony, this'll be like shooting ducks on a pond," I said. "Especially since she was facing prison time on both cases."

Blaine shrugged. "These are low-level property crimes, Ben. She wasn't facing much time, you know that. We'll ask the court to modify her probation. Get her into inpatient treatment for her oxy addiction."

Claire clacked a shiny green nail on the table. "When they hear Bigknife tell it, the jury will have to do a little more than bend over backwards to acquit your client—"

"You're living in a dreamworld. All they'll have to do is disbelieve a pill-popping thief and a backstabbing con artist. They wouldn't believe her if she said she had ten toes."

Claire snarled. "*And* the physical evidence, along with their own common sense."

"Put Bigknife on the stand. I'll set her on fire."

Claire took a breath and regrouped. "Face it. We've got facts on our side, and you've got the probable emotions of the jury, which means we've both got problems."

"But there's a way out of this for both of us," Blaine said, jumping into the fray.

"I'm listening."

He pursed his lips. "Convince your client to give us the name of the person who swung the axe. We'll dismiss all charges against Mia outright, and offer voluntary manslaughter to the other killer."

That jolted me. I hoped it didn't show.

Claire added, "Then we'll all be out from under this Godforsaken mess."

"Voluntary manslaughter," I said slowly. "That could be as little as a five-year sentence."

Claire nodded. "That's right, assuming the other killer has no criminal history."

"If that's a formal offer," I said, "I'll pass it on."

Claire folded her hands in her lap. "It's a formal offer."

"Do you think she'll take it?" Blaine asked.

I thought about that. "No," I said reluctantly. "I don't." But I didn't want the offer to get summarily yanked, so I said, "Not at first, anyway. But I'll work on it. It's a good offer. I'll do my best to make her see that."

Blaine made a face. "Tell her we've got the DNA of what I'm being told is probably Annie Black's son on the axe handle, so in time we might be able to convict him even without her testimony. If that happens, the offer is gone and she's an accessory to murder. She might as well come forward now, while she can still get something out of it."

"You know," I said, playing devil's advocate, "Annie Black doesn't have a son. On paper anyway. And the DNA does nothing to tell us who actually swung that axe."

Claire rolled her eyes. "Yeah, we get it. So I guess we're back to frying your client for murder."

"For what it's worth," I said. "I'll strongly recommend she take the deal. Like I said, it's a good one."

Blaine forced a smile. Claire didn't.

"What am I missing?" I said.

Blaine looked at me through one eye. "What do you mean?"

"I've known you a long time, Blaine. Can't see how you'd be content to come out of this so . . . so . . ."

"Diminished?" Claire said. "If she takes the deal, Blaine and I will come off looking like incompetent buffoons. That's what you mean, isn't it?"

I couldn't argue with that. I kept my mouth shut.

"I think Dean Curtis is as dirty as you think he is," Blaine said. "It's as simple as that. I wanted Curtis and Brown on the stand at that hearing last Thursday almost as much as you did."

"Hell of a risk for you," I said.

Blaine spread his hands. "What can I say? Fortune favors the bold. Bad things are already happening to Curtis."

Claire Riddle shook her head and looked away.

I focused on her. "Problem? What am I missing here?"

"Ask your buddy here."

"I'm asking you."

Blaine shifted his weight in his chair. "Claire's the best courtroom prosecutor in this office, but she disagrees with how I'm dealing with this case—"

"No shit," I said. "I can see that on her face. What are you not telling me?"

He crossed his arms and leaned back, a hand on his chin almost covering his mouth.

I leaned closer. "What?"

Blaine eye-balled me, stroking the stubble on his chin. "Two weeks ago, a guy called my office saying he knows who killed Paco Correa. Said he wanted to talk to me personally, that he was at The Rabbit Hole the night Paco Correa was supposedly murdered."

I tried not to let my sudden alertness show as I tried to recall the names Brackeen had given me—friends of Paco's that Brackeen interviewed in '93. I drew a blank.

"Who was it that called?" I asked.

Blaine's eyebrows went up. "He said his name was Jose Gutiérrez. He called the morning of the twenty-fourth, but I was at Keri's funeral. He called back in the afternoon and—"

"You sat on this for two weeks—!"

He held up a hand. "Let me finish. The second time he called, the receptionist patched him through to my assistant, who listened to his story, then came into my office white as a sheet." He pressed his lips together. "I took the call, of course."

"How come you didn't tell me before now?"

"Don't feel bad," Claire said. "He didn't tell me either. I didn't hear about it until this morning."

No wonder these two weren't getting along. The left hand was in San Francisco and the right hand was in Miami. I shook my head in disbelief at their relationship, then looked at Blaine. "Why?"

"I didn't buy the guy's story at first," Blaine said. "Thought he was a crackpot, someone playing a sick joke. But he insisted on talking to me because he didn't trust the cops."

"Understandable," I said.

"Yeah, I get it, but still." Blaine ran a hand over his face. "Our office has investigators that answer directly to me. I hooked Gutiérrez up with our best guy with instructions to put Gutiérrez up in a nice hotel and keep him safe while we checked out his story."

I thought about that. "You knew Agent Gordon was working on this. You should've notified her about this way before now."

"It took a while to vet this guy—make sure he was who he said he was."

"Caroline would've done that for you, better and faster than your investigator."

Blaine shrugged. "Yeah well, if you'll remember, I was busy at the time deciding whether or not to charge her with manslaughter for shooting a homeless man, so I rather doubt she was in any position to get anything like that done at all." He smiled. "She was on administrative leave, remember?"

"You know what I mean. You could've called the KBI—"

"Excuse me," Blaine's voice got louder. "I was elected DA, not you. I'll do the job the way I see fit." He shot a brief, hostile glance at Claire, then I got one. "I'm sorry you two don't like the way I handled it, but I couldn't just call the sheriff's office or the PD and let them handle Gutiérrez, now could I?"

I didn't want this to devolve into a shouting match, so I refrained from pointing out that none of his arguments explained why he'd kept Gutiérrez from the KBI. What I needed was information. "Gutiérrez probably had more to say than what you just told me. What is it?"

"Says he saw the news coverage and read your motion online. In '93 he heard the gunshots and saw Curtis and Brown dragging Correa's body behind The Rabbit Hole. Says he's willing to testify against Brown and Curtis for killing his friend."

"He saw them moving Correa's body?" I almost yelled.

I looked back and forth between Blaine and Claire. If true, there would now be enough admissible evidence to prosecute Curtis and Brown for the murder of Paco Correa, at least in theory. Without a body or a murder weapon, it would still be an uphill battle. There were other complications, including Gutiérrez's prior inconsistent statement to Brackeen in '93 that he wasn't even at the bar on the night of the murder.

I decided to make a point of it. "This is nothing like what Gutiérrez told Brackeen. I outlined what Brackeen said in my motion."

Blaine's condescending smile lingered on his face for a long ten count. "Yeah, I know, but—"

Claire cut in. "Gutiérrez was scared then." She shot Blaine a nasty look. "I figure that's the reason. Am I right about that? I just found out about all this, so I don't know. I'm just guessing in the dark here."

Blaine nodded curtly, annoyed.

Brackeen's instincts had told him that Gutiérrez was lying about not being at the scene of Correa's murder. Brackeen thought it was due to the shame Gutiérrez must've felt for having left his friend for dead, which was consistent with what I was hearing now. It was a promising development, but why did Blaine keep this from me for two weeks? Why did he keep it from Claire? That didn't make sense. Something else was in play here, but I couldn't see Blaine's cards.

I said, "Did Gutiérrez say he was the one who called 911?"

"I was caught off guard. I didn't ask him," Blaine said, shaking his head. "Neither did my investigator, sorry to say."

"Well, you've had two weeks to ask him—"

Blaine sighed. "We haven't gotten around to it yet, I mean, it's one of those questions that slipped through the cracks, Ben, I'm sorry. We'll get an answer for you on that as soon as we can."

"Jesus," I said. "Let me to talk to the guy."

Blaine shook his head. "Not a good idea—"

"He was friends with my father," I said. "And he knew my mother. He could be the key to this whole thing. I need to talk to him."

"Too many cooks in the kitchen," Blaine muttered.

"I'd settle for one competent lawyer," I said hotly. Then all this waffling gave me a thought. "Do you have him?"

"Have him?"

"Is Gutiérrez safe in a motel somewhere?"

"What the hell kind of question is that?"

"Is he?"

"Look," he yelled, shooting forward in his chair. He pressed his lips together and closed his eyes, sucking air in noisily through his nose. "I understand why you two are upset with me, I really do. But I wanted to keep a lid on this until after Thursday's hearing. Some of my staff knew about the calls already, and, well, you know how hard it is to keep stuff like this under wraps, so I made the decision not to share this information with anyone else." He looked at me. "I wanted you to have a crack at Curtis and Brown while they still felt cocky enough to fight back on the stand and maybe make a huge mistake. And as bad a public-relations nightmare as this has been for this office and for me personally, it's been a whole lot worse for Brown and Curtis."

"With Gutiérrez's statement in your hip pocket," I said, "you could have had both of them arrested right there in court after the hearing, after I had my crack at him. You could've charged them with Correa's murder right then. Problem solved."

"If I'd known the U.S. Attorney in the Southern District of New York was about to pop Curtis with sex trafficking, I might have done that."

"Might have?" I said.

"I wasn't quite ready to pull that trigger. You don't charge a billionaire like Curtis on a whim. I wanted the media . . . the inertia of this case, I wanted a tidal wave against Curtis so it would be all but impossible for him to use his money and his clout—"

"You wanted the media storm to peak," I said, "so there'd be as many eyes as possible on you when you charged Curtis with Correa's murder. Either that, or you got cold feet."

Blaine made a sad, patronizing face—the kind politicians like Blaine use to portray vast wisdom and sympathy for the misguided. "We both want the same thing here—your mother's murderers behind bars."

Claire said, "And if Blaine Swartzmiller somehow rode this wave of celebrity adulation he sees just over the horizon all the way to the governor's mansion, all the better." She focused on me, didn't look at Blaine. "This is the opportunity Blaine's been waiting for his whole life. If he can nail a predator like Curtis—President Collins' billionaire buddy—he'll be a hero to the right wing in this country and a darling of the Me Too movement in one fell swoop. Think about how unique a situation for kick-starting political stardom this is.

Might even get little Blainey on the cover of *Time Magazine*. Maybe he can even parlay this thing into a run for the presidency someday. Wouldn't that be something?"

Little Blainey? I suppressed a smile. Blaine had gone to the mat for me by getting Curtis on the stand where I could pummel him. Claire was going to be standing in an unemployment line later this afternoon. Maybe.

Anger flashed in Blaine's eyes. He leaned heavily back in his chair, his mouth tight. "What's changed here? A few minutes ago, Ben, you were thanking me for helping you get those two sons-of-bitches in a media crossfire. Whatever you think of what I'm doing, it's all risky as hell for me and my family, just like it is yours. And it was risky as hell to oppose that motion last Thursday and may not pan out for me at all. Right now, the whole world thinks Claire and I are idiots. You've seen the coverage. This might be the death of my career. Claire might blame me for that dumpster fire I let happen last Thursday, but now that you know I may actually have a way to nail Curtis and Brown, suddenly I'm this power-hungry politician because I kept a secret from everyone for a couple of weeks? That's pretty damn cynical. All I'm trying to do is hold these motherfuckers accountable for what they did to your mother and father. I'd like to think if we play our cards right, we can end up nailing Curtis for both murders. If having that as a goal is wrong, I stand convicted."

I took a deep breath. "Is Gutiérrez telling the truth? Is this even the guy Brackeen interviewed back in '93?"

Blaine nodded. "Near as I can tell, yes."

Claire said, "Even if he's not, whoever he is and whatever he's willing to say has served a higher purpose."

Blaine's face turned a shade redder than it already had.

"Meaning what?" I said to Claire.

"Gutiérrez has already caused the next domino to fall."

"Not yet, it hasn't," Blaine responded, "but it's ready to if we let it."

I threw up my hands. "What are we talking about here?"

Claire glanced at Blaine, who was watching me.

"Undersheriff Brown," Blaine said. "He found out about Gutiérrez coming forward and wants to cut a deal."

Conceivably, this was good news, but it hit me wrong, or something wasn't right, yet again. "How is it that Brown knew about Gutiérrez coming forward before I did? Before anyone at the Kansas Bureau of Investigation did?"

Blaine gave me an unblinking look. Politicians can do that—with their eyes, make you want to believe anything they were about to say. I could feel his magic trying to work on me. Until he spoke, that is. "His attorney somehow found out about Gutiérrez last Friday and called me."

I shook my head. "Come on, man, it's me you're talkin' to here. You leaked it to him to grease the skids—"

"I'm getting shit done, goddammit." He stood up and walked in a circle, running fingers through his hair. I took that to mean he'd said about all he was going to say on the matter.

I looked at Claire, then back at Blaine.

He sat down and cleared his throat, then abruptly changed the subject. "The acting U.S. Attorney in this district and two agents from the FBI are down the hall. I want us to discuss the prospect of cutting a global deal with Brown so the feds can go after Curtis federally on a whole host of other charges stemming from his activity here in Kansas. The search warrants they executed on all his properties last Thursday and Friday came up empty and they haven't been able to locate any people in his so-called inner circle that Matusak told you about. Someone tipped Curtis off, or maybe he cleaned house and dumped a bunch of witnesses in the Pacific after you filed your motion two weeks ago. Either way, the feds might be game to look for other ways to go after Curtis."

He glanced at his ADA. "Claire and I, of course, want to go after Curtis for the murder of Paco Correa. The prosecutor from your county is here as well. I can only assume that he's also interested bringing your mother's murderer to justice. Adding Brown's testimony to the crucifix connection you brought out in court last Thursday might very well bury Curtis."

"What does Brown's attorney want?" I said.

Blaine pooched out his lips. "Monet wants the moon, but he'll back off that during our horse trading like he always does. I think what he has in mind ultimately is something that lands Brown in state prison for less than ten years, which would be a good deal for Brown with everything he's looking at. But to get there, he'll need the feds and both state prosecutors' offices to be part of a global settlement agreement. Without it, Brown won't even consider cooperating."

"And all of you want my blessing to cut a deal with Brown?"

"Of course we do," Blaine said. "Let's take a break, and I'll get everyone in here."

45

TEN MINUTES LATER the table was elbow to elbow with state and federal prosecutors and cops, among them Agent Gordon, Taylor Greer (the prosecutor from my county), and the acting U.S. Attorney for the District of Kansas, Deb Walsh. Blaine, Claire and I got the last three seats in the room.

I knew Deb from my time as a federal prosecutor in the Kansas City office. In her younger days, cops and attorneys dubbed her Little Debbie because of her size and because she resembled the image of the little girl that still adorned the box of Little Debbie Snack Cakes—a spray of freckles under bright round eyes that brought to mind an old-timey girlish innocence. Now in her fifties, Deb still somewhat resembled the young girl on the snack box, but her look and the moniker belied her ferocity, as she would not hesitate to rip any defendant who took her to trial a new asshole whether they needed one or not. She mouthed her hello to me as she sat at one end of the long table directly across from Blaine, the rest of us sandwiched in between. I liked that our latest president hadn't gotten around to appointing a new U.S. Attorney in the district, and that we were dealing with a veteran prosecutor in Deb, not some hack political appointee with no real-world experience and an IQ in the low sixties.

Everyone introduced themselves. Of course, given the suspicion surrounding Undersheriff Brown, no one was here from his office, and no one from the Wichita Police Department was present either, which made perfect sense.

Also missing was the DA's investigator, which didn't. Blaine explained that his investigator was home battling Covid-19, then proceeded to tell us how Gutiérrez claimed to have heard gunshots and witnessed Curtis and Brown moving Paco Correa's body in the area behind The Rabbit Hole in '93, deftly pivoting and glossing over the so-called leak in his office that led to a call from Brown's attorney, Steve Monet.

"Long story short," Blaine said, "Monet wants to deal, but first he wants solid immunity agreements from the feds and the state prosecutors' offices involved, which is why all of you are here today."

Deb chimed in. "If Monet asks, tell him we're prepared to debrief his client tomorrow." She held up an envelope, looking to the two FBI agents at the table as if to make sure they were on board with this. "Got the proffer letter right here, ready to go."

A proffer letter, aka letter immunity, was informal and easy for her because she didn't have to get it approved by the U.S. Attorney General. More importantly, from the government's perspective, this type of immunity didn't give away anything. If agreed to by Brown, the feds would get the benefit of hearing all he had to say regarding his and Curtis's decades-long crime spree before deciding what, if anything, they wanted to offer him for his testimony. It was like an audition or a job interview of sorts. If negotiations fell apart and the USAO didn't want to use Brown as a witness, they could still prosecute him to the full extent of the law. The only thing that couldn't be used against him were any statements made during the proffer, which the feds wouldn't have had anyway without the proffer. Only thing Deb would be giving away was the time it took her and the FBI to sit down and listen to Brown's confessions. Window shopping, with no obligation to buy.

Blaine smiled. "Thank you, Ms. Walsh. That's a decent start but given his client's exposure to criminal prosecution and what he's up against here—meaning Curtis and his powerful contacts—Monet says his client is going to need more protection than that to come forward."

Deb shrugged. "Tough shit. I need to hear Brown's story and vet it first. I won't buy a pig in a poke. Monet's worked with me before. He knows how I work."

Blaine rolled his eyes and turned to Taylor Greer, the prosecutor from my county, and launched into another tiresome harangue, this one about why Greer should do his part to grant immunity to Brown for crimes occurring in his jurisdiction, freeing Brown to incriminate and eventually testify against Dean Curtis, in pursuit of bringing the full weight of three prosecutor's offices down on the disgraced billionaire.

Whatever I expected this meeting to be, this wasn't it. Nothing had been worked out beforehand; everyone seemed to be caught flatfooted, which I found disconcerting. This was the supposed brain trust. This was it. There wasn't a crack team of more sure-footed super-lawyers out there waiting in the wings.

I'd heard enough and cut in. "Blaine, you're making this way more complicated than it needs to be. If Gutiérrez's story checks out and you think he can hold his own on the stand, why don't you charge both Brown and Curtis for Correa's murder and see which one flips on the other?"

Deb and Taylor Greer nodded in agreement.

Blaine drew his head back. "But Curtis is the big fish. We don't want him to get away."

"With that federal case in New York, Curtis already has a hook in his mouth," I said. "I want both these guys to get their comeuppance."

Blaine slumped back in his chair. "Right now, all we got is the statement of Jose Gutiérrez, and given his prior statement and the fact that he kept what he witnessed to himself for almost thirty years, we've got next to nothing. These cases are cold and getting colder. We need to use the leverage Gutiérrez has provided to shore up the case against Curtis by dealing with Brown. Realistically, we'll need Brown's testimony to nail Curtis. Now's the time to act, before something happens to Gutiérrez. Ben, you know how this works. I thought you would want this. Monet has all but told me that Brown can give us Curtis for the murder of your mother in Taylor's jurisdiction. I guess I thought you'd want to go after Curtis for murdering your mother. That's what dealing with Brown the way I propose gets us."

I glanced around at the faces, all of them showing concern. Caroline looked away when our eyes met.

Finally I said, "I'll think about it."

"That's what I want to do," Taylor Greer said. "I need to think this through. I think we all do."

Deb stood, and in turn, the FBI agents followed along like a string of pack animals.

To the prosecutors in the room, Deb said, "Call me if you want to discuss this further. You too, Ben. I have grand jury in twenty minutes."

Claire and Blaine stayed seated while the rest of us headed for the door. I was last in line and Blaine called my name as I hit the doorway.

I turned and faced him.

His eyes shifted to Claire. "Can you give us a minute?"

She stood and passed me on her way out the door. "Time for the big-boy meeting, is it?"

Blaine gave a quick nod. "That's right. Before you get to your office, though, could you bring us some coffee?"

Claire stormed out the door, mumbling something about dumping coffee in Blaine's fucking lap.

The muscles in Blaine's jaw tightened. "Close the door and have a seat, Ben. There are a couple of matters we still need to discuss."

I shut the door and sat across from him.

Blaine sighed. "I get the impression Taylor Greer isn't up to this. My opinion—we need to convince him to let the state AG's office handle this in his jurisdiction. Regardless of who ends up prosecuting your mother's murderer, they need to strike a deal to turn Brown state's witness. With Brown on their side, they could nail Curtis for killing your mother. You'd be set for . . ."

I waited for the rest of it, but it wasn't coming. "Finish your thought."

"Nah. I don't know where I was going with that."

"I'd be set for what . . . for life? Meaning, after Curtis is convicted, I could file suit in civil court and score a big fat pay day. Is that what you were about to say?"

Blaine looked down at his hands. "Yeah. Sorry about that. I'm tired. I'm practically seeing double."

"You're not the first person to see dollar signs here. My sister—"

"We're real close to getting Curtis. You should consider asking Deb and Greer to do what I've suggested. Ask them to work with Monet. Brown will deal. He's the linchpin, but the prosecutors jockeying around in all these fucking jurisdictions have to cooperate to make it worth his while."

"Brown may or may not be the linchpin to get my mother's killer, but on the civil side of things I can't see that any of this matters. The statute of limitations for her wrongful death action ran out decades ago."

"I know you haven't had time to research this, but I have," Blaine said. "Ever heard of equitable tolling?"

He smiled at the question on my face.

"I'll email you the case law," he said. "The crux of it is the common law principle that wrongdoers should not be allowed to benefit from their wrongdoing, such as hiding the fact of a wrongful killing. In this case, a murder. It doesn't get any more wrongful than that. You've got a colorable argument to toll the statute of limitations. That'll get you to the negotiation table at least, and when you're there, Curtis's attorneys may want to settle up for another killing for which the statute of limitations hasn't run out."

"Keri's murder," I said. "Two wrongful deaths for the price of one. There's probably already enough meat on the bone here to negotiate a settlement with one of the ten richest men in the world, right? Thank God for silver linings." I failed to keep the cynicism out of my voice.

"I've offended you again."

"A little."

"I'm sorry, but just think about it, okay? This man has torn up your family. He's torn you up."

"Money won't fix that."

"You're right. But, fuck him. Fuck him for what he did to you. To your mother. To your . . ." His voice cracked. "Your wife. Monet let me know pretty clearly that Brown doesn't have any information regarding your wife's murder, but he gets us over the goal line on your mother's."

Us. I took a moment to compose myself. "I appreciate what you've done, and I appreciate what you're trying to do."

He looked away. There was a gap in the conversation. I tried to anticipate what was next. Seemed like we were through.

"You need to apologize to Claire," I said. "You were a real asshole a few minutes ago."

"I know. And I will."

I stood. "Better be on my way—"

"I get the feeling Deb and Taylor won't push to flip Brown on Curtis without your blessing."

I nodded. "I'll think about it."

46

"THIS CASE CAN be over for you today," I said to Mia.

I was sitting across from her at Pops' dining room table over Chinese takeout I'd brought back from Wichita after the meeting at Blaine's office. She and I were alone.

"What do you mean, over?" Mia said.

"Case dismissed. I spoke with the prosecutors a couple hours ago. They're willing to dismiss all charges against you if you'll tell them who killed Jimmy Ray."

"I told you. I'm not doing that."

"I know, but things are different now."

"How?"

"There's an actual offer on the table, and they're offering more than we ever thought they would. No jail time for you, no conviction. Nothin'. All you have to do is sit down with the ADA and Detective Riggins and tell them who killed Jimmy Ray. In theory, you may have to testify, but I don't think it will come to that."

She held a fork full of Lo mein suspended above the takeout box. Stunned.

"Before you tell me no, there's more."

She lowered the fork. "More?"

"They'll offer Tobias a plea to manslaughter."

"You didn't tell them Tobias did it, did you?"

"No, of course not. I'm bound by attorney-client privilege. Let me be clear here: What I'm telling you is, if you give them the name of the killer—Tobias—they'll offer him a plea to voluntary manslaughter."

"Voluntary manslaughter—that sounds almost worse than murder. What's that mean, exactly?"

"It's a reduced charge, Mia. Still homicide, still a killing, but done due to an admittedly unreasonable yet honest belief that circumstances existed that justified deadly force in defense of another person. That person being you, under the theory that Tobias thought Jimmy was forcing himself on you. Manslaughter carries a much lower sentence. If Tobias doesn't have a criminal history—"

"He doesn't."

"Then he'd be looking at a maximum of five years in prison, as opposed to life."

She shook her head, reeling from a temptation she'd vowed to resist. "What are my chances of being found not guilty at trial if I don't take this deal?"

"Fair. Decent. Given public reaction to what happened last Thursday, the prosecution believes there's a substantial risk of jury nullification on your case. Much more than before."

"Meaning the jury might not convict because they think Jimmy Ray deserved to die?"

"Something like that, but here's the deal. For a not guilty verdict, we'll need all twelve jurors to think that way."

"What happens if some don't?"

"Hung jury. Mistrial. If the prosecution is game, there's a new trial with a different jury and we do it all over again"

She took that in.

"There's something else you should know." I slid a copy of Bigknife's written statement across the table at her. "Your former bunkmate ratted you out."

Mia read the statement, seemingly breathing in the regret.

"She's a thief and a liar, Mia, and I'll make that argument to a jury if it comes to that, but Bigknife's testimony will be corroborated by some of the physical evidence in this case. This changes things. Makes it harder for any sympathizers I manage to get on the jury to hold out for a not guilty verdict during deliberations. Makes it more likely there'll be some horse trading, if you know what I mean. Jurors often get tired of holding on to their positions and just want to get on with their lives. So maybe they compromise and stick you with a lesser offense—murder two or manslaughter."

"I fucked up."

"If you take the deal, none of that matters. No trial, no doubt, you're free and this is over."

Her nostrils flared as she finished reading Bigknife's statement.

"This deal is a dream, Mia. It's as good as it gets. More than fair to you. And Tobias will be offered a damn good deal as well."

"I told Jimmy Ray he could have me . . . use me as his plaything for the rest of his life if he'd stay away from Amelia."

"You don't need to tell me this. In fact, I'd prefer that you didn't right now."

"Why?"

"If you don't take the deal, it might limit our options at trial."

"I know what you're doing. You're trying to avoid knowing for sure that I'm an accomplice to murder. You think you need to avoid hearing the truth from my lips."

"Depends on what the truth is, Mia."

"You want to avoid a situation where I'm on the stand and you damn well know I'm lying my ass off."

"I think you have a pretty good handle on the situation. Your public defender explain that to you?"

"Yeah, he said attorneys owe a duty of candor to a tribunal." She shrugged. "Something like that."

"Attorneys owe a duty of candor to the court, yes. But you have a right to testify, and the right to counsel, including privileged communications with counsel, so if I know *for sure* you're lying under oath, things can get complicated for me in a hurry and I want to avoid that. For those of us who weren't there in Jimmy's kitchen when he was killed, the truth can be a slippery thing."

"So, as I understand it from my last attorney, I can get on the stand and lie my ass off, it's just that if my attorney knows *for sure* I'm lying, he can't help me along by asking questions he knows I'll answer with lies."

"That's the situation."

"What if the prosecution asks me a question and I answer with a lie and you know it?"

"That's between you and your maker. I'm required to sit there silently and watch."

She smiled. "Don't worry. I'll make this easy for you. If I take the stand, I won't lie."

"You won't take the stand because you're taking the deal, right?"

"Wrong."

"Mia, the DA knows Annie Black's son's DNA is on the axe handle. She can't hide forever, and neither can Tobias. It's only a matter of time before they arrest him for murder. You can't stop any of this from happening, but you can save yourself and you can guarantee that he won't get more than five years in prison. You'd be saving both of you."

The muscles in her jaw knotted—she wasn't listening to me; she was somewhere else. "I was babysitting Amelia," she said. "She wanted to play on the swing set in the backyard, but I wouldn't let her. Jimmy Ray was in his backyard mowing with his shirt off. When he was finished, I thought it would be alright to take Amelia out back for a little bit. Get some fresh air—"

"Don't tell me any of this unless you're taking the deal."

She ignored me—kept rolling. "We went out there. I pushed her in the swing and then we kicked a ball around. But I could hear a mower somewhere and thought it might be Jimmy mowing his front lawn. I noticed that the shed where he kept his mower was still open. I didn't want to see him. I didn't want him to see Amelia, so I took her inside. I poured her some Kool-Aid, sat her at the kitchen table, and gave her some crackers. Then there was a knock at the door. Couple of Jehovah's Witnesses I had some trouble convincing to leave. When I finally got back to the kitchen, Amelia was gone. I hollered for her, looked out the window to the backyard. Checked upstairs. Went to the basement." She shook her head, her eyes alive with the terror of the memory. "I came out of the basement and went to the front porch, looking up and down the street for her, hollering for her. No Amelia. The Jehovah's Witnesses on their bikes were riding away."

She licked her lips. "I searched for maybe ten, fifteen minutes, combing the house, looking out the front and back doors, hollering her name over and over. I was about to call 911 when I looked through the back window for about the fifth time and saw her there with Jimmy Ray in his backyard. She was standing in the grass looking up at him. He was on his patio with his shirt still off. I bolted out the door, climbed the fence, ran through his yard and scooped her up. She had a baby doll he'd given her—one of those American Girl dolls that cost something like seventy bucks. I threw it at him and took Amelia back to my house. He sort of smiled at me when I threw the doll at him. Didn't say a word."

"Why don't we have Mason take us to Wichita right now?" I said. "You can tell this whole story to Claire Riddle."

She continued to ignore my advice and kept on.

"When I got Amelia away from Jimmy and inside my house, Tobias was coming through the front door. He saw I was upset and asked what happened."

"Was Annie with him?"

"No. He'd borrowed her Mustang to pick up Amelia for her."

"How long had you known him?"

"A few months." She started to cry. "I liked him a lot." She wiped tears away with a napkin. "I told Tobias what happened. About Amelia being in Jimmy's yard with the doll he'd given her."

"Did you tell him your history with Jimmy Ray? How Jimmy molested you as a child?"

"Yeah. Tobias wanted to know why I was so upset about just a doll so I told him what had happened in the past."

"Come on, Mia, let's go tell all this to Riddle. This story's too painful to tell twice in one day."

She shook her head. "No, I'm not telling this to the DA. What happened was my fault. More mine than Tobias's."

"What do you mean?"

"I was freaking out in front of Amelia. I basically snapped, so Tobias took Amelia upstairs and stayed with her a few minutes. When he came back down I was getting a steak knife out of a drawer in the kitchen. He asked me what I was doing and I told him I was going to go over to Jimmy Ray's to cut off his dick. Tobias had no plans to kill Jimmy Ray. This was all my fault."

"Okay, you keep saying this was all your fault. Tell me what you mean by that, since you're hell-bent on telling me the whole story right now anyway."

"I was trying to get out the back door. Tobias wouldn't let me. I dropped the knife during the struggle so I didn't hurt him. But I did everything else in my power to get away, wriggled around, dropped to the floor, hit him, bent his fingers back . . . screaming the whole time for him to let me go." She took a deep breath. "He finally released me when we heard Amelia crying." Mia pressed her lips into a line. "She was watching us from halfway down the stairs."

"Then what?" I asked. "You went to Jimmy Ray's house?"

She nodded. "Tobias went to console Amelia while I put the knife in my back pocket and ran out the back door, climbed the fence, walked right up to Jimmy. He was sitting there smoking a cigarette on his patio, watching me with a smug fucking look on his face. I told him to take me, that he could do whatever he wanted to me sexually for the rest of his life if he'd stay away from Amelia. Told him I had dreams about him. Good ones—the erotic kind. I could see that turned him on. I made it sound like he'd corrupted me so bad as a kid that I thought my time with him was the good ol' days and that I hadn't been fucked that good since." Her eyes were glowing with something beyond hatred at the memory. "Truth is, I *was* corrupted. I guess I still am. But he was so fucked up and perverted, he bought what I said. Like me wanting him was the most natural thing in the world and he'd known all along that this would happen some day."

"Would you have done it?"

"You mean cut off his sad little pecker?—yeah."

"But you never got the chance."

"Nope."

"Walk me through what happened."

"I followed Jimmy into his kitchen and he left me there. Said it would be just a minute. I think he went to the bathroom. Probably to pop a Viagra or something, who knows? That's when I propped his screen door open with a brick, planning my getaway after I cut off his . . . manhood, if you can call it that. I wouldn't. When he came back to the kitchen, he sat in the chair where, you know, where he was found, and he said, 'you know what I like.' He always had me start that way. With oral. I got on my knees. Unbuttoned his pants and I was about to get the knife out of my back pocket. Then—"

She looked down at the table. Her cheeks were turning colors. "That axe chopped into Jimmy's neck. I'll never forget that sound or the feeling of his hot blood spraying me, hitting me like a bucket of blood had been thrown on me."

When she finally looked up at me, she said, "After that, there was like this . . . weird kind of ringing in my ears, like the sound you hear underwater. I can't explain it. Tobias was saying we needed to get the hell out of there but I couldn't get my legs to work. He tried to pick me up but I pushed him away. I don't know why. It was like I was trying to wake up from a bad dream. He said he'd heard a car pull into Jimmy's driveway, then he ran out the back leaving me there on the floor in front of Jimmy. I heard a car door slam outside and, I know it sounds stupid, but it finally clicked what was happening and I knew I needed to run. I ran out the back across the yard, then climbed over the chain-link fence."

"What about the brick you'd used to prop open Jimmy's screen door? Did you move it, or was that Tobias?"

"I . . . I think it had to've been me, but I don't know. I don't remember opening Jimmy's screen door on the way out, but I don't remember picking up the brick either, or for that matter, dropping it when I climbed the fence. I guess I did. I remember running toward my house. I was seeing red."

"Okay, fine. You're somewhere in your back yard now. What happened there?"

"It's pretty straightforward. You know the rest from the reports."

"Jimmy's son saw you going in your backdoor covered in blood and he went and caught you before you could get your clothes off and into the shower."

Mia nodded.

"The knife you took over to Jimmy's. Where'd it end up? There's nothing about it in the police reports."

"I dropped it in a pan soaking in the kitchen sink on my way to the bathroom. I . . . I didn't really think about it. I just did it."

"When the cops got there, they had their murder weapon already. Steak knife soaking in the sink at your house seemed irrelevant. Didn't mean a thing to them."

Mia nodded again. "Guess not."

"Do you know where Tobias got the axe?"

"It belonged to Annie's uncle. Tobias borrowed it to take out an old stump for me two days earlier. Two days before . . . before . . ."

"Before Jimmy was killed."

Mia made a face. "Uh-huh. Anyway, after Tobias got the stump out we messed around a little, more than just a little, and he forgot about the axe. I found it leaning against the house by the back door that evening. Two days later he came to pick up Amelia for Annie, but also to get his uncle's axe which I'd put down in the basement."

"You must have told Tobias where you'd put it for him to have found it so quickly."

Mia nodded. "Yeah. I told him he could pick it up any time, even if I wasn't home. I told him there was a spare key under the flowerpot on the porch."

I thought about Tobias's blood on the axe handle. Killing Jimmy wouldn't have done that. "Tobias wasn't wearing gloves when he took out the stump, was he?"

"No. It took him half an hour. His hands were blistered, bleeding a little. I wrapped them in gauze for him. We kissed.

One thing led to another. Like I said, we were together. It was nice."

I had the whole story. Not sure yet what I would be able to do with it. Then a thought occurred to me. "Tobias—does he look anything like Russ?"

"Your investigator guy?" She thought about that. "Maybe. A little. But I'd say he favors Annie more."

"What about Bigknife's statement?"

"What about it?"

"She told the DA you told her that you had a plan to have Jimmy killed with the axe."

"I never told her that. She's a liar. You said it yourself."

"What did you tell her? Anything?"

"I didn't tell her who the killer was, just that I went over there to cut Jimmy's dick off. Ran into one hell of an interruption before I could do it. That's it."

"You told her the truth."

"Yeah, but the truth wouldn't have gotten Bigknife out of trouble, would it?"

"No, probably not. From what you told me, the only crime you're guilty of is attempted aggravated battery."

"For attempting to cut off his—"

"Yeah. But the state has no idea what you were actually up to, so that crime isn't even on their radar."

Mia thought about that. "Doesn't seem like cutting off that guy's junk should be a crime anyway."

I smiled. "I know what you mean."

"I can't believe Bigknife would say I planned to kill Jimmy. I never told her anything like that."

"You were her ticket out of the big house. She probably read the news story about the prelim from jail and told the prosecutor what she wanted to hear."

Mia's eyes narrowed. "What a bitch."

A long moment of silence played out. Mia wouldn't look at me. I thought I knew why. Finally I said, "You're going to make me try this case, aren't you?"

She bit her lower lip. "Yeah, I'm sorry. I appreciate everything you've done so far but I just can't give them Tobias. I just can't. I feel like this is all my fault."

I looked at my box of Kung Pao Chicken. I'd heated it in the microwave when we got home but it was room temperature again. "I understand. My opinion, you should take the stand."

"Won't they ask me who killed Jimmy Ray?"

"Yeah."

"What happens when I don't answer?"

"If you take the stand to tell your side of the story, you lose the right to remain silent. The judge could put you in jail for contempt for not answering the prosecutor's questions."

"For how long?"

I shrugged. "No more than six months."

She nodded. "I could live with that."

"If the jury finds you guilty of first-degree murder, you'll be in prison for the rest of your life."

"I know. My eyes are wide open."

Someone knocked on the front door. I heard a key working the lock, then Mason cracked the door open and poked his head in. "Agent Gordon is here to see you."

As I'd expected. Caroline called me on the ride home and said it was urgent that I speak with her.

Mason held the door, Caroline stepped in and shut it behind her.

"We were just finishing up," I said.

"It's alright," Caroline said. "This is perfect. I'd like to speak with Ms. Delarosa too."

"About what?" I said.

Caroline sat at the head of the table, the three us forming a triangle.

"About the DA," Caroline said, fixing her eyes on Mia. "Do you know him?"

Mia shook her head. "Never met the man."

"What's going on?" I said.

Caroline frowned. "I went to Blaine Swartzmiller's office after our meeting this morning. Told him I wanted Duke's written report about his debriefing with Gutiérrez. Duke is Blaine's investigator. I also wanted the video or the audio of their meeting." She shrugged. "And Gutiérrez's written statement if they'd release it. Also his contact information and where they were hiding him. You know, the basics."

"And?"

"Blaine said he and Duke never met with the guy. Allegedly, Duke didn't even record the phone interview. I say allegedly because why the hell wouldn't he? According to Blaine and Duke—who I talked to over the phone—Gutiérrez refused to meet with them in person."

I felt my eyes narrow. "So they really have no idea who this guy is or where he was calling from?"

"That's not exactly true."

"Explain."

"Blaine said the calls came from Mexico. He showed me the office phone bill. Duke traced the number back to an address in Juárez." Her lips tightened. "A man named Jose Gutiérrez lived there with a woman, Illeana. The phone was in her name. I just spoke with the Chihuahua State Police Chief. Jose Gutiérrez went missing on August twenty-fourth and Illeana, the girlfriend, hasn't seen him since."

"The day of Keri's funeral," I said. "The day Blaine said Gutiérrez called."

Caroline's mouth twisted. "Blaine said he and you were friends in law school. Good friends, he said."

"We were. I wonder why he kept this information from me if he was just going to give it to you so easily."

"Not so easily. Actually, I had to work him over pretty good to get it." She half-shrugged. "That was after I blew by his assistant and walked into his office unannounced. What do you think he's up to?"

"Taking him at his word, he's using Gutiérrez, or someone claiming to be Gutiérrez, or maybe some fictitious Gutiérrez, to leverage Brown into testifying against Curtis for the murder of my parents, but he needs two other prosecutors to cooperate to make that happen."

"You think Blaine might not be talking to anyone at all? Just making up this whole thing about Gutiérrez?"

"Probably not if Duke's involved, but anything's possible. If Blaine can get this done, he's golden. He thinks I should sue Curtis for wrongful death. He thinks there's a pretty good chance I come out of this thing rich."

"So that's his motive? Make you rich? You believe that?"

I shook my head. "Nope. My getting rich would be a way to get me on board with what he wants to happen. I've known Blaine a long time. I think he's anxious to claim his part in nailing Curtis for political gain. Dean Curtis is the only ten-point buck in this neck of the woods. Blaine's got a bead on him, and he intends to take a shot."

"Yeah, that part's probably true, but I have the feeling there's more to it than that."

"You wanted to know if Mia knew Blaine," I said. "What's that got to do with anything?"

Caroline turned to Mia. "You really don't know the DA?"

She shook her head. "No, not at all."

Caroline didn't seem surprised. "How well do you know Emma Hicks?"

Mia shrugged and said, "We both worked for Ricky. I knew her name and said hi when we were like in the same room. That's about it."

"She ever talk to you about going on dates with the DA?" Caroline asked.

"We weren't being paid to talk. We were being paid to leave when the date was over and keep our mouths shut, so no."

I cut in with a question for Caroline. "This woman—Emma Hicks—she told you she'd been with Blaine? As in, Ricky was the go-between, to put it delicately."

Caroline closed one eye. "Ms. Hicks told me Blaine was one of her regulars. According to her, he went to her exclusively. Told her he loved her. Said he would leave his wife for her. He told her his wife was frigid. Said they'd have sex maybe once or twice a year, if he was lucky. She believed him—that he'd leave his wife for her." Caroline leaned back in her chair. "Long story short, I think I've come upon a better explanation as to why Blaine is pushing so hard to get Brown a deal."

With this new information, so did I. "If Blaine was a regular with one of Butler's girls, he's probably in Butler's business laptop as a john. That'd be the same laptop Brown's men were looking for a month ago when they tossed Butler's house and kicked the shit out of him. Maybe they found it after all and Brown is blackmailing Blaine with it now, which is why Blaine is so damn eager to make this deal."

Caroline nodded. "That's what I think, but there's something else. Brown is also one of Emma Hicks' regulars."

Interesting intersection. "So it's possible that Brown had Emma steal Butler's laptop when he couldn't get hold of it any other way, is that what you're saying?"

Caroline wrinkled her lip. "I put that to Emma. She denies it. Told me she doesn't know anything about Butler's laptop and that Brown has never mentioned it. For what it's worth, I believe her." She shrugged. "I just thought you might like to know that Brown is a current client of hers."

"Current, huh?"

Caroline nodded.

"I'm surprised he'd leave the house for a date at this point," I said. "Date being a euphemism."

She smiled. "He doesn't. She comes to him. His wife left him so he's there alone." Caroline grabbed one of three fortune cookies sitting on the table and held it up. "You mind? I haven't had lunch."

"Six calories? Knock yourself out."

She cracked the cookie and pulled out the fortune, dropped it on the table. "Kind of puts that meeting we had with the DA this morning in a whole new light, doesn't it?" She popped half the cookie into her mouth.

It sure did. I thought about what to do about it. "Gutiérrez—the man missing in Juárez. We should try to get a photo of him to show Brackeen. See if he recognizes him."

Caroline pulled out her phone and tapped the screen a few times, then showed me a photo of a Mexican man in his fifties.

"The chief in Juárez emailed me this photo of Gutiérrez thirty minutes ago. I sent it to Brackeen. He says it's him—the man he interviewed and knew as Jose Gutiérrez in '93."

I said, "At least we know Gutiérrez exists. Or existed. What the hell is going on?"

"Damned if I know." She pushed away from the table and stood. "I better get going."

I followed her to the door. She swung it open and paused, looking at me. "Maybe hold off on giving the prosecutors your blessing on granting Brown any kind of immunity until I can figure out if Blaine is being blackmailed and whether or not Gutiérrez is even still alive. If he isn't, then he's being used as a chess piece."

"He's a chess piece either way. Blaine is going to pressure me to hurry the hell up and ask Deb Walsh and Taylor Greer to give Brown whatever he wants to testify against Curtis."

"Damn right he will. And I think we know why."

"Yeah, but Blaine knows something about me too. He knows I want to know what happened to my mother, who was behind it and why." I shrugged. "My father too. Both of them. Makes it tempting to give Blaine what he wants."

"I know, but you should hold off on that until we know the score." She glanced in Mia's direction. "The DA make her an offer?"

"Yeah."

"A good one?" she asked Mia.

Mia nodded. "Pretty damn good."

Caroline pooched out her lips. "I'd take it sooner rather than later. I got a feeling the clock is ticking on the guy who's offering it."

After Caroline left, Mia stood and came around the table with her box of Lo mein. "I'm going to eat this in my room and think about all this."

"Let me know if you change your mind about the offer," I said. "Caroline's right. Things could change in a heartbeat."

Mia spotted something on the table, then snatched up Caroline's fortune and read it.

"What's it say?" I asked.

"'A dubious friend may be an enemy in disguise.'" She gave me a lopsided grin. "Maybe this is your fortune."

"Maybe it's yours."

"What do you mean?"

"Tobias—seems like he's willing to let you take the fall here."

She looked away. "That's on him. I'm not a snitch."

"You'd go to prison for the rest of your life to protect him. Friends like that are hard to come by."

She cupped my cheek in her hand. "I'll be your friend too."

"Take the deal, Mia. Don't even think about it. Just take it. Let's go talk to the DA right now. Aren't you tired of losing?"

She took her hand off my cheek. "Yes, but I'd rather be a friend worth having."

She turned and went into the kitchen, then out the back door on her way to her room at the next-door neighbor's house. I heard her talking to one of Mason's men before the door closed.

47

I WAS LIFTING weights in Pops' basement on a Thursday afternoon when Rashonda called and told me a man claiming to be Jose Gutiérrez was on the line to speak with me. I was already out of breath, but the shocking news made catching it even harder. I turned off the blaring music and sat on an incline bench, my eyes burning with sweat.

"What's the caller ID say?" I asked Rashonda.

"The area code is local. No name. He's hard to understand, not because of his accent, but because his voice is awfully hoarse."

I'd briefed Rashonda on the latest developments regarding Gutiérrez, so she knew he was a Mexican national living in Juárez and that he'd been missing since Keri's funeral. I told her to patch the call through.

When she did, I said, "This is Benjamin Joel."

"You the attorney?" came a gravelly voice.

"That's right."

"Paula Joel's kid?"

"Yessir."

"I knew your father, and to some extent, your mother."

"That's what I hear."

"We need to talk."

"I agree. But it needs to be in person."

"That's what I want. Go underneath the wooden walk bridge that crosses the creek in Sellers Park. The one closest to the tennis courts. Look under the biggest rock on the west bank. You'll find a piece of notebook paper with a phone number written on it. Then call the number on a burner."

He evidently thought my office line or cell phone might be tapped, which wasn't all that farfetched, especially since I'd made it public knowledge that a wanted murderer named Elias Matusak had once contacted me on my office line.

I said, "I have a new burner ready to go. Never been used."

"Perfect. You're two blocks from Sellers Park. Call that number in twenty minutes. And Mr. Joel?"

"Yeah."

"No cops. I don't trust cops and neither should you. If I see one cop anywhere around you, you'll never hear from me again and you'll never know what happened to your father. I don't know how your mother died, but I know who wanted her dead, and why."

Before I could say another word—before I could get some idea whether or not this really was Gutiérrez—he hung up.

On my way up the basement stairs I called Mason and told him about the call and the bridge I was going to less than a quarter mile away.

"I'm on the front porch," he said. "Can I come in?"

"Yeah."

In my bedroom, I changed clothes, strapped on a Kevlar vest, and clipped a Glock inside the waistband of my jeans. Mason was in the dining room when I got there. He gave me the once-over and said, "This could be a ruse to get you away from the house and alone to take you out. Could be a sniper set up nearby. Also, the rock could be booby trapped with an IED."

"Possible. Gutiérrez has been missing from his home in Juárez for over two weeks."

Mason thought about that. "Gutiérrez might not be dead, but in this situation we have to assume he is. We should be braced for something big. Chief Bell needs to know about this."

"No. The guy said no cops."

"What the hell else would he say? This guy is just a voice on a phone. If he's bad, he's using your curiosity about your parents against you."

"I don't have a lot of time here. Do you still have the key Chief Bell gave you to the old junior high?"

I was referring to a building abandoned twenty years ago one block northeast of Pops' house that backed up to Sellers Park—three stories of crumbling red brick and broken windows. It was the tallest structure in the area.

"Yeah, but—"

"Think someone can cover me from the roof without being seen?"

"Sure. Actually, I have a guy up there now."

"Outlook, or does he have a rifle?"

"Barrets 82A1 sniper rifle."

I smiled. "Put him on the east side with a view of the park."

"Done." Then, "Why don't I go to the bridge? I don't have any kids who'll miss me if things go south."

"The guy said no cops."

"I'm not a cop."

"This guy won't know that."

"If he's got a sniper somewhere, or if someone's waiting under the bridge, you'll be on your own."

I grabbed the key to my truck. "Then I'll make myself a hard target to hit. Tell your guy to stay as invisible as possible and still cover me. I'm on my way."

I went out back to my pickup. Cruised south past my kids' school which was locked up tight like all schools were these days, or should be. The school resource officer was retired military—an armed guard waiting behind locked doors to greet anyone buzzed into the building after school started.

I turned left on Seventh Street, went two blocks and was in the park where the road veered left, turned to gravel, and ran parallel to the creek with the bridge. I went off the road and onto the grass, gunned the engine and got to the bridge as fast I could, slammed on the brakes, and bailed out on the passenger side, dropping down the creek bank into high grass with my Glock out and ready. No one under the bridge and I could see a piece of notebook paper half under a rock. I grabbed it and headed back to the house.

A minute later I was in the dining room with Mason. I called the number on the paper. The guy with the gravelly voice picked up on the first ring and said, "Get in your truck and drive around. I'll call with directions in ten minutes."

"Drive around? Where to?"

"Nowhere, anywhere. Just do it."

"Okay, but I'll bring my security guys with me. They aren't cops. They work for me. If you are who you say you are, that shouldn't be a problem."

"I know your wife was killed and you have to be cautious. Saw it on the news. And I read on the Internet what you filed with the Wichita court, so yeah, bring your guys. No cops."

"Did you call the DA? Blaine Swartzmiller?"

A moment of silence. Then, "Yes."

"When?"

"Couple weeks ago."

"Where from?"

"Juárez."

"How'd you get here?"

"Long story."

"I need to hear it."

"Not now you don't."

I wanted to keep him talking—see if I could figure out if this was the same guy who'd called Blaine and said he was Gutiérrez. "The DA is a friend of mine. He told me what you told him."

Silence again. Longer this time. Maybe he'd hung up.

I said, "How about you tell me what you told him, see if the two stories are the same."

He groaned. "We don't need to go through all that. I'll send you proof I'm Gutiérrez—"

"We *do* need to go through it. What did you tell the DA?"

"Told him I heard gunshots behind The Rabbit Hole and went to check it out because I knew Paco was back there. I saw Curtis and Brown dragging him off the front porch of the cabin behind the bar. He was dead. Obviously dead. I also told the DA I wasn't going to meet with cops, or the guy he put in charge of my safety."

"The DA's investigator?"

"Yeah, Duke was his name. Duke Shinliver. I looked him up. Guy used to be a cop. Gave me a bad vibe over the phone so I never met with him."

"Okay, so why didn't you call me?"

"That's what I'm doing."

"Yeah, but . . ."

"You want to know why I waited so long?"

"Of course."

"This will all make sense as soon as you see me. Bring your security, but you won't need them. I'll be alone. But no cops. Your burner will send and receive texts, right?"

"Yeah."

"I'll text you a selfie when this call is over. You can forward it to your grandfather's investigator, Brackeen, to confirm it's me if you want."

"I already know what you look like, but yeah, send the pic."

Silence yet again. Then, "How do you know what I look like?"

Caroline had shown me a photo she'd received from the Chihuahua State Police Chief. "You've been missing since August twenty-fourth. Some of us want to find you alive, so we made it our business to know what you look like."

"I see. What will you and your security guys be driving?"

I looked at Mason. "Black Tahoe?"

Mason nodded.

"Black Chevy Tahoe," I said to Gutiérrez.

"Get in the Tahoe and start driving around. I'll send a selfie now. I'll call back in ten minutes with more directions. If I see a cop—"

"You won't."

We ended the call and a minute later the phone dinged with a text.

Mason shook his head. "I don't like this."

I pulled up the selfie of an unsmiling, leathery old Hispanic. He was outdoors. Trees behind him. The weather in the photo matched the weather today. Bright and sunny, no visible clouds.

Mason gazed at the picture. "Is that Gutiérrez?"

"Yeah."

I checked the time stamp on the photo. Pointed it out to Mason.

He nodded. "Okay, so it's likely he just took the photo. I still don't like it. Call him back. Tell him you'll meet him here. At your house."

I thought about that, didn't think Gutiérrez would go for it.

Mason noticed my hesitation and said, "This guy hid his phone number close to your house, so he already knows where you live if that's what you're worried about."

"I'm not. I just think we better do it his way, at least for a while. You'll be the one driving. If you don't like where he's leading us, you can call it off."

I had several phones in my briefcase. I dug out the one I'd been using to talk to Caroline Gordon and called Chief Bell.

Worry lines formed in Mason's forehead.

When Bell answered, I said, "Chief, this is Ben. Need a favor. Something just came up and I have to leave the house. I'm taking Mason and his men with me. You mind seeing that my kids get home safe from school and stay that way until we get back?"

"Yeah, Ben, anything you need. I'll put some officers on it."

"Pops is at the doctor's office right now, but he'll be back in an hour or so."

"How long you figure you'll need us?"

"No more than three hours, I hope."

"What's going on? Something I need to know about?"

"There's a meeting I have to go to, that's all. Better safe than sorry."

Silence, then: "Taking Mason and his men with you. Can't say I like the sound of that, but I'm trying not to over-react here. You want a couple of my guys to go along with you? Might not be a bad idea."

No cops, but I couldn't tell him that.

"Not needed," I said. "Might turn into a pizza run for Mason and his crew."

"Which is why you called me. Pizza run."

"And beer, Chief. Look, I gotta go. I'll be in touch."

I ended the call.

Mason grinned. "Pizza run and beer. Wish I'd thought of that. You buying?"

48

I WAS IN the passenger seat of Mason's Tahoe with a phone, listening to the man I hoped was Gutiérrez give us directions. We'd gone west on Highway 160, then north through Conway Springs. Several turns later we were on backroads near a reservoir on the western edge of Sedgwick County—Undersheriff Brown's territory. I didn't like that and the scowl on Mason's face indicated that he didn't either. We'd been on the road maybe an hour and it was mid-afternoon. Mason drove and three of his men were behind me with AR-15s. All of us wore body armor and were sweating despite the air conditioner running full blast.

"You figure out where you're going yet," said Gutiérrez. At least I hoped it was him.

"Yeah, think so—what used to be The Rabbit Hole."

Mason glanced over at me. Concerned.

"That's right," Gutiérrez said. "Ever been there?"

"No, but I have a general idea where it is. Or was."

"You should be getting close now. In a quarter mile or so there's a small opening in the wall of trees to your right. Turn in there. You'll see the place."

"Why don't you meet us out front?"

"I can't."

"You can't? That doesn't make sense."

"It will when you see me," Gutiérrez said. "I'm sitting on the porch of the cabin behind the bar. This is where Paco was killed. I have to get off the phone now."

"No, stay on the line—"

The call ended.

"Sonofa—" I speed-dialed him. No answer.

Mason slammed on the brakes. Dust rose from the gravel road, obstructing our view for several seconds, then the cloud dissipated. I couldn't see a gap in the trees and there was no sign of the bar.

I tried to exit the Tahoe, but it was locked. Mason had activated the child-safety feature. I looked over at him and he grinned at me.

"Let me out," I said.

"No."

He looked back at his men. "Go see what kind of a jackpot we're headed into."

"We can't," said the one named Roger. "We're locked in."

"Well," Mason said, "when I unlock the door, bail out." Mason eyeballed me. "Stay put. I still have big plans for you when this is over."

"What about us?" Roger said. "Don't you have big plans for us too?"

"Yeah, don't get shot. Now get out." He pressed a button and the locks slammed open.

The three of them piled out, pushed the doors shut without making noise, then disappeared into the trees. Mason hit the child-safety lock, then smiled at me.

Ten minutes later we were still stopped, silent, listening with the windows open, when Mason's phone rang. He answered and Roger's hushed voice came through via Bluetooth. "Uh, there's a guy on the porch of what's left of a cabin alright, but he's tied to a chair. Hands and all, so there must be someone else in the area. You're not still sitting where we left you, are you?"

Mason put the Tahoe in drive and inched us up to five miles an hour. "We were. Movin' now."

"What's he look like?" I said to Roger.

"It's the guy in the photo you gave us—Gutiérrez."

My burner rang—the one I'd been using to talk to Gutiérrez the last hour. I showed the screen to Mason. "Gutiérrez's number. With his hands tied to a chair?"

To Roger, Mason said, "Gutiérrez isn't on his phone right now, is he?"

"Negative. Like I said, his hands are tied. He's just sitting there."

I put the call on speaker. "Who is this?"

"Don't come for me."

Odd way to start a conversation, but I recognized the voice and the crazy in it. Matusak. Probably on the move, breathing heavily while talking on the phone to me like he had been moments before he killed the assassin outside Brackeen's house in College Hill.

"Elias Matusak," I said, letting Mason and Roger know who we were dealing with. "How you been, big guy?"

"Shut up. If you get the sheriff involved, well, you know how that will end for Gutiérrez."

"No cops," I said. "Got it. How'd you get him here?"

"Swam into Mexico. Found him. Brought him back."

Mason smiled, shook his head, and mouthed *Swam into Mexico?*

Matusak said, "Have you reached Gutiérrez yet?"

"Working on it," I said, noting that if Matusak really didn't know the answer to his question, he didn't have eyes on the cabin. Could be a ruse, but it sounded like he was on foot, walking fast or running.

"I brought him here for you," Matusak said. "You're the only one I trust with him."

"What do you mean?"

No answer. He'd ended the call.

Mason gunned the engine, found the gap in the trees, and pulled into a weed-infested gravel lot, stopped in front of a weather-beaten building that looked more like an abandoned bait shop than a bar. On slats above a doorless entry was a sign with faded words: THE RABBIT HOLE. A vandal had hit the sign with spray paint to make it read, THE RABBIT's AssHOLE.

Mason put the Tahoe in park and said to Roger, "You clear the bar? We're coming through."

"Yes, but it's been a few minutes. Dark in there. Keep your eyes open."

Mason turned to me. "Matusak wouldn't have gone to all the trouble of bringing Gutiérrez to you if he wanted you dead, would he?"

I unholstered my Glock. "No, but when crazy and reason paddle the same direction, it's by accident, so don't let your guard down."

"It's never down." He pulled a matte black AK from the backseat. "Legend has it you can handle a firearm."

"Let's hope you don't get to see that for yourself."

His lips twisted. "Not sure how to take that. Let's go."

* * *

The bar was clear. We found Gutiérrez on the sagging front porch of the cabin as we'd been told. I checked him for weapons, then untied him while Mason watched the woods around us. The cabin was at the bottom of a bowl. A narrow winding stone path down the hill through the trees from the bar was damn near invisible from the porch.

Gutiérrez—a rawboned, ponytailed old doper in dirty Levi's and a T-shirt—stood up from the chair and rubbed his wrists. "And I thought this fuckin' place gave me nightmares before."

The cabin's door was off its hinges. Gutiérrez and I went inside. Mason kept watch from the doorway. Sunlight filtered through the canopy of trees and a gaping hole in the roof.

Gutiérrez gazed at me. "You look like Paco."

"I keep hearing that."

"He was a good friend. I wasn't, but he was."

"Glad to hear it. Never knew the man."

Gutiérrez regarded me. "I never knew my father either."

Silence. Finally I said, "Maybe you just tell me what happened back here in '93."

He nodded. Looked like he was deciding where to begin.

"Actually," I said, "tell me how Matusak got you here from Mexico."

He took a deep breath. "That crazy sonofabitch was sitting in my girlfriend's house waiting for me with a shotgun when I came in. He told me to sit and tell him what happened to your parents behind this bar. I didn't know this guy from Adam, or how he knew you. I thought maybe he was sent by Dean Curtis so I told him I didn't know what he was talking about. He smiled at that, then told me who he was in no uncertain terms."

"The second-coming of Christ?" I said.

Gutiérrez nodded. "That's when I knew he was the guy in the news who'd split from Curtis. He told me he'd kill me if I lied to him again. I didn't know how much he knew. So I told him what happened to Paco—actually what my wife told me she saw."

"What your wife saw?' I said, thinking maybe he'd been in Mexico so long that his English had gotten rusty and he'd misspoken.

"My wife, yeah. Paco went after Brown and Curtis for raping your mother and Curtis killed him. My wife saw that part of it too—the rape."

"Hold on, there's a lot to unpack here. First question—are you telling me that you didn't see Brown and Curtis dragging Paco's body off the porch of this cabin yourself? That your wife witnessed it and what you told the DA you got secondhand from your wife?"

"That's exactly what I'm telling you."

Mason had taken one step into the cabin. Before I could ask my next question he chimed in. "You have a wife *and* a girlfriend?"

"I had a wife. She died in '06. Breast cancer."

"What was her name?" I asked.

"Maria Delgado."

"So Maria Delgado saw Brown and Curtis dragging Paco's dead body off that porch right there and told you about it," I said.

"That's right."

"Brackeen spoke to a few people back in '93, but Maria wasn't one of them."

"Right. She saw those cops kill Paco so she ran as far and as fast as she could, went back to Mexico. We weren't married then. Weren't even an item, but she knew Paco and your mother. She and I didn't get married until '01. I didn't even know she was still alive or what she saw happen back here in '93 until years later when I ran into her at my cousin's wedding." He shrugged. "That's when we hooked up."

I shook my head. Nothing was adding up. "The way the DA tells it, you saw Brown and Curtis carrying Paco's dead body with your own eyes."

"Makes sense, cuz that's what I told him."

"Why the hell would you do that if it wasn't true?"

"Because when I finished telling Matusak what Maria told me, he suggested some changes to the story. Even wrote it down for me. Drilled it into my head. Biggest change he suggested was that I personally saw everything so I'd be able to be a witness in court. Said what Maria witnessed that night died with her as far as the law was concerned. Then he made me call the DA and tell it to him that way, with Maria completely left out of it. Told me to tell the DA that I wouldn't come forward and testify because I was scared. He told me playing hard to get with the DA at first would make me seem more believable. He said he'd help me lay low for a while until we saw what the DA did with the information I'd given him. Matusak wanted to make sure the DA was clean before he would allow me to give myself over to him. He thought maybe Curtis and Brown had gotten to the DA. Matusak was all over the place, but he was also kind of brilliant. Scary brilliant."

"Amazingly, Matusak is right about you not being able to testify about what Maria told you," I said. "It's inadmissible hearsay."

Mason chimed in. "Guy thinks he's Jesus, then a lawyer. Trajectory he's on, he'll think he's the second coming of Hitler by nightfall."

Gutiérrez half smiled. "Joke all you want. I'm not a religious man, but it seems like Matusak has been around longer than the rest of us. A lot longer if you know what I mean."

"You think he's Jesus?" Mason said, offended.

"Fuck no, something else. Something else, bad."

"You can tell me what you mean by that later," I said. "Right now I want you to tell me what you personally saw happen back here the night Paco was murdered. You, not Maria. I want the absolute truth."

"I was here." He nodded in the direction of the bar. "Not here in the cabin, but up there in the bar. Sometimes I did coke in a backroom. Never down here."

My stomach dropped.

He read me. "You may like Matusak's version better. Maybe you want me to start over?"

"No, stick to the truth."

"I saw nothing."

"Nothing?"

"Not back here I didn't. I was up at the bar. Paco and I were drinking. And I never did know where the hell your mother was that night. That's how it was with us back then."

"Tell me about your last night with Paco."

Gutiérrez nodded toward the bar. "Paco and I were drinking up there, like I said. We had our own booth. Played some darts. Five beers in, Paco tells me he's supposed to have some big come-to-Jesus meeting with Brown and Curtis behind the bar later. They'd been knocking his dick in the dirt, harassing him, trying to get more information out of him about the child sex trafficking ring they thought was doing business around here. But Paco had told them everything he knew, and he wasn't deep enough into the cartel's business to get them any more information. He was worried Brown and Curtis were going to arrest him and your mother because they sold coke to Brown when he was undercover. That's what Brown had on him. That's why he did what they told him.

"A few more beers into the night, Brown and Curtis show up dressed like a couple of scuzz buckets, make eye contact with Paco, then go out the back door. Paco followed. I was worried, but he came back a few minutes later. It was loud as shit in the bar and I was pretty well hammered, on more than just the booze, but Paco gave the impression everything was copacetic with Brown and Curtis. After that, I basically lost track of Paco."

"Lost track," I said. "Sounds like you were partying pretty hard."

"Yeah, and I was distracted, chasing pussy."

Nice.

"Is that how you refer to your eventual wife—Maria?"

He shook his head. "No. She had her eyes on some other guy that night. Anyway, I was in a back room with the door locked—what we called the VIP room—doing a line of blow with a stripper some guy had brought with him when I heard gunshots."

"What guy?"

"Some guy who owned a strip joint. He brought girls that worked for him into The Rabbit Hole all the time. Probably made him feel like a big deal. Life of the party. Like that. The girls would pretty much ignore him when they got there, though."

"This strip club guy—was his name Rick Butler?"

Gutiérrez thought about that. "If I ever knew his name I forgot it. I just knew the stripper I was with came with the guy who owned a strip club."

"What'd he look like?"

Gutiérrez laughed. "Fat as fuck. Just gross. I can't tell you any more than that because I couldn't stand looking at the sonofabitch any longer than I had to, know what I mean?"

I nodded. "Sure. But fatso was here the night Paco went missing?"

"Sure was."

The guy was probably Rick Butler, but I wasn't getting any more on the subject out of Gutiérrez, so I moved on. "You said you heard gunshots. I thought it was loud in the bar?"

"Between juke box songs not so much, so maybe that was it, I dunno, but the VIP room was basically a large pantry in

the back of the building, so there weren't any speakers in there
. . . which maybe explains how I heard 'em. All I can tell you
is that I heard fuckin' gunshots, okay?"

"Fine, you heard gunshots," I said. "Then what
happened?"

"I went into the bar, looked around, then checked the
restroom. No Paco. I looked out the front door and saw his car
still there. I remember thinking, *they fuckin' killed him*. Then
thinking I was just being paranoid because of the blow. But
the paranoia finally won out and I took off. Haven't been back
since. Until now."

"Someone called 911 about the shots. I heard the
recording." I looked into his eyes. "The caller sounds a lot like
you."

He looked down at his hands. "It was. I started to go out
back to see about Paco, then I saw a pay phone on the wall.
Fuck it, what was I gonna do? I didn't have a gun and even if
I did, I was all fucked up. I made the call and took off."

"See or hear anything else firsthand?"

"No. What I just told you is all of it."

"Okay. Exactly what did Maria tell you?"

"She was outside squatting in the trees because some girl
told her a pervert had put cameras in the ladies' room. I mean,
shit, in that place it was probably true. Fuckin' place
should've been called the Rat Hole. Anyway, she heard
screaming, got curious and went down the hill through the
trees. Saw Brown and Curtis dragging your mother into this
old cabin. Got close enough to see them throw her on a
mattress on the floor. Those two didn't even bother closing
the door. Brown was on her first. Maria saw they had guns,
and even if they didn't, there were two of them, nothing she
could do and she knew they were cops. So there she was,
behind a tree watching, paralyzed with fear, until Brown
stood, zipped up and went up the hill toward the bar. When
Curtis shut the cabin door, Maria went up to the bar looking
for me and Paco. We put it together later that I must've been
. . ."

He pressed his lips together. "I told Maria I was in the restroom but I was actually in the backroom with the stripper like I told you. Anyway, Maria found Paco, told him what she saw and he flew out the back door of the bar. Ran down the rock path you can still kind of see out there. Had his gun out ready to kill. When he realized Maria was following him, he told her to go back to the bar. She went back up the hill a ways, but got off the path and stayed in the trees and watched as Paco went up on the porch. Curtis must've locked the door, because Paco tried to open it, then picked up a rock and busted out the window."

Gutiérrez pointed at the opening near the front door—the cabin's only window frame. "That one right there. Paco was popping the remaining pieces of glass out of that window with the butt of his pistol when Curtis opened the door and shot him point blank in the chest and killed him. Brown must've heard the shot because he was there within half a minute. For a few seconds Maria watched him and Curtis trying to hold their shit together, then she ran. I never saw her again until my cousin's wedding."

"After Maria told you what happened, why didn't you tell someone?"

"Both of us left our friends for dead. Just left them there. That's not the kind of thing you want to admit. Even to yourself. And anyway, what did it matter? Where I'm from, you can't fight lawmen like this. You can't fight them here, our word against theirs. All you can do is run . . . stay off their radar. Look what they did to that cop that was sent to the scene."

"Officer Knudson. When he showed up that night it gave my mother a chance to slip away."

"But they got her later, didn't they?"

"Yes. Yes they did."

Silence.

So much of what Gutiérrez said and how he'd gotten here still bothered me. "Explain to me again why you lied to the DA and his investigator over the phone."

"That freak show, Matusak, told me I had to keep things simple for the DA. That I saw Brown and Curtis dragging Paco's body off the cabin's porch. He said these guys would never be brought to justice if I didn't." Gutiérrez frowned. "He also had a gun to my head during my call with the DA in case I forgot my lines."

"So you lied to the DA, saying you were an eyewitness. That was all Matusak's idea?"

"Yeah." Gutiérrez studied my face. "The news says you talked to this guy on the phone. What do you make of him?"

I shrugged. "He's mentally ill—belongs in a state security hospital."

"Maybe so, but he's very smart, or like I said, maybe he's just been around longer than us."

"That's the second time you've said he's smart and hinted that maybe he's a . . . what? Some kind of demon spirit?"

Gutiérrez gazed at me for a long moment. "You should have seen us crossing the border. He knew the routes better than any coyote I ever used. Like he'd done it a hundred times. More. Maybe not a demon spirit, but the guy seems to know a lot of shit he shouldn't, you know what I mean?"

"Maybe he went back and forth to Mexico for Curtis. Smuggling woman and children." I shrugged. "That could explain it."

"Could be. How else would he know?" Gutiérrez glared at me like the answer to his own seemingly rhetorical question bothered him. "There's lots of shit about him I can't explain. His Spanish is better than mine. As good as any Mexican native. Of all the things I've read about this guy, there's no explanation for that, except, like I said, that he's been possessed by something that's been around a hell of a lot longer than the rest of us."

At the word "possessed," Mason's face took on a look— equal parts disbelief, disgust, and more disgust. He looked away, as if the trees outside were more interesting than what he was hearing.

"How'd he get you to Kansas?" I asked.

"Pickup. Backroads. Had containers full of gas in the bed of a truck."

Before I realized what I was doing, I'd sat down on the warped floorboards and leaned back against the wall. Full-on autopilot. I must've needed to sit.

"You okay, Ben?" Mason said.

I closed my eyes. It felt like I was living one tic behind the present. Thinking one tic ahead was useful, but one tic behind was as useless as Jose Gutiérrez's inadmissible testimony.

"If you want me to continue to lie to the DA like Matusak made me do, Mr. Joel, I will. You deserve justice. Paco and your mother deserve justice."

I pulled my legs into my chest. Wrapped my arms around them and tried to imagine the scene here twenty-eight years ago. When I opened my eyes, I said, "We can't let the DA or anybody else know you're in Kansas. At least for a while. That okay with you?"

He nodded.

I held his gaze. "It's not for me to tell you what story to go with when the time comes. I'm not your attorney and I'm not your maker."

Gutiérrez looked around the cabin, then shrugged. "Where am I gonna stay until then?"

"We'll figure it out on the way back to Worthington," I said. "You hungry?"

Gutiérrez licked his dry, cracked lips. "Never been so damn hungry in all my life."

* * *

Mason took us home via Highway 54 through Wichita, where we grabbed takeout from Ziggy's Pizza. On top of feeding everyone in the Tahoe, I had two Classic Ziggys and a Big Time Pepperoni pizza to take home to Chief Bell and his men. Our second stop was the Sky Palace Motel on the east edge of Worthington next to the meat packing plant. Gutiérrez asked for a nose plug, but instead was given a new burner phone, bottles of water, and a firm admonition to stay put in his room.

Mason gave him a number to call if he needed anything other than a nose plug, which he said with a grin. Before nightfall, Mason promised to stop by with groceries and the booze Gutiérrez had requested.

It was almost five o'clock when we finally arrived home. I'd already removed the Kevlar when I gave Chief Bell the pizzas and thanked him for his help.

"I'll be damned," he said. "You went for pizza after all."

"Support your local police."

He laughed. "Got that right."

I found Pops hovering over the stove in the kitchen making spaghetti sauce.

"Beer in the fridge," he said, without turning around. "Grab me one, would ya?"

I pulled out two beers and set one on the counter next to Pops. I popped the top and took a pull. My kids were being loud in their room. Not fighting. Just loud.

"What's going on in there?"

"I got 'em one of those new PlayStation 5s and a TV this morning. They're playing some game called Madden." He shook his head. "Something like that anyway. Football video game."

"Sounds expensive."

He waved that away. "You do any good today?"

"Hard to say. Probably."

He turned and faced me.

I said, "You want to hear what Brown and Curtis did to your daughter?"

He picked up his beer. Popped the top. "No." He took a long pull, then another, then made a face. "Okay, tell me."

After I told him what Gutiérrez said, he set his empty beer can on the counter, opened the liquor cabinet, and pulled out a brand-new bottle of Old Forester and cracked the seal.

"Want some?"

I shook my head. "Think that'll help?"

"Won't hurt."

"I'm gonna go wash up for dinner."

Pops was pouring a shot when I left. In my bedroom I called Geronimo.

He picked up on the third ring.

"I need a favor," I said.

"Thought we were even."

"Not even close."

49

CARMEN DELAROSA PRETENDED to inspect a carton of organic blueberries in the produce aisle at a Whole Foods Market in Wichita. She had her eye on a skinny blonde in booty shorts who had her back to Carmen, inspecting the zucchini. A man beside the blonde picked up a red onion and slowly moved on, taking one last look at her backside as he did.

Carmen moved in. "Hey, blondie, what's your secret for looking so good?"

The blonde looked up, startled at first, then something like recognition registered on her face.

Carmen smiled and gestured toward the zucchini. "Let me guess—cocaine and veggies for dinner tonight?"

The blonde's eyes narrowed.

Carmen winked. "Your name is Emma, last name Hicks if I remember right."

Emma nodded. "Yeah, you look familiar, but I can't—"

"Mia's older sister, Carmen."

"That's right. I met you at . . . at . . ."

"My boyfriend's New Year's Eve party a couple years ago. You remember Geronimo?"

Emma nodded unconvincingly.

"We just got engaged," Carmen said, showing her the huge rock on her finger.

Emma gazed at it. Impressed.

"How you been doing?" Carmen asked.

"Fine, I guess."

They gave each other forced smiles, polite and meaningless.

Emma looked away for an instant. "I'm sorry about your sister."

"Yeah, me too. It's been hard."

"I can't imagine."

Carmen took another half-step into Emma's personal space. "Maybe there's something you can do to help."

Emma flinched slightly. "Um, I don't know what. I mean, I wish I could, but—"

"You think I ran into you here by accident? I didn't. I followed you. I want something."

"What?" Then, something hit her. "You want me to talk to the DA about Mia's case."

"Oh, do you know him?" Carmen said, secretly enjoying the moment.

Emma broke eye contact. "Oh, well, I thought that's what you were talking about. It seemed like you knew. I mean, the way you—"

"Knew what, exactly?"

Emma shook her head as if to reset her thoughts. "I'm confused. What do you think I can do to help Mia?"

"When do you see Undersheriff Brown again?"

Emma's face lost color. "Who says I . . . that I see him?"

Carmen laughed. "C'mon, girl. Don't play games with me."

Emma looked around furtively. "Okay, yes, I do. I'll see him tonight. I've seen him every night since his wife left."

"Good."

"It's *not* good. I can't get away from him. I feel like I'm being dragged through hell."

"I'm going to help you with that."

50

Friday night, September 17

CLINT BROWN CAME out of the master bath with wet hair and a big towel wrapped around his paunch. Emma Hicks watched him from the bed in a white tie top and skimpy red plaid skirt as he went to the liquor cabinet.

"What're you drinking tonight?" he said, his back to Emma.

"Glenlivet. Neat this time. I want to taste it."

Brown pulled two tumblers from the cabinet and set them on the bar. "Like the sound of that." He poured the Glenlivet, then put some ice in the other tumbler. Poured Wild Turkey over the ice like he always did.

He handed Emma her drink. Took a healthy pull from his and pointed at the large screen TV on the wall. "What are we watching? Lady's choice."

"Something nasty. The nastier the better."

Brown smiled, admiring the naughty schoolgirl outfit. "You're really somethin' tonight."

She took a sip of Glenlivet. Pretended to like it. She was good at pretending. "I work for tips. Pun intended."

Brown laughed, grabbed the remote, turned on the TV, and scrolled through some titles: *Milfs Exposed*, *Titanic Orgy*, *Schoolgirls in Heat*. Went with *Schoolgirls*, naturally, then ducked into the master bath with his drink. Came out in a terry cloth robe with the pistol he always carried to check out the cab and trunk of her Camry for unwanted guests whenever he met her in the garage. He set the pistol on the nightstand and fell heavily onto the bed next to Emma. He pointed the remote, hit play, and turned up the sound of the trailer—mostly women moaning in mock ecstasy. He took another sip of the Wild Turkey—gave a little moan of satisfaction.

Emma glanced at him.

He held up his drink. "Burns going down, just the way I like it."

Fifteen minutes later Brown finished his bourbon and set the tumbler on the nightstand. He took Emma's drink, tossed back the last of the Glenlivet, set her glass next to his, then rolled over and clumsily fell on top of Emma.

She lay there staring at herself in the mirror above the bed as he floundered to pick himself up. She could feel his hot breath on her cleavage. "You alright?" she said.

"I dunno," came the reply, a little slurred.

"Didn't you just get Covid a week ago?"

She sounded funny to Brown, but it was probably because his left ear was pressed against her chest. Then again, he felt wonky. What the hell was happening? He'd lost the last three seconds. Five maybe. He didn't know for sure. He rolled off her, seemed to be alright at the moment, sort of, so he got to his feet carefully.

"Yeah, I had it," he slurred, "but, uh, my symptoms were, uh, mild." He swayed, sagged to the floor, then sat up, shook his head, and tried to get his eyes to focus. Emma was saying something, but the words echoed and he couldn't make them out. She got out of bed and picked up the drinks. He tried to talk but no words came out. Just garbled sounds. He'd already forgotten what he was trying to say. He tried to watch her walk away but her image swam in and out of focus.

*   *   *

Emma shut off the TV and looked back in time to see Brown's head hit the carpet with a dull thud, then she went to the sink, dumped the whiskey, washed the tumblers, and ran hot water over the brown ice until it melted.

She placed the tumblers back on the bar and gave Brown another look. Then she put the bottle of Wild Turkey into a large purse, pulled out a phone and called Geronimo. He'd provided the roofies—crushed up powder—except he called it Mexican Valium which made her smile. Whatever the name, it damn sure did the trick.

Geronimo answered.

"It's done," Emma said.

"Security cameras off?"

She stepped over Brown and clicked through various views of the premises on the monitor by the bed, including the one of the front gate where there hadn't been any guards for three days. Brown had told her his bitch wife had drained his bank accounts and filed for divorce and the sheriff had finally folded to public pressure, putting Brown on unpaid leave and pulling his publicly funded security team.

"The cameras are on, but not recording, just like I told you they'd be. He doesn't record when I'm here. I'll open the gate."

51

Thirty days ago I'd been to Clint Brown's home under much different circumstances.

This time I had Mason and Roger with me. Also, Geronimo. For all Emma would know, we worked for him. I hoped to find Rick Butler's laptop, and I had rough idea of how I wanted to handle Brown, rough being the operative word. Other than that my plan was fluid. God only knew what we might find.

We came in through the gate Emma had opened for us and parked in a five-car garage next to her Camry. Mason and Roger split up to clear Brown's marble palace and search the place while Geronimo and I hiked up Brown's grand stairway on our way to the master bedroom, which Emma said served as Brown's panic room—three-inch-thick steel door, walls reinforced with steel sheathing, gun safe and escape hatch in the walk-in closet. All of us carried AR-15s and were dressed the same: combat boots, tactical shooting gloves, ski masks. Emma had said the cameras weren't recording, but we were guarding against Brown having a second system set up. We didn't want to take any chances that our faces would be caught on tape. For Mason, Roger, and I, there was another reason for the masks. We didn't want Emma to be able to recognize us when this was over.

Geronimo and I found Emma in the master bedroom. Her teeth were clenched and she was sitting on the edge of a wingback chair with a Sig Sauer P226 pointed at Brown, something that was lost on him because he was on his back, mouth agape, unconscious. The belt to his robe had come undone, exposing his pot belly. Mercifully, his nether regions weren't showing.

"You okay?" I asked Emma.

She nodded.

"That his gun you're holding?" I said, concerned she was thinking about killing him.

"Yes."

"Where is the gun safe?" Geronimo asked.

She pointed to the master bath. "Through there to the walk-in closet."

"Okay, fine. I'm going to check our good undersheriff's pulse, so, put the gun down."

She handed the pistol to Geronimo and said, "Sorry. He flinched and moaned a little, so I grabbed the gun just in case."

I knelt and checked Brown's pulse. Slow, but he would be fine. "That's smart," I said to Emma. "Let's have a look at the gun safe." Then to Geronimo: "Stay here with him."

I followed Emma into the master bath past a walk-in shower the size of Rhode Island on one side and a long makeup vanity with custom cabinetry on the other. The toilet had its own room next to the vanity. On the far wall was a pair of sinks and to the right of that was a walk-in closet big enough for a game of racket ball. The gun safe at the end of the closet looked like it might hold forty long guns and appeared to unlock with fingerprint ID.

I went back to the bedroom, told Geronimo about the safe. We dragged Brown through the rooms and pressed his right index finger on the scanner. Nothing. We touched his left index finger to the scanner—heard a metallic click. I pulled the door open as Geronimo dragged Brown away and dropped him to the floor like a sack of potatoes.

Along the back wall of the safe sat two M16s, an AR-15, and a sawed-off 12-gauge Mossberg. Between various pistols and stacks of ammo was an accordion folder. I pulled out the folder and smiled at what was underneath—Rick Butler's laptop and a two-inch stack of cash held together with a rubber band. The laptop was more beat up than I remembered it, which made sense because the last time I'd seen it Russ was chucking it off a bridge. It still had that AC/DC decal on it though. Rick Butler had seen Russ toss the laptop and had obviously found it in the brush on the creek bank only to have it stolen by Brown sometime later.

"That's Rick's laptop," Emma said.

I picked it up. "*Was* Rick's. He's dead, and ever since Brown has had it, it's been his ace in the hole against the DA." Then, to Emma: "Judging by Brown's interest in the laptop, it's likely Butler kept records of his clients—including your clients—on it."

She nodded. "Last couple of years, Rick talked about his list of clients a lot. He liked to brag about it. Made him feel like a big man. He flashed his laptop to a couple of girls one time. Said it was his black book. Called it his get-out-of-jail-free card. People thought it was funny that he had that stupid sticker on it like he was still in fuckin' high school."

I said, "So, the DA's name is in here? Maybe his credit card number? Venmo records, perhaps?"

She shrugged. "Probably. Everyone knew Rick made a point of gathering information on his customers, especially the powerful ones. He wouldn't shut up about it, like I said. Might be why he was killed."

I handed the laptop to Geronimo and said, "We're taking it with us."

"What are you gonna to do with it?" Emma asked.

Geronimo shot her look that said, *None of your fucking business.*

But it was her business. She was the DA's call girl. She was the one at risk for being used as a tool for blackmail against him. I wasn't sure if or how I would use the laptop, but if I could get past the password protection and Blaine's name was listed as a customer like I thought it would be, I was the one who now had an ace in the hole if I needed it. Fluid.

I ignored Emma's question and dumped the contents of the accordion folder on the floor—DVDs, three VHS tapes, an overstuffed Manilla envelope, a spiral notepad, none of it labeled.

I fanned the pages of the notepad. Only thing in it was on the first page. Someone had made a list of dates and locations starting in June of '93, ending in June of '98. There were eighteen entries and only one of them meant anything to me—the one dated July 10, 1993, the day Paco Correa was murdered. The location listed for that entry was an address in rural Harvey County. My first thought was, *Brown knows where the bodies are buried.*

I turned over the Manilla envelope and a large stack of photographs spilled onto the floor.

Emma gasped. I closed my eyes and looked away. Couldn't get away from the depravity fast enough, and could never un-see it either.

"What the fuck?" Geronimo said.

The scenes of middle-aged men raping underage girls hit me like a punch in the throat—took my breath away. One of the men was Dean Curtis, probably in his thirties, which meant the photo was taken in the mid-nineties. The girl he was with had a crude message scrawled in lipstick across her prepubescent chest—DADDY'S WHORE.

I glanced through the photos, wondering if some of the victims were the Mexican girls Brackeen had told me about—the ones Paco thought Brown and Curtis wanted to save from traffickers. If those girls had been murdered, their final resting places might be on the list in the notepad, along with Paco's.

The photos were taken from weird angles which made me think they were stills harvested from a video made by a hidden camera. Maybe Brown had pulled them off the VHS tapes or the DVDs for the instant impression they'd have on the public or a prosecutor when all-out war with Dean Curtis broke out and Brown was forced to release them in a final act of desperation.

The only other person I recognized in the photos was Jimmy Ray. He was nude, with a child, and it turned my stomach. I was glad he was dead. Judging by Ray's appearance, I guessed the photos had been taken in the last five years. God only knows how many kids he'd scarred in his lifetime.

Geronimo said, "This is Brown's blackmail material on Curtis and Ray."

"Kind of," I said. "Mostly it's the nuclear option of mutually assured destruction. The fact that Brown even has this stuff implicates him as well."

I looked up at Emma. She was crying. When she finally looked at me I said, "Get your phone. I need you to take photos of this stuff."

"Why? I don't want this sick shit on my phone."

"You're going to show the KBI what you found. They'll use what they get from you to get a search warrant for this place. You're the only one of us who's supposed to be here."

"Whatever you tell the KBI," Geronimo said, "leave us out of it. Understood?"

Emma nodded. "So, what'll I tell them? Brown'll say I roofied him. And I know for a fact that shit stays in your system for like, I dunno, twelve hours."

"Let's talk about that," I said. "Brown has roofies in his system, sure, but we're taking the Wild Turkey with us so he won't have that to corroborate his story that you dosed him. You'll deny knowing what the hell was going on with him. Guy was just wacked out of his fuckin' mind for some reason. Hell, he's got a date-rape drug in his system which might be a nice bit of irony for the cops to enjoy. From their point of view, Brown might've been trying to dose you just because he's a sick fuck but dosed himself instead."

Emma thought about that. "I could say he was acting funny, waving his pistol around, scaring me, got wobbly and passed out." She shrugged. "How the fuck do I know what he took? For all I know, the fat fucker just had a heart attack or something."

First thought was—what she said makes out Brown to be too unhinged, but then something clicked.

Emma noticed my hesitation. "Maybe he wasn't waving the pistol around, that's stupid."

"No, no, say he was acting crazy. Wouldn't be the first guy to go completely ape shit when his world fell apart. That works. He got into the safe for a gun while he was going cuckoo-for-cocoa-puffs and left it open." I thought about what we had so far. Liked it. "So, why'd you go nosing around in the safe? What'll you tell the cop that asks that question?"

Geronimo chimed in. "Only reason she would get in that safe would be to steal some shit."

She shook her head. "No. After everything I read about him, I was looking for a way to get away from him. And a way to nail the sonofabitch to the fucking wall."

I nodded, thinking a real-world call-girl-turned-thief might say exactly that in this situation. "They might think you were looking to steal something, just like Geronimo said, but we'll leave Brown's money in the safe to back up your story. Won't matter all that much to them after they get their hands on this stuff anyway. Right now, though, we got to get the photos taken and get the hell out of here, so go get your phone."

She returned wearing a terry cloth robe she'd gotten from somewhere. Mason walked in behind her and said, "Came up empty and there's no second surveillance system anywhere." Then he looked at the photos I'd spread out on the floor and said, "Aw, sweet Jesus."

Emma said, "I can't look at these."

"You have to," I said. "Just long enough to take the photos, then never again. You have to have seen them in case anyone asks you later—maybe in court—what's in them. Understand?"

Tears leaked out of her eyes.

I pulled out my phone and snapped a shot of the eighteen entries in the notebook. Emma saw what I was doing and followed suit. Then she proceeded to take photos of the depravity spread out on the floor. It was the kind of darkness that changed all who would see it. You knew in the instant you saw something like this that evil existed in the world and that it meant to consume the good. Sex crimes were different than any other kind of assault or battery, cutting its victims deeper in every way. Sex crimes are an assault on the spirit.

Deep down, even people who profess not to believe in such a thing as a person's spirit have to know that.

When Emma finished, we placed everything except Butler's laptop back in the safe where we'd found it.

I pushed the safe door in, careful to leave it cracked open, then turned to Emma. "Call the KBI hotline when you get home. Tell them what you got on your phone and where you got it. They'll send someone right over to your house, then they'll be here with a search warrant. Remember what we talked about."

After she left, I looked down at Brown. Roger walked up next to Mason. I glanced around at my crew. My crew of assholes who got me into this mess. "Load him in the Tahoe. By the time the KBI finds him, we'll have him as strung out as Emma tells them he is."

52

"BRING HIM OUT of it," I said to Geronimo.

Brown was unconscious, and in the same position Gutiérrez was in yesterday—strapped to a chair on the sagging front porch of the cabin behind The Rabbit Hole.

Geronimo knelt next to Brown in the gloom as Roger shined a light on them. We'd put pants on Brown, but left him shirtless and shoeless. Geronimo held a syringe and prodded Brown's arm, looking for a vein.

"How many times you done this?" Mason asked him.

"Done what?"

"Given a shot?"

"First time," said Geronimo as he jammed the needle in and depressed the plunger, shooting black-market Flumazenil into Brown's system to reverse the effects of the roofies. "Kind of interested to see how this goes."

Ten seconds later Brown came to and glanced around at the four of us in ski masks standing before him, his face clouded with fear and confusion, his breathing labored. Finally, he said, "Where am I? What the . . . what the fuck is happening?"

Silence.

"Who the fuck *are* you?" he half-yelled in a slurred voice.

I shot light from my phone on the cabin and the trees around us to let him know where he was—to stoke his fear. As I did, my phone burred with an incoming text. One of

Mason's men was informing me that the KBI had arrived at Brown's home. The search of Brown's home was underway.

"Why'd you bring me here?" Brown said.

I ignored that and put some gravel in my voice. "We got your blackmail file on Curtis."

"It's not a blackmail file," Brown said. "It's an insurance file. Curtis turns on me, I turn on him."

Geronimo slapped him upside the head as Mason put the piercing light of a tactical flashlight in his face. Blood dribbled out of his mouth as he clamped his eyes shut against the light. He tried to smile and said, "If you kill me, I got a man who uploads everything I got to the press. That stuff in the safe was just the tip of the fucking iceberg."

Geronimo hit him again. Harder. Blood and spittle flew from his mouth.

"We don't give a shit about Curtis," I said. "We don't work for him."

"Who do you work for?"

"Ourselves," I said.

"Yourselves? Why? What the fuck do you want?"

"Got someone here to talk to you about that," I said.

Jose Gutiérrez stepped onto the porch as Mason pulled the light out of Brown's face. Brown slowly opened his eyes and saw Jose Gutiérrez coming at him. Gutiérrez wasn't wearing a mask. He bent down so Brown could get a good long look at his face.

Gutiérrez smiled. "Remember me?"

"Yeah. You look like something I saw floating around in my toilet this morning."

Gutiérrez grabbed Brown by the throat and slammed him against the cabin and held him there with the chair tipped back. "Twenty-eight years ago, I saw you and Curtis back here. Watched you drag Paco off this porch."

"You must be Gutiérrez," Brown croaked.

Gutiérrez let go and straightened up. "Now you're getting' it."

Brown wheezed, hacked up something bloody and spit it out. "We back here so you can live out your revenge fantasy or something?"

Gutiérrez sighed. "Hardly. I cannot pay the men standing here with revenge. None of us can eat or drink or smoke revenge. Revenge isn't going to buy us the company of beautiful women. Revenge will never suck my cock on the beach, and it won't bring back my friend. I'm not a man of principle. If I were, I wouldn't have let you and Curtis get away with killing Paco. If I were interested in justice, I'd be hiding in some hotel the DA put me up in right now, waiting to testify against you and Curtis in court, hoping Curtis didn't get to me first. But I'm like you and Dean Curtis. I'm a practical man, and I aim to get mine."

"If you let me go, I can get you a lot of money."

Geronimo laughed. "You can't even afford security, *pendejo*."

"I have cash," Brown said. "Hidden . . . on my property. You'll never find it on your own."

"How much?" I said.

"Hundred grand—my bug-out money."

Gutiérrez grunted. "A hundred K won't do."

"What about Curtis?" I said. "He's got the kind of money we're looking for."

"What do you want? I'll talk to him. I'll tell him you found my insurance file and you'll keep it quiet for a price. How much you want? A million? Two?" He looked at the five of us, including Gutiérrez in his gaze. "Each," he said.

I ignored that last part. "Curtis is in federal lockup in New York. All his calls are recorded. How's he going to get to his money?"

"We'll . . . talk through lawyers . . . like we always do. It's against the law to record that. I ran the jail so I know lawyers' conversations with clients are privileged, off limits. That's how we'll get around it."

"Five million in cash," Mason said. "Personally delivered by you to us right here, this Sunday, ten p.m. You got an hour to bring us the hundred grand from your place. We'll be here.

If those two things don't happen according to schedule, we'll kill you and release your so-called insurance file on Curtis to the cops and the press. Get that message to Curtis."

Brown nodded. "I'll get you my money. And five million in cash won't be a problem for Curtis."

Lies. We didn't care.

Gutiérrez looked and me and Mason, nodding, like he was pleased. So far, this had gone well. Couldn't have gone better.

Mason stepped forward and cut Brown loose from the chair, then cut the rope around his wrists.

"Your truck is out front with keys in it," I said. "It's got just enough gas to get you home. We'll know if you cut and run. Come back in your Camaro."

Brown stood, massaging his wrists, as something dark welled up in me—I slammed Brown against the cabin and put my Glock to his head.

"Don't do it," Mason said. His hand was on my shoulder. "Be smart, man, we're real close to getting the money here. Real close to getting what we want, don't fuck it all up."

I slammed my fist into Brown's gut. He doubled over, went down, crawled off the porch. I didn't feel good. Something was still telling me that shooting Brown in the head would help with that.

Geronimo pulled Brown to his feet. "Shake it off, *pendejo*. You only got an hour to get back here with the money."

Brown, still half doubled over, staggered off into the trees and up the hill toward the bar.

Mason said, "Let's get the fuck outta here."

*   *   *

I was on the roof of the school across from Pops' house with Mason when Caroline Gordon called at one in the morning.

"You awake?"

Winding down, I didn't tell her. Trying to anyway, but failing miserably.

I glanced at Mason. We were sitting in lawn chairs, close enough to the edge to see Pops' front door, but far enough back that it would be difficult to spot us from the ground.

"I am now," I said to Caroline. "What's up?" As if I didn't know.

"I wanted you to hear this from me first. We searched Brown's premises with a warrant a few hours ago. We got 'em, Ben—Brown and Curtis both. Not exactly sure of the specifics, but we got 'em on rape and human trafficking and probably multiple murders if everything plays out like I think it will."

Mason nodded. It was quiet and Caroline's voice carried.

"Did you arrest Brown?"

"Yeah but listen to this. He wasn't at his house like we'd expected. Washington was late and was passed by what he thought was Brown's truck on his way here ... started following it. Called in the tag, and yep, it was Brown's truck alright. Washington was in an unmarked Crown Vic, so he called for a trooper to get the truck stopped, but about then Brown must've got paranoid and ran his speed up to ninety, then promptly, well ... long-story short ..." Caroline laughed, "the fucker ran out of gas."

Mason looked up at the sky laughed to himself.

"Washington ordered him out of the truck at gunpoint and out comes Brown, no shirt, no shoes, all sweaty and pale and get this, not one firearm in his truck. Didn't even have any ID or a cell phone on him. You'd think he'd at least arm himself, given the danger he's in from Curtis. And you'd think he'd have surveillance cameras running at his house, but he didn't."

From Caroline's perspective, Brown was acting crazy, which would corroborate Emma's story about Brown acting completely unhinged, waving a gun around, and leaving his safe open. Sometimes things go your way. I smiled at Mason. "That's truly bizarre," I said to Caroline.

"Yeah, he was strung out as hell," Caroline said. "We think he's on something."

I made a face. "Sounds like he might've snapped. You question him yet?"

"No, but that didn't keep him from talking. Washington got him cuffed and waited on the trooper, who brought Brown to me while we were still searching his place. I told Brown what we'd found in his gun safe and he looked genuinely confused, then angry. Looked like his mind was going a thousand miles an hour when he finally asked me if we found a laptop with an AC/DC sticker on it in the safe. When I told him we hadn't found any laptop, he completely flipped his shit. Started yelling about how the DA had set him up and how the KBI was in on it. Said he had Rick Butler's laptop in that safe, and that the DA's name would be in it."

"Persecution complex, wild conspiracy theory," I said. "Sounds like he probably is on drugs."

"Yeah, he insists Emma Hicks—who he referred to as the DA's whore—set him up, then stole the laptop from him to save the DA from being outed for frequenting a call girl."

"Interesting, since Blaine is actually seeing Emma Hicks, who is actually a call girl who worked for Butler."

"I know, right. What a fuckin' mess."

"Did Brown even realize how bad an idea it was to admit to having Butler's laptop?"

"Not at first, no way. He was so fucking mad and fucked up. You should have seen him. At one point he went off on a rant about how . . . I think he was saying Gutiérrez, how Gutiérrez and his men had just kicked the shit out of him. Then he wondered out loud if it really was Gutiérrez he'd seen, or just some guys sent by the DA."

Mason shook his head then turned away to hide a smile.

I said, "Did Brown ever say how he ended up with the laptop?"

"No, he didn't go that far, but the answer to that question probably isn't good for him, especially since Butler was murdered. Keep in mind, I never even asked Brown a question, so . . ."

"So, no *Miranda* warning necessary. Everything he said will be admissible in court, assuming he's not flown too far over the cuckoo's nest."

"That's what I'm thinking. Even if everything he said gets thrown out, though, whatever cards Brown held before tonight, they're gone now."

"Given what Emma told you about her relationship with Blaine," I said, "are you thinking there's something to what Brown is saying—about the DA setting him up?"

"I'm worried about that, but I called Emma. She tells me she didn't steal any laptop and that Blaine had nothing to do with this. She said she's not even seeing him anymore."

Good girl.

"Okay," Caroline said. "I gotta roll, things are moving fast. Brown finally lawyered up and called his attorney, who is on his way to our Wichita office. Blaine is coming too, so this should be interesting. I called the FBI and they're sending an agent as well. Full court press on this sonofabitch."

"Good."

"Oh, it's better than good. I don't want to oversell this, but we found photos of a lot of victims in the safe. Two of them we know went missing in '98."

"After the death penalty was reinstated in Kansas."

"Exactly. Blaine is pushing for a deal tonight. Something that puts Brown in prison for the rest of his life but takes the needle out of his arm in exchange for a full confession and his testimony against Curtis on all of it. The murder, the rape, the trafficking, all of it."

"Sounds real good, Caroline. Thanks for the update."

"There's more. We might—let me stress the word, *might*. We might already have information about where Paco Correa is buried."

I closed my eyes. "Thanks, Caroline. I won't get my hopes up, but this sounds promising."

"I'm sorry, Ben."

"About what?"

"Guess I'm just sorry that you had to go through all of this, that's all."

I thanked her again and ended the call.

Mason pulled a flask from inside his jacket and tossed it to me.

"You might not feel like celebrating," he said. "Especially with a sonofabitch like me. But if you do, go ahead and have a snort."

"What's in here?"

"Blanton's single barrel."

"I suppose that's high-dollar stuff."

"To me, yeah. Not to someone in Dean Curtis's tax bracket."

I unscrewed the cap and took a hit. It burned. "Fuck Dean Curtis."

Mason studied my face. "You like it?"

"No."

"Really? That's the good stuff."

I gave the flask back to Mason.

"That's not the good stuff," I said. "Keri was the good stuff. I gave up the love of my life to dig up some old bones."

Mason took a pull and winced. "This is my fault. I know that, and I'm truly sorry."

Silence.

I shook my head. "When we knew what we were up against in Dean Curtis, Keri and I talked about backing off. Going back to Idaho and leaving this place behind a second time. Maybe Curtis leaves us alone if I do that. I wished I'd done that now. This has cost me more than I ever . . ."

Mason studied my face, waiting for the rest of it. Finally, he said, "More than you ever what?"

"I was going to say imagined. But hell, I knew the risks. That's why we thought about leaving. I made my choice, and now I have to live with it."

53

AFTER I GOT back from mass on Sunday morning, Russ called. I wasn't expecting that. I took it in the living room.

"Mia is innocent of murder," Russ said. "She might be guilty of something else, but not murder."

"Only thing she might be guilty of is attempted agg battery," I said. "For going over to Jimmy Ray's to take off his junk with a knife. I know the story."

"You know about Tobias?"

"Yeah, you have a son. Congratulations."

"He's not my son. Kinda wish he was, actually."

That threw me. Russ stayed silent. Then I finally got it. "Oh my God, not Annie's father?"

"Afraid so. I feel bad for this kid, coming into the world like he did only to end up in prison for ending some bullshit that should've been handled a long time ago."

"The DA offered to drop the case against Mia if she'll give them the name of the killer and agree to testify. Said they'd even offer a sweetheart deal to whoever it was that killed Jimmy Ray. Manslaughter plea—be a five-year pull for Tobias."

"That's actually really good news," Russ said. "Tell Mia to go ahead and give them Tobias's name and take the deal. Let her know it's alright and that she'll never have to testify. The main reason I called was to let you know that Tobias is turning himself in and confessing tomorrow morning. Annie's turning herself in too. They're doing this together."

"Have them hold off, Russ. I'll need to talk to Mia about all this. And I got something else in the works that might work out a little better for everyone involved."

"What is it?"

"Can't tell you that. You don't work for me anymore. Call me back tomorrow."

He was trying to apologize again for getting me involved in this mess when I ended the call.

* * *

Two hours later I was making a sandwich in the kitchen when Caroline Gordon called. She informed me that Clint Brown had agreed to the DA's terms and been debriefed extensively about his decades-long human trafficking conspiracy with Dean Curtis, Jimmy Ray, and Ricky Butler. The KBI had several digs going on at the same time at the spots described in the notebook which were confirmed by Brown as the burial spots for multiple victims. So far they'd uncovered the skeletal remains of at least ten children—and one adult she thought was probably going to be Paco Correa. She asked if she could swing by my house tomorrow to take a buccal swab of the inside of my cheek for DNA comparison. I told her that would be fine.

"They killed Officer Knudson themselves," she said. "I figured they'd hired that one out, but that's not what Brown says. He says Knudson walking in on them behind The Rabbit Hole was their first real experience with shit going off the rails, so they were caught off guard."

"Curtis didn't have his murder-for-hire connections yet?"

"Exactly. He got busy with that later. Has the state AG called you? He's taking over the case regarding the murder of your mother."

"He hasn't called."

I felt hot, flushed, and left my unfinished sandwich on the counter and walked out onto the back patio for some air. The skies were full of dark clouds and the smell of rain was in the air, but the neighbor lady had a sprinkler running in her garden anyway.

"I'll let the AG tell you the rest of it," Caroline said.

"How about you tell me."

"He wanted to be the first—"

"To hell with his dumbass protocol."

Caroline cleared her throat. "Brown said he and Curtis drew straws . . . to decide which one of them would kill your mother."

"Who drew the short straw?"

"Curtis. So it was up to him to kill your mother, and he did the dirty work himself. Like I said, Brown said this was before Curtis outsourced his killing. The necklace left behind, of course, corroborates Brown's story."

"Whose idea was it to make it look an accidental overdose?"

"Brown's. Your mother was an addict. He thought no one would question it, and no one did until Ricky Butler laid eyes on you and spilled the beans in an inebriated haze."

I spotted a lawn chair and carefully lowered myself into it.

"Ben?" Caroline said.

"Yeah."

"You okay?"

"Yeah, I guess."

"The state AG is charging Dean Curtis and Clint Brown with the murder of your mother tomorrow. Curtis as the principal, Brown as an aider and abettor."

"Okay, sounds good."

"Where are you?"

"Home. Sitting outside watching a storm roll in. I take it that Brown isn't claiming any responsibility for killing Keri."

"He figures Curtis was behind it, like the rest of us, and no, he says he can't help us with that."

The neighbor lady came out of her back door and worked the water tap, shutting off the sprinkler. She looked over and waved at me. I smiled and waved back.

"Ben?" Caroline said.

"Yeah?"

"Maybe you oughta go inside now and take it easy. You sound . . . kind of flat."

"Sounds like a good idea."

*   *   *

Thirty minutes later I was still outside in the lawn chair when the state AG called. He repeated everything Caroline had told me, but it sounded different with all the window dressing a professional politician throws in because they can't help it. He seemed out of sorts by the end of the call, his speech riddled with awkward hesitations and repetition, like maybe he thought I wasn't comprehending what he was saying.

A few minutes later the wind kicked up and I stood to go inside. Then my phone buzzed with a call from District Attorney Swartzmiller.

"Blaine," I said, sitting back down.

"We finally got the sonsofbitches!"

"That's what I hear."

I could hear him breathing heavily into the phone. "Caroline just called. She's worried about you."

"I'm fine."

"Maybe it doesn't feel real?"

"Been down the rabbit hole a little too long, maybe. The, uh, *Alice in Wonderland* rabbit hole I mean. Not the bar. I feel like this whole thing was . . . is, a bad dream."

He chuckled. "I'm starting to think the whole world has been down a rabbit hole since the beginning of time. One giant rabbit hole in outer space." He laughed again, which sounded forced to me, like a politician's laugh. "I want to be there for you. Anything you need, just call, you know that, right?"

"Thanks, Blaine. Appreciate that. More than you know."

"Good, good. Hey, while I got you on the phone, has Mia given you an answer on that plea offer?"

"We need to talk about that."

"Yes, we do."

"In person, I mean."

"Alright. You free tomorrow?"

"I'm free now. How about you come on over."

"What? To your house?"

"Yeah, my grandfather's, actually."

"Ben, I was up all night Friday night and I've been working this case until late last night. My wife—"

"You should come over now. No Claire Riddle. No investigators. Just me and you on a Sunday afternoon."

"I'm supposed to go with my wife—"

"Anything I need, right Blaine?"

Silence.

"Or was that just bullshit?"

Another five seconds of silence. Then, "I'm on my way."

54

AN HOUR LATER, Mason escorted Blaine Swartzmiller into Pops' dining room. Blaine was in jeans and an untucked golf shirt, looking as haggard as I'd ever seen him.

"Jesus Christ, Ben, your guy patted me down and took my gun."

I was sitting at the head of the dinner table. "You won't need it in here." I pointed at a chair next to mine. "Have a seat."

Mason left as Blaine sat to my right. I slid my laptop in front of him. It had a decal of the rock group AC/DC on it I'd gotten from the dollar store this morning. Not the exact same decal as was on Butler's laptop, but close enough.

He looked down at it. "What's this?"

"Really?"

He pooched out his lower lip, blanching uncontrollably, then shook his head.

"Well, then. Guess everything I heard about you hooking up with a high-end call girl was total bullshit. Good. I was trying to do you a solid, but if the stories aren't true you don't need my help."

I reached for the laptop. "I'll hand this over to Caroline and the KBI like I should've done in the first place."

He pulled the laptop closer and glared at me. "Where'd you get this?"

I shrugged. "One of my security guys found it in the yard this morning at dawn's first light."

"The fuck they did."

"Turns out, one of those guys out there guarding the place is a certified computer hacking forensic investigator. He hacked into it for me. He says this laptop contains the business records of a place called Strictly Confidential Escorts. He said your name's in here, but it must be another Blaine Swartzmiller. And there's probably some explanation for how your cell number ended up opposite that name. Here's the good news. There are records in here of the time and location of each date this guy supposedly had with a girl named Emma Hicks, so I'm sure you'll have alibis galore to show that this Swartzmiller isn't you."

His lips were bloodless. "What do you want?"

"My client is innocent. All I want is for you to do the right thing."

"What about the other killer?"

"Let it go. You don't know who it is, but it isn't Mia. And dismissing the possession case against Annie Black would be a nice gesture too. Brown planted meth in her purse when she wouldn't have sex with him. After she got charged, he came back and raped her to show her how much power he had."

"I flipped Brown on Curtis yesterday—made you a multi-millionaire."

I laughed. "If that's true, I'll be looking forward to donating to your campaign for governor someday."

He glared at me for a long moment. "Monet cornered me in the hallway yesterday, off the record."

Monet was Brown's attorney. I waited for the rest of it.

"He told me he was concerned that his client might cook-off during the debriefing and start accusing me of setting him up. Said his client swore up and down that he'd had Butler's laptop in his gun safe and that my name was in it along with a long list of other johns. Said that's why I sent Emma to his house—to drug him and steal the laptop, then call the KBI about the blackmail file. I assured him I hadn't set anybody up and didn't know anything about any laptop."

"How much of that is true, Blaine? A quarter? Half?"

He grimaced. "A lot of it. Enough. How'd you get that fucking laptop?"

I smiled. "Like I said, it just showed up in the yard."

Blaine shook his head. "Monet also told me Brown swore to God that Jose Gutiérrez kidnapped him last night."

"How could that be? Don't you have Gutiérrez in some sort of witness protection somewhere?"

"I never said that."

"That's the impression I got."

"That's the impression Monet had too."

I looked him in the eye. "Because that's the impression you meant to give us, Blaine."

Silence.

"Did you do it?" I said.

He looked away. "Do what?"

I smiled. "Set up Brown."

He stared at me. "I could ask you the same question."

I gave him a look of mock surprise. "Really?" I leaned closer to him. "By the way, where *is* Gutiérrez?"

"I should ask you the same thing."

"You're the one on record interviewing him. Keeping him somewhere safe, out of reach of Brown and Curtis."

His jaw clenched. "I spoke with him on the phone one time. At least I think I did. Fact is, it could've been anyone. He's been missing ever since. I told Caroline the truth, but Monet doesn't know he's in the wind."

I nodded. "Damn. Nice bluff, counselor."

His eyes blazed. "Compared to you, I'm just a fuckin' amateur."

"Don't know what you're talkin' about."

He grabbed the laptop and stood up.

"Put it down, Blaine. No way you're not getting out of here with that."

He smashed it over the top of the hard cherry back of his chair multiple times. He stopped when his hands were empty and his face was glistening with sweat and component parts and shattered glass were strewn about the room.

"Well, shit Blaine! You've gone and scratched the hell out of my grandfather's chair. You also owe me a laptop."

He was breathing heavily. "Tell your grandfather I'm sorry about the chair. I'll pay for that, but it was Butler's laptop so I don't owe you shit. See you at trial. I'm withdrawing my offer to Mia."

He turned and headed for the door.

"I lied," I said.

That stopped him. He looked back.

"Kind of." I tilted my head in a side-to-side rhythm. "That was my laptop you just trashed, so I'll take a check or cash." I reached into a soft-shell briefcase at my feet and pulled out Butler's laptop. "Here's the real thing. Got names in it, too."

He was still out of breath. "You son of a bitch."

I smiled. "Uh-huh."

He stared at me for several seconds. "What about the person that killed Jimmy Ray?"

"After you dismiss the case against Mia, invite five of your favorite reporters to your office and show them the pics of Jimmy Ray raping children. Then announce your finding that in the view of the DA's office, the killing was justified."

His forehead creased. "Defense of others?"

"Yeah, to include Annie's five-year-old girl."

"You don't think that's a stretch?"

"The way the law is written, yeah, but in reality, no. The way I see it, it was a perfectly justified killing. Nothing was stopping Jimmy Ray. And Brown and Curtis. Not you, not me, certainly not the law. If someone hadn't killed Jimmy Ray and set all this in motion, he and Brown and Curtis would still be out there putting more women and children in the ground."

He stared at me for a moment. "I'll dismiss the cases against Mia and Annie Black first thing in the morning." A rush of air huffed out of him. "Then do I get the laptop?"

"Sure, once the statute of limitations runs out."

"There is no statute of limitations for murder."

"Yeah, I know. I feel real bad about that and how this went down." I motioned to the chair he'd been using. "Have a seat, stay for dinner? Steak, baked potato, corn on the cob?"

He walked to the door, reached for the knob.

"I'm sorry," I said.

He froze with his back to me. "For what?"

"I didn't handle this right. I needed it to be over. I'm just, so damned tired."

He turned. He looked shrunken. "Do you think Brown has any sort of a backup of what's on that computer?"

"No idea. You might ask him. Get him to pinky-swear that he doesn't."

"It could be out there in the cloud somewhere."

"Could be. Secrets have a way of getting out and the cloud is . . . well, the cloud. Clouds can rain."

Blaine's eyes were dead and his color was off. He looked sick.

I said, "Caroline already knows about you and Emma."

"I figured." He hesitated. "Don't know if it'll help, but the stuff in Butler's computer might be useful in putting names to the victims we found."

"I'm working on a way to get Caroline those records without implicating you further."

He looked at the laptop. "You'll need to come up with something better than a delete button and a story about finding that thing in the yard."

"Already done."

He grimaced, then turned and reached for the knob again.

"You know you have to quit seeing Emma, right?" I said to his back.

He looked at me, then closed his eyes.

"Either that," I went on, "or give up those big gubernatorial plans of yours."

He yanked the door open and left.

55

Tuesday, September 21

TWO DAYS LATER I left a note for Pops in the kitchen at four-thirty in the morning and took his fishing boat to our favorite spot on Worthington Lake and watched the sun come up. Mason and his men were back in Texas, and for the first time in a long time, I wasn't carrying any burner phones.

At nine the air was still and warm and I was sitting in my seat on the casting platform when my regular phone buzzed with a call from the interim US Attorney in the district of Kansas. I set down my pole and answered the call.

"Good morning, Deb."

"You have a second?"

"Got more than that. The fish aren't biting."

"I wanted you to hear this from me. I just got a call from the US Attorney in New York. Dean Curtis was found dead in his cell this morning."

A cold darkness struck at my core and I threw out the most naïve thing I could think of to say to lighten my spirit. "Natural causes?"

She laughed softly. "Suicide by hanging."

"Ah, the circle of life."

Deb forged ahead. "That's the ME's preliminary finding, anyway, but it's total bullshit. Two days after landing in the Metropolitan Correctional Center, Curtis was found by jailors on the floor with a bedsheet around his neck while his cellmate was lying in bed, sound asleep. At least that's the cellmate's story—that he slept through a suicide attempt going on at the foot of his bed. Curtis claimed his cellmate tried to kill him, but prison officials sided with the cellmate and called it a failed suicide attempt."

"After all that, he should've been on a suicide watch."

"He was. But less than twenty-four hours after Brown's arrest, MCC's psychiatrist took Curtis off the watch and they assigned him a different cellmate like they're required to do."

"And that cellmate killed him?"

"No. They assigned Curtis a cellmate but never moved the new guy in with him, even though they were required to do so by the prison's own rules. Curtis was put in a cell in the special housing unit by himself last night at eight. They found him dead at six-thirty this morning with another sheet around his neck."

"When's the last time anyone saw him alive?"

"Last night at eight."

"He just comes off suicide watch and they don't bother to check on him all night?"

"That's right. The most notorious inmate in the country, and they never checked on him. Oh, but MCC's records say they did. Every half hour just like they're required to do. But they didn't."

"The jailors falsified their records?"

"Yeah, and they've both already been arrested for that."

"There's got to be surveillance."

"There is. Of the jailors fucking around on the Internet and sleeping at their desks at central control all night. But there's no video of Curtis's cell door or any of the doors of the other inmates in his unit. The camera that should have caught all this was shut off last night."

"Jesus—they didn't even bother to make it look believable."

"There wasn't enough time to get fancy. That's how close we were to the untouchables, Ben. Curtis was set to be debriefed by the FBI this morning. An hour from now, actually."

"He was going to cooperate?"

"Yeah, when he found out Brown was arrested he fired Benowitz, hired a new attorney, and was going to bring everyone down with him."

"Who's everyone?"

"It's called hyperbole, Ben. You've seen all those old photos the press has been showing of Curtis with Hollywood types, heads of state, royalty, other famous billionaires, presidents from both parties—"

"Yeah, yeah—"

"Some of those people. That's what I'm talking about. We know from flight manifests who all visited Curtis's Caribbean island, but Curtis claims not all of them were there to swim in the ocean and eat conch salad. Curtis was going to tell us which ones partook of forbidden fruit."

"Sex with underage girls?"

"Yeah." I heard the disgust in her voice.

"Curtis went nuclear for his final play," I said, almost to myself. "He have any visual proof to back up his claims?"

"Dunno," Deb said. "We may never know."

"Did anyone bother asking Curtis's new attorney that question?"

Deb laughed. "Yeah, and he has no idea, but what the hell else is he going to say at this point?—'Sign me up, I'd like to be the next one to die.'"

The boat started rocking gently and I realized I'd heard a motorboat in the distance behind me. When I looked, it was moving away. My lids felt heavy and the glare off the lake had my face contorted into a full-on squint. I got sunglasses out of my bag.

"I don't know what you think about all this, Ben. Maybe you're glad the fucker is dead."

I slipped on my sunglasses and thought about that. For a brief moment in time, I'd gotten to Curtis, had him on the witness stand. How many people get to face down their demon like that? But a snap of the fingers and the dark world Curtis belonged to had whisked him out of a Wichita courtroom and swallowed him whole in a New York jail cell and he was again nothing more than a tiny sliver of the aloof untouchable evil that is beyond all of us.

Was I glad Curtis was dead? I decided against a definite yes. "I take my joy where I can find it. I'm a cup-half-full kind of guy. Thanks for calling."

I started the engine and made for the boat ramp. Halfway there, I got that familiar sensation of detachment, like maybe I was just a kind of moist robot. A two hundred fifteen-pound cyborg with wind in his hair. I didn't feel real.

*   *   *

I dropped anchor fifty yards out and put on my waders. Climbed out of the boat and slogged through the waist-high water toward my truck on the shore.

When I got there Elias Matusak stepped out from behind it with a shotgun aimed at my midsection.

He eased to within four feet of me and dropped a knife and a cutting board on the ground between us and gripped the shotgun with both hands. "I came for your tongue."

Adrenaline spiked. My Glock was holstered underneath the waders, not that it mattered in a situation like this. I'd be cut in half by the shotgun before I could get a hand on it.

Sunlight glinted off Pops' white Silverado on the road in the distance behind Elias.

I said, "Did I not do your will?"

He cocked his head. "My will was done. Nothing more. You pretend to have a say, but nothing you do is your own doing and the gifts you possess are borrowed so when I ask— who are you?—what could you even say that would be true?"

I needed to keep him talking, distracted.

"I'd say I'm the pretender," I said.

"You are the poem, pretending to be the poet." He looked at the knife on the ground between us. "It's a hard lesson, and a judicious cut."

"The great physician taking what he must to save the patient," I said.

"When you see the public reckoning and the names spewing from Curtis's lips, there will be many who laud you and you will be filled with boastful pride and when you go to wag your stump for a tongue it will be impossible for you to forget that bringing down these men was not your doing but mine."

"You want all the credit for this shit show, you got it."

His face was stone.

A pulse thrummed in my temples. "No names will be spewing from Curtis's lips. No trials, no public reckoning. Curtis is dead."

He lifted his chin, then reset his feet. He hadn't heard.

I held his eyes. "How could you not know that, Elias? I thought you were God."

He made a noise in his throat. "That tongue wags to the end."

"The government's going to say he committed suicide."

"He would not do that."

The Silverado in the distance had closed in and was now at a spot where I could not focus on it without moving my eyes to the left, but I saw enough to know it had stopped in the roadway.

"There are limitations to my present form," Elias said.

"I see that."

"You see so little, but that will change when you sit upon the precipice with me in paradise as I cast demons out of men and into swine. We will watch as hogs rush into the lake and choke. Now bow down and give me what is mine."

Yeah, right. When hogs fly.

Movement. Pops was out of his truck.

"Pray with me," I said.

Elias widened his stance, changed his grip on the shotgun and curled his finger around the trigger.

I closed my eyes. "The Lord is my shepherd; I shall not want. He maketh me to lie down in green pastures: He leadeth me beside the still waters." I opened my eyes and saw his filling with tears. "He restoreth my soul: He leadeth me in the paths of righteousness for his name's sake. Yea, though I walk through the valley of the shadow of death, I will fear no evil: for thou art with me; thy rod and thy staff they—"

A red plume flowered from his head and a warm mist wet my face and he dropped face-first on the cutting board. In the distance, Pops got back in his Silverado with his old Remington M40.

*   *   *

When Pops pulled up I was wiping my face with a towel I'd pulled from the F350.

He got out of his truck and glanced at Elias prone in the grass, blood making a pool around his head. "Catch anything?"

"A couple flatheads is all. I threw 'em back."

He looked up at the sky. Glanced around. "Well, you know what they say. 'A bad day fishing is better than a good day working.'"

I glanced down at Elias. "Turns out that's not entirely true."

"Want a beer?"

I nodded.

He pointed to the bed of his truck. "Six-pack in the cooler."

"Cold?"

He shrugged. "As cold as they get."

EPILOGUE

Tuesday, December 21

I WOKE UP on the side of the bed where Keri used to sleep. I showered, ate breakfast with the kids, then drove them into town for their last day of school before Christmas break.

Three hours later I was on my way to Manny Hernandez's office for a retirement party I was told about only yesterday. When I walked through the front door, I was met with an empty reception room. So much had changed since Keri and I had set up an office here in August. Now Keri was gone, and I'd terminated the month-to-month lease with Manny at the end of September. I hadn't been here in two and a half months.

"Hello?" I called.

"Back here," Rashonda's voice called back. "In Manny's office."

Rashonda smiled as she rushed past me going the other direction in the hallway, chasing after the sound of a ringing phone at the front desk.

I found Manny behind his desk with clear rubber tubing draped over his ears and under his nose. Prongs jutted into his nostrils. He was watching the news on a giant flat-screen TV on the wall to his right. He muted it, swiveled his chair to face me, and smiled. He looked as sick as ever.

"Thanks for coming on such short notice." He motioned to the chairs in front of his desk. "Have a seat."

I did, raising my brows. "Am I early? I was told the party started at eleven-thirty."

"You're right on time." He looked at his watch. "Fashionably late, actually."

"Where is everybody?"

He beamed.

I glanced around the room. Law books. A few lawyerly knick-knacks like the scales of justice and the gold bust of an eagle. "Where's the spread? In the conference room?"

"Spread?"

I shrugged. "Punch. Hors d'oeuvres. Maybe an olive plate? Cake? I could use a bit of cake about now."

"I think there's leftover coffee cake in the kitchen if you're hungry. Not even a week old."

I shook my head. "I'm good."

Something caught his attention on the TV. It was footage from almost a year ago—a shirtless man in a horned fur buffalo cap and face paint with other rioters milling about the senate floor.

He grunted. "I would've thought it'd be harder to break into the capitol building than that. The jihadists must still be kicking themselves."

"Manny?"

He looked at me.

"Where's the party?" I said.

"Your grandfather says you're not interested in buying this place."

"Don't have the cash flow. I didn't know you knew my grandfather."

He chuckled. "Not real well. He's not sure you'll ever even practice law again. Tells me you're mowing greens at a golf course."

"Lately I've been cutting down dead cedars, but yeah, I enjoy it. I can actually see the progress in my work."

He studied me. "I always thought with law, it was like I went to work moving a pile of shit from point A to point B while some other lawyer was moving it from point B to point A. We both had jobs, but nothing got done."

I laughed. "The attorneys got paid, though, right?"

"Of course." A smile tugged at his lips. "You really don't have any interest in buying the office from me?"

"No. Sorry about that."

"What if money was no object?"

"You just gonna give it to me?"

"No, but what if I did?"

I shook my head. "I still don't want it."

"Just gonna mow greens for the rest of your life, huh?"

I shrugged. "I'm talkin' to a guy about a little something, but I'm probably not gonna do that either."

"Guy? What guy?"

"Mason—the security guy who came up from Texas after Keri was murdered."

He nodded. "Is it legal work?"

I shrugged. "Yeah, I guess. Pretty much, anyway."

"Sounds too vague to be legal."

I laughed. "You're the life of the party, Manny." I looked around in mock observance. "If there was a party."

"How's the pay gonna be with this job?"

"It's not about the pay. They'll call me if they need me for a project somewhere, but like I said, I'm leaning toward not accepting the offer."

"Your creditors won't care for that."

"I'll figure something out. Always do."

He suppressed another smile, opened a drawer. Pulled out a packet of papers and pushed them across the desk at me. An emboldened caption told me it was a settlement agreement with Dean Curtis's estate.

I dragged it a few inches closer. "What the hell is this?"

The figure on the front page by my name had a "3" behind a dollar sign, then enough zeros tacked on that I thought there was a typographical error. Maybe a couple of them. Someone's finger might've bounced on the zero key.

"A gift from the guest of honor." Manny nodded at the paperwork. "This can be your retirement party too, if that's what you want."

I counted the zeros, then stared at Manny. "Thirty million dollars?"

"That's just your take. Your sister and your grandfather get fifteen mil apiece."

I didn't believe it. I stared at Manny, thinking his image would dissolve and I'd wake up in bed.

But Manny wasn't going anywhere. He jutted out his lower lip and nodded. "Your sister brought your grandfather in. They both told me that when the subject of suing Curtis's estate came up, you shut down. Didn't want to talk about it."

I flipped to the back page and saw that it was signed by the executor and the estate's attorney. My sister and Pops had already signed.

"That's the settlement agreement being offered for your mother's and Keri's wrongful death claims. Sign it, and you release any and all other claims against the estate, including any claim you might have for the death of your biological father, Paco Correa. You'll get a lump sum check for the whole amount in less than six weeks."

I flipped through the agreement, the thrill of Curtis's money surging through me like a drug, then came the sickening memory of how this was even possible. "When did they come to you? Pops and my sister—how long ago?"

"Before Dean Curtis was in the ground." He shook his head. "Benny, you have to understand, that when I got to drafting the demand letter, I got to thinking about you and your kids and I . . . well I called your grandfather about approaching you and he told me to add your name and your wrongful death claim for Keri to the mix."

I opened my mouth to say that wasn't his call but the words died in my throat.

Manny's forehead puckered. "I meant to approach you for permission, but in the end decided it would be easier to ask for forgiveness with millions of dollars' worth of mea culpa in my hand."

I glanced around the room, trying to quell the sorrow welling up in me. "I'm not mad. I don't know what I am."

"Your sister and grandfather were convinced you'd never sue. That to you it would be like trading Keri's life for money. But that isn't what is happening here, Ben. Not at all."

I gritted my teeth against all the conflicts crashing around in my head.

Manny gave me a gentle look. "You okay with this?"

I took a moment to compose myself, remembering the case law Blaine had sent me about equitable tolling—the common law principle that wrongdoers should not be allowed to benefit from their wrongdoing, such as hiding the fact of a wrongful killing. "Do you think equitable estoppel would've barred Curtis's estate from successfully pleading the statute of limitations on my mother's death?"

Manny leaned back in his chair. "I made it sound that way in the demand letter." He gave a knowing smile. "Sounds like you were more interested in suing than you let on."

I sighed. "The DA—old law school buddy of mine— turned me onto a theory to get around the statute of limitations on my mother's wrongful death. He sent me the case law. I got curious and read up on it one day."

He cocked his head. "Could be one hell of a lawsuit, but if you go that route I won't live long enough to see it through. We might have a little trouble proving Curtis sent Gans to kill Keri. In the end, the executor and the estate's attorneys decided to throw some money at us to make us go away. A lot of money, actually. They threw some to the Knudson family too, I heard. There'll be others."

He watched me for a moment.

"What?" I said.

He glanced at the paper in front of me. "That's nuisance money. You could hold out for more. Maybe you get it. Won't hurt my feelings one little bit. But that is a bird in hand. No telling about the two birds in the bush."

Thirty million would change my life, not necessarily for the better, but it would change everything. Getting more would not bring Keri back. Mostly I just felt very tired right then.

Manny leaned forward. "You gonna sign the agreement?"

"I guess. What's your cut?" I regretted the question the instant I said it. It didn't matter. I wasn't thinking clearly.

But Manny smiled. "I'll be happy if you don't report me to the ethics board."

"Aw, Jesus, Manny, who the hell cares? I'm sorry I asked. You're retiring, right?"

"Yeah, and I'm dying, so there's that. This isn't for me. How 'bout ten percent instead of the ambulance chasers' thirty? I have family to think about."

"Rashonda probably did half the work."

He laughed. "At least. I'll give her half of my cut, how's that? Make it her retirement party too."

I liked that. Lives were going to change. "Draw up the contract."

He nodded, pulled a pen from his shirt pocket and flipped it across the desk at me. I signed the agreement.

I thanked him several times before finally standing to leave.

"You should take a vacation," he said.

"As a matter of fact, I'm leaving with Pops and the kids tomorrow. And that's just the start."

"Of what?"

"A long sabbatical." I nodded at the agreement. "Maybe longer than I'd intended half an hour ago."

* * *

Christmas

So it turns out swine can swim. Which is just one of the reasons I would never sit on a precipice with Elias and watch them run demon-possessed into a lake and drown. But I did get to watch a colony of them rush into the surf and swim in the crystal-blue waters of the Bahamian archipelago. Swimmin' piggies! Who knew? We swam with them and they blew brown bubbles out their butts in the water. My children laughed and laughed.